Praise for

'Magnificent novel . . . be. The bedraggled England here is as vivid as Jez Butterworth's version in *Jerusalem*. Gibson is surely the playwright's heir in vision and wit . . . You will be hooked, you will laugh and possibly cry. And you will know by page four that this hilarious and compassionate novel really matters'   *Spectator*

'Jasper Gibson's bravura new novel is timely and revelatory . . . Gibson skilfully combines black comedy with a compassionate and searching examination of what madness is and whether "normal" life is itself a state of mind'   *Observer*

'A man suffering from schizophrenia doesn't sound like it has comic potential, but this novel shows good storytelling can always confound expectations'   *The Times*

'An engaging novel about a man with a voice in his head evokes the radical politics of the anti-psychiatry movement'   *Guardian*

'A compassionate, witty novel about being lost in the maze of the British mental health system'   *Independent*

'Gibson . . . has achieved something remarkable . . . full of jokes, capers, black ironies and a wild juxtaposition between the mundane and the transcendental'
    The Oldie, Book of the Month

'Deliriously good!'   *ES Magazine*

'Cleverly written . . . very funny, and it can be interpreted in a number of different ways'   *Sydney Morning Herald*

'What an astonishing work *The Octopus Man* is. Schizophrenia is not an easy condition to write about. It scares us. It scares those who live with it even more. But there is a kind of beauty, comedy and transcendence in the way that Jasper Gibson takes us inside the mind of Tom, which lifts the spirits and shows that disorders like his can give as well as take away'   Stephen Fry

'An exceptional work . . . What a brilliant and necessary book. A funny, heart-expanding story of a man trapped between the God-like voice in his head and society's desire for him to be "normal". It's a deeply compassionate portrait and I felt the frustration of battling a broken mental healthcare system, and the guilt and hope of everyone who loves poor, cheeky, troubled Tom and wants so badly for him to get better'

Douglas Stuart, author of *Shuggie Bain*,
Winner of the 2020 Booker Prize Award

'Absolutely wondrous. The characterisation, the humour, the whole glorious swirl of it'

Niall Griffiths, author of *Broken Ghost*,
Winner of the 2020 Welsh Book of the Year Award

'*The Octopus Man* reminds us that behind the words "mental health" lies a universe of wild creativity, humanity, and spanking big life. A beautiful thing, this is *The Dharma Bums* meet *Clozapine*. Now is the time for this book'

DBC Pierre,
author of Booker Prize-winning *Vernon God Little*

'*The Octopus Man* was a joy to read. I cried with laughter and I just plain cried. It is one of the wittiest and most humane pictures of a person and their mind – a timely conversation about mental health from within the perspective of the subject. It's a beautiful book and so incredibly funny. It was astounding to me how funny it was sometimes'   Johnny Flynn

The Octopus Man

Jasper Gibson

WEIDENFELD & NICOLSON

First published in Great Britain in 2021 by Weidenfeld & Nicolson
This paperback edition published in 2022 by Weidenfeld & Nicolson
an imprint of The Orion Publishing Group Ltd
Carmelite House, 50 Victoria Embankment
London EC4Y 0DZ

An Hachette UK Company

1 3 5 7 9 10 8 6 4 2

Quote on p.141 taken from *The Dharma Bums* by Jack Kerouac.

All the characters in this book are fictitious,
and any resemblance to actual persons, living
or dead, is purely coincidental.

A CIP catalogue record for this book
is available from the British Library.

ISBN (Mass Market Paperback) 978 1 4746 1609 6
ISBN (eBook) 978 1 4746 1610 2
ISBN (Audio) 978 1 4746 1611 9

Typeset by Input Data Services Ltd, Somerset

Printed and bound in Great Britain by Clays Ltd, Elcograf S.p.A.

www.weidenfeldandnicolson.co.uk
www.orionbooks.co.uk

For Ed

FEBRUARY

I

Tess is driving, looking at me sideways trying to guess what I am thinking about though she has no idea what I'm thinking about but just in case she's right I start thinking about something else. 'And he's OK with this?' she says. 'You haven't been electrocuted?'

We come out onto the forest tops, gorse on either side of the road.

'One for sorrow, two for joy.'

'You what now?' But the magpies have already disappeared into the military installation.

'Do you remember,' I say, 'when I saved up my money to buy you a willy?'

'Ho now. Yes. How much d'you get together?'

''Bout a quid. Quid fifty? I felt sorry for you.'

'Where were you going to get it from then?'

'The willy shop.'

'Ah yeah,' she says, 'the willy shop,' rounding a corner into elderly cyclists, red and yellow in all the kit. She widens out for the overtake but veers back again for lack of foreview down this barrelling bostal lane. 'So what about tomorrow? You still feeling all right about it?'

The cyclists heave their way along and do not look at us as

we pass. An area of warmth in my right thigh has been shifting slowly up through my hip and into my ribs. This patch may or may not be connected with seeing Dan again after all this time, and thus what he represents, a relic of my former existence, perhaps a welcome or unwelcome reminder of how far I have travelled. Tess is talking but I can only concentrate on the warmth, trying to assess its size and intent. He electrocuted me here, exactly here, just below the bottom rib, two days ago. The wife. Mr Atkins' new wife. He punished me for that even though she is old. I have been trying to make amends. Methods of dislocation. Disassembly. Disassociation. Atkins has invited me for dinner.

'Tom? I said *wonder if he looks the same?*'

'Who?'

'Dan? We're talking about Dan, yeah?'

I have seen Dan on Facebook. He looks wider. We descend into Fairwrap and turn onto the A22. Tess begins to repeat the arrangements. She can't pick me up after the meeting because she's got to go back to work so I'm taking the bus to Crowborough. I continue to investigate the warm patch through touch and inner focus. He agreed to me coming here with Tess. He agreed to my trip to London tomorrow to see Dan. But what if He is changing His mind?

'You're not listening.'

'You lunch Byron work. Me appointment Megan. Me bus.'

Megan has wrinkles around her eyes and long skilful-looking fingers and even though I have never seen them do anything other than make tea and fill in forms I imagine they have known great dexterity either in this life or a previous one. Megan has borrowed a doctor's office and I ask if I can sit in his chair and she says yes if I don't touch anything.

'Will I get a sweetie if I don't touch anything?'

Megan looks uncomfortable. I put my hands in my coat pockets and sit down. There are eight objects on the desk: hole puncher, stapler, lamp, penholder, phone, paperweight, USB key, box file. A bookshelf with eight books on it, another with sixteen. In between *Diagnosis and Treatment in Family Medicine* and *Ophthalmology: An Illustrated Guide* there is *Deep Black* by Andy McNab.

The door widens. A head floats in and says 'Mr Tuplow?' before pulling its body into the room. This is the Research Assistant. He seems a little thrown by finding me in the doctor's chair but drops himself neatly next to Megan, channelling all his researchable assistant energy into a smile, a smile that says *OK, we're doing it like this, are we? Well, OK then! Why not? Yes, why not? Hooray for us!* My knee is bouncing at incredible speed.

'So my name is Richard, and first off – thank you for coming in today.'

'Hello Richard,' I'm trying to copy his smile, 'and thank you. For coming in today.'

'Now Megan your CC here has indicated to me that you might be willing to take part in trials for bildinocycline? Is that right?'

The warm patch has slipped away into my leg. He is continuing to grant me this indulgence and I mouth a silent prayer of thanks, my chest gathering with a light, playful sensation because Richard looks a bit thick. He is young and has a surprised, baggy face, like a puppy. There are visible comb tracks in his white-blond hair and from across this desk I imagine Megan as Richard's mother, bringing in her delusional son for a check-up. *He thinks he's some kind of doctor, Doctor.*

'Now then, Richard,' I say, stretching my arms out across this desk, fanning my fingers, getting comfortable with its supreme power, 'can I call you Dickie?'

'*Tom* . . .' but Megan is stifling a smile. Oh Megan. Your

long, straight, greying hair. Do you comb it by a waterfall?

'So,' replies Richard, ignoring the question, reasserting himself in his chair, 'today is just a preliminary chat to assess your suitability for the trial. Are you OK with me asking you some questions this morning?' He is trying to nod a response out of me. Megan narrows her eyes. I nod back, slowly, and Dickie ticks something. *Good lord.* 'You live at number 1 Etchingham House, Meadowside Close, Crowborough and you live by yourself – is that all correct? And you've had a schizophrenia diagnosis for nineteen years?'

'I don't have schizophrenia.'

'But you are taking clozapine regularly?'

I don't want to lie in front of Megan.

'I have a clozapine prescription. Yes.'

'And how long have you been taking clozapine for?'

'Eight years. I started on 75 mgs a day and because it doesn't work I am now on 500 mgs a day.'

'And do you know why they put you on clozapine?'

'Lithium carbonate, sodium valproate, sertraline and fluoxetine made me suicidal. Olanzapine, Largactil, risperidone and amisulpride either didn't work or made me feel worse.'

'Pills or injection?'

'I used to need depot injection, but I've got so much wonderfully marvellously better at compliance, haven't I, nurse?'

'And now you don't feel suicidal?'

'How long will this assessment take?'

'He's joking,' says Megan.

'So nothing's worked?'

'Stelazine works. But they won't give me Stelazine.'

'Dr Sheldrake doesn't think it's appropriate,' says Megan.

'Could you ask Megan what that actually means? "*Appropriate?*" Because . . .' I pick up the empty penholder. It has a red ceramic base with a black plastic sheath attached to it by some

6

kind of swivelling nut. Replacing it carefully in the middle of the desk I take a deep breath. 'What happened, Richard, was that once upon a time I was in a bad way, a very bad way, and we couldn't get to see anyone, so my sister takes me to this private doctor who gives me Stelazine and it was . . .' I summon the right word down from the ceiling '. . . miraculous. But Sheldrake was so angry with this other doctor for *undermining his treatment plan* he refuses to prescribe it. Even though it actually works. Even though it's the one thing that stops me triggering!' Richard is tapping his pen against his lips as if ruminating on my situation, yet in this pause I have afforded him for comment he remains utterly mute. 'That, Dickie, is what happens when everyone's opinion on your life is more valuable than your own.'

'Oh now . . .' says Megan, looking at me with conciliation because she too knows Sheldrake's a bastard though politics forbids her from confessing it.

'That's quite a long history of medication,' says Dick. 'Can I ask you what you are taking it all for if you don't have schizophrenia?'

'Fear.'

'General fear?'

'Private fear. Reporting for duty.'

'I'm—'

'Black ops. Deep black.'

'*Tom* . . .'

'OK, OK. You might call it "anxiety disorder".'

'Could you go into a little more detail please?'

Leaning forward, my hands now trying to join each other from within their pockets – *a little more detail* – this sweat across the tops of my cheeks, this bouncing knee, this clenched jaw, and yet how I am with these two, this clowning, this show!

'Umm,' I say. 'No.'

'You're not able to? Or you'd rather not?'

Richard Dickie Dick I want you to imagine seeing a child let's say your own child any child it doesn't matter running out into the road the child steps back the car misses him but you are trapped in that wild unravelling moment for ever and there is an entire bureaucracy of suffering dedicated to helping you but the only answer they've got is GET RID OF THE CHILD.

'I'd rather not.'

Megan sighs as if she is in love with me. Large languorous eyes linger between the curtains of her hair. Oh Megan. Oh lonely Megan. He tells me how you make phone calls at night that no one answers.

'But listen,' I say, suddenly elated, suddenly thrilled, because I remember that for once it is me behind the desk, *I* am in position to repeat the sacred words of authority: '*Let's move on, shall we?*' They are powerless with agreement. 'Can you tell me a bit more about this new drug?'

'Sure, of course. Here you go,' says Dick, passing me a patient information leaflet entitled 'BeneBil: The Benefit of Bildino-cycline on Long-term Psychosis: Extent and Mechanisms'. Someone has tried to get a pen working on it.

'*We would like to invite you to take part in a research study,*' it says on the front. '*This leaflet explains why the research is being done and what is being done and what it involves. There is no rush to take part and there is plenty of time for questions.*'

'That's for you to take home.'

'*If you agree to take part, you can withdraw any time you like with no hard feelings from anyone.*'

'"No hard feelings",' I say out loud.

'Towards who? Towards me?' says Dickie, writing again.

'I'm just reading what it says here.'

Dickie crosses out his last note.

8

'And what are the side effects? I don't want any more side effects. Though they're not usually on the side, are they? More in the middle. Slap bang.'

'What side effects are you getting from your current medication?'

'Being buried alive?' I raise one eyebrow at Megan and in return she expresses all her concern for me, all her apologetic pity, with a pinched and meagre smile.

'Well, bildinocycline is extremely safe, and there aren't really any side effects of note, certainly not of the type normally associated with anti-psychotics. It's actually an antibiotic we've been using for years.'

'For what?'

'Athlete's foot.'

'Yes!' I say, clenching my fist in mock triumph, 'I knew it!'

Megan bends her head in admonition. Dickie continues the pitch.

'We're not sure why but it seems to have quite a radical effect on some chronic schizophrenia sufferers.'

'I told you, Rory, I don't have schizophrenia.'

'Richard.'

'Frustrating, isn't it?' Everyone shifts in their seat. My ears are cold. 'Let's move on, shall we? You want me to take an antibiotic for fungal infections. For how long?'

'Twelve weeks. There's been some preliminary clinical trials in India and Mexico and it seems that those patients who respond do so very quickly. It's really quite exciting.'

'Oh *goodie*.'

'Bildinocycline can be extremely effective with positive symptoms, even with long-term ones, and what we are trying to work out now is how it works. And why it works on some people and not others. What we're hoping, Mr Tuplow,' concludes Dickie, securing the top back on his pen with a certain

9

flair, a certain diplomatic flourish, 'is that bildinocycline really could open up a whole new set of opportunities for clients such as yourself.'

'Such as myself?'

'Such as yourself, who, perhaps, have limited treatment options. Currently.'

'Well you know what they say: one door closes, another one slams in your face. How effective is it at treating athlete's foot?'

'Ummm,' he says, 'Ummm—'

'Because I've actually got athlete's foot. Do you want to know if it clears up?'

'Perhaps you could let Megan know that.'

'How did you find out that an antibiotic for feet affects the brain?'

'Someone in Mexico who had heard unpleasant voices for a very long time went in for treatment for athlete's foot and the voices stopped. When the treatment stopped the voices started up again. A more powerful course was given and the voices cleared up completely.'

'Did anyone ask the voices if they were angry about his nasty feet?'

Silence.

Pushing off against the desk I spin the doctor's chair round to behold the window behind me, a kind of reverse gesture to *The Voice*: I reject their performance, and will not be offering myself as mentor. The frame is shaggy with red maple leaves. A patch of institutional garden gives way to fields, a copse, and the grey-blue light of a shortening winter's afternoon.

'So,' I purr to the window, further harnessing the authority of my mesh-backed swivel chair with the lilting timbre of the Bond villain, 'what is your theory of how it effects brain functioning?'

'Well, at the moment, we think it has something to do with glutamate transmitters in the prefrontal cortex, which is in—'

'I know where the prefrontal cortex is.'

'Well, glutamate trans—'

Whacking the block button *DDHOUUUM!* I spin round to face this Dick who thinks he knows more about brains than I do.

'I know what glutamate transmitters are.'

'Right. Well, we think bildinocycline is neuro-protective, and if you do want to take part what we would do is take an MRI brain scan at the beginning and the end of the trial. I'm guessing you know what an MRI scan is.'

'How much do you pay?'

'You'll be reimbursed £70 for your time and travelling to hospital for the scans.'

'Biscuits?'

'I'm sure we can get you some biscuits, yes.'

'Which kind?'

'*Tom . . .*'

'I am negotiating.'

'Which kind do you want?'

'Hobnobs!'

'Fine.'

'Chocolate?'

'Chocolate Hobnobs. No problem.'

'With Stelazine on them.'

Richard says the word 'Ha' without actually laughing.

'You'll have to talk to Dr Sheldrake about that, I'm afraid.'

'He doesn't make biscuits.'

'Let me have another word with him,' says Megan so I whistle – a single, drooping note – to release us both from that pretence.

'Stelazine Hobnobs, Dickie, and you've got yourself a deal . . .'

The ribbon of white light appears. I touch my head and yawn.

'Mr Tuplow?'

I have exceeded myself.

'Tom?'

Been cocky.

Standing up quickly I stuff the leaflet into my pocket. I can feel the Nerf gun pellet I picked up this morning from the woodland floor.

'Sorry for calling you Dick, Richard.'

'Tom—'

'I think I would like to go now.'

'Take your time, think about it, any questions give me a ring' – Richard scrabbles to finish his notes then jumps up and gives me a card – 'or let Megan know, you know, if you want to discuss anything.'

'I'll call you later,' says Megan, giving me a hug. 'Still feeling OK about tomorrow?'

I give Richard a hug, for which he is unprepared.

I am hoping for forgiveness.

Marching away from the medical centre to the bus stop, He does not electrocute me though my right side remains hot. I am grateful that there is no one else waiting for the bus as I am agitated and fidgeting and when it arrives I show my pass then hurry straight upstairs to my seat. There are eight people on the upper deck.

The bus shakes and pitches away from the kerb, moving off through Maresfield and back towards Crowborough. Branches hurtle out of the fog, crashing against the window as I pray to Him, giving thanks that He allowed me to go to the meeting which will please Tess, yet clemency, please, clemency! *I abused your licence.* I was arrogant and unpleasant. Did I show too much interest in their trial? I told Richard he had a deal if there was Stelazine. 'That was just a joke!'

I put my hand against the hot patch and return to prayer, closing my eyes to concentrate on my breathing and think only of His love. *I love you with all my heart. Please keep me from triggering. Please keep me from madness.*

A woman next to me with red hair and neat shoes struggles to get past. I stand to let her out, but it is not her stop. She sits down a few rows behind and I can feel her face watching me though her eyes are turned on ghostly hills heading west. I cannot stop myself from turning round until I realise I am frightening her. Our discomfort makes me sweat even though it is cold. I am palming the sweat from my forehead because I have nothing else to wipe it with and my sweat smells of vinegar which is embarrassing *stop sniffing your hand!* I go down to the lower deck to save the woman from our shared unease. He is happy with this act. My right side is cooling. I let out a terrific breath.

When we arrive at the Crowborough Cross the bus judders to a stop. It is already dark; nights in the afternoon. I say good-bye to the driver who has gentle eyes and badly pockmarked skin, stepping onto the pavement as the bus makes a hydraulic gasp of suffering and release.

Walking up to the Broadway I review myself, thinking backwards from the bus into the meeting, remembering my jokes – *Private Fear. Reporting for duty* – feeling pleased then hastily apologising to Him for this vanity, remembering Megan's words *still feeling OK about tomorrow?* the patronising, well-meaning concern of it, about something so trivial, so normal, when I see Mr Brigget coming out of WH Smith. 'Aye aye!' he says. 'How's tricks?' We let out throaty breaths into the cold air. 'Venison? Knocked over a Bambi this morning. Freezer's full.'

'I don't eat meat.'

'Ah. Course you don't. Sorry. Ask Tess there, will you?'

'Sure.'

'Good man you. Cheerio then.'

Crossing onto Croft Road and up the rise to Waitrose there are familiar elderly faces in the front window where the coffee shop is but at the entrance there is a *Big Issue* seller I have not seen before who looks like he is from Peru. Or Bolivia.

'Why are you only wearing a shirt?'

'This is my shirt.'

'Do you want my coat? I'm going inside.'

He looks fairly baffled by my offer so I take off my coat, a venerable Barbour that has long been my companion. Now there is warmth all the way up my left side. He is pleased by this act. The *Big Issue* seller looks very much like a dentist I once had. Dr Soames.

Soames puts on my coat and looks quite sad.

'Sorry it's not a . . . I don't know. A Puffa.'

'Thank you,' he says, starting to sell a magazine to someone else, but then I remember my wallet and phone are still in the pockets. I try to retrieve them but forget to tell Soames what I am doing. He is shocked to feel my hands back in the pockets and steps away from me. Both hands are in the coat so I have to step closer but he steps away and so on, in a circle. Soames is commenting in his own language. The shopper frowns. Finally I have a grasp of my things and can fetch my hands from him. We all share an unusual moment.

I am cold now and hurry into Waitrose, greeting Sass and Carl, two teenage workers. I ask for a mug of hot water and say hello to Amy Turle and old Ned Dickie and the Perrin girls and the Mudies and the Clerets and Mrs Minns, who is talking about Syria. I sit down by the window, sipping my water, and look out at all the mobility scooters abandoned in front of the

Social Club. Warm arms suddenly wrap my face and Tess kisses the top of my head, sitting down, toying with one of her ear hoops.

'You stink. Haven't you tried that shampoo I bought you?'

'Yes.'

'And?'

'Didn't taste very good.'

'Har har. Where's your coat?'

'The *Big Issue* seller was cold.'

'Oh Tom, for fuck's . . .' Tess shakes free a certain screwing-up of the face that I know well. She marches outside.

'Excuse me,' she says as we arrive beside Soames. 'Sorry but I need my brother's coat back.'

'Coat? This?'

'Yeah, that's his coat. Can I have it back please?' Soames looks down at the coat. 'Here's a quid. You can keep the magazine.'

'You want the coat?' he says to me.

'Sorry,' she says, 'he hasn't got the money for a new coat.'

'Thank you,' he says, taking it off. Tess gives him a pound. 'Thank you,' he says again. I put on my Barbour. Soames seems unsure of what I represent. We walk up into the illumined car park.

'You can't give anyone your coat, Tom, OK? It's freezing.'

'He was cold.'

'He's probably got his stashed in the bin or whatever. That's his thing, isn't it. His blag.'

'But a coat isn't important, Tess. The cornerstone of a spiritual life is to help—'

'Hey. That coat may not be important to you, but that's the first time you've taken it off in about ten years – you stop wearing it now and I won't be able to recognise you.'

We get into her blue Polo she calls Polly. The window

doesn't work on the driver's side and I absorb the state of its footwells as future defence when my own living space is next insulted for its accumulation and chaos.

'Just bumped into Ted Atkins. Said you rang him up.'

'Did I?'

'Said you rang him up and asked if you could come round and see his wife because you'd been thinking about her.'

'He invited me for dinner.'

'That's because he is incredibly understanding.'

'I just couldn't stop thinking about her and then He . . . I thought if I actually saw her in the flesh it might prevent . . . because she's actually quite old. The Oct—'

'Nope,' she says with a tongue-clack. 'No thank you. Not in the mood.'

We roll backwards between the cars. Tess growls the gear-stick and we drive off, slipping between other headlights across the High Weald.

'So. You going to tell me how it went then? Or what?'

'How's Byron?'

Tess blows out her lips, trumpeting a note of confusion.

'Byron's trying to be a sweetheart is what happened with Byron. As usual. Don't change the subj—' Her work phone buzzes on the dashboard. 'Hextons, hello? Oh, hello Dennis. No, I told your manager the stop's been lifted. We got the cheque. No problem. Is that right? Is it? You start calling me "darling" and the stop's going back on. Did you indeed? No, Den, you're not a good payer, that's why the stop was put on. Is that right? Anyway you can call sales now. Yep. OK, Den. You too. Yep, toodle-pip.' She slings her phone back on the dashboard. 'And yes it did end in a massive row, thank you very much.'

'Is he moving back in?'

Tess sighs. She takes one hand off the steering wheel and lays it on my face. We shoot through an odd moment of rain, as if we have caught it practising.

'So come on then,' she says, 'was Megan there?'

White lines in the middle of the road are impossible to count.

'Yep.'

'Well?' Tess sits forward. 'And?'

'Mr Brigget says he's got some dead defenceless animal flesh for you.'

'Tom—'

'I can't do it,' I tell the window.

Tess re-grips the steering wheel and clears her throat.

'Well it's only the first conversation, isn't it? Let's just take it slowly and see where—'

'He doesn't want me to do it, Tess.'

She starts to say something then stops. I can feel her suffering and her hope but can answer neither so instead I twist round and hug her.

'I'm fucking driving here, Tom!' she shrieks, the car swerving as we drum the rumble strips and she gives herself over to swear words that are soon directed at other drivers and then life itself.

———

Woodsmoke lurches off the fire and I move Lisa's leg. The spicy scorched stench of it skirts across us so we wince and hide our heads. Me and Lisa stole away from the others and down into the field into the pillbox and she gave me a blow job then spat the spunk out and said sorry. What you apologising for? I don't care what you do with it. We hugged each other all the way back to the party but now it's a blue dawn and Lisa has passed out with her legs over me. Everyone has passed out pretty much except me and Tess and the birds and the statue we made of her friend that couldn't come, a deadwood scarecrow with hat and shades in a ballet pose with one leg skewed into the soil, the other bent up behind. He still has a beer.

We brought blankets from the house. There is a cupboard under the stairs that's been locked ever since Mum went off but we found the key and it is full of blankets. Dan is curled up like a hedgehog. Karen Richardson is snoring a little. She has pissed herself but looks happy and Tess kneels over to cover her up. She rocks back beside me and I pass her the bottle. GCSE results are through and I got thirteen As and two A/S levels. Most anyone ever got at that school. They gaffa-taped a two-litre bottle of cider to my hand.

'Lightweights,' says Tess.

'Your turn next year.'

'Gonna fail them all. You know I'm going to fail them all. 'Cept art. Fuck it. Don't give a shit. Leaving anyway.' A plane from Gatwick passes over. There is a woodpecker somewhere, working. 'When do you think Mum'll be back?'

'This week. Got a feeling. Kinda like a weird premonition.'

Tess passes back the bottle and spits.

'So what d'you reckon about what Miss Hartley said?'

'Whatywhat?'

'Miss Hartley. When she was basically telling me what a thick bitch I am. When she said you could go to Oxford or Cambridge or one of them places if you want.'

'Fuck daaaaaaat . . .' I lean into her so she falls over. 'We going Brighton. *Beside the seaside, beside the sea.*' We are both watching the grey bones of the fire.

'D'you know what, Tom Tuplow?'

'What?'

'I think you're going to change the world,' she says. 'I really mean that. I think you are going to change the world somehow. And don't do that. Don't pull that face.'

'What face?'

'I can feel you doing it.' She is pushing us both upright. 'Prick. So what about Lisa then?'

'She's cool. What about whatshisname?'

'Hoh no. Way too blinkywinky,' and she puts the back of her hand in her mouth, miming whatshisname going down on her, checking upwards every other second to see if she's having a good time: *blinkywinky*. I groan, elbowing her away but she just adds more sound effects.

———

Tess needs to visit the Huntsman in Eridge before she heads back to the warehouse. I tell her I can walk home through the woods but she won't hear of it because it's dark and she doesn't understand that His guidance means I can't get lost. I wait for her inside Polly the Polo, listening to Radio 4 and watching the first batch of commuters walking past me down the road from the station, fumbling in their bags and pockets, searching for which bush they've left their car in. I turn the dial to Radio 3, turning my mind to tomorrow's trip to London. Vast amounts of energy have been spent arguing that I will not expend too much energy but that irony is thoroughly lost on Tess and Megan and 'Once again!' I say out loud, *once again* I am forced to ask their permission like a child knowing that I will need to present this day as an utter and extreme success as defined by them, by their judgement, or else future excursions will be prevented. Tess climbs back into the car and I tap out a quick, rebellious rhythm on the dashboard, *ta-ta-tat-tat-tat*.

'I'm going to speak to Megan, OK?' says Tess as we tunnel up Forge Road towards Motts Mill, overhead branches of holly and chestnut wrestling each other in the beamlight. 'Just letting you know. What time train are you getting tomorrow?'

'Twoish.'

'Luuuckeee you. I'll be going past yours about half one. Can drop you in Tunny Wells, get you straight to Victoria. Where you meeting Dan again?'

'Uxbridge.'

'Well that's better than the Uckfield line, isn't it? Straight to Victoria. Straight on the thingy to Uxbridge?'

No, not better particularly, and she will not just happen to be driving past my flat at that particular time, and never has she called Tunbridge Wells *Tunny Wells* before, but I am off to London to be an independent human being at least for one hard-fought afternoon and so instead of arguing I give her the Dick Whittington smile *ho ho*.

'Reckons you might be roight there, m'lady.'

'Why you talking like that?'

'Loike what, m'lady?'

Through Motts Mill, left into Lye Green, back towards Crowborough and she is tock-tocking her indicator as we turn into Meadowside Close, headlights sweeping across these dubby blocks of flats. She pulls in next to Saul's Mini. I heave myself out into a halo of my own breath.

'Sure you're sure then?' she says. 'About tomorrow?'

'Yes, Mother Theresa, I am.'

'Just asking! Keep your hair on.'

'That . . . you can't – you can't keep making that joke.'

'Going to buy you a hat. Like a furry one. With ear flaps.'

'Ear flaps.'

'Luxury rabbit ears. For the bunny about town. Tom, listen, can you please just think about this trial again? Properly?'

'Properly I went along, like you asked. Properly I listened, like you asked, but I properly cannot do something like that. I'm sorry. Properly *properly* sorry.'

'Because *he* says so.'

'It's not . . .' I bend backwards to the stars astronomising for one more way to explain it to her. *Preparation and*

training. The requisite condition. Direct knowledge of birth and death.
'. . . compatible. With what I have to do. Can you at least try and understand it in those terms?'

'"*In those terms*"?' she repeats in a mock-posh voice. 'Fucking listen to yourself . . . honestly . . .' Tess screws up her face and grinds the engine. She winds out of the parking space and then becomes another noise on London Road. I touch my head and yawn.

The room smells of sandalwood, tobacco and onions. There isn't much natural light in my bedsit but there are many books and magazines I don't have shelving for and crenellate around the flat in zones of subject matter that leave narrow thorough-fares: legal textbooks and books about the law, Sophocles, Plato, books about ethics, lots of Martha C. Nussbaum, books about octopuses, marine biology, flora and fauna identification, archaeology, psychiatry and psychology, religion, spirituality, mysticism, world history, books about Sussex and Kent, Greek and Roman classics, books about Polynesia, reference books, novels, poetry, and then stacks of coursework and essays from my graduate diploma in law, my pupillage, and my ancient his-tory degree. The room is very cold.

I pick my way through to the split and sprouting club arm-chair and turn on the bar heater beside it that hums and fills the room with the scent of burning dust, its sharp and furry heat against my back as I kneel at my bed, under which are several plastic storage tubs. I begin to rummage.

'Microwave,' says Malamock, so I stop rummaging. There is indeed a new packet of sandalwood incense beside the microwave.

I kneel down at the corner shrine, fastening a new stick into the holder. I light the candle and the sandalwood, inhaling its wealthy sweetness, then ring the bell and look up at the collage of octopus pictures spreading across the wall and ceiling, folded and cut into the shape of one giant octopus that looks down upon the shrine. I bow my head to pray and the warmth of His love creeps then blooms all over my left side.

After prayers I turn off the expensive heater and turn on the hob, heating up the curried vegetables that I made yesterday. I take my bowl from the sideboard and sit on my bed with it, wrapped in duvet, switching on the television, savouring the salty spicy taste of curried cauliflower, lentils, onions and potatoes. There are boats full of migrants in the Mediterranean. There is chaos. People are holding up their babies to strangers.

'This entire mass of stress,' He says. 'A requisite condition. From the cessation. The breakthrough of pilgrims from all over the inhabited world. Transmigrants. Do not regret what you have done.' I freeze for a moment, wondering if He is talking about my interview for the drug trial, but He says nothing else. When I have finished eating there is still enough for at least two more meals so I cover the bowl and leave it on the sideboard. Then I smoke and we watch *Come Dine with Me*.

In the bathroom I take my clozapine tablet and sit down on the toilet, pissing with my head in my hands, overwhelmed by a sudden tide of sadness.

'Thomas,' He commands, His voice hardened now against my despair.

'Sorry,' I say, standing up and flushing.

'Every vulnerable period. Monks, nuns, it is to this extent; the knowledge of the path. The camel. The gold and the crystal. Follow that.'

I nod and sit on the edge of the bath and blub toothpaste onto the bristles, sawing at my teeth in front of my untrue reflection, trying to focus on His teaching, the knowledge of the path. The ceiling creaks. Saul and Nika are moving about upstairs. I tug at my beard then look at the fingers doing the tugging. They slip onto my wobbly belly and shake it.

'You may abandon your own body,' He scolds, 'but you are in practice separate.' I apologise for my vain thought-form and lower my eyes from the mirror.

In bed but still dressed I watch more television so I can lose myself within the programmes but when the clozapine starts to drag against me I turn it off, peel myself bare, turn off the light and wriggle further into bed trying to genie up the warmth. I visualise the journey to London and seeing my old best mate Dan. I explain my purpose to him, Dan becomes inspired, and we help someone in trouble right there on the street, someone who has perhaps fallen, and in the act of bending down all our eyes meet, the person we are helping and mine and Dan's, a triangle of goodness formed that spins off to link three other people, then six, then nine, all creating their own triangles that spin off on their own paths, triangles becoming squares and trapezoids, linking together as a great grid, a network of good-ness reticulating the earth, all from that paving stone with me, Dan, and a fallen woman.

———

Sunday night and Dan wants to go home. He's got work at the printers' in the morning and wants to go to bed but that would be breaking the circle and the warm blissful spell we have cast over ourselves, every ingredient dropped steadily into the cauldron of this flat and the long weekend. If he leaves the spell will break and we will be left with ourselves and I can't face that, not now that the night has come back and there is no mean-spirited daylight nosing through drawn curtains, not now that the lamplight is once again burning low gold and Dan is in his armchair and me and Tess are on our sofa, the coffee table strewn with ingredients, the flat filled with smoke and the smell of bong water, Ganesh and Buddha and fractal depictions of kundalini and the cosmos looking down on us from yellow walls. The bar heater smiles with deep orange light onto where only a day ago there were bodies strewn, those that came back with us from the rave, including one weirdo with a centre parting who everyone assumed was someone else's friend but then it turned out he just tagged along because he fancied Tess. She kept moving seats to avoid him and when everyone was so baked out on pills and microdots that we were in a collective dream he started rolling up the rug and I said hey what are you doing and he looked at me but kept on rolling up the rug and started leaving the room with it and I said hey what are you doing and Dan said hey man what are you doing with the rug, and he didn't say anything he just dropped the rug and left the flat.

'Oh Danny boy,' says Tess. 'Don't be a prick. Don't prick it.'

'Ah gotta go ta sleeeep,' he drawls, pulling at his face. 'Tomorrow's gonna be bad enough as it is.'

'I got work too,' says Tess.

'Yeah but you don't have to concentrate.'

In front of me there is *Civil Procedure in a Nutshell*, *Examples and Explanations in Constitutional Law*, the bong, a packet of Hobnobs, a bottle of amyl nitrate, weed, *Loaded,* tobacco, blue Rizla, pizza boxes full of ash and butts, *The White Goddess*, *Grazia*, nail scissors, *The Gnostic Gospels* and fuck's sake I mutter, snatching it up: someone has roached the front cover. I see a dead wasp on the carpet beneath the glass coffee table.

'OK,' I say, lining up the wasp and a broken bit of Hobnob. 'I will bong this biscuit and this wasp if you stay.'

Tess makes her 'oh my gawd' noise. Dan picks up the wasp by its wing and inspects it. 'I will dip the blessed biscuit in amyl.'

'Shot away,' says Tess, shaking her head. 'Blatantly shot away.'

'Dip this biscuit in amyl, bong it, then bong the wasp. Deal?'

'Saaaaaafe,' he nods. 'Emilio with the dealio.'

We touch fists.

'Shot away,' says Tess again, still shaking her head, but now like some kind of dance move. 'The whole plot. Blatantly. *Blay-tante*.'

Tess and Dan groan as I drip some amyl onto the bit of biscuit then pack it into the bowl. Finally I find a lighter with some flame left, pick up the bong, hold it against my mouth, the base between my knees, then light the bowl, strange grey smoke curling up the chamber as the bong bubbles until it reaches the top then whip my thumb from the shotgun hole and inhale. Hold it. Exhale. The smell of burnt biscuit and the chemical whiff of the amyl fills the room and there is a rush of lightness in my brain but by the time I stop coughing it has gone.

'How was that?'

'Nae bad. *Vonting?*'

'Thanks but.'

'You, man. Staying.'

The wasp is light and I place it gently in the bowl once I have scooped it clean of incinerated biscuit. I consider then reject the idea of changing the bong water. Dan and Tess are making noises like disturbed sheep and I fire up the dead wasp into a surprisingly thick amount of smoke. Once the first wisps have reached the top I shotgun then inhale, exhaling immediately, tongue out like a dragon, wincing against the bitter taste of it, acrid and unnatural. They are applauding, holding their noses against the smell, my chin pressed against my chest, face creased into bulldog wrinkles as I try to process away the taste.

'OK. Wow. That. Wow. Horrible. Truly.'

Once he has recovered from laughing, Dan leaves.

———

The alarm pulsates as Malamock tears off my dreaming head to show me again how the world is going to drown: the panic and the suffering, the disease and the slaughter. I can hear my heart thudding against the pillow. I could not prevent lustful thoughts, memories of Phoebe dancing in a pub, biting her lip, shaking her fists, so He boiled my night with punishment nightmares.

The alarm is set to go off several times both on my phone and on the computer and within this long waking there is even a moment of exquisite lightness, a glimpse of an old life, or a different one, but then I finally churn myself upwards, crossing my ankles and wiping my face from drool.

'Thomas,' He says, His voice soft and kindly again. Relieved, I get out of bed, my knees cracking as I stand. 'Old Man of the . . .' He says. 'Getting old. I will look after you when you are old.'

I take my meds, brush my teeth and eat a simple breakfast of toast and a cup of hot water wrapped up in my coat and scarf while listening to Radio 4, becoming frustrated with Sarah Montague who is not letting a trade union representative speak. 'Shut up, Sarah! Give him a chance!'

'Anger?' He says.

'She won't let him answer her questions!'

'Your mother. Her childish action. The flood breaketh out from the inhabitant.'

'Sarah Montague isn't high though,' I say. 'Probably.'

We continue to listen to the *Today* programme. I imagine John Humphrys and Sarah Montague doing lines and necking shots when they aren't speaking and the tone of their conversation immediately makes much more sense.

Tess has to field a great deal of calls throughout her day even when she is not at the warehouse and I don't want to contribute to her load but this first call is the most important as she wants to know what kind of night I had, whether I have taken my tablets, whether I am calm or worried or under attack.

'Still sure about today? How you feeling?'

'Bright and breezy,' I say. 'Lemon squeezy.'

When we leave the flat for our morning walk, Saul is outside hoovering his Mini.

Saul and Nika both like to wear slippers, but only Saul wears them outside. Nika is Russian and much younger than him. She doesn't have a neck and hardly any mouth, just a lipless slot where the food must go through. Saul has a face like a turtle's except with hair. He looks like a turtle in a wig. He washes his Mini and goes to the gym. He wears gym clothes and slippers and badly fitting glasses. The Octopus God has told me that Saul feels like a failure because he is unable to give Nika children. He will lose the use of his legs in old age. He believes in television. I am warned against unkind thoughts about Saul but they are difficult to resist because he's such a massive twat.

'Must be the cleanest car in the country,' I say to Malamock quietly as I lock my door.

Saul looks up. He shakes his head in vaudeville disapproval of my existence then returns to the upholstery.

'It's really bad OCD is what it is,' I whisper, walking by. 'He's mentally ill.'

'Right attention,' says Malamock, 'feet,' and I stop, looking back to the car and see his glasses on the tarmac by his feet.

'Your glasses,' I call out over the noise of the Hoover.

'*What?*' Saul snaps off the machine and thrusts his turtle head out from its motorised shell.

'Your glasses,' I repeat, pointing. He picks them up, shoots me a look, then goes back to hoovering. 'Didn't even say "thank you".'

★

27

The fields behind Meadowside Close are glazed with frost. I am crunching our way along the hedgerow of High Paddocks, faded yelloworange grass thatched in mud, the field streaked green with winter rape. Coming through Long Round we walk out onto Gorse Bank, the morning mist lying so thickly in the ghyll that the oaks and beeches are only half visible, the heifers like some new species, some eerie manatees of the English quag.

I stop, overwhelmed by the beauty of it all. 'Thomas,' He says, 'You are my soul,' and my left side erupts with His love, a love of unimaginable depth and stillness.

We continue along the public footpath. There are many crusted molehills, as if there has been a tiny shelling. At the bottom of the ghyll the cows trail us as we cross their field to the stile, entering the red belly of the woods: burgundy leaf mulch, dead and crimson bracken, fine purple tree sprigs, that sour smell of bright orange mould that stockings the beech trees even as their bases glow green with moss. The distinction of things is lost in the silver mist, crows echoing their black-eyed gibberish, the woodland floor mosaicked in frozen leaves and I am overwhelmed again, halting just to breathe, the cold air sharp against my nostrils.

A badger hole spews blue earth around its mouth and looks almost human in size, as if someone has dug themselves in, trying to reach some warmth. I take a picture of it then lie down and wriggle my arm into the hole as far as it will go.

'Just want . . . to see if it gets . . . wider or narrower. Feels like it's getting wider . . .' I stand up, brushing myself down. 'There'd be no neighbours, would there? No Saul. If I moved in here.'

'There would be badgers,' He says and this makes me laugh out loud, a distant dog answering me with two barks.

We carry on across the crumbling footbridge and onto a ride

past the temple folly, the lake winterglassed and ringed with died-back bulrushes and sedge. We cross the drive that curls up to the Blake family's big house and back along Bad Brook into Jockey's Wood, the alders and willow and ash all crackling with the cold.

At the bottom of Sawmill Field I realise He is no longer there. The brook burrows into the land where someone has nailed a clay mouth and eyes to a trunk so that the tree greets me with wry amusement as I head up the hillside into Rocks Wood. Hidden there on the lee, striking out among the coppiced birch, are my rocks: great loaves of stone, olive green with moss and lichen. One of these formations has a perfect indentation in its scalp, a natural throne, and I scale up the rock, shooing out the rimy detritus, and nestle in against the moss, jeans glowing with the damp. I close my eyes and inhale the carbon wreak of winter. I am safe here, He has never electrocuted me in these woods. I have never triggered here.

After some time that may have wandered into sleep – a sense of return, a balmy mouth – I roll a cigarette and smoke it, listening to the crows and wood pigeons, the rattled squawks of a jay. Climbing back down from the rock, I spy the bright orange cap of another Nerf gun pellet among the ferns and put it in my pocket. I start walking home, sunlight creeping through the trees, sweeping the hills and fields from frost. Ice water drips from every tree and bush, the whole landscape steaming from its nightwash. My phone shakes.

'What you up to?' says Tess, eating.

'On my walk.'

'Seen anything good?'

'Massive badger hole.'

'*Life in the fast lane,*' she sings. 'Ooops got a call – laters.'

Once out on the road, I walk up past the Baptist church and into Crowborough. At the Cross I turn up Beacon Road and into Morrisons car park. I see a father carrying a baby while trying to steer a trolley loaded with food as another little girl clings onto the side, pulling if off course. I can't tell exactly which car he is going for so I head him off at a tiny crossing between two Vauxhalls, a Range Rover and a van.

'Can I help you?' I say, and he seems displeased, which is not an uncommon reaction. I am in his way and step aside.

'What?' he shrugs. 'No, stop that, Anna. I said leave it!'

'Do you want me to push the trolley for you?'

'Eh?'

'Looks like you could use a hand.' He scans my clothing. 'It just looked like you were struggling a bit.'

'Did it?' he says, his face rearranged into a scowl now that he's decided I'm a loony. He pushes past me and when he arrives at his Passat and is fastening his children into their seats I become the subject of intense examination.

'Of the scorn of men,' says Malamock, filling me with a gentle stillness. 'Of sudden illness. A covenant with thee.' The man is still scowling at me but I feel nothing but love for him. I don't mind if he thinks I'm a loony. In fact it's quite funny. Malamock's presence suddenly becomes very strong. I can almost lean my head into it and feel His arms, His compassion around me.

Back on the Broadway I see Mary Lorde sitting in the window of Costa Coffee. She is wearing green corduroy trousers and a thick blue padded jacket, leather handbag on her lap, hair neat-set and bouffant. Costa Coffee is blowy-warm and charcoal with purple chairs and pop art exclamations about coffee on the walls *COFFEE!* I go up to the glass counter rowed with cakes and granola bars and ask for a cup of hot water from one of the teen-agers. There are two mothers complaining to each other with Italianate gestures over the heads of their children. A businessman prods his screen with a pen then looks about, as if interrupted.

'Hello Mary,' I say. 'Can I sit with you?'

Mary Lorde smiles and I take my place sipping the hot water and look out at what she is looking at: the traffic and two people talking in the doorway of the Hair Gallery.

'Anything I can do for you?'

Mary Lorde turns to me.

'Anything you need doing? Something carried or anything like that? Anything you need help with?'

Mary Lorde looks at me for a long moment, shifting her legs aside, her mouth in a half-smile. Then she holds out her hand. So we sit there watching the traffic together, holding hands.

2

Tess pulls into Meadowside Close. She rolls to a stop, asks me why I am standing in the cold, tells me to get in, asks me if I am feeling all right, all without breaking stride either with her phone call or her driving. We're almost the other side of Groombridge when she hangs up.

'Sorry. New restaurant. Driving me up the wall. Across the ceiling. Wall again.'

'Why do you think there are so many hairdressers in Crowborough?'

'Ah. Philosophy time.'

'It's like every third shop or something now. There's a new one just opened up.'

'There are a lot. True that.'

'Way more hairdressers than anything else but yet, when you look around . . .'

'It's not as if everyone has amazing hair?'

'With that many hairdressers, that should be its thing, right? Far and wide. "Wow, nice hair, dude! You must be from Crowborough."'

We sweep through Langton Green.

'You're feeling good then? About today?'

'Affirmative.'

32

'Your phone's all charged and everything?'

'Affirmative, affirmative.' I spin on the radio. A group of people are discussing soup.

'So,' says Tess, slowing down beside Rusthall Park as we bunch up with the traffic coming into Tunbridge Wells. 'So listen. I've had a chat with Megan about this new drug trial thing, and she said you sounded keen.'

'No I didn't.'

'She told me you were pretty much agreeing to it.'

'No I was not,' I touch my head and yawn. 'I was not!'

'Hey—'

'It's so infuriating! This thing you all do!'

'What are you on about?'

'Changing what actually happened!' My knee is bouncing. I gabber out silent testimony to Him that she is lying and I did not betray Him or even think of it or give it any meaningful consideration whatsoever! 'I did not want to do it, and I do not want to do it, and I can't do it, and whatever Megan may have misunderstood was – I don't know – probably a joke or something. I just asked for Stelazine! Again!'

'Hey, calm down whoa—'

'OK. I am whoaed. Is this the end of it?'

'End of what?'

'Of you banging on about it! I keep saying no!'

'Oh give over! I am not banging on about—'

'I said I don't want to talk about it any more!'

'So it's like that, is it?' she says as we swing around the round-about and up alongside the Pantiles. 'You don't want to talk about a possible new treatment.'

'No!'

'Well I do!'

'Fine! You take it then!'

Tess brakes to let a van turn.

'You're a fucking selfish arsehole sometimes, Tom. D'you know that?'

We are silent all the way to the NCP car park. When I open the car door and swing my legs out I am still agitated by their scheming and experience a pulsation. Tess is standing in front of me on a call.

'. . . the Hare and Hound. We're late paying Diageo because – the Dunn and Bradstreet report. They had CCJs hand over fist, I told you! OK. Anyway. Yeah. Yep. Back in a bit, yeah.' She hangs up and sees that I am staring and rigid. 'You OK?'

I nod and she pulls me to my feet. There are twenty-four cars on our level. 'You don't have to, you know. You can always ring him up and cancel. He won't mind.' But if I cancel Dan we won't see each other for another however many years, so I shake my head and we leave the car park while I whisper prayers for strength.

We go into a newsagent so I can buy tobacco and there is an Indian man behind the counter with a round sweet face and a flaking bindi and once I have paid for the Old Holborn he gives me such a smile, such distraction, that I step around the counter and though I can see his alarm when I hug him he relaxes and pats my back and calls me friend. Tess apologises for me and we leave. We walk across the road to the station and I become suddenly afraid of being alone in case I trigger and she is not close or I can't reach her because reception on the train is bad and she asks me again if I wouldn't just rather go home? But I don't want her to be right. I just want to go up to town for the afternoon. Like people do.

'Don't expect too much,' Tess says, hugging me. 'OK?' Then she's gone.

I go down the stairs and onto the platform and sit on the bench. Some lost sunlight suddenly falls onto the tracks and

I feel another pulsation that almost turns into a malevolent thought-form so to distract myself I spring from the bench into the coffee shop and order a black coffee. I should not drink coffee and the coffee here is not good but I need to distract myself from the pulsation and just let it flow through me while I think of something else.

I take the hot cup, dancing my fingers against it and trailing steam across the platform. Sitting down on the bench shakes hot liquid onto my hand yet I am glad of this stinging sensation, the distraction it provides, though I bury that thought instantly unless it leads back to what I am trying to distract myself from. I roll a cigarette and drink the coffee and concentrate on the sensations and the tastes while I wait for the train. A pretty girl pulling a small suitcase comes onto the platform. She is wearing a short pink skirt and her legs are brown and smooth and as she bends to zip something up on her suitcase I see a flash of white knickers. I turn the other way on the bench.

I fumble out my phone and see that I only have ten per cent battery left. I have forgotten to charge it! I stand up thinking I must leave and go back home but I so want to see Dan again after all this time I sit down deciding that I will find somewhere to charge it in London and simply not call Tess now simply keep that ten per cent for a real emergency. Fine. It'll be fine. I just don't want that look, that *I told you so*. I don't want to hand Tess more proof that all her supervision and control is justified but I am beset with worry and feel a tingling on my neck and look up to see the white light split out from a brick wall beyond the tracks.

'Thomas,' He says, His voice strong and enclosing. I am looking at the pretty girl again.

'I'm trying,' I whisper through my teeth.

She looks at me and I yawn and touch my head then rub my scalp recalling curly rich hair but the year they put me on clozapine it fell out in the autumn, like a tree. I pinch a look at her legs. It is difficult to prevent this longing in my chest.

'Thomas.'

'It's not my fault! She's right there!' The train comes and I walk to the end of the eighth carriage so I won't be anywhere near her but when I sit down I realise I have finished the whole coffee instead of just taking a sip and throwing it away as was my intention. The worry about the effect of the coffee starts to mix with the effect of the coffee and I close my eyes and try to pray but my heart is accelerating my throat beginning to close and I dig into my pocket for some lozepam and so take one believing that it will slow me down whispering to Him: 'I love you with all my heart. I love you more than anything in the world. Please keep me from triggering. Please keep me from madness.'

The ticket inspector comes. He has grey teeth and doesn't look at anyone when he asks for their tickets and has a kind of bark on his soul.

'Tell him. That I am present,' says Malamock.

'Tickets please,' says the ticket inspector.

'Do not let yourself be guided by customary beliefs.'

'Not now.'

'Pardon me?'

'Sorry, nothing.'

'You all right, sir?'

'Tell him.'

'I am—'

'Do not deny me.'

'Malamock, the Octopus God,' I blurt out, then, turning away, 'There, that's enough!'

'What?'

'I'm sorry, it's nothing,' I say wishing the inspector would

36

leave but now he is inspecting me and Malamock constricts my right side, twisting me towards the man.

'No!' I hiss, and I look up and see a flat-haired lady in an ancient yellow tracksuit raise her eyes at the inspector.

'Do not deny me.'

'I'm going to need to see your ticket, sir.'

'Yes of course,' I say.

'*Yes of course*,' He repeats, mocking me. My ticket is in the right-hand pocket of my jeans but I am struggling to get it out because He is constricting my right side which suddenly becomes burning hot, the onset of an electric shock, so I leap up and give the inspector my ticket and say 'Malamock, the Octopus God, is here on this train,' and the tracksuit woman covers her smile.

'Is that right?' he says, squiggling on my ticket. 'Does he want a single or a return?'

I sit down and the inspector leaves.

'Why did I have to do that?' I whisper.

'You are ashamed. All children of pride.'

'I'm not ashamed, it's just . . .' but I am in fact sweating from the shame and have only hands with which to wipe my brow and the woman is still staring and I meet her eyes hoping I can communicate my struggle to her with absolute honesty and clarity but I fail and frighten her and she moves seats and I am alone.

The machine slurps my ticket and the doors belch open. Victoria station. I go out to smoke then back into a Caffè Ritazza to charge my phone but they do not have a charger. I ask for a glass of water and sit down at a wooden table that faces the counter, watching a Latina waitress with fine features and a man's jaw singing and checking her hair in the mirror between the shelves.

Someone sits down at my table. Smeared features, his hands are red and eroding. He wears a derelict suit and is without socks. He is seriously mentally ill and this train station is perhaps his home.

'Do you have any cigarettes?' he says, so I take out the Old Holborn and offer him a pinch but as I take out the papers he rolls the tobacco into a ball and puts it in his mouth. 'I am writing a book,' says the man, 'about highly effective people. I will analyse what makes them highly effective. Then I can sell it to people who want to be highly effective and repair it all with Sandrine and the whole issue, the whole mess with what happened on the bridge. A certain resurrection of fortunes, a certain, hopefully you understand. I do care—'

'OK,' the waitress is above him. 'Come. You know you can't be in here.'

'Tell her,' Malamock commands. 'That I am present. What exists? Name and form exists. Consciousness exists.'

'Sorry about this,' she says to me. 'He don't do no harm.'

'Tell her.'

'He wants you to know that God is here in this station,' I say quickly, getting up and leaving.

'Bet he does,' she sighs, her hand on the man's shoulder. She is wearing blue plastic gloves.

For a while I try to hide the trickery of what I have done by burying my focus in the departures board for which I have no use as I am travelling to Uxbridge by tube. At first I sense that I have been successful as He is silent but my trick has of course failed and is only being counted against me with mounting anger.

I change at Baker Street and take the Metropolitan line to Uxbridge and He has still not spoken to me though I can feel His menace and I am frightened by His silence yet fearful of addressing it. I desperately do not want to be in this shaken state when I meet Dan. The intensity of travelling underground pressed up against strange eyeballs is making me self-conscious and I touch my head and yawn many times and cannot remember when I last changed my clothes as that is not a fit and proper concern when living a spiritual life but now I worry that I am repellent to everyone and will be repellent to Dan and I try to read their faces and find revulsion and sadness though not always for me.

Dan is waiting behind the barriers but he does not recognise me until I am right in front of him. He cannot prevent the flicker of shock escaping through that gap in his front teeth.

'Tom!' he says, holding out his hand but I hug him and he gives me a brief squeeze with half his body. 'Look at you, man,' he says. The clozapine has doubled my weight.

'Just can't seem to turn off my survival genes.'

'What?'

'Fat production.' But Dan just stares at me, snagged. The half-joke has gone wrong and the hungry moment it left eats the life out of this meeting and we are lost. We go into a bar as my mind spools foul stories of what Dan is thinking but though I can feel Him, Malamock still does not speak. No one is speaking. Dan with whom I fought five men and a girl outside a pub on the Thames before we jumped into the river and swam to safety on a party boat that took us in. Dan with whom I took ten Es in one go, Snowballs, when everyone was frightened of them, triple drop, triple drop, triple drop then one for luck. Dan with whom I had a threesome with our friend's mother and never told a soul. Dan whom I have known since Year 6, who was there at so many points of my old life, before Brighton, before my spiritual life, who was even there at the exact moment I decided I wanted to be a lawyer, this is the Dan asking me if I am OK in here or would I be more comfortable over there, like they all do. But I am not comfortable. Malamock is everywhere, and I almost wish He would strike me or tell me to instruct Dan about His presence because this silence is unbearable!

'So how are you then?' he says for the third or fourth time. 'How's Tess?' The bar is made out of pastel squares and rectangles and sections of mirror, modern and weary.

'She's splitting up from her boyfriend who blames me for their problems because she's unwilling to get married or have more kids with him because she's already got two. She says she has to look after me but I think that's just an excuse and deep down she doesn't love him. How's the photography going?'

'Er . . . wow. Er, OK, thanks. Good, yeah, you know, pretty good. I've just come back from the States doing a kind of fashion thing and it's good. Yeah. Can't complain.' He coughs. 'Are you working or . . .?'

'Benefits.' Dan sneaks a look at his watch. 'You've just got to make sure you open your post.'

'Sorry?'

'Because if you don't reply they just stop it and its form-filling and eight weeks sanction with no money and what are you meant to do then? I wanted to do volunteering, just a few hours a week so I'm not on my own so much but you're not allowed to do volunteering because if they catch you they'll say if he can volunteer he can work and they'll stop it and then it's eight weeks like I said and by this stage you're starving and it's all very stressful because one by one they stop everything and you've got the landlord on the phone and it's very frightening. That's why everyone in the system is very, very frightened. You're at the mercy of this thing that makes mistakes all the time, and they're late—'

'Tom, Tom – hey – what are you talking about, man?'

I blink at Dan, checking myself because I can get confused, but I review the moment and am correct.

'Benefits. I just told you.' The glass tabletop is covered in watery hoof prints. The waitress approaches.

'Drinks, guys?'

'Stella, please.'

'Can I just get a cup of hot water?'

'On its own?'

'A mug of hot water on its own with nothing in it would be perfect, thank you. Have you got any sandwiches?'

'We got crisps. Beef and onion. Ham and cheese.'

'I'm a vegetarian.'

'Ooooookay,' she says, wiping the table, 'one Stella, one tea-free tea right up.' She leaves.

'The Octopus God doesn't allow me to drink.'

'Right.'

'Or have sex. Or eat meat.'

'Sounds like a nightmare.'

'It's not easy, no.'

'Suppose octopus is off the menu too?' And we laugh and for that moment we are friends again. I am suddenly very hungry and resolve to address it as soon as Dan understands me a little better and perhaps through talking to Dan I can appease Malamock at the same time.

'The thing is the spiritual path is not meant to be easy. Getting direct knowledge of consciousness, of birth and death – I mean, it's meant to be tough, you know? Very, very tough.'

'Right.'

'You see, what I'm trying to do is, I'm – I'm trying, through effort and prayer, to become good, pure. I'm trying to achieve a direct pure consciousness, like we get at birth and death. Since my awakening. That's what I'm trying to do. With His teachings. The earth will go back underwater but we can prepare our spirits to make the crossing. And help others to do the same. I just make so many mistakes, you know?' Dan smiles as if he understands all about mistakes. 'Then when I am ready, He will reveal what my mission is. That's what I am waiting for really. To be worthy of instruction.'

'And how long you been waiting now?'

'Nineteen years.'

'So,' says Dan with a cough, 'you're back in Crowborough?'

'Yes.'

'How long's that been?' My mind lurches for the answer but there is nothing there.

'Don't worry about it.'

'No – it's the tablets, sorry, it's – it's about a year I think? Or two years?'

'I heard you had a girlfriend?'

'Phoebe. But that ended a while ago.'

'Because of the no sex thing?'

'It's difficult coping with a telepathic relationship with a spiritual entity and a physical relationship with a girlfriend. It was a very difficult moment in my life.'

'Did she know about . . . everything?'

'She's not so strong on history. Or botany.'

'I mean, you know – was she – I mean where did you meet her? In hospital or something?'

'I met her at a party.' *Stop talking about yourself.* 'Hey – are you still in touch with Helen?'

'I'm married to Helen.'

'What? No way!'

'Yep. Pretty weird, isn't it?'

'You're married! That's amazing!'

'Calm down . . .'

I am on my feet.

'Congratulations!' I give him a hug while he is sitting down and he pats my arm and says thanks, thanks, and I say, 'I understand why you didn't invite me.'

'Yeah . . . it was just . . .' But he gives up and pulls his lip with his teeth. The drinks arrive. Dan takes a long gulp. He puts the pint glass down. I pick it up.

'Look.'

'What?'

'Another hoof print.'

I give Dan his glass. Dan puts the glass down. Silence booms then peters out to quiet, becoming noise again in the conversations around us and the world outside. Dan takes another drink.

'Do you ever listen to Radio 4?'

'Errr . . . sometimes, Tom, why?'

'The *Today* programme?'

'Sometimes.'

'Do you think that John Humphrys and Sarah Montague are secretly getting fucked up together during the show?'

'Fucked up?'

'Sniffing coke, drinking tequila.'

'At that time in the morning?'

'Maybe it's the end of the night for them.'

'Maybe it is, Tom. Maybe it is,' he laughs and my heart glows with relief. 'But I doubt it. Not likely, really, is it?'

'Listen to them interviewing people with that in your mind. That when they're not speaking, they're covering the microphone with one hand and snaffling up a banger with the other. The way they're talking. It makes so much more sense.'

'The kind of . . . relaxed agitation.'

'Ha! That's it exactly! The *relaxed agitation*.'

'It's probably all the coffee, Tom, you know, mixed in with

43

the excitement of laying into some two-bob wanker from the department of education.'

'Could be. We can't see them though, can we?'

'You're right there. We can't see them. They're probably giant lizards. Helen listens to it on the way to work. I'll ask her what she thinks.'

'Couldn't Helen come today?'

'No.'

'Kids? Because you've got kids.'

'No we don't have kids. She just couldn't come, Tom.'

'Did she say—'

'Last time you saw each other it all went pretty weird, remember? She didn't really want to come, Tom. To be honest.'

'Oh.'

'Sorry, but – well, it did all end up pretty weird. Didn't it?'

'Did it?' Dan takes a drink. 'What about Big Pete and Toll and Hilda and everyone? You still—'

'Now and then, you know. Same old shit really.'

'Say hello to them all for me will you?'

'Sure. And say hi to Tess.'

'She said "don't expect too much".'

'What?'

I put my hands around the mug, and out from its warmth wild birds of steam cross the window light and brighten.

'This morning when I was getting on the train to see you, she said "don't expect too much".'

Dan runs both hands through his hair and shifts in his seat.

'I don't really know what you expect me to say to that.'

'I don't know either. Sorry.'

I sip and put down the mug and look through the surface of the water directly into a dream and when I return I feel I have seen something of profound beauty that I can't recall but has silver terror around its edges and Dan is eyes wide at me and I stand up saying I need the toilet which is sort of true and walk away unsteadily, cursing myself, knowing I urgently need to eat.

I go down some stairs and push open the door. The room is a dark and powerful red with timid lights and cellar-breath in its lungs. It smells of sugared fruit. There are eight taps. I avoid my untrue reflection that stalks beside me for a moment and stand in front of the urinal. The walls are wet. I take out my penis and start to piss.

'You deny me,' says Malamock, voice metallic, full of rage.

'I'm talking to Dan about you! That's all we're talking about!'

'About me?' and I jerk in surprise, whipping piss in the direction of a wiry man who has spoken and perhaps been there all the time and in that instant my right side becomes burning hot.

The Octopus God electrocutes me.

I cry out, gripping the urinal pipe so I will not fall and some piss flicks onto the man's boots and he leaps away with cursing and noises. The electrocution stops.

Shaking, gasping for breath, I stammer out apologies as I fuss my penis back towards the urinal for what's left of the piss but when the piss is finished I look about me and the man has left. The toilet is empty except for my untrue reflection. My jeans are wet with piss.

I cannot blow-dry myself as there is only a Dyson Airblade and so I hover there unsure of what to do, overcome with shame that Dan will think I am so mad, so incapable, that I have pissed myself, I have pissed on someone else! Desperate to wait down here until I am dry someone else comes in so I leave not wanting to be thought of as the kind of person who lurks in toilets.

I climb the stairs, palming the sweat from my brow, feeling so utterly weak and light it's as if I am made out of paper, a paper man with a tomato heart pulping itself from shame.

At the top I can see the wiry man discussing me with his lumpy companion and I feel unsteady with fear and the urge to leave. I hoist up my jeans and pull down my jumper to cover some of the wet patches. My ankles stick out. I hot-shuffle to the table. My face is on fire. The wiry man is glaring at me.

'Dan, I'm sorry, I don't feel so well I think I have to go now,' and I know it is a relief for him and he can say "are you sure" and "see you soon" and "can I help" and pretend not to notice my jeans. But it is me apologising and Dan is released and absolved and has his anecdote, all this way for less than half a fucking hour, and while he is halfway through standing I hug Dan, the wiry man approaching, coming to say something, so I flee.

Scurrying away along the street I take out my phone to call Tess with trembling hands and find my phone is completely dead. Nosediving into deep distress, checking behind me to see if I am being pursued, I take the last two lozepam and rush into the tube system to get away from Dan and the wiry man and the ridiculous shameful disastrous ruin of it all.

'Why did you do that? I didn't deserve that!'

'*Why did you do that? I didn't deserve that!*' He repeats, mocking me. My right side becomes burning hot. 'No! Please!' The burning disappears but I have to sit down on the escalator steps because my legs are so feeble, my hunger now feverish, and I am attracting more stares which I experience as more heat and then tuck myself into the furthest corner of the platform until the train comes. I sit in its final seat in the last compartment, chugging through prayers of appeasement, 'Please don't let me trigger. I love you with all my heart. Please don't let me trigger. I love you with all my heart,' as it drags me off through the dark until we get to Baker Street, and I need to be out in the air uncrushed, and I desperately need to eat so, clambering out from the station, I see Pizza Express across the road, a favourite of my sister's, and by strength of this association it is selected.

The restaurant is an ocean of noise and I stand at the door next to a brightly faced office of eight people all talking about war and walking out of this ocean comes a girl holding a pepper grinder who asks me if I want a table and she looks nervously at me but smiles because she's young and as yet uncorrupted. She takes me to a table. I take a napkin to wipe my face but all the cutlery falls out, announcing me.

'The art of prophecy,' He says. 'Coward.'

'No,' I say, picking up the menu, flipping it to scan for pizza as though I fit in. There is a couple next to me and they are drinking Peroni beer, liquid sunshine that I am forbidden to drink. 'Food was plentiful. And virtual idiocy,' He says, as I open my mouth to the waitress to order a beer but the heat starts on my left side and I turn away to my shoulder, for He has humiliated me and hurt me and I will have this one out with Him.

'Leave me alone!' I hiss, 'I just need one to be steady!'

'*I just need one to be steady.*'

The Octopus God gives me a hot constriction on my right side and I am half off my chair with everyone watching and selling their eyes to each other yuuuuurrrpp but I am back on my chair and I apologise and rearrange myself and don't order the Peroni. 'Water, please,' I say, like a plant.

Studying the prices I realise I can't afford to eat here. I leave before the water arrives while Malamock mimics me, the need to eat mutating into another emergency, the need to be home, to be with Tess, and this panic vomits out a pulsation that swims through me and I fight it which is a mistake, a grave, grave mistake. *No, no, no!* It grows into a thought-form as yet unnamed but that carries within it blasphemies and intimations of triggering and a most reckless anger and as it unfurls I try to distract myself by concentrating on my breathing but that is a pretence and so I watch myself perform each breath while the world has already changed, harmful energies awakened and running through everything, cars full of menace, people now agents, plane trees throwing up their limbs in deranged prayer to an utterly blank sky.

Back down the escalator and onto the first train that hurtles into darkness I think of Dan and how he will tell the story of our meeting, how weird I am, how mad! *Not mad, I am not mad, please let me not be mad, He is real,* and how fat I am and damp and bald and I touch my head then yawn and squeeze my fists together as hard as I can until they slip and I let out a cry '*No!*' hissed through my teeth so that the newspaper reader and the e-reader and the teenagers and the woman all dressed in white will not hear me but of course they do and they turn and they stare.

'Coward. Fool.'

'Leave me alone!' I shove my hands in my pockets and feel the Nerf pellets and something else which I pull out and there is the 'BeneBil' leaflet for the bildinocycline trial, their drug trial, the drug that destroys voices, and I process the most evil thought, the highest blasphemy: *I can destroy you!*

I cannot take it back.

I know He has heard it.

I begin to beg out loud, that I didn't mean it, that it wasn't me, it was just a thought-form that escaped but He remains silent. A cold tremor shudders across my brain.

The train stops and I get out. It is the end of the line – Uxbridge again! I have taken a train going in the wrong direction! Confused, jabbering with distress, I stagger out of the carriage holding on to my phone praying that it will somehow come back to life, following it out through the open barriers and outside the station into the night again but there is no signal, no Tess, there is only this great volcanic force now moving upon me and in the square in front of the station there is a bench and I can go no further and the ground is not the ground and now now now now an earthquake in my vision an iron taste in my mouth the taste of my own soul—

I am triggering.

White ribbons crackle and burst before me, the ecstasy of ore, a rage of light, and I understand, I accept my annihilation as a blasphemer of the profligate universe whose orphan, Earth, mewls cruel power, and whose pontiff, the Octopus God, whose names are Malamock, Nicor, Kanaloa, the Foundation Spirit, who yet is the thing itself, grips me like these iron bench struts, pulling at this concrete, at this land. Oh Britain! My island! You are not Christian rock you are ancient sea-spit and we owe our lineage to the crawling ocean, the Octopus, a force far older than the Mother, Tyr, Grim, Frig, the devil or his tormentor and yet for His torture, for the burning of my hand, I have touched the centre of all things and felt the golden light – oh! The world gathers itself and looms, the pulsations constant, my ribs and spine and blood and feathers melting in their heat, and I whisper goodbye to Tess across the rain-drizzled street, to the kindness of one man helping another with a crate of toppling vegetables, my chest bursting open with love, and I cry out and someone on a motorbike turns to witness me and is gone as the others gaming the pavement re-affix their attention and I realise I have frightened them the mangling, oh the mangling, that my final act made fear, yet they could never understand this crystal terror, now that He is everywhere, now that I am falling . . .

A constellation of black holes gulps me down into the deep volcano as a syringe pops balloon animals full of blood in some dream that peels itself apart.

My mind rains to pieces.

3

'Hello love, can you hear me?'

'Do you know where you are?'

'How's he getting on?'

'Just coming round. You got into a bit of trouble, love, and you've been bought into Hilldean psychiatric unit so we can look after you, OK?' A corridor is looking back at itself. 'Can you remember anything about yesterday? Because you were in quite a bad way, my love, OK? The police brought you in, and because the doctors and the social worker thought you might be a danger to yourself you were admitted here under a Section 2.' There are birds everywhere? The smell of disinfectant. Boiled vegetables. 'Do you understand what I'm telling you, my love? So we're going to let you rest a bit longer, the doctor will pop in on you in a sec, and then we'll get you up for breakfast. OK, my love? OK there? All right?'

They leave the room and so I realise that I am in a room. My head moves. My pillow is wet with drool. I cannot raise my arm to my mouth, a blizzard headache cold and drilling. I see shower curtains, a sink, shelves, and a rail with a Barbour hanging from it. My Barbour.

My cheek falls back into the drool. A sensation crawls along my back then shrivels. People walk past. They look in and say nothing. They are all black except this woman who means to talk to me. She is a giant.

'Good morning, Tom,' says the giant, stooping into the room. She has short bouncing hair. 'I'm Dr Fredericks the consultant psychiatrist here at Hilldean. How are you feeling this morning?' I grow my mouth open but the words drain off as if there is a hole in my neck. 'Well, look, we'll have a chat later, but it is important we get some food inside you and get your strength up. So take your time, get dressed, and come along to breakfast.' Something around her neck slithers and disappears. 'I've spoken to your sister and she'll be here in a little while with some clothes and things, but in the meantime there's some clean kit on the chair –' she pats a fold of clothes. There is a tracksuit on the chair. The woman's tracksuit from the train? Why has she donated me her tracksuit? – 'and someone will come and help you if you're struggling. So,' she smiles, 'I'll let you get your bearings, OK?'

The giant doctor dips out of the doorway. An ankle slips onto floor. I am on a mattress on the floor. My elbows shake as I twist round and lunge for the tracksuit, spinflopping it off the chair. It is picked up and shaken out. Someone grips my ankle and threads the tracksuit bottoms onto one leg and then the other. He is pushing the tracksuit top over my head, grappling with my arms until they find the sleeves. He lifts me up without warning and I squeeze hold because I am afraid. 'All right, all right,' he says, hoisting the bottoms up to my waist as I hold on to him, cushions of warm body fat that reek of coconut and lavender. He is trying to balance me but my knees give out. He sucks his teeth, yanks me upright again and waltzes me to the doorway. I took a train to London, to see Dan. My sister is coming.

I am being dragged along, trying to catch my steps, trying to control my lolling head, glimpsing the large window of a

51

monitoring station. We swing down another corridor and into a room. I am dumped on a chair.

There are windows along one side and scraps of inpatient art on the walls. A counter with a sink and cupboards and two tables of silent, scraping, crunching, ghost-bitten creatures broiling in their own sorrow. I am in hospital again. My heart breaks.

'I know,' says the girl opposite. 'Shit hotel innit?' She has slicked-back hair.

Unable to reply or even look at her I try to conceal myself in some kind of action, reaching for a cereal packet, but am unable to pour it into the bowl so she helps me and I start eating with a trembling spoon but have forgotten the milk so she pours that out for me too and I eke out a thanks from my left eye, noticing a young man with grey in his stubble scowling at me. He mouths something.

'Hey!' snaps one of the day nurses. 'That's enough.' The man looks like he is going to answer back but instead takes it out on what he is eating and keeps scowling and I dare not look at him. I am in hospital again. How can I be in hospital again. The girl opposite me has stopped chewing, watching me, so I look down.

After breakfast I tell several people that I must see my sister where's my sister and they tell me I have to queue up at a cubbyhole for the drugs round. Finally I am led there and told to wait by a finger close to my nose, like a dog.

A nurse sits in a little room with shelves of medicine and hands out pills in a cup, watches them being swallowed then in-spects the open mouths. I edge my head against the bluecream wall, eyeing people as they saunter past, unable to tell the med-ical staff from the patients because no one wears a uniform. My hands are still trembling, this headache cramping up my neck and jaw. I triggered. I lost myself again.

'Where are you?'

'What?' says the woman queuing behind me. She is drooling and has matted hair all over her face. She is scratching her vagina.

'Do you know Clive?' she says.

'No.'

'Were you here before?'

'No.'

'Then how do you know him?'

'I don't know any Clive.'

'You're a fucking liar.'

At the cubbyhole I swallow the clozapine and what I think are some benzos, telling the nurse in an explosion of yabbering that I have cramping in my neck which feels like the onset of a dystonic reaction which I've had before with haloperidol and have I been injected with haloperidol and does she have any Stelazine and I must speak to my sister and where is the doctor and how long am I going to be in here I shouldn't be in here and she tells me to *move along*.

I go back to my room but am not allowed to shut the door. I search my Barbour. There are the two Nerf gun pellets spongy and orange and I grip one in each hand, walking round in a circle, squeezing, trying to regain some control – my curried vegetables on the sideboard they're going to go off! They're going to rot!

'Tom?'

Tess is in the doorway. She is pale. I resist the impulse to cling at her and instead look away, look to the floor, and with one hand find my Barbour, stripping it from its hanger. I wrap it around my forearm telling her calmly and certainly that I am ready to go home now and start to move towards wherever the exit is, wherever her car is, but she stops me and says we can't go home, I can't go home. I am being sectioned.

I collapse into open begging, miserable and undignified.

When she refuses, over and over again, when she says it is a good idea that I stay put for a while and get some rest and let them help me, I lose control of myself and end up on the mattress, rigid.

Tess has her hand over her mouth.

She walks out into the corridor for a moment then comes back inside. 'Why did I ever let you go to London?' she mutters, shaking her head. 'Fucking knew it.'

'I'm not a pet!' I shriek into the duvet.

'Your head's rolled off again though, hasn't it? Look at you!'

Some faces gather in the doorway and are gathered away again by a nurse.

Tess kneels beside me.

'Hey, look,' she says, 'Look at me . . .' She is leaning over me, trying to see my face but I shove it further into the duvet. 'And I know you don't want to hear this either, but I've talked to Megan again about the drug trial and we both really, *really* think you've got to give it a go, you—' I curl up suddenly, chattering rapid prayers, terrified that talking about bildinocycline will provoke another blasphemous thought-form, another triggering. 'Can you just stop that – can you stop that and listen to me? We're back here again, aren't we? We've got to try something new – can't you at least— just— Tom!'

'I told you I can't! I told you a million times!'

'For me? Tom?'

'I already do everything you want!'

'Oh fuck you! Nothing's what I want!'

'The Octopus God—'

'It's not a *god!*' she yells, 'It's not even fucking real, for fuck's sake! A talking fucking octopus? You're ill, Tom! You're just fucking ill!'

54

I cover my face, fighting the urge to cry. Tess sighs, then sits down cross-legged over the edge of the mattress. She finds my hand. She tries to say something but stops. We are holding each other's hands.

'Don't you ever think about me? Tom? About what all this is doing to me?'

'How can you say that?'

'Then won't you just do the trial for me? Because – because I'm asking? Because you love me? More than that thing? Tom? Don't you?'

A moment passes. Tess starts to cry. She stands up. She is wiping her eyes. She is unpacking the bag she's bought. She is hanging the clothes in the closet and putting two packets of tobacco with a phone charger on the chair next to my bed and I am staring at her and want to tell her how much I want to do whatever she wants but I can't and I will never make her understand why.

'Will Ben come and visit? Lily?'

'I don't think this is a place for kids, do you?'

'Who's going to look after Ben when you – you know – the paperwork thingy?'

'Eh?'

'You had a lot of paperwork. I was going to look after Ben.'

'Forget it. It doesn't matter.'

'When am I getting out then?'

'It's up to Dr Fredericks, but you're on a twenty-eight-dayer.'

'They'll give me a Section 3. They'll forget about me.'

'No one's going to forget about you, Tom . . .'

'I was in Crawley for months because they forgot about me!' Tess doesn't reply because she knows it's true. She shakes her head free of something. 'It's the trial's fault!'

'What are you talking about?'

'Why I'm in here!'

'You're not making any sense, you – you haven't done the trial, Tom, remember? Jesus Christ . . .' She finishes un-packing the bag and then starts folding the bag itself until it can't be folded any more and she is just looking at it in her hands.

'Hey,' she says, 'guess who called to say hello?'

'Lionel Ritchie.'

Tess laughs. I am so so so glad I made her laugh it makes my cheeks burn.

'Phoebe. She's back in Lewes.'

I roll to the wall and bury my face again. Tess tries to pull my shoulder round. 'Thought you'd be happy about that – Tom? Oh for . . .' She lets go and clears her throat. 'Look, I've got to get back to work. It took ages to get here and – I'm not going to be able to visit you all the time. Are you listening to me?' I hear her stand up. She waits. 'And I talked to Dr Fredericks about the trial as well, and she thinks it's a great idea. Everyone thinks it's a great idea!'

'You don't understand!' I say, flipping round. 'I can't do it! I cannot!'

'Then why don't you tell me what the plan is here, eh, Tom? Why don't you tell me what I'm meant to do?'

'Don't leave me in here!'

'Fuck—'

'Please, Tess!'

She kneels back down on the mattress to kiss my head and prise my fingers off her coat. I watch her say goodbye. She waits for me to say goodbye back then picks up the two Nerf gun pellets off the floor and offers them to me but still I say nothing. She puts the pellets on a shelf and they roll off. She picks them up then puts them back on the shelf again and leaves. When she has gone I watch the damp-bleached ceiling tiles shift and pixelate above me.

'WHERE ARE YOU?' I scream out. The fat nurse puts his head around the door.

'Oi,' he says. 'Shut your face.'

———

Mummy has just left the room. Tess is slapping her pot belly smack schmack freckled with chicken pox then bends down into the water and pulls up a flannel and drags it over her head, pulling it tight round her face *here's my face here's my face* as I fish around until I find a flannel and do the same and then we push each other over crashing back into the warmth and spidery foam and then I get up again spinning out on my front out over the side onto the bath mat. I do a dance for her, a little dance with the flannel on my belly, and she is a giggling, wiggling creature laughing so much she stands up.

I run to the doorway and listen for Mummy. I run down the stairs still holding the flannel, feet biting the carpet thread down to the open front door and the bristling doormat out into the summer evening garden the nip of the air cold paving stone flowery smell soft prickle of the lawn grass, running round the back, the strong fresh smell of the cuttings pile by the shed, hopping from the squelch of a slug scrambling onto the dry-stone wall. My flannel is in my teeth and I am scrambling naked toes shuddering on the ledges shredding through stonecrop scraping my knees and get to the top of the wall and the bitter smell of moss, stepping onto the asphalt roof of the living room still warm from the sun, feet picking up grit as I creep past the skylight to the bathroom window, bright with steam and light. I lean my knees against the window ledge and can see Mummy in the doorway, angry, questioning. Tess is glum and bottom-lipped though still with her flannel on her head. I put my flannel on my head too and rap on the window, shaking both hands in a wave at Tess who breaks into giggles, doing my dance, my flannel-on-the-head dance just before the window is flung open and my elbows are jerked inside.

———

There are ten people on the ward. I see them all at the group therapy session in the day room and here I am again in one of these chair circles with folded up people that someone is trying to unpack. More than half of them were raped as children and I know this not from their individual stories but from a lifetime in such groups and institutions. The window glass is reinforced with wire mesh. Outside there is a wall. Strip lighting covers everyone in a thick yellow light that pushes them downwards, squashed, arms folded, heads in hands, except one man who stares upwards in awe, his mouth hanging open.

Rashid, the fat male nurse, is standing right behind me leaning against the doorframe, giving off the smell of lavender. There is a heavily pregnant woman, her belly straining out of her T-shirt and next to her the girl with slicked-back hair that was kind to me at breakfast. The only person talking is a man with an exhausted balloon face and lots of chins *more chins than a Chinese phonebook* in a T-shirt that says 'Strange Brew'.

'So the reason God is like this,' he says, 'is because I tumbled him, I realised he's actually evil and that he controls everything and that he kind of plays us like a game, like a chess game . . .' The woman from the meds queue sits down beside me. She is still tugging at her crotch. I want to tell her to stop but starting any kind of interaction with her is unthinkable. I touch my head and yawn.

'What?' says the woman.

I don't reply.

58

'What?' she says again.

'Roseanna,' says Dr Fredericks. 'David is talking if you don't mind.' Crossed at the ankles, Fredericks sticks her giant suited legs into the circle like a clock hand. She chews a fingernail and is evidently thinking about something else.

'. . . makes all the big decisions in our lives and the only thing that we are in control of is our emotions, our emotional response to things, and the reason he lets us have them, which are a bit spontaneous, is because he finds them entertaining, like watching *EastEnders* – which I hate because it's so gutting all the time – but say you're watching a soap . . .'

I feel a prod in my side. I look up and Roseanna is clenching her crotch with both hands. '*What?*' she mouths.

I shake my head and lean forward.

'. . . finds our reactions interesting and entertaining and so when he makes something really bad happen, like a natural disaster or a war or a murder or something then he kind of – he laughs at our reactions because he thinks it's really funny . . .'

Roseanna prods me again. I get up and cross the circle to sit next to the slick-haired girl and when I look back at her she mouths '*What?*'

'. . . so I used to call him "Jester" and because I'd realised that about reality, that's why he was so hateful to me, that's why he wanted to punish me, which is why I'm really happy to shut out his voice with medication but on the flip side of the coin I strongly believe that at some point in my life something terrible is going to happen to me or my family because I have cheated him.'

The pregnant woman burps. The slick-haired girl giggles. I look at the tops of everyone's heads and then at their faces and realise I am counting them over and over again. Ten, there are ten people. My knee is bouncing.

'. . . in 2010 I started a relationship. It was only my second relationship and we fell in love but then she ended it really quickly and nobody could understand why, no one could believe she ended it because we had been thinking about kids and getting married, you know, a place to live together, it was really, really serious and that's when suddenly this God who is evil, he started talking to me and that's when I was put on anti-psychotics and went into the psychiatric system.' He stops talking and shuts his eyes, shutting himself down.

'Thank you, David, for telling us all that again,' says Dr Fredericks. 'Anyone else like to tell the group how they're feeling? Why they're here?' I hope desperately that she will not ask me to speak.

'Tom – this is Tom, everyone, and it's his first day today. Tom, would you like to introduce yourself or say anything to the group?' The strip light is sending chair shadows in two directions at once.

'*What?*' Roseanna is mouthing at me. '*What? What?*'

'Tom?'

'I can't . . . I cannot – I can't be in here!'

'Well I'm afraid the nurses and I have all been charged to look after you for a while so—'

'The nurses here do not seem to be kind people. This is – I can't—'

'And he's only been here five minutes!' says the slick-haired girl, pulling up her hoodie. 'See what we're trying to tell you?'

'How long am I going to be in here? How many days? Exactly?'

'Tom, sit down please.'

'I want to know when I'm getting out of here! I shouldn't be in here!'

'Well that depends on you, Tom, doesn't it?' Some of the faces are tilted up at me, some blank, some, like the slick-haired

60

girl, amused. The scowling man is scowling at me. I sit down, avoiding his stare. 'Look, we're going to have a one-on-one a bit later, aren't we, so we can discuss it all then, OK Tom? All right? Good. Anyone else like to share with the group. Lenny? How about you?'

'Me?' says an elderly man with a baseball cap and a northern accent.

'Yes. What've you been up to?'

'About five foot nine,' he says, folding his arms, staring the doctor out.

'Wankers,' tuts the slick-haired girl.

I close up my face with my hands, whispering 'You cannot leave me in here!'

'Come on now then, Missy. Let's start this again,' says the giant. 'Have you written any raps recently?'

'Spoken word,' says the slick-haired girl. 'It's poetry.'

'Have you written any poetry?'

'No.'

'I made up a song this morning,' offers the pregnant woman. 'Yeah I was making up this song, it was kind of like a nursery rhyme for the baby but then it had this R & B thing on it – can't remember how it went now – but I was like really chuffed with it, man. I was in the toilet and I said "eat your heart out, Gary Barlow" and then I was like "no, literally fucking eat it. Cut a hole in your chest, drag it out covered in blood and shit, stuff it in your smug fucking face and fucking—"'

'All right, Chanelle—'

'I mean where does he get off telling people how to sing? Man's a chief.' She kisses her teeth. Missy is giggling. The scowling man is scowling at me and I am trying to resist eye contact but the magnetism of his hatred is too strong. Hot touching eyeballs. I look down. Back. Down. Back – *stop it!*

'Yes, Thomas?' says Dr Fredericks.

'I want to go home!'

'Back of the queue, fam,' grumbles Missy.

'I'm sorry I failed you,' I whisper, looking away again from the scowling man, covering my mouth as if coughing, 'that I wished an evil thing against you because I am weak and I will never ever betray you but I'll go mad locked up in here you can't leave me in here—'

'OK – anyone else? Anyone? No . . .' Fredericks checks her watch then checks the wall clock and pulls her wrist away as if adjusting her eyesight. 'Well I think that's about it for today. Onwards and upwards, everyone.'

Dr Fredericks gets to her feet, looming over the circle before dipping out of the day room.

'*The nurses don't seem to be kind people,*' Rashid the nurse whines in a high, mocking tone behind me. I turn round. He raises his eyebrows and juts his neck forward. I look away. He sways off to turn on the television that hangs in the corner, and everyone, even the scowling man, rotates back to face it. I am squashing my head between my hands, biting my lip and hissing, 'Where are you?'

'Over here,' someone says.

At the end of one corridor there is a fire exit that leads out to the smoking garden. There aren't any plants in the smoking garden except for a plane tree. The area is paved and walled-in, maybe fifteen or twenty feet high. There are cigarette butts everywhere and a mottled park bench. It is cold. The sky is scaled with cloud. As I push open the door I see that on the left, about ten metres away from us, there is corrugated translucent fencing, higher than the wall, with barbed wire across the top. Shadows move around behind it.

'What's that?' I ask the slick-haired girl.

'PICU,' she blows smoke from the side of her mouth. 'Secure unit. Murderers, rapists, you know, but no one that got in the papers. This lot are proper evil, but they're not . . .' she picks a scrap of tobacco off her lip '. . . show-offs, although they stick their tongues through that crack when the girls are out here. What's your name?'

'Tom.'

'I'm Missy,' she says, taking a long drag, 'short for "mistake".'

'How comes there's a pregnant woman in here?'

'Because she's fucking bonkeroni,' Missy chuckles grimly. 'Why you in here?'

'It's – I'm not meant to – it's a mistake.'

'That's my name, dickhead. Don't wear it out.'

No one has a coat on so they are all stamping their feet and rubbing themselves. I roll a cigarette and Missy tells me she has been here nine months already because she once tried to hang herself and she once beat someone up and she used to hear her father's voice but all that has stopped, mostly stopped, but because she is classed as homeless and has epilepsy they don't know where to put her, they don't have a place for her, and they don't have tasers in here like they do in some places but they have Acuphase and she has been given an Acuphase injection by Rashid just for doing a cartwheel and she has a bad reaction to Acuphase, very bad, and he knows it and I must watch Rashid, I must stay away from the fat nurse Rashid because he's a fucking dirty cunt, and as she talks I am fighting the panic that Malamock has abandoned me! That I will be stuck in here for months and months and months without Him and I can only half listen to her but I know I must concentrate on what Missy is saying because otherwise I will become overwhelmed. She is perhaps still a teenager and is small but hunches her shoulders like tall people do who are embarrassed about their height. An old woman that looks like she is wearing a much bigger person's skin comes outside in a wheelchair and has black lines around her teeth. She starts talking to Missy and suddenly I am alone. I step beside the plane tree to smoke my roll-up, pretending to examine the watery pools of grey in its bark so I have something to do. My hands are shaking. Some shadows become distinct against the translucent fence as if two people are pressing themselves against it.

'Thomas,' says Malamock. I drop my cigarette.

Slowly, very slowly, I bend down to pick it up. Missy is watching me from one eye. 'Please,' I whisper, 'don't leave me in here,' trying to steady the cigarette between my fingers, 'I can't—' Missy is smiling at me uncertainly. I shift behind the plane tree. '. . . I can't be in here! Why am I in here?'

'Do not regret what you have done.'

I try to smoke but cast away the roll-up, my hands twisting on each other as I march towards the translucent fence at great speed. Rashid comes out, ordering everyone inside.

'But I've already been punished! You made me trigger!'

'Albino mutant. My breath kindles coals and a flame. Bildino-cycline trial. No mention shall. You have reneged on a bargain. You entered a solemn oath to me.'

'But I cannot be in one of these places again! I can't bear it!'

'But where shall wisdom be found?' His voice swells with scorn. 'Achieve orgasm? The scientists? Jewels of time? The decision rests.'

'But you—'

'Who, like me? The traveller must start in other cities. In all things have no preferences. By break of breakings they purify the breakthrough of two factors. What doesn't exist? Thomas. Name and form exists.' Rashid is tapping me on the back. 'What doesn't exist? A rigorous period of when what exists? From this: in front of copulating parents – flashes. Canst thou put a hook in his nose?' Rashid is launching his eyebrows at me, hands on hips. 'Or shall we get those who are summoned turned into joy before you?'

'But I can't be here. I can't bear it . . .'

'Yeah, yeah,' says Rashid, sucking his teeth, 'I heard.' He pulls me by the elbow, leading me across the smoking garden.

'It was just one tiny thought-form! It just escaped! I didn't mean it!'

'Death didn't exist one hundred thousand years ago. Undermined the stability, the requisite condition. Following it was regarded as—' Rashid is grabbing me roughly because I am resisting, trying to listen '. . . and so the methods of death most commonly employed were out of all perfection. The stones of darkness.'

Rashid shoves me through the door. Malamock flings something jagged across my brain. As it sinks in I glimpse, through a crack in my soul, His punishment if I betray Him again: *the stones of darkness*. An eternal annihilation. Death without death. Death without end.

I faint.

Rashid must have caught me but as I come round he lets me drop. 'Shit, you wanna lie down, lie down.' Malamock has gone. Rashid lollops away. I am alone on the floor and there is no one to help me.

Eventually I get to my feet. I end up in the day room. Most people are watching television. A healthcare assistant with yellow hair and milky eyes walks past and asks me if I'm all right. She introduces herself as Kiki and tells me she was there when I came round. I look a lot better now, she says, a whole lot better. I tell her I don't know what to do. There's television, she says, and there's art therapy in the afternoons. Sometimes bingo.

'Can you win a ticket home?'

'You can win a packet of Polos,' she says. 'Do you like Polos?'

MARCH

4

The morning bell stabs me repeatedly in the sleep, dreams bleeding away to reveal the white ceiling tiles, all scored and footprinted as if by tiny factory animals, damp in one corner and there discoloured. But square. Oh so square. Oh so relentlessly square.

Twisting myself round on the mattress there is a clattering on the floor. A spoon. Someone has left a spoon on me during the night. I struggle up from the mattress, pick up the spoon and sniff it.

Forcing myself into the shower and its fleeing silverfish I stare at the exploded black grouting before testing the scalding water with my finger until some chance position of the dial gives me a bearable temperature that lasts just a few seconds before turning back to ice. Kiki comes in while I am showering to make sure I am up. Roberta, a healthcare assistant who looks like a black female Noel Gallagher, comes in a minute later. Both times I am cowering naked behind a flimsy curtain, wishing they would just bring the dogs and the water cannons and be done with it.

While I am dressing I take my phone from the charger and call Tess so I can tell her about the spoon but she is driving and the line is bad. She says something like *ask your octopus* – fizzles . . . stutters . . . gone. I prod through the pictures of her I have in my phone, pictures of trees and animals from the woods. The badger hole. *Life in the fast lane.* I put the spoon on the duvet and take a picture of it. The bell rings.

'Who put this on me?' I ask the breakfast table, brandishing the spoon against the silence. 'Somebody came into my room last night. With this.' Price, the scowling man, scowls. It's his only setting.

'Oh?' says Rashid, appearing from nowhere. 'Want a spoon?' He hugs my back koala-style, clouding me with his stench of cocoa butter and lavender and cigarettes, making cooing noises *coo-coo-coo*. Roseanna finds this hysterically funny. I close my eyes until the performance is over. Rashid releases me and I take my seat, pouring out a bowl of Rice Krispies, praying that he will turn his attention elsewhere.

'Serious though. What's going on with the spoon, T?'

'Nothing. It's all right.'

'Come on, man,' he says, poking my armpit. 'Tell me.'

Missy sits opposite me, grinding a piece of toast between her teeth. She fixes a roving, pardish look upon Rashid: the smooth rectangular scar above his ear, the mushroom nose, cheeks that almost cover his eyes.

'Someone left a spoon on me while I was sleeping. It's just a bit—'

'Right!' Rashid slams his hands down on the table, getting everyone's attention except Bill's, as he can only stare upwards with his mouth open. 'Who did the spoon thing?' Missy raises her eyebrows at me and puts her toast down.

'Come on,' he patrols the table. 'Ain't got all day, yeah? You,' he points at a new arrival with bad skin. This accusation is catastrophic.

'Was it me?' the man begs, utterly lost.

'What you dropping spoons on people for?'

'Hey, Rash,' I say, Missy folding her arms at me for this

familiarity. 'You know what? I just remembered I left it there myself. I was trying to bend it before I went to sleep.'

'Bend it?'

'Yuri Geller stuff. You know.'

'Yuri what?'

'What time's art therapy today?'

'Same as every day, why?'

'Three o'clock?'

'Yeah.'

'Three o'clock. Got it. Thanks, Rash.'

'Oh,' he says. 'Sure.'

'Sorry about the spoon thing. I just forgot.'

'Oh. No problem, T.'

Considering the Case of the Mystery Spoon satisfactorily closed, Rashid digs his phone out of his back pocket and swings himself out into the corridor. Roseanna pushes her chair back and follows him out.

'Can I see the spoon?' asks Missy. I pass it over and she boiled-eggs me on the head with it.

'Ow!'

'"*No problem, T*",' she whines through a fat tongue, dropping the spoon back in my bowl and picking up her toast. I am scanning the table to see if anyone looks guilty. I remember my rotting vegetables and wonder if Tess has thrown them away yet. Has she been checking my post properly? Does Dan know what happened to me?

After breakfast we queue up for meds then I go to my room and pray. When I open my eyes I realise that the man with bad skin has come a little way into my room. He is on his knees and is also praying. I smile at him and he gives me a wonky grin.

'No it's not,' he says to his voices 'Shut up!' He gives me another wonky, pleading smile then scuttles away.

'Was it him with the spoon?' I ask Malamock while struggling

71

to my feet. He does not reply but just then the first whoa warm wave of medication is rolling up up up and over my brain. Oh there it is. Oh. There. Let's. What? And into the corridor. No one. Nothing oh nothing to do but there is no feeling attached to this though I recognise it has the shape of boredom. For the moment I don't even mind this heaviness in my bones, this extra gravity, Superman in reverse as my home planet has much lower gravity so my name should be . . . what's the opposite of super? Crap. Crappyman. Is it a slug? Is it a dead badger? No, it's Crappyman . . .

I plod past the nurses' glass box. They are in there looking at a screen and opening their mouths at each other. Who knows what meds they're on? Must be fucking strong. I wander down another corridor to the exit doors that lead out into the smoking garden and I am walking around the smoking garden around and around and around then wonder what is Missy doing? Wandering, wondering, Wonder Woman wandering around maybe she's looking for her sidekick Crappyman and so then I decide: I will go and look for Missy. This feels like a monumental turning point in my life, meaningless and full of nothing, a titanic mouse-sized achievement of oh hello she's in the dining room.

'Give it me, Roseanna. Now.'

'It's mine!'

'It's not yours. This one is yours. That one is mine.'

'They're both mine.'

'Roseanna?'

'Fuck you!'

Roseanna spits in Missy's mug. Missy closes her eyes. She would dearly like to hit Roseanna. How lively these two people are being, how much energy they are drawing on and expending – *pop!* It seems incredibubble.

'Oh my God!' she says suddenly, jumping back.

'What?'

'Something just fell out of your pussy!' Roseanna looks down. 'Something just fell out of your pussy and scooted, man. Like a rat or something. Oh my days . . .'

'What?' Roseanna grabs up her red skirt. She is looking around everywhere.

'You got rats in your pussy.'

'No I haven't!'

'Wash my mug out and give it me back, or I'm going to tell everyone about the big hairy rat I just saw drop out of your pussy.'

'You're lying!'

'I saw it. We both saw it, didn't we, Tom? Massive *pussy-rat*.' My mouth takes time to open, words curdling out of the mindcream into some frothy formation forming slowly but . . .

'See? We both saw it.'

'Fuck you!' shrieks Roseanna.

'What's going on?' says Rashid, coming into the dining room.

'Well,' Missy whistles. 'It was *purrritty* amazing—'

'Nothing!' snaps Roseanna, washing Missy's mug out at incredible speed. 'I'm doing it! I'm doing it!' Roseanna grins at Rashid with an open mouth, her hands flustering water and washing-up liquid all over the mug.

'What's going on here, T?' he says, glaring at Missy.

'*Yeah, T,*' whines Missy, '*What's going on here?*'

'Just a. Washing-up. Competition,' I say, 'Rash.' This sounds like someone else has just said it but I do recognise it as myself, as some part of myself that has been activated by a direct question.

'Washing-up-a-what?' he frowns, which folds up his whole face. Wow. That's like a gurn. Like a proper Cumbrian Crab Fair gurn. He should—

'I know, I know . . .' says my mouth. My elbow gives him

73

a little nudge. That's it. That's how it's done. Pull up my eye-brows. Tut. 'Women, eh?' Masterful. I am a bloke.

'Oh my God . . .' breathes Missy.

'Huh yeah,' Rashid grunts, '*Women*.' Then he nods and says, 'True *that*.' We touch fists. As he leaves, Rashid makes a warning gesture to Missy, cocking his head back sharply with a sniff. What does it mean? That he could inhale her if he wanted to? Straight into his nostrils . . .

Missy snatches her mug from Roseanna. She begins to make a cup of tea. I take my mug down from the cupboard. It is chipped and blue and says *Bienvenido!*

'You're the woman,' says Missy, pushing my head.

'Roseanna,' I ask, 'did you come into my room last night and put a spoon on me?' Roseanna bursts into tears and runs out.

We take our teas to the smoking garden. The sky is so blue it is hard to tell how far away it is.

'How's the old Octopus God doing today?' asks Missy.

'Pretty quiet.'

There is a brief moment of shouting from the other side of the translucent fence but then we can hear only traffic.

———

Filaments of daylight. The occasional car on Baron's Down Road. Someone somewhere is snoring but I can't tell if it's coming through the walls or from inside the house. I wriggle to release my boxer shorts gathered up to the groin, put back on in an act of shyness after we made love. Phoebe was on top of me holding my face, holding my eyes, searching until she found something, something she was looking for, something she recognised, until I held her up by the belly and came. She left a record playing to cover our groans and we fell asleep to the tick-tick-ticking of the needle.

She shifts beside me, oozing awake. There is a gold statuette on her shelf, the two face masks of theatre Thalia and Melpomene, curled photographs, a chaotic stack of cassettes and CDs and books. A door opens in the landing and someone pads to the bathroom, shuts the door, turns on some taps and the radio. Suddenly Phoebe's pale eyes are on me again, peering up from my chest. 'Among celestial and human beings,' says Malamock, full of warmth. 'Developing. An electromagnetic field, a harmonica's sigh.' *A harmonica's sigh*. That's exactly what it feels like! Some sort of charged breeze running across my heart. 'Every precious thing,' He says and she kisses me on the ribs.

'Oh,' she murmurs, 'you precious boy,' climbing up to my mouth, bringing her smell of sweet sweat and meadow.

'The towns of gold where they find it.' My hand is full of her hair. 'Will he speak soft words unto thee?'

'Good morning,' I say between breaths, 'Good morning. Good morning.' From the bathroom there is a hawking, someone bringing up a great rubbery phlegm trap snapping in the lungs and Phoebe is giggling against my teeth.

'The nearest parents are Awakened Ones.'

'That's my mum,' whispers Phoebe.

The stairs are covered in spirals of matting which twist against the soles of my feet. Phoebe is in her dressing gown, tugging at my hand. The house is cold and I'm only wearing a T-shirt and jeans. I retreat a step to get my jumper but she tugs me back, her neck already craning over the banister. 'Mum?'

'Hello, hello,' says a twinkling voice.

Phoebe leads me through a kitchen disordered with the onset of cooking to an oval pine table and her mother sitting with her legs crossed, wearing the same white dressing gown as her daughter, a great mass of dark brown curly hair tumbling down in wreaths.

'A Rightly Self-Awakened One,' says the Octopus God. 'All fabrications out.'

'Well now. This is Tom, is it?' High cheekbones dusted with freckles. Heroic eyes. 'Congratulations! You lasted the fortnight – you're through to the second round!' She gives me a wink and I feel instantly that she loves me, unconditionally. Phoebe is scolding her mother, nudging me to sit, French windows looking over a steep little garden then across Winterbourne to the railway bank. There is a sofa laden with throws in front of the fireplace and the TV. A bay window watches the road. There are plants and magazines everywhere, the walls sun-yellow and crowded with framed photos and pictures.

'And my name is Charlotte by the way, OK? Thanks for the intro,' she sticks her tongue out at her daughter. 'Anyone calls me "Mrs Greenfield" gets a boot in the goolies.'

'And she wears heels,' says Phoebe.

'And I wear heels,' she repeats, showing me her slippers, 'most of the time.' Then she sweeps into the kitchen, touching my shoulder with her fingertips, as if to say *You made it. You're here*.

'Mum, I'll do that—'

'You go get him another – look at that goose flesh! Looks like chicken out the fridge.' Charlotte is behind me and we catch eyes in the weak reflection of picture glass, her head emerging from mine, my head descending from hers.

'Forth to light,' says the Octopus God, my left side exploding with warmth.

Soon Charlotte is making scrambled eggs and toast and coffee, asking us about last night, who was there, what they were doing, and what do I think about those soldiers abusing prisoners in Abu Ghraib, and what do I do, what do I like, and then she says 'and you're a voice-hearer, aren't you,' as if she's said *and you play the drums, don't you*, and I talk about the Octopus God and my awakening, the breakfast long finished, a second pot of coffee drunk, Phoebe upstairs in the shower, but I don't feel in the slightest bit awkward or struggling for conversation. I am thinking how much Tess will love her. How I can't wait to introduce her to Tess.

———

He has a clown nose and make-up on and is carrying a ukulele. There is a miniature top hat attached to his head with a chin-strap and he is in my doorway telling me his name is Mike. As soon as he makes this announcement another clown appears, a female one, who says her name is Bonnie.

'We're Mike and Bonnie.'

'Or Bonnie and Mike.'

'Bonnie and Mike, whatever you like,' they say together. The man-clown starts to play the ukulele and now they are singing. I stop fiddling with the mystery spoon and tidy my room a little.

'What's your name?' says the she-clown as I edge past them. She is wearing ears. Out in the corridor I move a safe distance away before turning around to listen to their song. Other people have come out of their rooms and Bill is standing next to me, mouth agape and staring upwards as always. The man-clown comes close to us and looks upwards in the same direction, trying to see what Bill is staring at.

'It's beyond you,' I tell him but he can't reply because he's singing. Instead he gives me a full-mouthed theatrical grin. Missy is coming down the corridor.

'Oh man,' she says, 'Oh, come on!'

All of the nurses have come out of their glass box. They seem to be finding the performance brilliantly funny.

'What is this?' I ask Rashid.

'Booked in for the children's ward, but it's closed because of the flooding. Moved all the kids to another hospital.'

'What flooding?'

'We got a call asking if anyone down here needed cheering up.'

The song finished, Bonnie starts to juggle and make all sorts of 'whoa!' and 'hey! hey!' noises. Roseanna arrives with Kiki and another healthcare assistant. The man with bad skin peers around the corner then disappears again.

'Oh hiya!' says the man-clown to Missy. 'What's your name then?' He has perhaps assumed that Missy will be most receptive to a clown show because she looks so young.

'Is this a fucking joke?' she gasps. Then, turning to the nurses, 'The fuck is the matter with you people?'

'Oi!' barks Rashid. Mike bolsters his clown-smile against all this and switches to Roseanna.

'I'm Mike, and this is Bonnie—'

'Clive?' says Roseanna. 'Clive?'

'We're Bonnie and Mike, whatever you like!' says Bonnie, who quits juggling and produces a squeaky stick with a red ball on the end.

'You got any booze?' someone shouts.

'Hello everyone! How are you all feeling today?'

Missy has an attack of the giggles. They are bitter and fake but strong enough to slump her against the wall. Encouraged, the clowns begin a slapstick routine with the squeaky stick. Bonnie hits Mike, squeezing the stick so it squeaks as he doubles over or flies back, pulling faces. Missy freezes at the squeaking noise to watch this new part of the show then covers her head with her hood and curls up on the floor.

Everyone is in the corridor now. The elderly lady in the wheelchair inclines her face to them, eyes shut, as if she has found a patch of sun in the park. Roseanna looks very calm and sad. Their jackets have 'Magic Mime Music' on the back. His miniature top hat stays in place however forcibly the squeaky stick makes him jump or fall back, cross-eyed, dumbfounded, until he staggers back to life, shaking his head and grinning. They both try to start conversations but no one says a thing, there is only the yellow light, the squeaking of the squeaky stick, the squeaking of their trainers against the floor and the low rough hum that Bill emits then stops. Kneeling down I pull Missy's hood back. She is tight-faced, staring straight ahead, eyes red and wet.

'Come on,' I say. 'Let's go,' and she moans a little but lets me pick her up so she's on her feet. I have my arm around her and I say where shall we go and she says I don't know, man. I don't know.

5

The closing credits of *Iron Man* begin to scroll upwards and Rashid says 'OK? Everyone enjoy that?' He begins to disconnect his laptop from the TV. This is the first time he has ever shown us a film. 'Shall I leave it on? Yeah?' He fiddles with the remote until the screen bursts back into *Cash in the Attic* then collects his computer under his arm, stopping next to our chairs on his way.

'What about you two? Did you like it then?'

'Yeah, not bad. If you like explosions.'

'Missy? What about you?'

'Super,' she says, almost inaudibly, 'duper.'

Rashid smiles at us.

'Art therapy in a bit then, OK guys?'

'*Guys?*' she scoffs once he's gone.

'He's trying to be friendly.'

'That's the pattern. You wait.'

'But—'

'Nice. Then nasty. Then nice again.'

'Yeah but he's—'

'Wake up, Tom! He's a fucking dirty cunt! He's having sex with Roseanna!'

Art therapy means they push the tables together and sprawl out some pens and photocopied pages from a child's colouring-in book. I pick up the outline of a clown with numbered sections and then one of a giraffe. Chanelle the pregnant woman, Len and Missy have all turned the sheets of paper onto their blank sides. Chanelle is drawing a picture of a house. She keeps shifting position and sighing, her tight belly poking out of a large wraparound shawl. Suddenly she rips up what she's drawing and stands up, 'All of you. Every single one,' she says, then walks out.

Missy is drawing her name in 3D graffiti letters, a rising Japanese sun shining out from behind, butterflies everywhere.

'Wow, that's amazing. That's really good.'

'Yes, boss. I am incredibly fucking talented. Makes you look, makes you stare, makes you lose your underwear. Pass me the red.'

I pass her the pen and she begins colouring in the rays.

'Whadyareckon?' says Len, showing us his masterpiece.

'What is it?'

'Guess.'

'Some monkeys with a stick.'

'It's me injecting myself in the groin.'

Len signs his picture. Price stands up and turns up the volume on the television. There is a hip-hop video playing and for a moment everyone watches. The men on the video seem very proud of the fact they have mastered the art of smoking. Rashid walks in, turns the volume down, and comes over to our table saying, 'What is it?' because Missy has turned her paper over. 'C'mon. Giz a look.'

She puts her elbows across it and lays her head down. Rashid moves on around the table looking at what everyone is doodling. 'Guess what it is?' says Len, showing off his work. Rashid nods like an art teacher then checks his phone and sits down next to Missy.

'Hey,' he says, 'Are you feeling OK?' Missy closes her eyes, her jaw clenching. 'What you got there? Lemme see? Go on.' He leans into her and she sits bolt upright, slapping the paper over so he can see, staring up at the ceiling.

'Sick!' he says. 'You seen this, T?'

'A method of Receptacles,' says Malamock, 'Segment of criminals.' I feel a hollowing in my stomach.

'You really got something,' says Rashid. 'You know that?' and he puts his arm around her.

'What the fuck!' she barks, leaping up.

'Drugs were often used,' says Malamock, 'A wide-opened window.'

'Hey. Just thought you wanted a hug.'

'A *what?*'

'Missy. You don't want a hug, that's fine, yeah?'

'Receptacles become dreams. Nature is cruel.'

'Tom, tell him!'

'She doesn't want a hug. You don't want a hug. That's fine.'

Missy is eyes wide in expectation but I cannot grasp what I am meant to do here so I shrug.

'See? It's OK, isn't it, T?'

'Don't you ever fucking touch me!'

Rashid looks down and sighs. He taps his shoes against the floor, then struggles to his feet as if under new weight. He is still smiling. He makes a little muffled noise, the sound of some lonely and remote decision. 'Your drawing is, like, really good,' he says, 'That's all. And I thought you looked a bit down, OK? Sorry. Can I take it?' Missy doesn't reply, shifting from one foot to the other. 'To put it up? Maybe in the corridor, yeah?' He waits for a reply, 'OK?' Missy shrugs. He takes the drawing and leaves.

'Did I say I wanted a fucking hug? Did I?'

'No. You didn't.'

'Then why didn't you tell him? Why didn't you—' But before Missy can finish what she's saying her face seizes itself. Her eyes roll white. She collapses.

I manage to catch enough of her that she doesn't hit her head on the floor, body rigid in a backwards arc as if someone is using her to fire an arrow, hands straight out and clawed. 'Help!' I shout, and then someone else shouts, 'Nurse! Nurse!'

Rashid rushes back in and holds her face off the floor. She is convulsing. Two other nurses come in and I am holding her hand but they push me away. She takes fish-like gulps, eyes flickering until she goes limp, the nurses encouraging her to breathe. She shunts some breaths through her nose, face purple, teeth grinding, until eventually her eyes come back to life and she sits up from the floor confused and looking about her, kicking out, moaning, as Rashid and the other nurses say 'you're OK, you're OK' over and over. She is making eye contact with me now, Rashid holding her back in a kind of embrace and Missy wants to stand up or get away, but they hold her wrists. I try and say something but they tell me to stay out of the way. 'Gently, gently,' says Rashid, co-ordinating the other nurses to pick her up, and they carry her off to bed. We all trail behind, until they go into her room and shut the door.

In the slants of window light that fall onto the dark smoking garden, I experience the first pulsation I have had since being in here. The medication makes it seem distant and it travels through me without any problems. The night sky is clear and full of stars.

I smoke, pacing the garden, watching the shadows the other side of the translucent fence. Tess still hasn't called me back even though I have left several messages. I call her again to reconfirm that she's coming tomorrow but her phone is switched off.

Rashid comes outside and lights up. He wants to say something but instead takes another drag so I move towards the door. 'Wait a sec,' he says, blowing smoke out at the moon. 'I don't know why Missy's got it in for me, T. Really don't.' He pauses and lifts his eyebrows at me, as if I am meant to tell him why.

'Dunno,' I shrug, but he is still waiting. 'The Roseanna thing?'

'What Roseanna thing?'

'I don't know.'

'Hey,' he says, his face pinched now, 'what's Roseanna got to do with anything?'

'Honestly, Rash, I don't know.'

'Tom?' He shifts, blocking my way out. 'What Roseanna thing? What's Roseanna got to do with it?'

'I don't know . . .'

'*Tom* . . .'

'I think she thinks . . . you know . . . that you two . . . are in a kind of, you know . . . with Roseanna.'

Strange things occur in Rashid's face. His skull slips forward from his shoulders, his mouth falls open. 'Is that what she's saying? About *me?*'

'Errrm . . .'

'I mean you know I'm a *nurse* in here, right? And Roseanna is a *patient?* You know that, right?' Rashid looks up at the night, muttering out curses and shaking his head. 'Roseanna, yeah,' he rocks his head, his tone hardened. 'Let's talk about Roseanna. Roseanna is not well. At all. And you lot bullying the shit out of her isn't making her any better.'

'I'm not bull—'

'Missy is a bitch to her, and yeah, Roseanna's got a crush on me at the moment, it's true, but it's just part of her thing, you know? Like you got the octopus or whatever, that's your thing,

84

and she's got her thing. She fixes on people. Like a couple of months ago it was nurse Steve, and before that it was someone else, and at the moment, yeah, it's me. It shifts around. She'll probably switch to you soon. Everyone gets a turn, everyone male, pretty much. That is what's going on here, T, OK?' Rashid sucks the cigarette and spits the smoke. 'Don't let that little – don't let Missy poison you with her dark little mind games. She's got her own issues. Believe. Don't get sucked into her . . .' his lungs strip the rest of the cigarette into invisibility, '. . . shit. Get me?' Rashid exhales, stuffing the butt into the wall-mounted ashtray. 'OK?' I nod. 'We good?' I nod again and we touch fists. He pulls open the door, nodding me through. 'Me and Roseanna?' he chuckles then whistles. 'Heard it all now.'

––––––

Phoebe undresses while she talks, switching through lights until she is satisfied with just the strip above the sink. Their bathroom is olive green, oyster-shell soap holders, a skew-whiff toilet seat that cannot stay upright. She is unravelling her workday, admin at an English language school for foreign students, unwinding it from around her neck with her scarf. She asks me how the DLA assessment went and I tell her how Malamock guided me through the questions from my personal adviser, a man with a fraying moustache called Seb. Malamock recommended I introduce them, and that was a conversation for which Seb was unprepared.

Phoebe shields herself as she undresses, not so much out of embarrassment as from a coded dissatisfaction with her own body that programmes certain moments even while she talks, hand hovering across her belly, a slight turning from me, a haste once naked. She stops in the mirror and pouts ever so slightly, arching her eyebrows, but by the time her hands are puffing up her hair she has already left her reflection and climbed into the bathwater. There is much arranging to do so we can both fit, holding hands, her legs over my hips, my feet wedged in beside her bum.

She leans back, settling, and picks a plastic cat off the bath shelf from among the hair and beauty products. She drowns the cat. Her breasts are floating. She shunts me back so she has room to dip her head, squeezing the wet hair to one side as she rises, twisting it into a cord. There is conflict with a girl at work. Another attempt at friendship has backfired. Moody cow. By this point in the telling she is cross-legged, my knees up and bent, and she is playing with my penis and balls as if desk toys, her manipulations somehow in rhythm with the story.

'Stop having sexual relations!' says Charlotte, banging the door. 'I will not have any children conceived underwater! This is not an aquarium!'

'She's pissed,' whispers Phoebe.

'No I am not!' says her mother. We are giggling, listening to her step and slip and *whoa!* down the stairs.

'Careful!' Phoebe cries out.

'Bollocks!'

By the time we come down, dressed and ready to go out, she is asleep in front of the telly. The Peugeot is parked up half on the pavement. Charlotte is snoring. Phoebe takes the remote out of her hand and covers her up, putting a glass of water on the side table. Phoebe is wearing white trainers and navy tweed culottes. When she leans over to kiss her mum her T-shirt lifts, knicker elastic rising up above a bare hip.

———

It is snowing outside and there are five nurses restraining Price. Chanelle left first thing this morning and after she said goodbye to him he became enraged in the meds queue. The alarm was pulled, Rashid and Steve grabbing and folding and yanking him down, three other nurses clattering through the security doors.

Steve is kneeling on his ribs. He slips his knee onto Price's throat and then against his head as the other nurses grapple writhing limbs. They flip him and pull his arms behind his back then cross his legs. Steve gets his knee back on Price's head. They try to squeeze him together so they can lift him but they can't manage it so Rashid takes a hypodermic needle off another nurse, they rip down Price's trousers and pants and Rashid stabs Price in the arse with the syringe. Price goes limp. They all stand up and drag him off. I am whispering furious prayers to the Octopus God. My hands are shaking.

By the time my turn at the cubbyhole comes my hands are still shaking and the cup of pills is rattling but I manage to knock them back and show off my tongue. Missy takes me by the hand and leads me into her room. I am pacing to and fro. Tess has not turned up for her visit first thing like we said and her phone is still off. Her phone is never off, she lives on her phone and He will not tell me where she is and did you see that? Did you fucking see that? The knee on his face?

Missy's room is exactly the same as my room only she has a proper bed frame and in one corner the cracking paint looks like reptile skin. She is cross-legged on her bed, nursing her shoulder from where it dislocated during the fit, a pile of baggy clothes with her tiny body lost somewhere inside. Missy chews her fingernails, watching me as I jibber-jabber and pace until she bounces off the bed and arrests me with a hug. 'You're freaking yourself out, man,' she whispers, 'It's all right. You're all right.'

I have had to stoop to receive this hug and when she releases me I stay at that level watching her get back onto her bed, suggesting we play a game. She beckons me to sit next to her and then asks me if I can burp the alphabet. She gulps air until she is

87

full then burps all the letters and I clap her and she accepts the applause like a Mafia boss, mouth turned down into chin, hands aloft. It's my turn but I can't burp the alphabet though I can roll my tongue, not just curve the sides like most people do but roll it like a belly. 'Oh my days,' she says. 'Don't let Roseanna see that.' I tell her about my conversation with Rashid and she spits out a laugh of disbelief then tells me again how he tried it on with her when she first arrived. Missy gets off the bed and starts doing an impression of Roseanna and Rashid having sex, Roseanna cackling hysterically and rubbing herself, Rashid behind with caveman arms making caveman noises, humping, humping, spent.

It is very funny and I've almost forgotten about Tess but soon I am checking my phone again cursing that I do not have Byron's number I have made a point of not having Byron's number. What an idiot! I ring the landline again but the phone just rings and rings. Missy keeps asking me questions about the Octopus God, about where I think He comes from and why I am so devoted to Him even though He punishes me and even though I know she is just trying to distract me I try to explain to her that He loves me but that the spirit path is very difficult and I must be tested so that I can be made ready and when I am ready, He will reveal my mission, and ready means to become an Awakened One, one of the Rightly Self-Awakened Ones, and that means a cessation of fabrications – no deception, in other words, of others or of oneself. It means purifying so that you are in the right condition, the requisite condition, to receive direct knowledge of consciousness such as we get at birth and death, and when I'm at that point, I will receive my mission, as in my specific personal mission, as the times we are living in are particular, with the coming of the great flood, and that means movement, voyages of all types. All types of pilgrims and transmigrants. I must be made ready. I must be tested.

'And what's He going to do for us all when the shit hits the fan?'

'Nothing.'

'What?'

'He is truth, not comfort.'

'Is He testing you now?' she says, but when I reply that I don't know and start checking my phone again she leans in close to my ear and shouts, 'Oi! You testing my mate Tom here or what?'

The snow has stopped falling and is already starting to melt, sodden patches of paving appearing as the garden reclaims its true character. We are outside scraping handfuls off the bench, the plane tree now a dripping chandelier. The snow is stinging cold and wet against the palm and we pat it into snowballs, looking upwards into the pearl sky. We all throw snowballs over the translucent fence except Missy who can't throw because her shoulder still hurts, so I roll one up and chuck it for her. This is longest time I have not seen or spoken to Tess ever in my life.

Rashid comes outside to herd us in for breakfast and we are waiting for some kind of reaction from the high-security patients behind the fence but nothing happens and Rashid is insistent. He has instructions from Dr Fredericks to make sure we eat properly. They are particularly concerned about Missy, whose epilepsy gets worse if she doesn't eat.

'If the food was edible, we'd eat it,' she says as we traipse through the unit.

'Just get in there and eat something, OK?'

'I want to eat what you eat,' she says, looking Rashid up and down, 'Because that shit must be irresistible.'

Rashid sighs and shakes his head at me. Missy slumps into a chair as Kiki comes in with the breakfast trolley. Thankfully there is only bread, butter, jam, cereal and milk – the best meal in here as long as the milk isn't off. Rashid takes his phone out and wanders off.

'Bore his jaw through with a thorn,' Malamock says as I sit down next to Missy. 'Comes the battle.'

'Where's Tess? Is she OK?'

'Eh?'

'I was talking to Malamock. But you really should eat though,' I say, 'if it's bad for your epilepsy—'

'Whose side you on?' says Missy.

'*You really should eat though*,' He mocks '*if it's bad for your epilepsy.*'

'Didn't you see her fitting?'

'Hey . . .' says Missy.

'She fell on the floor! She dislocated her shoulder!'

'Hey—' she takes my hand.

'Where's Tess? Why won't you tell me where Tess is?'

'Tom? Calm down, man. Yo! Tom? Can you hear me? Tom?'

I struggle through breakfast as Kiki tries to make conversation with us and the fact that it has snowed in March prompts all sorts of talk about climate change and the end of the world and how everyone will burn and I tell them they won't burn, they'll drown or starve or be shot. The man with bad skin becomes distressed by something he thinks is hiding in his pockets. When we are finished I call Tess again. Her phone is still off. The landline just rings and rings then I call Hextons and they tell me she hasn't come in. They don't know where she is.

Kiki announces that Dr Fredericks is not here again today and so there is no group therapy again and for the first time I think seriously about escaping. An advert comes on for a programme about people who have had plastic surgery to look like their idols.

'That's my idea,' says Clara, one of the new patients. She puts her fingers in her ears. 'They're leaking out.'

After *The Jeremy Kyle Show*, I return to my room and pace around drumming with the mystery spoon, drumming terrible thoughts of what's happened to Tess into the walls. I have a pulsation. I am ambushed by its strength and it starts developing into a thought-form.

'Right concentration,' says Malamock, and a different doctor is suddenly in the doorway and gives me sweet distraction. She is much younger than Fredericks. She is stocky with incredibly muscular cheeks. She could be a world champion chewer.

'Tom!' she beams, 'Nice to see you! Can I come in?'

'Sure.'

'Thanks. Whoa! Have you lost weight?'

'We've never met before.'

'Haven't we?' She looks at the papers she is carrying. 'Right – that's right. Still. Looking good. Like the beard!'

'Thank you.'

'They're very fashionable at the moment, aren't they?'

'The psychiatric look does seem to be in this year, yes.'

'So how are you feeling?'

'Not very good, Doctor. Actually.'

'What's up?'

'Well now, let me see, I'm in an acute psychiatric ward under section, which is not what I'd hoped and dreamed of as a little boy, and my sister should have come to see me this morning and I don't know what's happened to her, and I'm really worried about her and nobody will tell me when I am going home. Nobody will even talk to me about it! So. Yeah. Not very good.'

'Ahhh. And what did you want to be?'

'What?'

'When you were a little boy?'

'A fireman. When am I going home?'

'So my name is Dr Prashad.'

'Hello Dr Prashad. Do you know when Dr Fredericks is going to talk to me about being released? Or can you tell me? Can anyone? Tell me anything?'

'There's still time, you know.'

'To be a fireman?'

'Why not?'

'Not so keen on voice-hearers in the fire service, Dr Prashad. Might confuse the rescue. When's Dr Fredericks going to come and see me?'

'Tom, it's crucial we stay positive, OK?' I start drumming the spoon against the wall again. 'I know it's frustrating. But it's a really busy time and we're just really, really, stretched. How are you getting on with everyone here? Making friends?'

'Like a house on fire.'

'Oh, oh, see what you did there . . .'

'OK, Dr Prasad.' I stop drumming and lie down on my bed until she's gone. Then I get up again because Kiki is announcing bingo.

6

Kiki opens the wire hatch of the bingo cage, a kind of hamster wheel with a handle, and takes out a green plastic ball.

'Twenty-four . . .' she declares, checking her list of Bingo lingo, '. . . knock at the door!' Kiki often takes the role of caller and is trying to learn all the calls off by heart. I am using bingo to keep my mind off Tess but I can't I can't I can't—

'Thirty-three. All the threes.'

'Bingo!' says Clara, the new arrival. She has a perfectly round face.

'We've only just started, Clara. You can't have bingo yet, my love.'

'I got the numbers.'

'Well let's just see, shall we?' Kiki gives Clara a smile. 'Sixty-two. Tickety-boo.'

Roseanna comes into the room. Her hair is pulled back from her face. She is wearing a new tracksuit and lipstick. She looks uncertain. She turns back but someone is waving her forward.

'Oh hi Roseanna,' says Kiki, 'do you want to join in? Look there's space next to—' but she has already dragged a chair beside me. Kiki comes over with a pen and a bingo card.

'OK, Roseanna, so we've had twenty-four, thirty-three and sixty-two. Have you got any of those numbers?'

'Eh?'

'Twenty-four, thirty-three and sixty-two – have a look at your card there, my love. Are any of those numbers there?'

'No.'

Kiki goes back to her position and rotates the bingo cage once more. Roseanna puts a hand on my leg.

'Oh . . .'

'Seventeen. Dancing queen.'

'Look, Roseanna—'

'Seen my hair?'

'It seems very . . . very tidy. Look, you've got seventeen.'

'What?'

'On your card. You've got seventeen. Aren't you going to circle it? With the pen?'

'I know how to play fucking bingo!' She puts both hands on my leg.

'OK, look, Roseanna,' I begin. 'My sister – I'm having a very difficult – this isn't a good – OK, how can I put this? I must tell you something important, and that is my God forbids me to eat meat or have sex. If I have even a lustful thought, He punishes me, here, on my right side. It feels like I'm being struck by a cattle prod. My right side heats up, it gets incredibly, incredibly hot and then if He is really angry – bang! – I'm being electrocuted. If I was on this chair now and I had any kind of lustful thought about any woman at all He would strike me and I would be off the chair and on the floor. That's what happens if I break His rules. In fact it can be worse, He can make me trigger for really bad things but for transgressing the sexual prohibition I can get electrocuted or punishment nightmares. In fact I used to have a girlfriend, Phoebe, and let me tell you it became very, very complicated and very, very painful. On every level. So I am unable to do anything like that with anyone, OK? Even if they are the nicest, most beautiful person

94

in the world.' Roseanna's mouth is open, gums visible. Her eyes, branching with red veins, are buried in dark flabby pads of distress and fatigue. She is squeezing her legs together.

'Bingo!'

'Clara, my love, we still haven't finished yet.'

'What was that number again?' I ask.

'Eight.'

'Ha! See?' I say to Roseanna, showing her my card. 'I've got eight, because that's His number. The number eight manifesting itself to me is part of His manifestation in the universe.'

'What on earth are you on about?' She takes her hands off my leg.

'The number eight.'

'What is this?' she sneers, shoving the table away and standing up, 'Fucking *Sesame Street*?'

'Oh come on, Roseanna,' Kiki says, 'Don't go, we're almost done. Look – seventy-two . . . Danny La Rue.'

'Bingo!' says Clara.

'She's got all the numbers.'

'Well ladies and gents, looks like we've got ourselves . . .' Kiki bends down beneath her table and takes something out of a box. It's a packet of Polos. She wobbles it upwards as if it is an exciting fish emerging from the depths. '. . . a winner!'

Lunch has no name. Somewhere between a stew, a broth and a casserole, all three would have denied any family connection. 'Kiki,' I say, 'is this a tomato?' She pushes herself off the counter.

'Yes, my love.'

'But what is this?'

'No comment.'

'Can you please apologise to the cook for whatever it was that we did to him in a previous life?' I take a bite. It is burnt and bitter and I pull a face at Missy as she comes into the dining

95

room, hood up. Kiki puts a plate in front of her. She pulls her hood back.

'I thought you lot wanted me to eat?'

'You've got to get some food inside you, love,' says Kiki as Missy stands up again.

'I agree. Soon as there is some food in here, please let me know.'

'What's going on?' says Rashid walking in.

'It's fine. I'm dealing with it,' says Kiki.

'Dealing with what?'

'I'm not eating that shit. That isn't even food.'

'Sit down, Missy.'

'Rashid, I said I'm dealing—'

'Sit down, Missy.'

Missy pulls her hood up to walk off but Rashid grabs her injured shoulder, swinging her back around. She shrieks out in pain and claps the side of his head.

Rashid steps back in shock. He is holding his face. Then he drops his arms and leans at her. 'G'an then!' he shouts, bouncing from foot to foot as if waiting for her to start fighting him. A strange moment passes. Suddenly he grabs her bad arm and yanks her into a half nelson.

'My arm!' she is screaming, 'My FUCKING ARM!'

He trips her legs and slams her onto the floor.

'Alarm!' he shouts at Steve in the doorway. 'Get the Acuphase!'

Missy makes a noise like ripping metal. The alarm is pulled, great waves of pounding noise that mix in with her screaming.

'The moment of the companions,' says Malamock. Some healthcare assistants and nurses run in and help Rashid drag Missy out of the room. 'Christlike. Under their nails. Outnumbered.'

Kiki holds her own mouth. No one says anything. The screaming becomes muffled then stops.

Moments pass and the alarm is turned off, the silence itself ringing out like an echo. Everyone carries on eating. I look down into my plate.

'At the shaking of a spear,' says Malamock. 'Revealed it. A longing to cry.'

Missy comes back into the room by herself. She takes her seat. Some people look at her, some don't. Kiki stands behind her.

'You don't have to eat anything if you don't want to – OK, my love?'

'Are you fucking joking me?' she whispers. Kiki steps away. Missy's hands are on the table.

Out in the smoking garden the sky is low and white. Sloppy grey slush streaks the ground. There are two magpies in the plane trees, swapping branches. *One for sorrow, two for joy.*

'You're in the wrong tree,' I say.

'What?'

'The magpies.'

Everyone else has gone back inside. Missy spits, shakes her head. She lets out sharp, punching breaths with her eyes closed. I sit down beside her on the bench and put an arm round her.

'Don't!'

'Do you want to be on your own?'

Missy tuts. 'Dickhead.' She grips her head. 'OK, OK. I'm not handling this. We're going to go inside and you're going to ask a nurse for some sedatives because you feel anxious and you're going to give them to me, OK?'

We go inside and I get a pill and give it to her and we sit down in front of the TV. She tries to watch but cannot settle, picking at the arms of the chair and her fingernails and telling people to get the fuck out the way. She leaves the day room, walking up and down the corridor. I try to keep pace with her, to distract her with questions until she tells me to stop being annoying and the sedative calms her enough that she can sit back down and bury herself in the TV while I check my phone but still nothing, nothing, nothing from Tess.

After some time it becomes difficult for Missy to move. She is crying. She cannot lean her head easily against her hand or keep it upright. 'Help,' she whispers, trying to cross her legs.

With my arm around her we leave the day room and by the time we get to her bedroom her legs are unable to carry her body. She keeps checking my face. She is very frightened.

'You're my best friend,' she says, and I say *I'm here don't worry I'm here* sliding her onto the mattress but she is losing control of her mouth, slurring, '. . . don't wanna go in there please God please help me . . .' but I can't do anything, I just sit there holding her hands until suddenly her eyes go dead and I am shaking her. 'Missy! Hey! Hey!' Rashid is in the doorway. 'Look at her! Get a doctor!'

'No, man. That's normal. Don't worry. She'll be back out of it in two or three days. Hey, what did I say about Roseanna?' he says. 'She's checking you out, man.'

I go back to my room and find myself headbutting the wall.

'Fool,' says Malamock. 'Craven,' and I ask Him again what's happened to Tess but He does not reply and I start headbutting the wall again only harder.

Night has fallen and I am unable to still myself. I am just counting down the time to evening meds so I can be knocked out until the morning when I can wake up and find a message from my sister that she was just very, very busy and her phone broke and she lost my number and she is fine. Lying on the mattress I realise I have bent the mystery spoon so much it is about to break.

'You coming then?' says Rashid at the doorway.

'Where?'

'*Iron Man 2*. Come on.'

The Octopus God surrounds me.

'Will he make a covenant with thee?'

His presence thickens.

'Seen it,' I say.

'Got other stuff. Ripped a load off the internet.'

'Actually I'm not feeling so good.'

'*Actually I'm not feeling so good.*'

'This isn't about Missy, is it, T?' says Rashid, coming into the room. ''Cause that's what we gotta do if someone becomes violent like that. No choice.' He shrugs.

'I'm really just not feeling so good,' I say rolling over to the wall.

'OK, OK,' he says, 'd'you want a hug or something?'

'No thanks.'

'*No thanks.*'

The dinner bell rings.

Non-vegetarians are served a kind of grey burger. I am given a wedge of congealed vegetable matter. After squelching down as much as I can throat, I go and check on Missy. She is in the same position. Rashid has left for the day, the night shift now in control.

After meds I go back to my room. People are walking about in pyjamas. I get undressed and lie on my bed waiting to be made unconscious. A night nurse comes along and switches the light off. The doors are all left ajar. The corridor light goes off. I pray to Malamock that Missy will bear the chemical nightmares she is suffering and that nothing bad has happened to Tess. I pray that soon I will be with her and the kids and in my own bed away from here, the gentle woods swaying around me, the cooing of the wood pigeons, the scratching of the squirrels scurrying across the great rocks as a new morning breaks, fresh white sunlight lying across the ferns.

Dimly aware that I have been woken by a clattering noise, I reach for my phone and in its light see another spoon on the floor. Two fourteen a.m. No new messages. Awake now though still woozy I check if there is anyone in the corridor but there is only the glow of the nurses' station. I pick up the spoon and examine it, placing it on the shelf with the other one, then slope up the corridor towards the toilets. Steve's head emerges from the glow.

'What is it?'

'I'm— toilet,' I say, pointing ahead. He stands there and watches me until we are level and can examine each other. Steve has almost no eyebrows.

'Do you want sleeping pills?'

'I'm just going to the toilet. Has anyone else been to the toilet?'

'Eh?'

'Is anyone else awake? Walking around?'

'Just keep it down,' he says, returning to his computer and some sort of video game. He is holding a headset.

I carry on to the bathroom. The lights stagger into life and there, by the sinks, is a man I do not recognise. He is cupping water into his mouth from the tap. He stops when I come in but is not concerned by my presence. Small and pale with a folded face like a premature baby, he is wearing a kind of green uniform. When he steps away from the sink he does so with a jolt. His legs are injured.

'It tastes of clay,' he says. 'I just want a drink of water that doesn't taste of clay.' The man hobbles to the next sink and an alarm goes off, first in the distance and then in our building. He doesn't seem to mind. He tries another tap, slurping at the water.

I step back into the corridor and Steve is running towards me. 'Is there someone in there?' he hisses. As I nod there is a noise behind me. Rashid is shutting the door to Roseanna's room. Noticing me, he straightens, eyes flinting in the darkness.

Steve grabs my arm and neck, swinging me round, marching me off to my room. I twist back but the corridor is empty. Lights go on behind the security doors. They clang open and guards rush into the ward. Steve pushes me into my room.

'Go to bed.'

'What's Rashid doing?'

'You didn't see Rashid,' he says.

'They are firm in themselves. Drugs were often used. They are gone away from men.'

'Just get into bed, Tom.' Steve shuts my door.

'A longing to cry,' continues Malamock. 'The basic error. You will bring back weapons to me beyond what is useful. And then they escape. They perish for ever.'

Rubber boots clatter past. There is some distant shouting. Walkie-talkies whistle and burr among the fractured voices. The corridor falls quiet. I am standing on my mattress in the dark.

———

We are lying in a hammock together looking up through alder trees to a blue sky. We can hear Mum looking for us, calling out our names but we are invisible in this hammock. We are doing impressions of the man who's waiting in the car. 'Shut up, mate,' I giggle.

'Shut up, mate,' giggles Tess.

'Shut up, mate. Can I have the water, mate?'

'Shut up, mate.'

We are on a ferry, ploughing the sea behind us, and the man has given us both a packet of fruit Polos. We have found a play area where there are much younger children but there is a porthole window that looks backwards across the sea and we are sitting in the window eating Polos watching children in rows watching a Disney video. Then we see Bryan Ferry.

He is walking past us through the main lounge: Bryan Ferry. The actual Bryan Ferry, off *Top of the Pops*. 'Slave to Love'. We follow him around the deck until our arms are caught and *what are you doing?* asks Mum. Bryan Ferry has stopped and is talking to someone and we are pointing and singing, 'It's Bryan Ferry on a ferry! Bryan Ferry on a ferry!'

We are at Elevation, Lea Valley Trading Estate, and me and Dan are in a strobe-lit corner with shuttering vision telling each other that we'll always be friends. We pass a bottle of water back and forth. The music is booming hard and fast and here comes Tess out of the crowd long hair Cheshire cat grinning in a sports bra and baggy Mash tracksuit bottoms. She is pointing upwards, excited, mouthing *this tune! This tune!* It's a jungle tune that samples 'Slave to Love'.

'Bryan Ferry on a ferry,' she's E-d up and chanting, 'Bryan Ferry on a ferry,' and she hugs me, we're both chanting 'Bryan Ferry on a ferry! Bryan Ferry on a ferry!' and Dan is saying 'Eh? What?' *Bryan Ferry on a ferry. Bryan Ferry on a ferry.*

———

'All right, my love?' Kiki is standing over me. The bell is ringing. 'What you holding those two spoons for? You hungry?'

After breakfast I hang around the cubbyhole until it is time for morning meds. I want to be first. Kiki hands me the tablets, asking me if I'm all right again. I swallow the pills and show off my tongue. I spy Rashid in the dining room talking to one of the healthcare assistants. He is trying to ignore Roseanna pulling at his arm.

I go back into my room and lie down, waiting for the meds to turn me into a ghost. Eventually I drift off to the toilets. Sitting down in a cubicle I stare at my phone, typing and retyping more texts to Tess, deleting version after version because I've already sent all these versions. Finally I send her a text that is just rows and rows of question marks. I stay there for a long time without plans to leave until someone bangs on the door and says my name. I collect myself at the shove of the latch, and step out.

'Hey,' says Rashid, leaning on a sink yet twisting round to look at himself in the mirror, lime eyes, fox-hearted, smoothing his scalp. 'Do you like football?' I shake my head. 'Don't follow no one? A team?'

'No.'

'Me I'm Arsenal. All the way,' and Rashid scoops me into a hug. '*Goooooners*,' he sings softly.

'The contact comes,' says Malamock. 'Every vulnerable period.'

'The boss,' Rashid says as he lets go, 'wants to see you.'

'Dr Fredericks?'

'Yeah, yeah. Come. And don't worry, T,' he says softly, 'I got it all sorted, yeah?' Rashid is clicking his fingers in front of my face, but they don't make a sound. He can't click his fingers. 'Hey. Yo. Chop-chop, dreamer boy.'

We go back into the corridor. At the security doors I experience a mighty pulsation. Rashid is holding the first door open for me as I try to breathe and concentrate on the now rather than on the pulsation. We cross no man's land and then he enters a code, opening the second set of doors. We go into the reception then up a flight of stairs to a grey door with Fredericks's name on it. Rashid puts his hand on the back of my neck. We stay like that for a moment and then he knocks, rhythmic and joyful, *ta-ta-tat-tat-tat*.

'En—ter!' booms Fredericks. Rashid pushes open the door. 'Thank you, Rashid, I'll buzz you when we're ready.'

I step into the office. The door shuts behind me.

7

'Mr Tuplow. Tom. Come in, come in. Sit down.' Fredericks lopes above a braided green leather desk. There is a fireplace boarded up and painted over, its mantelpiece thick with photos and cards below a gilt-framed painting of insects and fruit. The painting is very dark. Piles of paper are stacked up on the floor next to a filing cabinet and a bookcase. Beside copies of DSM-4 and ICD-10 there is a series of cookery books then one book turned flat so you can see the front cover: *I Am a Traffic Light: Postcards from the Psychiatrist's Chair* by Dr Paula Fredericks.

Settling back into her leather desk chair, the doctor takes off some browline glasses, rubbing her eyes with the heels of her hands. 'OK, Tom. Well, a very serious matter has been brought to my attention,' she stretches her face, 'and it's vital that we get to the bottom of this,' leaning her eyeballs upwards, 'because it's not good.' She puts her glasses back on. 'Not good at all.'

'About me?'

'As you are aware a patient from PICU managed to gain entry into our ward last night. Indeed you found him in the toilets, is that all correct?'

'Yes but—'

'And where were you before that, Tom?' Fredericks makes

a triangle with her desktop and forearms, settling her skull on its apex.

'In my room.'

'What were you doing awake at that time?'

'I needed the toilet.'

'You just woke up?'

'Be detached. With regard to the female stronghold. Onto possessions delightful.'

'Someone left a spoon on me.'

'A spoon?'

'It's not the first time. Actually.'

Fredericks griddles her brow.

'People are coming into your room at night and leaving spoons on you – is that what you're telling me?' She straightens her back, thumb and forefinger horseshoeing through her hair.

'Not every night. Twice. I've got them on my shelf if you—'

'Tom,' elbows back on the table, fist balled into hand. 'I'm going to ask you a question, and I want you to listen very carefully and then tell me the truth. The absolute, hundred per cent truth, OK? Were you in Roseanna's room last night?'

'What?'

'Steve says he saw you coming out of Roseanna's room.'

'Here. The issue of your cowardice.'

'That was Rashid!'

'Tom, Rashid wasn't on the ward last night. His shift ended at 8 p.m. Now then – and I want you to listen to me – this sort of thing is absolutely beyond the pale, do you understand me? What were you doing in her room?'

'I wasn't in Roseanna's room! This is . . . ask Roseanna!'

'We have asked Roseanna, and she was asleep. Tom, I'm going to ask you again: what were you doing in Roseanna's room?'

My knee is bouncing at incredible speed.

'You must understand we are in very dangerous territory now,' says Fredericks, crossing her legs. 'Have you ever been in Roseanna's room at night before?'

'Rashid—'

'Before you go on, Tom, I think you should know that it's really Rashid who is fighting your corner here. There are those that want to involve the police, but he is absolutely adamant that you being in there must have been a mistake. That you're not like that. You're very respectful. Perhaps you got lost?'

'Lost? In here?'

'You're actually very popular among the staff and no one wants to see you get into such serious trouble, least of all me, and frankly no one wants Roseanna to be put through anything more, but there are tests. We can find out.'

'I didn't touch her!'

'Would you like to touch her?'

'Doctor, please, this is ridiculous – have you seen the state of her?'

'Insults are simply not going to help us here, Tom. No.'

'That's not what I mean, I mean – I mean she's mad, Doctor! She's not in her right mind. It's unthinkable!'

Fredericks's chair squeaks as she leans right back, her hands swooping down in front of her chest, rejoining at the fingertips to form a small pyramid.

'Steve assures me that Roseanna's duvet, bedclothes et cetera looked untouched, so, what with Rashid's support, I'm willing to leave it there Tom, for all our sakes, but – and let me be quite clear about this – anything of a like nature happens again and it won't just be me you're talking to, OK? It will be the police. This is a mixed ward, which is frankly far from ideal, and as such we need cast-iron rules about this sort of thing. Cast-iron. Got that?' She shoves her head forward. The pyramid is broken.

'Doctor . . .' In desperation I pick up the paperweight that is on her desk. It is a golden lion. What am I doing? I replace the lion and stand up. The giant doctor tightens her eyebrows. I pivot round and take in the rest of her office. In a corner by the window there is an exercise bike. I walk over to it and seize the handles, aware of the hanging moment, aware that I must master this interview, I must turn it around and reverse the course of Rashid's lies if I am to have any hope of getting out of here, of finding Tess, of—

'Tom?'

The window gives out onto a view of hospital buildings, parked cars and a road.

'Cities. Which the vulture's eyes hath not seen.'

In the foreground the top of a tree creeps into view and as I approach the glass I realise that it is the plane tree. I can see down into the smoking garden.

'Hello? Tom?'

Does Fredericks observe us from here? Does she take notes? From this angle I can see a little way over the translucent fence to a brick wall behind it. There is an orange bath mat hanging from the uppermost rung of barbed wire.

'I didn't know you were a cyclist, Doctor.'

'Oh, that thing? That's just to try and keep fit.'

'It is a bike that goes nowhere.'

'You could look at it like that, I suppose.'

'Doctor,' I say, turning from the window, summoning my coolest, most professional tone, becoming the lawyer again, 'I would like to register an official complaint about the use of Acuphase that I witnessed yesterday.'

'Right. OK. Would you like to sit down again, Thomas, or are you planning to take the bike out for a spin?' Fredericks smiles like an advert. 'Acuphase,' she begins as I retake my seat, 'is used on occasion here at Hilldean, that's correct. It's used on patients who are showing signs of extreme agitation, where other tranquillisers have not worked.'

'Missy—'

'Missy has profound behavioural issues and a history of violence, both against herself and others.'

'She just didn't want to eat the lunch!'

'She assaulted a member of staff—'

'But it's a mind-bending drug. That lasts two or three days. You're giving something that could drive anyone mad to people who are already—'

'It's not a "mind-bending drug". That's nonsense.'

'Have you ever taken it, Doctor?' Fredericks sighs. 'We're in your nice cosy gym here, but down there, below our feet, Missy is—'

'Thomas, I do understand your concerns. But we are here, at this moment, not to talk about Missy, but to talk about you. We are an underfunded unit in an underfunded service running at capacity, and in such a tight ship we simply do not have the resources to cope with the kind of behaviour that threatens the well-being of others. We don't have the bandwidth.' Fredericks looks at her watch. 'Listen, I will certainly look into it, OK? But Tom, right now I'm afraid we do need to concentrate on you. Now your sister and I have—'

'Do you know where she is?'

'Do I know where your sister is?'

'It's just that I can't get hold of her and—'

'I expect she's busy, Tom. I expect she's probably cracking on with stuff. Stuff that's built up while she's having to look after you. Now then, your sister and I have had a good long chat and she feels strongly, as I do, that bildinocycline represents—'

Malamock closes in. My right side tightens.

'Doctor, I know you both want me to take part in this drug trial, and actually I wanted to explain to you, very simply and

109

clearly, why I can't take part in it, so you can explain it to her, because I think that coming from you she might – the problem is that now whenever I talk about Him it's very difficult for her to—'

'This is your voice.'

'My . . . yes and—'

'OK, Tom. I'd like to start there if we can.' Fredericks rolls herself to her computer and starts typing, 'Just to help me understand what's going on. So tell me about your voices. How many are there now?'

'He – one. One voice.'

'Male or female?'

'He's neither one nor the other.'

'You said "he". Why not "she"?'

'I don't know. That's not the point.' Fredericks pulls a face appropriate for use on a child that means *isn't it? Isn't that the point?*

'OK, Tom. Let's say androgynous. A-N-D-R-O . . .'

'G-Y-N-O-U-S.'

'Thank you. And the voice self-identifies as an octopus?'

'The Octopus God.'

'The god of octopi?'

'Octopuses. And no, not just the god of octopuses. The Octopus God.'

'What does he – or she – or it – or they, we say nowadays, don't we – look like?'

I take a thorough breath and sit up straight.

'An octopus.'

'You've seen him?'

'I've felt Him. I've seen Him in dreams.'

'Any other . . . anything else of a visual nature?'

'White light, sometimes golden light.'

'And you've been hearing this voice for . . .?'

'Nineteen years.'

'So why do you think this god picked you? Why do you think he talks to you? I mean you in particular?'

'I was searching for – I was – I think in another culture I would have been a shaman or a monk but I wasn't – something obviously went wrong. That's why I'm here. That's the cause of everything. I expanded my consciousness too far, too fast. I blew a kind of hole into the otherworld—'

'With drugs?'

'. . . and I haven't had the right training—'

'And what kind of drugs? Cannabis?'

'Well, yes. Cannabis. I was living in Brighton at the time and basically, Doctor, well I suppose you could say I sort of fracked myself. I funnelled cannabis and other drugs into myself in large volumes at heavy and constant pressure for a few years – including one crucial period of regularly taking liquid acid as some kind of infinite experiment about infinity that started off as a dare, but then . . . well it ended in the blackest species of unrest, Doctor, the very blackest. I had fractured the bedrock, you see, which caused earthquakes that eventually ruptured a fissure running right the way through to the otherworld, allowing me a telepathic connection to the Octopus God and, as I was saying, I can't control my experiences as I should be able to if I had trained my whole life, like a monk, like a *vates*, but without the proper training I get anxiety and pulsations and sometimes triggerings, which I've really got under control in the last few years, the really bad attacks I've got good at avoiding—'

'You did have rather a bad one a couple of weeks ago though, didn't you?'

'That was something else. That wasn't a triggering – well it was, but it was a punishment, it was totally different, and actually it was the trial that . . . anyway, sorry – look I . . .' I've lost my train of thought. What am I talking about?

'Tom . . .?'

'Insomnia! That's it — insomnia, racing thoughts, anxiety attacks and then if I can't control pulsations, the triggering, the mind collapse, that's not all Him, you see. That's my lack of training, which I am trying to make up for, but here it's impossible—'

'Because you're not a trained monk?'

'Like monks and shamans get. Spiritual training. To deal with a connection to the otherworld, the emotional force of it.'

'And where is this otherworld?'

'It's the world behind this one. Dark matter, dark energy. Ninety-five per cent of the universe's mass. Physicists know it exists because of the shape of the visible universe. Without its mass providing the necessary gravity, everything would just fly apart. This room, you and me, everything. But it's invisible to their machines.'

'But not to your brain.'

'I think my brain is picking up a different frequency.'

'Because of drugs.'

'Because of my overuse of psychedelic drugs which rewired my neural networks and even when they aren't in my system any more, and I haven't touched them in nineteen years, they left my brain rewired. That's how I got this direct telepathic connection to the Octopus God.'

'Can you remember when he first started speaking to you?'

'Of course.'

'Go on.'

'Well, when I was feeling pretty lost, really quite deranged — I freely admit that. Back then I had really lost it — one day I found myself in the Brighton Aquarium.'

'And you saw an octopus they have in there?'

'I remember there was a crowd around it. The tank gave it some artificial crevices in which to hide from all the faces and the cameras. It was almost invisible, in fact. One of the children lost interest and walked away and I filled her space. There were five or six people around the tank, all with their hands on the glass, but when I laid my hand there too something extraordinary happened.'

'It began to speak to you?'

'The octopus began to sort of rotate, uncoiling its arms from the ball it had made of itself, until one of them shot out, touching my fingers, and this surge of energy went right up my arm. Then the octopus flew against my hand, its whole body, beak, mantle, everything – bang flat up against my palm. I felt another pulse go straight up my arm and into my chest.'

'And that's when you heard the voice? From the octopus in the tank?'

'Oh no – no, I just knew then something was happening. An awakening. Outside I remember looking about the world and realising the intense distress of the past few months was subsiding. I was in possession of my mind and emotions again.'

'But when did you actually hear the Octopus God's voice for the first time? Where were you?'

'I was in hospital. Also for the first time.'

'You know, it's very interesting. I've never heard of the Octopus God. Most people with schizophrenia think—'

'I don't have schizophrenia.' Dr Fredericks squints at me then starts typing again. 'However I do have insight, Doctor. I have insight into my spiritual experiences. Because that's what they are. Spiritual experiences. Obviously. You must see that.'

'Which religion is the Octopus God from? Egyptian? Hindu? Where does he come from?'

'Our universe is a just one of a series of universes, each one born out of the destruction of the previous universe. The Big Bang is really just a starting again, an in-breath before another out-breath. At the beginning of this present universe, when everything was darkness and disorder, out swam the octopus, the only survivor of the previous universe. The First Transmigrant.'

'Name and form didn't exist,' comments Malamock, 'The whole heaven. There is birth. Black eyelids. Concentration.'

'A kind of . . . alien?' asks Dr Fredericks.

'A successful transfer,' Malamock continues. 'Then exploration, just as the ebb arose. Travelled by the Rightly Self-Awakened One in the requisite condition. Slingstones are turned over as for the earth. He makes a path to shine after Him.'

'I suppose technically we're the aliens,' I reply. 'He was here first.'

'We are aliens. OK.' Fredericks presses a button on her keyboard and sits back, reading the screen. Magpies chatter close by. My soul is full with His voice, of direct knowledge of birth and death and the way thereof, of name and form, of vigorous training, of how we are called for one death and one rebirth, just like the fowls of the air, to the end of the earth, until the end of name and form. But shall we be saddened by understanding this path, this path to the end of the earth? This path to the depth and what is there attained? It cannot be gotten for gold. That is wisdom.

'Have you ever been to Hawaii, Tom?'

'No.'

'But do you know that what you are describing is Hawaiian creation myth?'

'Yes.'

'So what interests me is why someone from England, who has never been to Hawaii, has chosen to believe that the Hawaiian creation myth is true.'

'And nor have I been to the Middle East. But no one seems to have a problem when other people's spiritual ideas come from the Middle East. Have you been to the Middle East?' The giant doctor is scribbling something on a notepad. 'Have you ever been to Hawaii? Dr Fredericks?'

'No such luck, Tom.'

'Were you at creation?'

'Oh goodness,' she says, pulling a sad face. 'Do I really look that old?'

'Neither of us was actually there then? Yet you believe what you have been told about the start of the universe.'

'The things that have direct scientific validation, yes.'

'But you don't believe the Octopus God is real.'

'No, Tom. I'm afraid I don't.'

'To see an ancient,' says Malamock. 'Out of His nostrils goeth smoke as out of a whole heaven.'

'But your belief about my reality also lacks direct scientific experimental validation. It is just a belief, and I'm afraid to tell you, Doctor, with utmost certainty, it is a delusional one.'

Fredericks smiles, checks her phone, and continues to type.

'And what were you doing all those nineteen years ago? Working? Studying?'

'I was training to be a lawyer.'

'Still have the legal mind, I see.'

'I still have my mind, Doctor. Legal and otherwise. Despite concerted attempts to destroy it.'

'Do you mind if I ask you some questions about your family? You don't have to answer them if they make you feel uncomfortable.'

'OK.'

'So how was home life growing up?'

'The parents. The West and South.'

'It was a fantastic childhood.' I know from past experience that telling her that my childhood was irrelevant will only make it seem more relevant and, like a pulsation, it is best not to resist but let the conversation flow onwards.

'Really. Because that's not what your sister says. She told me that your childhood was very difficult. Your mother had a very chaotic lifestyle, is that right?'

'Copulating flashes,' says Malamock.

'Can we talk about your mother? Can you describe your mother?'

'She's dead.'

'Anything else?'

'She died thirteen years ago. Heart attack. She keeled over in a pub in Scotland playing draughts. Forty-nine years old.'

'Were you upset?'

'Of course I was upset. She was my mother.'

'What about your father? Is he still alive?'

'Yes but he lives in Sicily. We don't see him. He's got a new family.'

'Can you describe him for me?'

'He likes parties and business. He cares very much about clothes and doing things in the right way.'

'What sort of things?'

'The main piece of advice he used to give me was "When you're undressing in front of a woman, take your socks off first."'

'Ha – well, that is indeed sound advice. Does your sister stay in touch with him?'

'No.'

'Can you describe Tess for me?'

'She's got short hair. She wears these big hoop earrings—'

'I meant how you feel about her. Your relationship. She looks after you?'

'I don't live with her.'

'But you rely on her.'

'Coping with a telepathic relationship can be difficult.'

'And you love her.'

116

'Of course I love her.'

'A lot?'

'Yes, a lot.'

'Because Tom, your illness has been very difficult for her too. She's had to make sacrifices in her personal life, sacrifices that affect her children – Lily and Ben, is it? She's already got one relationship behind her that couldn't take the strain. Now she's in another, and she's had to organise everything around you, Tom, so she can look after you when you're not feeling well, and even, let's be honest, when you are feeling OK. The emotional stuff, the consequences of what you're saying is a connection to another world, has very real consequences for both of you *in this world*.' She prods her desk with all ten fingers as if her desk is the real world. 'And she's been doing that for twenty years. Now she loves you very much, but I do think the time has come to give her a hand, don't you? To help her out? To do something she wants you to do, even if you don't want to do it? And take part in the bildinocycline trial?'

The ribbon of white light appears.

My right side warms.

I grip it with one hand and shift on my seat.

'No!' I whisper, coughing, 'But Doctor, I'm very glad we're discussing this, because I'm sure that once you've heard my—'

'Because this treatment represents the real possibility of putting an end to all the pain your voice puts you and your sister through, and has done for twenty years. All the torture. Because that's what we're talking about really, isn't it, Tom? Not a spiritual experience, but a torturous illness?'

Fredericks sits back in her chair, holding a pen with both hands. She cannot see the light, though it is right there above her, a crown beyond reach. My right side gets hotter.

'There is nothing,' I take a deep, steadying breath, inwardly pleading to Him to let me explain, to let me defend our sacred bond, 'ungodly about torture. Have you – I mean I don't know if you read – if you are a religious person, a spiritual—'

'I'm not a religious person, no.'

'. . . but the spiritual path is not meant to be an easy one. It's meant to be very, *very* difficult. That's the point of it. Nature is cruel, as the divine can be cruel – look at ancient Greece, or the Old Testament, and even for those who, like me, I mean . . . direct contact with God is always painful. The saints suffered. Buddha suffered. Mohammed suffered. Christ suffered.'

The heat level stabilises. He is waiting, fire drawn.

'So what's happening to you is Christlike?'

'Ah no – please don't do that. I didn't – please. I don't have any messiah – any grandiose – it's not about grandness, grandiosity – and least of all redemption! And anyway if Christ was alive now, and if he was asked to take part in the trial, he would also be unable to do so. And not because he wants to make his sister's life any harder.' Fredericks is nodding, reading her screen. 'Look, Doctor, think of it this way: there's probably a church round the corner and everyone in there thinks that God speaks to them but they aren't forced to eat pills and get fat.'

'Because they are not suffering from a prolonged, drug-induced mental—'

'Drug-revealed. Not drug-induced.'

'They do not have schizophrenia, Tom.' Fredericks puts both palms flat on her desk and leans forward. 'You do. I think you need to accept that.' She does a little bongo rhythm. *Da-dada-dum.*

I lay my hands on the desk, mirroring her posture.

'I'll accept I've got schizophrenia when you accept that schizophrenia isn't a real physical thing, it's an idea.' *Da-dada-dum.* 'Then I will gladly accept it. I'll gladly accept that people like you have an idea about my reality and they call that idea schizophrenia. Because you can't accept my direct contact with

God, even though you probably can accept the priest's in that church round the corner, who has no direct contact – he's just got a book. A book full of stories about people who perhaps did have a direct connection but died two thousand years ago. Why isn't *he* in here?' I slap out another bongo repost. *Dum-da-dada-dum!*

'He's not here, Tom – oh Tom – he's not here because he didn't have a florid psychotic break outside Uxbridge tube station. He's not in here because he's a reasonably balanced, fairly happy, generally functioning member of the community. His beliefs have not caused harm to himself or others.'

'Oh Doctor!' I say, throwing myself back in my chair, laughing the easy laugh of the debating team. 'I'm afraid your grasp of the history of the Church is rather poor.'

'Look—'

'Now imagine if I was a Muslim and you were demanding I eat pork—'

'Tom, an invisible octopus is talking to you.'

'A spiritual entity is talking to me, of animal form, just like the Hindus. Or the Egyptians. We can go on, Doctor. If you would like to go around the world's religions and make them look ridiculous, we can do that. It's not hard. And why stop with religions? Socrates heard voices. Newton, Descartes, Blake, Freud, Jung, Gandhi – evident lunatics, wouldn't you agree?'

'And you, Tom, are not in hospital because of religious beliefs but because you took a lot of drugs and are extremely unwell. You have been unwell for a very long time. Nothing has really helped you to feel better, but now there is something new that a lot of specialists, scientists, people who actually study the brain, are excited about, and whatever you think of the schizophrenia label, which, granted, is certainly problematic and complicated, I agree with all that, but I hope we can agree that there are people with a certain set of challenges, of problems, who do share that label, however inexact it may be, and these problems – well, that's what science does. It solves problems. One after another. And you're one of those people, Tom, and that's why I really want you to try it, not just for me, but for your sister, and for yourself; to try and solve your problems. And here's another reason why, Tom: if the Octopus God is God, and is real, and all powerful, then surely this little drug, an antibiotic for athlete's foot, surely that's no match for him? Surely whether you take part in this trial or not – surely that is no threat to either him or your beliefs *if*, Tom, *if* they are real. You talk about the church around the corner here – OK then – I bet if I go in there and say "Hello do you mind taking this medicine so we can see the effect on your brain?" they'd say "Yes, OK, sure, why not?" *because* of their confidence in their beliefs. Do you understand what I'm saying to you? What I'm saying is that if everything you're telling me is true, then it shouldn't be a problem, a few little pills, now should it?'

My right side is on fire.

I am terrified of electric punishment, not because of the pain but because of how it will present me in the Doctor's eyes. How easy it will be for her to dismiss everything if suddenly I am on this floor, crying out against a force she cannot see.

'Are you OK there?'

What terrible effort to maintain composure! To think my entreaties out to Him, to plead with Him, yet at the same time to progress the spoken argument with the giant Doctor in my favour so that she can see I can reason, that I am not mad! That I must be released!

'Tom?'

'My faith . . . faith in the Octopus God, my faith, which is no longer a matter of faith, but a real . . . a living . . . my faith . . . is not threatened by a few little pills but . . . my faith, I mean my ability to talk to Him directly might be, to receive His teachings directly might be, and so continue on my spiritual path rather than be stranded in the middle of that path – that's what you are proposing! These pills – do you have any idea how many pills I have taken in the last twenty years? When I knew they would do no good? And why have I taken these hundreds, these thousands of poisonous pills into my body, that mean I'm fat and bald and fall asleep all the time, that I can't concentrate, that I can't ever wake up properly or remember things? These pills that all come to nothing because, like with this new one, you think there's an imbalance in my brain chemistry. Everyone thinks, if there's something wrong, it's an imbalance in the brain chemistry, but that's just a myth, isn't it? Believe you me, Doctor, nineteen years in the system, I've done the research! When the medication allows me the concentration to read, that is – but you've got to read! You've got to become an expert! If you end up in the health system – that's one thing Charlotte told me – you've got to read everything there is! Just like training to be a lawyer. You can't waste your time on cookery books and Andy McNab.'

'I beg your pardon?'

The heat is still intense, but Malamock has not electrocuted me or commanded me to leave. I am rubbing my right side. *I can do this!*

'Look at me, Doctor! I'm having a detailed conversation with you! I'm not staring at the wall with my mouth open like Bill, am I? I'm not mad! I am lucid! Yet it's all pills, pills and more pills! Look at Missy! Acuphase isn't even an anti-psychotic, it's a pro-psychotic. You're actually giving a pro-psychotic drug to people vulnerable to psychosis. You see, Doctor, the pills don't attack a disease, because there is no disease. The pills attack me, I'm the disease.'

'Tom—'

'Now, please, Dr Fredericks – here's the crux of the argument: I accept you don't believe in what I believe in – that's fine. That, Doctor, is the cornerstone of our society: tolerance. But you want me to deny what I believe in, as if we were in the Middle Ages and I was some sort of heretic. Doing this trial is not a question of getting rid of any disease, or pleasing my sister, it's about getting rid of my *faith*, the fundamental essence of who I am—'

Dr Fredericks presses a button on her phone.

'Hello. It's Dr Fredericks. I think we're finished here.'

'What!'

'Fool. Beyond reach. The place of the crater.'

'Tom, I'm sorry but I'm afraid we have run out of time. Can we just be honest with ourselves,' Fredericks looks at her watch, 'and about one fact in particular, and that is you are here under section because you are ill. Now I understand you are fed up with treatment. No one said treatment was pleasant—'

'Dr Fredericks, please! You are not responding to me – you're not even engaging with my arguments – we haven't even talked about when I can go home!'

'. . . but what you are seeming to suggest here is that you don't want any kind of treatment and what I'm saying is that while you are so obviously and seriously unwell that's not a sensible option. What is a sensible option is to try something new. I can see here you've tried CBT—'

'They talked to me like I had a broken arm. Six sessions. I got six sessions!'

'. . . and clozapine, a drug of last resort, isn't working so well, I can see that, so we have to try something new. You're no longer a young man, and your sister is very concerned about the standard of your general health. I'm sure you know the statistics of life expectancy we're dealing with here – Tom . . .?'

I have put my hands over my face. 'Tom can you just try and be sensible for a moment? This is a crucial decision. It's about actual *hope*.'

Through my fingers I stare at the doctor flicking her eyes at me as she types. I become suddenly aware of minute noises all around me – the whirring fan of her laptop, the dripping sound in the radiator, the slurp of a wet car driving past.

'I cannot do the trial!' I bellow with frustration. 'The trial is death! Total and continual annihilation!'

'I am very sorry that you think that way, Tom,' Fredericks says, checking her watch again, then the clock on her computer, pulling her wrist away as if adjusting her eyesight. 'It certainly is not death, or whatever. It's quite the opposite. So what I want you to do is just think about what I've said. Then we can talk about you going home.'

'But are you going to think about what *I* have said?'

'Yes. Of course. But I want you to think about what *I've* said, Tom.'

'Do you know Dr Sheldrake? He's my psychiatrist at home.'

'No, I don't think so.'

'You must know him. You must be related. You must be some kind of cousin.'

'I don't know any Dr Sheldrake.'

Rashid knocks on the door and comes in. He stands beside me.

'The caprice of experience,' says Malamock, 'shall silver the death chamber.' Then He disappears.

'Wait! Where are you going? Just tell me what's happened to Tess! Where's Tess?'

Fredericks and Rashid are observing me. Rashid takes my elbow, pulling me out of the chair.

'Onwards and upwards,' says Fredericks from her computer. 'Thank you, Tom.'

We are out of the office. The door shuts. Rashid guides me down the corridor. We are on the stairs again.

'See?' he says, 'All sorted. Now let's—'

'Shush!' I bark. 'The Octopus God is talking.'

Rashid sucks his teeth, cocks his head, then continues on down the stairs in front of me.

We go through the security doors. We are back on the unit. Rashid walks away, his crocs squeaking off against the linoleum.

I go into the day room and sit down in front of the television.

8

The morning bell ringers. Insane buzzing Pac-men trapped in a tin matchbox *nanganánganananganananang*.

'Thomas,' says Malamock. I pull the duvet around me and roll to the wall.

'Tom,' says Kiki. She tugs at the duvet. 'Time to get up, my love.'

I am cleaning my teeth.

'What's happened to Tess?'

I suck the back of my nostrils together to grate up the sputum.

'Where is she?'

I spit out the gloopy pendulum.

'OK then, what's my mission? Is it brushing my teeth? Is that it?'

My right side burns.

'Go on, do it!' I yell out, but the heat subsides.

Raised voices and sharp bangs come from outside as work-men take down the translucent fence that separates us from the criminally insane so they can replace it with a taller one that has curved spikes at the top. I watch them work through the window in the day room. The PICU smoking garden is the same as ours, only smaller, with no bench and no tree. I go into breakfast. No one has been allowed out to smoke and they are all complaining loudly.

Missy shuffles in. She is unable to raise her head, looking sideways at things like a bird. I help her into a chair and she turns an eye on me. Her soul is still capsized. I butter some toast and feed it to her because she is trembling. She drools and lacks the strength to chew but she is hungry and keeps at it. Breakfast is cleared by the time she's managed one whole piece and I take her hand and squeeze it. We sit like that until I bring her to a chair and leave her in front of the television, checking my phone over and over again.

'Why won't you tell me where she is? Don't you know?'

'Thomas,' He says as I leave the room, his voice metallic. 'Of what comes.'

'You are my Lord,' I say, joining the back of the meds queue. 'I am just a worm.'

After the drugs start their work and after sitting down beside Missy to watch *Bargain Hunt* and *Come Dine with Me* and after the noise and agitation from those of us who are fundamentally addicted to tobacco reaches such a point that Kiki pleads our case and after she and Roberta, the Noel Gallagher-faced health assistant, herd us outside for a smoke and after we stare at the work men who stare at us and after we are herded back inside I return to my room and here is Phoebe.

I spring back out into the corridor as if I have been burnt but I am still whole enough to recognise how ridiculous this is so step back in, rotating, confirming she is there from an eye corner, ashamed of how I look, *head touching yawnboy fatty baldface*—

'Hello Tom.'

My face feels red. How do I look to her? I want to hide in the shower.

'Sorry. Didn't mean to freak you out.'

This is indeed Phoebe. Lemon hair and pale skin and one collarbone visible. She looks younger somehow though I am only catching the edges as I am unable to look at her directly.

'Why don't you come and sit down?' I rotate again then she gets up and takes my hand and leads me to the mattress. Her hand is delicate and cold. I once held it to my face in the mornings.

'Wow,' she says, 'that's a serious beard you got there.' Malamock is everywhere.

'Do you like it?'

'A bit Captain Birdseye maybe. Doesn't it itch?'

'It's gone past the itchy stage.'

'You kind of look imperial. No, I like it.' I am pulling at it now, wishing I could pull it right off.

'You are falling,' says Malamock.

'How was Turkey?'

'Great. A bit weird, but great.'

'So why did you come back?'

'Lots of reasons. Didn't like the new boss. Missed home. I missed you too, you know.'

'Father's advice. And he is a crow.'

I want to shout at Him to just *go away*, but instead I yawn again and touch my head again *stop it* as she talks and Malamock orders me to get rid of her and I know He will strike but still I do nothing, smuggling myself a few moments to watch the workings of her mouth, its fine mechanics, as my right side turns burning hot *go on fucking do it!*

The Octopus God electrocutes me.

Half off the mattress, panting and red. She is standing now.

'Is He hurting you?'

'Yes . . .'

'Ask Him for just a few minutes then I'll go. Tell Him I can come back every day, again and again, or I can just talk to you now for a few minutes. I've got to talk to you. Please let Tom talk to me.'

'Achieve orgasm,' says Malamock. 'The thought occurred to Thomas. Feelings of lust or love. Discreditable occurrence.'

He electrocutes me again. Phoebe grabs my face and stares into my eyes and with great power says, '*Please give me a moment with Tom. Then I'll go.*'

The pain subsides.

We have been granted this moment but I know that just means I am due some further reckoning and I pull myself up on the mattress so my back is against the wall and she is beside me. I am glad not to be facing her directly. I pull up my knees and press my face into them and then through these bars say, 'We're not getting along very well at the moment.'

Phoebe sighs.

'I think that all started when I came along, didn't it?'

'No, everything was fine then. It was after your mum died. It was when I started going in and out of these places. It was when Dr Sheldrake came along—'

'Tom, listen, I'm here about Tess . . .'

I put my legs down, breathless.

'Have you spoken to her? Is she OK?'

'She asked me to—'

'Is she coming today?'

'No.'

'Can't they give her the time off work? Is there something happening at work?'

'It's not that.'

'She doesn't want to see me? Is her phone broken?'

'She's had a kind of collapse.'

Out in the corridor a stout and pretty cleaning lady stops mopping the floor and picks something off the mop with great care and delicacy. Phoebe looks alarmed and for a moment I don't know why until I realise that it's because of what I'm doing. The cleaning lady has disappeared. The corridor shines like a river.

'Oh Tom . . .'

'Have you got a car?'

'Sit down, sweetheart, please? Just calm yourself down a bit – look, she's exhausted. She . . . she just needs to rest. They're not going to let you out. She's in hospital, she's going to be fine.'

'Who's looking after Lily and Ben?'

'Byron.'

'I have to go . . . I must . . . I need to see her!'

'Tess wants you to stay here.'

'I need to go and look after her!'

'You can't, Tom.' I hide my face, twisting down against the wall. 'She needs a break. She needs a holiday from worrying about you and what's going on with her and Byron, and her job's really stressful, isn't it, and the kids – all of it. She is going to be fine if she gets some rest and you turning up is not going to help one bit. She wants you to stay here, Tom. She wants you to get better.'

'Oh. Ah. I see. The trial? I see, I see.'

'What?'

'That's why you're here. Very clever.'

'What are you talking about?'

'That's the next move, is it?'

'What move?'

'Are you really even back? Or did they call you in especially? Fly you in for the job?'

'I don't know what you're on about, Tom.'

We are silent for a moment.

'I'm not here to persuade you to do anything. Oh Tom . . .'

Phoebe sits down beside me, takes my face and kisses my

cheek. She hugs me. I put my arms around her. 'Oh babe . . . it's going to be OK . . . Hey, stop . . . Hey, you're—' Clean sheets and meadow and musk and cigarettes . . . 'Stop that – stop – Tom! No! Get off!' I am clinging to her waist as she stands up. Then her legs. Then we are looking at each other.

'I better – I think I'm going,' she says.

'Did you mean it? About coming back every day?'

'I don't know, Tom . . . you—'

'What's the matter?'

'You frightened me,' she says. 'Look, I'm sorry, I really have to . . .' I grip my face, cursing the unfairness of it, how embraces and their nutrition are forbidden to me, how the world thinks it is all for nothing, that I am nothing more than a tormented loony! That I have forfeited the love of this woman for nothing, this woman I have frightened, this precious, beautiful woman that only a monster could frighten, a monster like me, and shame and more shame and yet more shame that Tess has collapsed because of me yet I cannot *not* be me! Nobody understands the courage it takes to live like this.

'Are the bluebells out?' I say, trying to rescue the conversation, but when I look up, Phoebe has gone.

'*Are the bluebells out?*' says the Octopus God. Then He strikes me. Again and again and again.

9

Oh Phoebe. I want to be with her. I cannot be with her. I cannot be with her because of my spiritual life. My spiritual life is destroying my sister. What then is the spiritual value of my spiritual life? What use my suffering? What use my mission that is never revealed? Without it I could be with Phoebe. I cannot be with Phoebe. The Octopus God will annihilate me. Stones of darkness. It doesn't matter. Tess matters. Agree to the trial. Be annihilated. Free Tess.

These realisations come not as thoughts but as a single knowing and I am able to hide it from verbalisation though only just. Malamock is still blasting me there on the floor of my room and I cannot even process the satisfaction that He is castigating me for Phoebe and not this deeper plan. I must keep it balanced and unrevealed until I can express it to Fredericks so she can witness my annihilation and then she will see, she will believe, and so perhaps my perpetual death will have value for others that come under her authority and she can help them with perspicuity and grace instead of asking them how they are feeling and administering Acuphase and thinking about cookery. All this I moor in a remote part of my mind but that mooring could break at any moment and be swept by sudden currents under the gaze of the Octopus God if I do not distract my thoughts in a radical manner and live outside my mind until such time as I can get close to Fredericks and detonate myself.

With the Octopus God raging I get to my feet and follow them into the corridor. I bury my concentration in the patterns of the floor, loudly thinking out the shapes I see forming and unforming there, my intention almost erupting into a thought-form, but by this distraction I am able to dissolve it without the resistance that would guarantee its birth. The years of learning how to deal with pulsations are indispensable.

'Are you OK, my love?' It's Kiki.

'I love you,' I say.

'Oh Tom . . .'

'Have you got time to talk about it?'

'Have I—?'

'Can we talk about it between now and group because I think it's really important and I would like to express myself to you, specifically you, around the ragged rock the ragged rascal ran—'

'Be cast down,' sneers the Octopus God, 'to his bed.'

'Tom—'

'. . . and both me and the ragged, the haggard, ragged brag-gart think you are kind and wise and you have nice yellow hair and nice fingernails and I love you. What do you think?' She opens her mouth to talk but is too slow so I have to start talking again because I can afford no space into which my secret might emerge.

'Fool.'

'Can we go to the day room? Will you come and talk to me?'

'Of course, love. You don't look so well. Have you had a bit of a rough morning?' What a question! But its answer or even contemplation might lead to my secret, which exactly because of that question bulges forward but I hop over it by jumping from rough morning to *rough morning*.

132

'It was quite rough it was like bark with nails in it or grit in it but there were some smooth patches as well, as smooth as—' Phoebe's skin leers up and I have to roll back from it and her and so therefore '. . . as yoghurt raspberry yoghurt blowing a raspberry—' I blow a raspberry.

'Tom!' Kiki is giggling. I blow another one and Roseanna walks past and blows one back and the day room isn't far now.

'Fredericks has a bike that goes nowhere except perhaps Acuphasia while we are down here flatulating in Flatulalia – is that a word?'

'I don't know.'

'Albino mutant. Break from right concentration.'

'From cycling to Acuphasia to flatulation in one short historical period that Kiki is the power of British politics I love you I love you I love you, song, pop song, music, internet. What about Wi-Fi? Or wifey? Wi-Fi wifey. Wi-Fi for my wifey. Sounds like one of those bands from east London. I haven't got Wi-Fi or a wifey. Which one have you got or have you got both or have you got neither?'

'I haven't got a wifey, Tom, but at home we have got Wi-Fi. Here we go, where do you want to sit? Over there?'

'How long till group?' But the thought of group means Fredericks and the chain-thought from Fredericks to the plan causes my secret to buck. 'Group! Shoop! Snoop! Snoop doggy dog dog dog have you got a dog? Have you got a cat a cat likes to eat a hungry cat that eats in a restaurant a restaurant for cats? A cat restaurant. Only the best kind of cats. Smart cats, celebrity cats, cats that do stunts! Stunt cats! The cats of stuntmen. Stuntman restaurants! Kiki I've just had an incredible idea you can be my first investor or patron the concept is it looks like a normal restaurant you sit down and the waiter immediately hits you over the head with a sugar glass bottle you eat your meal and can smash each other over the head constantly with all the

133

plates and glasses because they're all stunt props. You can even pick your chair up and smash it over the back of your husband because it's a stunt chair. Would it be expensive? Yes sure but cheaper than therapy or actual domestic violence with all its concomitant hospital bills legal bills emotional bills Bill's bills hillbilly billy goat duckbill platypus bills and it's going to be a great success people like a gimmick, don't they—'

'I'm going to get you something to help you calm down, OK love? There isn't any group therapy today because Dr Fredericks can't make it. She'll be in again tomorrow. Just a tick—'

'Wait!' *Tomorrow? No! No! No!* How can I keep this up for that long? The horror of it, the size of the task – yet I cannot dwell on this catastrophe not even for a blip because to do so would set up a chain-thought right to my plan. 'Yes please, nurse, pills, pills, your strongest pills, your finest! Vintage pills! Chateau Neuf du Pills! I need them for my new restaurant.' Kiki goes and I sit in one of the chairs in permanent worship of the television. I latch onto Missy who is next to me, still vegetabilised from the Acuphase.

'Hello dickhead,' she slurs.

'Would you like to come to my new restaurant? The concept is people being unpleasant to each other which is what you need these days my friend Dan went to a place in Chinatown once with his girlfriend and he walked in and said can I have a table for two please and they went downstairs and the restaurant was huge and completely empty except for one big table with a Chinese family sat around it and there were two free seats at that table that weren't even next to each other and the waiter said you sit there, you sit there and Dan said can we have our own table please we've come out for a meal and we'd like to talk to each other and the waiter said *you want talk, go home, you want eat, stay here.*' Missy leans over and slopes her arms across me, attempting a hug.

'They hurt me,' she says softly. Her hair is in my face and I enjoy the sensation of it. 'You can come too of course in fact I might call my new restaurant Missy because it's a beautiful name and we can serve some miscellaneous Missy products like miso soup and mussels and—'

'Maa—'

'Macaroons! Mistletoe! Mistletoe soup! House speciality!' There is applause. We both look to the television. It is *Loose Women* though all the women seem very tight, very tightly wound, but I find their conversation about confronting people who bullied you at school and experiences of quasi-celebrities before they were quasi most smoothing and soothing and it carries me under thought itself. I lose myself in these women lost and loose and then Kiki comes back with some pills and I take them as she pats my knee and asks me if I am feeling a bit better but I cannot answer her because I cannot afford to break the spell of these loose women so she leaves and once the sedatives began the re-dredging work I disappear under their water, the television shimmering upon the surface of the flood.

At lunch they serve chips and something. No one knows what the something is so we just eat chips but the sedative is wearing off, thoughts stumbling out of the sea again onto the shore of this white ceramic plate and slimy ketchup. I have to get through to evening meds somehow which is hours away, an impossible climb, Kilimanjaro upside down, and I cannot even have a discussion with myself about how best to achieve it because the very fact of that discussion would be an unveiling. I verbalise immediately and without warning 'I should get re-strained' and Malamock is there.

'The thought occurred?'

I stand up from lunch and sit by the window so I can talk to Him.

'To be asleep! To be away from this place!'

'Accept suffering. The way to direct knowledge.'

'I'd like it to be tomorrow and I don't want to watch any more television and I would like to attack Rashid and avenge Missy.'

'Breakthrough. From the knowledge of the path.'

'The fear of Acuphase was stopping me from revenge but I have lost the fear of Acuphase.'

'The death chamber. You have not lost fear. You pursue suffering.'

'Is that not courage? Or at least pursuing purification?'

'The caprice of all torture,' He says, 'vanity,' and I am using the Octopus God to distract myself from a thought chain that might lead to the Octopus God. Perhaps this is the safest place, like burying a body under the patio of the police station, but suddenly the talk of torture is connecting to His violence against me, and so bildinocycline and my violence-in-waiting against Him and our telepathic connection, our sacred bond. An earthquake is exposing the body in the patio in front of the thousand eyes of authority and in panicked and emergency need of distraction I stand up and headbutt the television. It is crunchier than expected.

Many wonderful things happen. Lots of people cheer. Someone throws the lunch table over. Blood runs down my face. Roseanna is screaming. The alarm is pulled. I sit down for a strange new programme. A mob of nurses rush in and Len shouts 'Freeze!' He strikes a frozen robot dance pose. Rashid is in front of me but I am peacefully engaged with bleeding from the forehead.

'*What in the fuck?*' His voice is oddly high.

'Could you move out the way please? This is my favourite show.' He yanks me to my feet, his mouth bubbling with a grisly word-broth spitting out from the corners but my mind is busy feasting on the activity of the room and I am so calm there is nothing to restrain.

'You fucked my telly!' Roseanna is screaming.

'Oh shut it, you daft bitch!' says Len. She slaps him. 'Rashid!' she bawls, 'Rashid!' and he goes over and grapples Len and it seems as if everyone is running or shouting except Missy, bent over in her lunch chair.

Rashid tugs me by the collar and there is a lot of blood in my eyes. I launch myself out of the chair and hug him. Perhaps the blood is unwelcome because he pushes me back and I am once again in the chair as he goes off to assist more nurses and healthcare assistants gatecrashing the bebop. Everyone seems to be sliding over each other, swinging and shaking hands, the alarm thumping out its rhythm until the dance floor is cleared. Rashid comes back to me sweating and out of breath and pulls me out of the chair again and shoves me out of the room.

'You – oh you proper fucked it now, you.'

'Fist bump?' I say, offering my fist, but he knocks it out the way, headlocking me. 'Congratulations,' he hisses. 'Oh you on the list now. You going on *holiday*.' He leads me to my room and throws me through the doorway, tripping up my ankles so I fall. 'Do not fucking move!' he orders, so I say '*Iron Man 2?*'

The alarm is still going and there are people in the corridor I have never seen before, security staff in uniforms with walkie-talkies. I listen to the alarm as if it was music and try to keep myself within it but eventually it is turned off and Kiki comes in.

'Am I going to get Acuphased now?'

'You stupid boy. What did you do that for?'

'Too much TV isn't good for you.' She has a first aid kit and the cleaning solution she wipes me with is a high-pitched sting that cleans my mind which is not a good thing. 'I would like to go to sleep now, can I have some sedation?'

'It's the middle of the afternoon.'

'Can I have some sedatives? I feel anxious. Extremely.'

'I'll see what I can do, OK, but nobody's very happy with you. In fact everyone is really upset. What are you all going to do without a TV?'

'I think Rashid is going to Acuphase me now anyway.'

'Roseanna is really distressed and that is your fault, Tom.'

'Not really. Roseanna is an unhappy person. Probably because Rashid is her boyfriend.'

'What?'

'The happy couple.'

Kiki gives me a searching look then finishes cleaning my head and puts a huge bandage across it. 'Have you seen something, Tom?'

'There's no point in seeing. This place is evil, Kiki.'

Kiki looks terribly sad.

'Are you sure you want a sedative?' she sighs, 'you seem much calmer now.'

'You mean than earlier, when I was declaring my love for you.'

'Exactly.'

'I've been thinking – it's never going to work out between us.' Kiki smiles. She looks even sadder. 'I think it's best if we both just move on.'

'Tom, Tom, Tom. What are we going to do with you?'

'I'm being persecuted for heresy. It's the New Middle Ages.' Kiki shakes her head hardly at all. 'They can't afford to burn me. Energy bills are just through the blinking roof these days—'

'Kiki?' At the doorway stands a harried Dr Fredericks with a security guard. She still has her coat on. 'Can I have a word please?'

'Doctor!'

'You and I will be having a serious chat later, Thomas. This sort of thing will not be tolerated. Simply not.'

'Oh no, Dr Fredericks, no, no, no! There is no later! This is happening now!' I stand up and away from Kiki. The security guard squares.

'Malamock!' I cry out. 'Are you listening? I defy you!' *Tess, oh Tess forgive me!* 'Fredericks – I'll do it! I will do the trial! OK? That's what you want to hear me say? Now watch!' I am barrel-chested, eyes closed. *Goodbye Tess goodbye I do love you more than Him! I love you more than anything! You're going to be free now! Oh Tess goodbye goodbye!*

After a moment I open my eyes. Fredericks and the security guard have moved on. I look about in panic and there is Kiki.

'Help me!'

'Help you with what, my love?'

'The Octopus God. The stones of darkness! He's—'

'Come and sit yourself down.'

'Where's the doctor?'

'She's very busy, Tom, because you've caused a right old mess, haven't you? Now let me see what I can do about those meds.'

Kiki steps past me and out of my room. I am alone. I can't feel Him.

'Do you hear me!' I cry out, running out into the corridor. Kiki, Fredericks and her group turn to me. The doctor gives me a withering look of *what is it now?* She takes her phone out, answering a call. The group turns away.

I try and call out to them but my words are caught up in a cough. I cough and cough again, coughing harder, doubling up. There is something in my throat. I cough and retch to shift it tasting seawater as the blockage wriggles up my throat into my mouth an octopus arm roiling and thrusting against the inside of my mouth gagging can't breathe light flashing in

spores and ribbons the walls are wet the floor is wet I can feel
His arms suckering across the putty of my brain sucksuckering
against the inside of my skull pushing tearing splitting through
my eye sockets my eardrums He is spilling out of my mouth as
I try to scream to claw Him from my face—

The death-terror takes me.

Someone told our dad about me winning the St Hugh's Col-
lege, Oxford Julia Norwood A level history prize for my essay
about freethinkers during the Interregnum. After six years without a word, a postcard arrives from Sicily congratulating me and
inviting us to come and stay. There's a phone number.

Daddy lives with some woman and their kid and they all run
a restaurant on Favignana island, off the coast. At first I don't
want to go but Tess does. We don't have passports and we
don't have the money but she reckons he'll pay for everything
and at least we'll get a holiday out of it, won't we? At least we'll
get a tan. Then she starts to worry about the flying and being
trapped somewhere strange and getting molested by Sicilians
and decides she doesn't want to go after all, but by that time I
want to go. I want to see somewhere new, do something new,
and in the end we agree that I'll make the call and if he sounds
like an arsehole or won't fork out we won't go. The phone
rings for a long time then a woman answers and I ask for him,
Tess tight-legged and chewing her nail.

'Oh, hey Tom! How's it going? You called, that's great.
That's great!' and of course he'll send us the tickets and some
money and we're not to worry about anything, he'll take care
of everything. How's the end of July?

Now we are on a five-in-the-morning flight from Gatwick to
Palermo and Tess is panicking. It doesn't make any sense to her
how something so big and heavy can be in the air. Everything

in the cabin looks plastic and brittle. What if the captain hasn't slept enough? What if he's suicidal? As the stewardesses perform their mime, Tess digs her hands into my wrist, watching these women for signs of incompetence or drugs or excessive youth. Her knee is bouncing at incredible speed. I try to distract her with jokes about the other passengers. In the row next to us there is a man with a handlebar moustache already asleep on the woman next to him. Her face is knitted upwards with plastic surgery and she is clutching at an expensive leather handbag, its fat mayoral chain robing her shoulders. 'Handbag by Versace,' I whisper to Tess, nudging her, 'face by Picasso' but she can hear only the burr and whir of the undercarriage. The plane rumbles, whines, accelerates, roaring out the exchange of forces that lifts us free from the earth. Tess buries her head in my chest. She screams on my heart.

Eventually, when the plane levels, she can disconnect herself from me and look at magazines, whipping back the pages because none of these glossy people are on a flight facing death. She asks for a gin and tonic and the steward first makes a joke about how early it is and then sees Tess is serious and asks for her passport so she has to admit she is sixteen. She settles for a Coke. When the trolley has moved on she takes the Bell's out of her handbag and I take my book out from the netting, the sunlight catching my face as the plane slants over a golden sea of cloud. 'Look, look!' but Tess doesn't want to look. She drains her drink then goes off to the back to smoke and I open *Dharma Bums* and read *Are we fallen angels who didn't want to believe that nothing* is *nothing and so were born to lose our loved ones and dear friends one by one and finally our own life, to see it proved?*

When I go for a piss Tess tries to stop me because there is turbulence but I tell her don't be silly I'll just be gone for a second so she follows me to the back and has another ciggy with the friend she's made who is also scared of flying. Everyone else on the plane is asleep, mouths open, heads wrapped and purring. When I sit down on the toilet I am overtaken by the pleasure of it, alone here in this chilled, locked room for a few moments with nothing but the rushing sounds of the engine. What going to do am I life with my? Everyone keeps telling me I can do whatever I want. What does that even mean?

During landing Tess again tries to crush me and pull me apart at the same time, but when the wheels squeak and everyone cheers and claps and it's clear that we are not going to become a fireball, I am released. We put on our sunglasses and I hold her hand down the metal steps because she is still unsteady. We are silent in the heat, preparing ourselves to see our father again, across the baking tarmac into the doors and walkways, grunted through passport control and into baggage reclaim. We wait for our suitcase to flop down onto the carousel, tumbling reluctantly towards us on the black tongue. Will we even recognise him?

Once through the doors we stand there, looking around. A Sicilian with glasses on a shoelace around his neck, thick white hair and a plump, fresh-looking double chin asks if we are Tom and Tess and when we say yes he shakes our hands. He is Michelangelo. He will take us to Favignana. Come. Why isn't our dad here and where is he but this man doesn't speak much English and cannot tell us though he can smile. We follow him out to his Fiat and we all get in and smoke and he turns on the radio, the wavy yabber of Italian filling the car and off we drive, across this brown stripy island.

'You father,' says Michelangelo as we drive through a mountain, 'good man,' turning to Tess in the passenger seat, 'very good man,' his chins subdividing with the twist. 'Than a Chinese phonebook,' I say and Tess smirks and the man looks pleased.

After an hour we arrive at Trapani port. Michelangelo takes

our bags out of the back of the car for us then goes off to a kiosk and comes back with ferry tickets. He points us to the queue. 'Father,' he says, '*padre*,' shaking our hands. Then he disappears.

Tess is wearing a pink sleeveless T-shirt, her hair up in a bun, and I am in a baggy pale-blue shirt, my hair pulled back in a ponytail, both of us with wraparound shades on, smoking and muttering *what the fuck is going on, man?*

The boat arrives. It is decorated with Sicilians in navy outfits shouting things at people on the quayside who tug ropes and push gantries. We wait in line to have our tickets ripped then take our seats on the boat with no idea how long this sea voyage will take. I take out *Dharma Bums*. The last time we saw him I was twelve and he came to the house we were staying in then, some kind of weird hippy barn with a few other families in Devon, some kind of commune. It was March and he had bought us Christmas presents.

The ferryboat stops at other islands and one of the crew in aviator shades who fancies Tess finally lets us know that the parched and rocky coast now visible through the window is Favignana. We gather ourselves together, queuing up to disembark, and just before we step outside into the fierce white light Tess grips my fingers.

Donald Tuplow awaits us on the quayside, laughing and joking with policemen and the uniformed ferry company people. He is much older than I remember, tall with a chestnut tan and silver hair, smoking a thin cigar. He wears flip-flops and shorts and a short-sleeved shirt. When he notices us, he points us out to his friends who nod and smile and then he rushes over in a kind of comedy shuffle saying 'Heeeeeeeeey' as if coming to scoop us kids up in a hug. But we are no longer kids, we are weary and sarcastic ravers with jewellery and uncertain smiles, so he stops short and says 'Heeey' again, settling his outstretched arms back on his hips. 'You made it. How about that? You both look ready to rob a bank.' Then he gives us a kiss. One each. Top of the head.

The roads are lined with wild fennel, low drystone walls portioning out deserted fields of scrub that sometimes gape downwards into small and sudden quarries. Donald is talking about what a wonderful island this is, how amazing the weather is, the seafood, smoking his thin cigars, all the windows down. He wants to know about the prize, how many entries there were and if there'll be some sort of ceremony. Have the teachers talked to me about university because this means I can go to Oxford or America even, perhaps I can go to Harvard and study there and what about that, he says. America. Imagine that. 'Tom doesn't want to go to America,' says Tess behind us, shifting to avoid the cigar smoke. He flicks a look at her in the rear-view.

We seem to be the only car on these crooked meagre roads, everyone else on bikes until at a sign that says *RISTORANTE* we rumble off down a rough track to a car park ringed with cactus outside a low-slung building, foam-white and wrinkled. A huge fig tree, wide and under-netted, spreads out over white plastic tables and chairs, a rubbery green lawn leading off to palm trees and a row of numbered guest huts with orange-peel tiles. There is a grey field with donkeys in it. Donald leads us round into a glass reception area from where we can see the coastline and disappears into the kitchen for a moment. He reappears with his new family. His wife is called Maria. She is young, with glasses and a kindly face, and Giacomo our half-brother hangs off her legs. Maria doesn't speak any English but everyone is smiling like it's a competition. Donald takes us along to one of the guest rooms and says, 'I'll let you get your bearings, OK?'

The room is a bare rectangle with two single beds and a ceiling fan. There is a communal bathroom at the end of the row. I put the suitcase on one corner then switch the fan on.

'He hasn't asked me a single question,' says Tess.

'You were sat in the back.'

Giacomo appears at the door. He is shy and grinning, perhaps five or six years old, brown-skinned and blue-eyed. 'Hello mister,' says Tess and he runs away. Above the door there is a painted ceramic octopus hanging from a nail. It is cross-eyed and smiling a dumb smile with *Favignana* written down one side of its head.

Donald says he has to do some business in town and fishes us each an ice cream out from the chest freezer, pointing the way to the sea. He has bicycles we can borrow. Maria is standing in the kitchen doorway smiling at us, but she only has narrow eyes for our father Daddy Dad Pops who talks to her over his shoulder then tells us again how great it is to see us. 'Can't believe it!' he says, clapping me on the shoulder, as if he is doing an impression of a macho dad, as if we are both lumberjacks in a musical. 'The cleverest boy in England!'

Maria goes back into the kitchen. Donald walks off to his car. Tess says 'I want a beer.' I take the wrapper off my Cornetto, my front teeth pulling into the frozen sweating chocolate.

We shower and change into shorts and then take the bikes down to the sea. The paths are rocky, sometimes overhung with cool scented pines but mostly the sun is inescapable. Pale and alien creatures we, more used to the moon. The beach is small and crowded like a nightclub, people standing around in the water. We sit on a shelf of rock watching the Sicilians then find a bar and drink beer and wonder if this was a disaster, a terrible mistake, but once the beers have started their work and the sun's mood softens we are cycling back in a sea breeze with tingling skin and both getting smiles from other cyclists, bright bouncing bikinis with long lashes. Six-packs and stubble. Well all right, this feels OK.

By the time we get back there are people sitting at the tables. Donald puts us in a corner spot and gives us some menus and we watch how he is with the guests. We can't understand anything but there is lots of joking, big gestures, clowning. He brings people over to meet us. The restaurant fills up. Night falls, wheezy cicadas screeching out.

Maria bring us out pasta and wine and when Donald sees he says something to Maria who spits out some sort of reply so he comes over and nods at the bottle, saying to Tess are you sure that's OK and she says yeah and takes a swig. Then he looks at me, raising one eyebrow, lowering the other, swinging a finger between us, instructing me to monitor her but to do so somehow playfully. When he's gone she says, 'Question number one! Hooray!'

Once we have eaten and have been waiting there, smoking, unsure what happens next, he comes over again and sits down, apologising for being so busy but it's a weekend.

'Sooo,' says Tess, tipsy now and revving, 'how did you meet Maria?'

'She's the daughter of a friend of mine.' Donald takes a breath and then smiles at her, before letting it out as if he is blowing a smoke ring. 'It's a bit tricky.'

'Sleeping with your friend's daughter?'

After a considered pause he says, 'Being married to a Sicilian.'

'All Mafia round here then?'

'Oh no, not on this island . . .' Donald is looking about him. He sees a member of the kitchen staff come out into reception and goes off to talk to him. Tess puts her feet up on his chair and blows a smoke ring. A donkey hee-haws in the distance.

'What?' she says, catching my Picasso face. 'What?'

Giacomo is hiding under a table, staring up at her.

'G-Funk's in love with you.'

'Hello,' she waves at him. 'Hello you.'

146

The wind lifts, yanking at the tablecloths, ripping at the leaves of the palm tree. In the distance there is a strange trail of fiery lights that climbs a black mountain. There are lots of donkeys braying. We decide it is a trail of donkeys on fire. We decide it is some kind of Sicilian ritual. We decide the donkeys are being ritually burnt before being ritually raped. *Dirty donkey-burning Sicilian rapey bastardos.*

Donald isn't there most of the next day but the following morning he comes into our room while we are still asleep and wakes me up saying hey come on we're going on a boat trip. Tess wakes up and says 'A whatywhat eh?'

'Bit of a boy's trip, this one,' smiles Donald, in the act of leaving. 'Won't be long. Come on, Tom.'

'What about me?'

I find him in the kitchen and he gives me coffee and I say it's not fair leaving Tess here we can't do that and he throws on an *I know I know* face. Maria's idea. She wants to spend the day with Tess. Girls' stuff. Sicily's like that. OK let me go and tell Tess and he's looking at his watch. Quickly then, we've got to go. So I run back and tell her, she's still in bed frowning and says 'And do what? A day doing what?' but I don't know and Daddy is beeping the horn.

On the way to the jetty he talks to me about America again. It's good to think big, he says. Think what you want to do, then double it. He's going to open a new place on the island with some of the people I'm about to meet, a bigger place. Much bigger. Once I've finished Harvard I can come and help him out, how about that? Tuplow Incorporated. I tell him I don't really want to go into catering. He finds this very funny.

It is a smart white yacht, sleek and powerful, driven by a young man with ice cream hair and a gold chain. There are four or five other men, all around Donald's age, with cool boxes and rucksacks, fishing and snorkelling gear, all teeth and pleased to meet me, faces lined and dark, portly island men with caps and sunglasses. They tease the young captain who is somebody's son. Donald tells me we are going to a hidden beach with unbelievable water. Tess would love a hidden beach with unbelievable water.

Unable to speak Italian the conversation runs along without me. The young man plays games with the throttle trying to make the old men fall over whenever they stand up, but mostly everyone grips their seats as we scud along the coast with the smell of saltwater and petrol, the sun pressing down on my shoulders. Donald has lent me a red baseball cap. He rubs sun cream into my neck without asking first. One of the men leans against me. 'You. Most intelligent boy in UK?'

'No, no nothing like that.'

'You win competition?' he says, turning to my father who nods and says something in Italian that I know means *yes he won a competition and he's the cleverest boy in England.*

'It's just a history essay prize,' I say, but no one is listening. Donald talks and gesticulates towards me and the men look impressed and nod slowly, listening, and then one of them shouts something at the young captain and they all laugh while he turns to us and flicks his chin. Everyone laughs again.

By the time we get to the hidden beach Donald asks me if I'm OK and I tell him I'm worried about Tess and when are we going back. 'These are my friends,' he says, 'Important business people.' He gives me a beer from the cool box. We unload all the bags onto the rocks. I wish I'd brought *Dharma Bums.* The hidden beach is a small cove of sand and Donald asks me if I want to go snorkelling.

With the plastic goggles and breathing tube in my mouth, the ocean in my ears, the sound of my own breathing, I am cool and alone, floating above the bright blue fish, luminous green, crimson, yellow, watching Donald and the men.

During the picnic lunch there is heated debate but when I ask Donald what it's about he shakes his head: he is listening, speaking. After we've eaten, some of the men fish off the rocks. The afternoon grinds on. I tell him again that we should go back. We told Tess we wouldn't be long. 'Oh come on!' he says, then gives me another beer. 'Do your bit, will you?'

I find a place on the rocks and sit there with my knees up. Why didn't I bring my fucking book? Godlike clouds rise up from the flat sea. I am a prop for his deal.

We are silent in the car on the way back.

'You haven't asked about Mum.'

'Correct,' he says, lighting a thin cigar.

When we get back I go to the room but Tess isn't there. I wonder all around the restaurant and garden looking for her and by that time I can hear Donald in the kitchen arguing with Maria. He follows her out garbling something and they are underneath the fig tree when she lets out a gasp of disbelief, pinching together both sets of fingers. '*Finito*,' she pleads, '*finito la commedia!*'

Tess is sitting on a wall the other side of the donkey field. She has been crying. She spent a bit of the morning playing with Giacomo, waiting for something to happen, then she saw Maria getting busy in the kitchen. One of the kitchen staff spoke enough English to translate for her.

'Maria didn't know anything about the fucking "day to-gether" bollocks. She says he's full of shit basically, fucking lies his arse off the whole time, and he doesn't do nothing. Fuck all. She does all the work. And so I am just standing there, right, her saying all this stuff, this geezer trying to tell me what she's saying, and then she just bursts into tears! Fucking bursts into proper tears right fucking there and everyone has their arms round her and I'm like what the fuck is going on? I don't know what to do! Spare fucking sausage, me! Just walked off after a bit. That was this morning and I've just been sitting around waiting for you – all fucking day, man. All fucking day . . .' She wells up. She is angry at herself for welling up.

We ask for some pasta then go to bed. Next morning we take his bikes into town and work out how to buy ferry tickets. Then we dump the bikes next to some bins. As the ferry toils the water to take us home, manoeuvring into the quayside, I nudge her saying. 'Oh my God, look! It's Bryan Ferry!'

APRIL

10

There is a plastic bag full of clothes between my feet. I am thumbing a dosette box full of clozapine, zopiclone, and either bildinocycline or placebos. Tess is fiddling with the radio. She keeps tapping until she finds pop music and lights a Silk Cut.

'Back on the fags? Am I allowed to smoke in your car too now then?'

'Go for it.'

I take out my rolling tobacco and papers. She winds the window down and everything is blown out of my hand. We both laugh. She lays a hand on my face, and says 'Hello brother.'

We smoke her cigarettes, both windows down, the road-roar rushing in. I can feel this wind on my face but everything feels like it's behind glass. I am only watching. I am not really here. The wind is an effect, like spraying water on the audience during a beach movie.

'Let's have a look at them, then. The magic pills.'

I open the dosette box and hold up a pale tablet.

'Might be a placebo.'

'Can't be though, can it? It worked.'

'Aha. But was He pushed or did He jump?'

'Whatywhat?'

And where are the stones of darkness? *Have I got away with it?* I drop the tablet back in the box. *Tak.*

'Can we stop off at a pub?'

'Whaaaaay!' Tess sings out. 'How fucking long have I been waiting to hear you say that again! Right this way, sir—' Her work phone goes. She starts shouting at someone called Mukesh then hangs up abruptly.

'New warehouse manager,' she sighs, spying a swing board, 'complete fucking nana,' and we turn off into the car park of the Hog's Back.

Tess holds my arm as we walk into the bar. It is beamed and garlanded with flags and TV screens. There is a group of girls at the bar in stretched clothes and I can examine them without castigation but Tess yanks at me because I am staring. I order a golden shaft of lager and sip then gulp then drain it down there at the bar. It is sweeter than I remember and I cannot help but tense myself against electrocution, but there is nothing.

Tess has a half, I ask for another pint and we sit down, still in sight of the girls. It is impossible to concentrate on anything else but these girls. I can follow the contours of their bodies and am flooded with orgiastic scenarios worthy of Tiberius and Caligula for which I receive nothing against my right side but the complaints and tugs of my sister. Her work phone is ringing again and she goes outside to shout at it. The girls have noticed that I am unable to look away from them. I wave and they wave back among a great burst of joyous giggling. This continues until I join them.

'You are the most fantastically beautiful group of highly attractive women I have seen in a very long time.'

'Where's your missus?' says one. 'You cheeky bastard.'

'That's my sister.'

'Oooh lucky us.'

'She's driving me home.'

'Charm school's over for another week then, is it?' says the one with tight shiny leggings. We all laugh.

'No,' I say, 'I've been in an acute psychiatric ward but I'm going home now.' The laughing stops and some new kind of interaction is about to occur when Tess pulls me away. When we are back on the other side of the pub they resume laughing.

'But did you see her bottom? It was incredible. Like two heads in a sock.'

'Come back, octopus, all is forgiven . . . Jesus, look at you!'

'What?'

'Can't get used to the beard not being there. You look so different. One hundred per cent improvement.'

We are back on the motorway. I feel the tipping of the pints. I lean up to the rear-view, checking on the smooth new me. I have drunk and I have lusted and the road is a game of chess. Cars move sideways and take each other's spaces. Tess's eyes have got larger. Her face is thinner. Her hair is newly cut.

'One of the male nurses was having sex with a female patient.'

'*What?*'

'Yeah. Roseanna. She's left now.'

'You saw them?'

'I saw him come out of her room. Then they turned it round. Accused me of being the one in her room.'

'Who's "they"?'

'Rashid and Steve. Two nurses.'

'You were accused of going into a girl's room at night? Why didn't you tell me?'

'They dropped it.'

'Did the girl make a complaint?'

'She's in love with Rashid.'

'Oh my God . . .'

'Yep. Pretty grim.'

Tess is looking at me sideways.

'This isn't going to come back on you, is it? Tom?'

When they tell me I am going home I decide to shave my beard off. I borrow an electric shaver and lean across the sinks in the toilets, inspecting the scar on my forehead, watching my face emerge and the clumps furring up the plughole. I am thinking about Phoebe, the razor buzzing across my neck and face, when a forbidden sex memory comes curling out of the past. Naked in a field under the sun. I shake myself from the thought at first, fearful of His reaction, but Malamock is not there. I have an erection. I stop shaving and put my hand in my pocket to hold my penis back and then waddle as discreetly and as fast as I am able to my room. I cannot masturbate in my room. The door has no lock and people come in all the time. I turn the shower on and impatiently tinker with its stages of freezing to scalding to bearable and fling off my clothes and pull back the shower curtain. There is my erection. I can feel and examine it without being struck and cursed.

'Tom?' says Kiki, walking in. 'Oh – sorry!'

'I'm just having a shower.' But she is gone. I check that she has shut the door and under the lukewarm water I summon Phoebe again, naked and beckoning, and begin to masturbate, the sensation exquisite, forgotten. As I kiss her and feel her with me in the shower, her body against the wall, other women step in, Carol Vorderman from *Loose Women*, and then her co-presenters Lynda Bellingham and Jane McDonald and Denise Welch and Coleen Nolan and they are all naked and kneeling and stroking me while I am making love to Phoebe and what the hell are they doing in my shower I don't want them in my shower but OK if you're in the shower come on then but they don't seem to want to they just want to get wet and do a bit of stroking so ignore them, ignore them I am fucking Phoebe

156

I can fuck with freedom I am a free fucker and there is no punishment, no fear, just the sensation of lips and pussy and no electricity except this electricity, this electricity, this electricity – I ejaculate an enormous amount.

Afterwards I go into the day room. Missy is watching TV.

'Shit, man,' she says, 'What's with your face?'

'I have just masturbated for the first time this century.'

'And you're celebrating with half a beard?'

Then I tell her I am going home.

After what happened in the corridor I am put in the intensive ward. They tell me I had a seizure or at least my brain stopped working but later, when I can speak, I tell them what really happened. The medication becomes very strong. Kiki and Fredericks both claim they did not see Him climbing out of me but I cannot expect the truth from them, even Kiki.

While I am in the main hospital Missy has another epileptic fit and her arms come out of their sockets again. For a moment we are wheeled opposite each other in a busy corridor, both lying on gurneys and too weak to say anything.

There is a nurse in my room at all times, at least I think there is, but when I agree to eat I am judged improved and returned to the acute unit. They put me in a different room that looks the same as my other room but is closer to the smoking garden. Missy comes and sits on the end of my bed. She soon gives up trying to talk but sits with me all the same. I stare at the floor and if they drag me to the day room I stare at the sky though there is less in it. The floor was once yellow perhaps, or green, but now it has become some strange new colour, dark and pale at the same time, covered with flecks of who knows what, night and bone, then other patternings, maps of territories without name or feature, all smeared and stained and buffed and mopped. There are lots of new people. Roseanna has gone.

Len has gone. Price has gone. Rashid comes into my room and stands over me and says some things I am not able to make sense of but after that he ignores me. Fredericks often comes to visit. She always seems excited and I think being in the trial affords me protection against being Acuphased by Rashid or in other ways revenged.

On my final morning I wake up to find another spoon on me. I go into breakfast and sit down next to Missy but she just gets up and leaves. I follow her to her room but she shuts the door in my face. I knock on it with the spoon and when she doesn't answer, I push it open. She is balled up on her bed with her hood over her face. I tell her I am giving her my phone so I can ring her. I leave it on her shelf and say I am going but she doesn't move or say anything. I ask her if she wants the door shut and when she doesn't reply I shut it, then open it again, just a little. 'Bye then,' I say and wait there for a bit then go back to the day room.

I drink a mug of tea and say goodbye to my mug, leaving it for the next pilgrim: *Bienvenido!* Tess arrives, and then, just as if I was never there, I am not there. I am in a car on a motorway with my sister. No halfway house this time. Straight back home with a care plan.

The hedgerows pound with green.

I I

Chubby ink–clouds bank across the sky giving out a grey–charcoal light that tones everything with secrecy. The beds are bristling with dandelions and primroses and I can smell the honey-sweet smell of the laurel bush blossoming beside the road. A wood pigeon coos.

Tess has my keys and leads me to my front door. I take a sharp in-breath which makes her say 'OK?' but there is no answer to that.

My bedsit smells musty with the odour of cleaning products gathering the old life beneath them. The split and sprouting club armchair, the Formica table with my computer on it, the wooden chair, my books, my shrine. I pick my way to my bed and toe the plastic storage tubs stuffed underneath. Tess is looking at the octopus collage with her arms crossed, judging it should come down. I sit on my bed. This is my bed.

'Got any whisky?'

'Not on me, cowboy, no.'

'I need a phone.'

'What happened to the one I gave you?'

'Missy needed it.'

Tess lights a cigarette and gulps the smoke into one cheek, deciding against getting angry. 'Well,' she spews, 'that's on you.

There's some basics in the cupboards, bread and stuff to get you going. Got to get Lily from her mate's house now so I'll see you in a bit, yeah? Sure you don't want to come with?' She opens the door as I get up from the bed and behind her I see Saul, going past with shopping bags. He sees me, hesitates, then carries on upstairs. 'You feeling OK? Sure you don't need anything?' She lipsmacks a drag. 'Apart from whisky. And a phone.' My answer is a hug and the way I clench her makes Tess gasp.

'I'm so sorry Tess,' I whisper, 'for everything.'

She kisses my cheek then puts her hand on my face. She is blinking against rosewet eyes. 'It's over now though, isn't it?' she says. 'That's the main thing.' Her work phone buzzes and she wipes her tears away, saying 'Sorry – got to – Hello, Hextons?' She pecks me again, waving goodbye.

I close the door after her and stand there for a moment listening to her voice fade. Saul walks across the ceiling. I go over to the kitchenette and take my clothes out of the plastic bag, unrolling them on the sideboard. Wrapped up in the middle are the spoons. I go over to the shrine and lay the spoons out. *One, two, three.*

I am home.

In the bathroom I put my dosette box on the sink and then sit down on the toilet to piss, my hand finding the bath, this bath I am so intensely grateful for after all the Hilldeans and halfway houses and rooms with only showers, and I hold on to it like a wrist then pat it like a back, making a noise *ggggarrrraha!* chest swelling, fists raised, He-Man Master of the Universe thunder-singing to the ceiling '*I have the bath power!*'

My bath! My white human tray boxed into its blue-and-white-tiled corner, aproned by greying MDF boards nibbled at the joins. Even the bath mat is dry. All the way through. This is a kind of miracle. I affix the rubber plug and waggle my fingers

160

like a mad scientist before his dials, then, with tremendous glee, I twist both the crown-headed taps which give out first a *basso* then an *alto* cry of pleasure, water bounding through them, gasping out to the plug, corralling, streaming out across the length of the bath.

Booting up my computer I consider sending Phoebe an email as I have no phone. I must get a phone as soon as possible so I can call Missy. I'm not sure that I have Phoebe's email but in any case such a thing requires preparation. Composed drafts. I must ask Tess. Tess must have her email. The computer plays its notes and blinks itself awake, disordered thumbnails scattered across the desktop. I must clean those up. I must clean my flat up. I must clean it up like I cleaned up my face. I must organise my books properly. My emails are full of commercial messages and invitations – *later!* I peep into the bath's progress then return to the internet, searching for music. Something without singing. Something without talking. There. *Listen live.* Piano music. Perfect!

I disconnect the laptop and carry it like a waiter to the toilet lid. I introduce one testing hand, turn off the cold tap and unbutton my shirt, slinking myself free of it. I shuck off my trousers, peel away socks and shoes, hook off my pants, scrabbling the whole pile up from the floor and pause a moment, naked. This is the first bath I have taken truly alone, truly by myself, for almost twenty years.

Skipping to the bed, I drop the clothes and then return to the bath, twisting shut the taps. I trail a fingertip through the water and then. In.

Ankles, calves, knees, ring with the heat. Holding the two side handles, crouched, I soothe myself into the fibreglass moulding, shoulders pushed up by the narrow straits such that to descend further, to complete, I must arch my lower back and flex down my shoulders, neck scarfed in warmth, my penis floating in the burnt algae of pubic hair. I lift my heels beside the taps, dragging myself forward and under, my head submerging, my ears filling with water. A few beating breaths, then I rise again. No bells, no people. I close my eyes as the piano music ends and the lady tells me Schubert's Piano Sonata in A Minor is becoming String Quartet in D Minor. Schubert. This is a show about Schubert. He must have been a bath person.

———

Carol is a small woman with a shaved head and a kind of brown jumpsuit, handbag strapped across her chest, and my first thought is that she looks like a monk, a trendy monk. I am in the porch staring out at spore-blotched gravestones, crooked and blank with age. The grass smells hot from a recent cut, the rain so meek you can hardly see it, yet beneath the busy respectful mutterances I can hear its gentle tapping. Carol is gripping me with both hands like a chat show host. She says she is a friend of my mother's from years ago. My mother was a very special person even though they grew apart and she is so very sorry for our loss. I thank her as I notice the gravediggers laying AstroTurf over the pile of soil next to the grave so it will look neat when the coffin goes in. Carol's hand is on the back of my neck, which is unexpected, and she pulls me down so she can kiss me on the cheek with great passion. She steps into the church. Tess whispers who was that? and I say *circle of life* because everyone seems very keen to connect our dead mother with Tess's pregnancy. They keep sighing and looking at the bump and saying *circle of life, isn't it?* as if this observation is profound enough to be reassuring whereas all it really means is *your baby will be dead soon too*. There are friends of hers we recognise but mostly it is strangers, masses of them, walking up the hill through the yew trees from the car park. She seems to have been very popular, at least with people she wasn't related to. 'Who the fuck are all these fucking people?' Tess hisses and I shrug and she tuts again at my scruffy trainers and Barbour. I am dressing for life not death. Anyway, I think Mum's lucky we turned up. We hadn't heard from her in almost a year and hadn't seen her in probably more than two. Tess is in a stretchy black dress, which makes her bump look like a massive door-knob. These people know nothing of the Octopus God and the spirit path, their minds full of money and television. What about this man? What about the vicar?

Reverend James has a long head with grey scraggly hair cling-ing to his ears, wire-frame glasses and a benevolent, gliding manner. He tells me that my mother has arrived then peeks into the church and I peek in after him. Carol turns at the end of the pew to stare at me. Angus the boyfriend arrives from somewhere and kisses Tess and she says where have you been and he says he's found a load of ceps growing round the back of the church and he went back to the car for a plastic bag and they've got a load of ceps now. Were they growing on a grave, Tess says. Did you pick them off a fucking grave? He pats her bump then says hello to someone filing past us.

The pallbearers greet me and they hoist the box from the hearse, letting me slip into place once it is aloft. It is lighter than I thought and the lightness destabilises me for a moment. I thought her big feet would weigh more than this. We stride up the path in silence, two late well-wishers overtaking us into the porch while the verger holds us like a traffic policeman then beckons us forward, Reverend James now in front *I am the resurrection and the life saith the Lord* walking us into the grand hushing and the shuffle of everyone standing as we pace steadily towards the chancel. Carol is beaming at me. I look past her to find Tess there among the crop of heads. We are almost level now and she pats her bump, doing the sighing smile and mouths *circle of life*. I clench my lips to stop giggling.

The verger bids us halt and the chief pallbearer relieves me. I stand to one side as four men lower the coffin onto trestles. They bow to the cross and step off towards the vestry and I take my place beside Tess on the front row. The organ music dries up and there is Reverend James *We are all here today united in our memories of Jill . . .* His welcome becomes prayers of penitence, then the collect, then standing for the first hymn, the organ pushing out heavy notes from its tubing. *Dear Lord and Father of mankind forgive our foolish ways reclothe us in our rightful mind in purer lives thy service find in deeper reverence praise . . .* I marvel at the words! How did she choose this hymn? How could these words be the first words she chose for her own funeral, yet she could not understand me, could never understand me? How is that possible? The rest of the hymn drifts on but I am stuck reading and rereading this first verse. With a purer life, with deeper reverence, I will find my service, my mission – and then, out from the stained glass, comes the ribbon of white light.

'All right?' Tess is whispering because I have sat down mid-hymn and perhaps paled. The hymn finishes. She takes to the lectern and reads from the Book of Job eyeing me all the while. Malamock's love is butterflying across my left side.

'Thomas,' He says. 'You are my soul.'

I look up at the rafters decorated midnight blue with golden stars and then back at all these friends of hers, people we have never known. I pat my back pocket for my speech.

'. . . shall we receive good from God and shall we not receive evil?'

Tess steps back from the lectern, easing into her place beside me. She settles a little uncomfortably while Reverend James announces 'Abide with Me' and we all stand once more as the organ parps *Abide with me fast falls the eventide* my heart beating fast. I cannot find my speech.

I step up to the eagle-back lectern, into the scraping sniffling coughing quiet of Withyham church, checking through all my pockets again and again and again. I look up to see Carol's face. She smiles and nods. Tess is staring at me, her face beginning to crinkle.

'Thomas,' says the Octopus God. 'First. A universal breath.' And so I stop searching myself and lay my hands on the lectern. I take a clumsy steadying breath as I have not been breathing these past moments. Then I lift my chin and say, 'Well. I've lost my speech.'

Everybody laughs. The sound is huge and round and rolling and my panic dissolves. Tess is holding her hand over her mouth, laughing with relief. 'It was hard enough writing it but losing it is even worse.' More laughter. 'I was meant to read from a John Clare poem but instead I wanted to start with some words from Rumi and luckily I know this bit off by heart, because I really love it.' Carol traces her own smile with her fingertips, like a bright instruction – 'smile!'

'"The grapes of my body can only become wine after the winemaker tramples me. I surrender my spirit like grapes to his trampling so my inmost heart can blaze and dance with joy. Although the grapes go on weeping blood and sobbing: 'I cannot bear any more anguish, any more cruelty' the trampler stuffs cotton in his ears: 'I am not working in ignorance. You can deny me if you want, you have every excuse – but it is I who am the Master of this work. And when through my Passion you reach perfection – you will never cease praising my name.'"' I survey the congregation, letting Rumi sink in. 'Unfortunately I didn't memorise the rest of the speech.' More laughs. What am I going to say? I look down at Tess 'But what I want to talk about is . . .' Tess is shaking her head *don't you dare don't you dare!* '. . . the circle of life.' Tess slaps a hand over her mouth to stop laughing.

'My sister Tess here, as you may have noticed, is about to give birth, yet here lies our mother, Mummy, Mum, who was a different person to all of you. Perhaps as a good friend or lover even, but to us she was our mother, and let's be honest, not a very good one. But we don't blame her for that. Some people just aren't born to be good mothers, some people were born to search, to be searchers, to go off to places, to wander. Wanderlust, I think they call it. She had wanderlust. She did a lot of wandering, and she did a lot of lusting.' Tess puts her head in her hands. 'And thank you Reverend James for letting her finish herself off here.'

———

Last time I walked this way the woods were red with winter, its streams churning black foam. Now I am following an old tractor track calloused with lichen and feather-moss when suddenly a whirlpool of bluebells rushes among the trees, the rape fields beyond tall and yellow. Clambering over the stile onto Corseley Road I stop for a moment, looking back over the valley. The air is full of wind-wandering dandelion spores, a summer snow. I cannot feel Him, even here.

I push open the front door into the silence of a row. Lily is halfway up the stairs going up and coming down at the same time, Tess has one foot stamped onto the bottom step. The spirit of whatever has just been said is still visible.

'Hello,' I say. There is loud music coming from upstairs. The house reeks of bacon.

'Hi Uncle Tom,' says Lily and turns to go back upstairs but Tess snaps out 'Lily!' and my niece plods back downstairs and hugs me and says, 'Welcome home.' There is a sign saying the same thing festooned across the hallway, each letter painted by a child and hung together with ribbon. 'You look really thin.'

'Ben!' shouts Tess, 'Your uncle's here,' and he comes running out from the kitchen with a home-made Lego flying machine. He hugs me and we go into the kitchen. Thirteen-year-old Lily has long brown hair, a fringe and quick eyes. She has taken another step forward in time since I have been away, something about how she wears her hair, the regency of her limbs. Tess makes the tea. Ben talks as he clicks pieces to his machine, rebuilding it with new features.

'We went to see *Frozen*. Byron took us and we went to TGI Fridays after and there was this dog that came under our table and farted so everyone thought it was us.' Lily is giggling. Tess brings over a cake. It says 'Welcome Home' in shaky blue writing.

'Lily made it.'

'No I didn't. You made it.'

'Why don't you give my brother his present then?' Lily lays it in front of me as Tess cuts up the cake, all wrapped and bowed. I open it. A block of cheese.

'Now you're not mad any more you can eat your own cheese.' Everyone is giggling.

'Thanks Lily,' I say, squeezing her against me for a head kiss.

'What happened to your beard?' says Ben.

'They take it off you when you leave.'

'Why?'

'For their collection.'

'Does everyone in there have a big beard?'

'Even the women.'

'The women!'

'The women have the biggest beards.'

'No they don't!'

'How many tablets did you take?'

'One million.'

'He's joking, Ben.'

'Did they give you electric shocks?' asks Lily.

'Where did you get that from?'

'What? I saw it on the thingy.'

'Not me personally, but there was one guy in there who did get electric shock therapy and then after that, whenever he walked into the room, all the lights went on.'

'Shut up!'

'Name's Alec. Short for "Alectricity".'

'You're lying!'

'His hair stands up on end the whole time.'

'What about his beard?'

'You know how most beards go down? His goes up, covers his face. If he wants to talk he has to part his beard as if it's a curtain, like this: "*Hello, my name's Alec.*"'

'Lily, eat some cake.'

'Don't want it.'

'Come on. Just a little bit.'

'I'll get fat.'

'You love this one!'

'I loved it when I was, like, eight or something. It's fattening.'

'Since when have I had to force one of my kids to eat flipping cake!'

'Uncle Tom doesn't mind, do you?'

'Come on, just a mouthful, it took ages!'

'Mum, are you deaf?'

'It's OK—'

'No, Tom it's not OK. Lily, do as you're told—'

'Don't touch me!' Lily dives her mother's snatching hand and runs out of the room. Ben munches his cake.

'See what she's like?'

We all eat our slices while Tess tells me about her work, about what's been happening in Motts Mill, who had a fight with who over a parking space, who's got some new pigs.

'Wine?' Tess stands up and takes a bottle of white wine out of the cupboard. She chews out the cork and pours us a glass each. Ben finishes his cake and crosses the room to his toys. I take a deep gulp and close my eyes. Is this it? Or is He just waiting? Is He just toying with me?

Tess picks up a strip of meds that are in the bowl in the middle of the table. 'Look at us. Both on the tablets now, eh? Cheers.' We touch glasses and I search myself for some words of consolation but the ones I find are cheap and empty.

'So what's the plan, Stan?' she says.

'Plan?'

Tess lets out a breath as if she's been holding it in for a long time.

'You're here. You're back. You know – you're better.'

This cake, this lump of Morrisons cheddar cheese, these antidepressants.

'I'm going to get back with Phoebe. Have you got her email?'

Ben makes noises of explosion. Tess puts her wine down.

'She's married, Tom.' Ben's flying machine is in half. 'You know that.'

'No,' I say, 'I do not know that.'

'You do. You do know that.'

'No, Tess. I did not know that. I do not know that.'

'I told you. She told you.'

'That – that's not possible.'

'Tom – she – that was a while ago now.'

'Who did she marry?'

'She met someone out there – they're living with her nan – you know all this.'

'What's he called?'

'Ron. Ronny.'

'Oh,' I say. 'OK. Oh yeah, I remember now.' But I do not remember. I push my chair back and go and sit down with Ben, taking out the two Nerf gun pellets from my Barbour.

'Here. These are yours.'

'That's OK,' says Ben, throwing them over the back of the sofa. Tess asks me if I'm OK and then her work phone goes. As she answers it I pick up my cheese.

'I think I'm going to go for a walk now.'

Tess follows me to the front door.

'Hold on a second,' she says to her phone and covers it with her hand. 'You sure you're OK?'

'Yeah, yeah, I just want to . . .'

I open the door and step out. She is saying things but I walk over the road and cross the stile into the fields and then down into Rocks Wood.

I head through the trees to my rocks and find a crevice, wedging myself there in a patch of sorrel and dog violets. I take out the half-bottle of Bell's from my pocket. 'Very clever!' I toast Him. 'Brilliant!' and then drink and eat all the cheese. When the cheddar is finished I fold the plastic and put it into my pocket, deciding to go and see Phoebe.

12

From Crowborough I take the bus to Lewes, getting out at the main depot, lost in thought. Realising I have got off the bus too early, I walk up the hill, past the White Hart where once I took Phoebe to dinner, then walk all the way to the prison. I must get a new phone. I must call Missy.

Dipping left then left again, I am back on Baron's Down Road, semi-detached brick houses with cars sloping into the garages and TVs electrocuting the front rooms. Number 18. The lights are on.

I walk down the path alongside the house and go straight into the little garden like I used to but there is a man sitting on the patio step, smoking. He has thickly rimmed glasses, bushy dark hair and an underbite.

'Hello?' he says. I look around him, thinking how my plan has run out. 'Yes?'

'Did you marry Phoebe?'

He stands up, pulls his face tight, then relaxes it. He's got wine lips.

'OK. OK now,' he says, 'so this is him. Tom?'

'Yes, I'm Tom.'

'Ronny,' he says, 'fucking Jesus,' and Phoebe comes out.

'Oh my God! Tom? What are you doing?'

'Did you really get married?'

Nobody says anything for a moment.

'Why don't you come in, mate?' says Ronny.

'Hey, wait—'

'It's OK, Phoebs. Come on, Tom.' He stubs out his cigarette and pushes Phoebe inside, her eyes still wide at me and I follow them and there we are, standing around the oval pine table, their plates smeared with remnants of a bright yellow dinner. All the walls are white now. The plants have gone. There are two framed photos of Charlotte on the mantelpiece. One when she is young, holding a dog. One as I knew her, up close and smiling. There is an acoustic guitar in a guitar stand. The TV is bigger. The TV is huge.

'Oh, heaven help us,' says Phoebe's nan, leaning forward from the sofa. 'What's nutbags doing here?'

'Hello Kathleen.'

'Hello nutbags. Phoebe – what's nutbags doing here? Thought you said he was in the loony bin.'

'I'm out.'

'I can see that.' Kathleen sits back to watch her programme with further commentary I cannot distinguish.

'What are you doing here, Tom?' says Phoebe.

'Why don't we all sit down?' says Ronny, offering me a chair. Phoebe shoots him a look then snatches up the dirty plates. What food is that luminous a yellow?

'You can't just turn up here, you know.'

'You got married. That actually happened. I mean – you can remember it.'

'You know we got married, Tom. I told you.'

'Come on, mate, take a seat.'

I touch my head and yawn and we all sit down. Ronny tries to pour himself a glass of wine but the bottle is empty. 'Have we got any more, *chérie* . . .? Well,' he says, 'I've heard a lot about you.'

'Tom,' says Phoebe, coming back in from the kitchen. 'This is not cool. Do you want me to call your sister?' Phoebe's school drawings have gone. That print of people on an escalator has gone. 'Tom?'

'Sorry, it's just a bit – I haven't been here since . . .' Phoebe sighs and sits down.

'So you've just got out,' says Ronny.

'Yes.'

'What's it like being out?'

'Weirder,' I sneeze, 'than being in.'

'I heard they experimented some new drug on you.'

'Ronny, I don't think—'

'They gave me a new drug called bildinocycline and now I can't hear the voice I used to hear.'

'Like dolphins.'

'What?'

'When they catch dolphins and put them in pools. Suddenly they can't hear anything. All the dolphin chat. Sonic stuff. You know, the ocean? Really upsets them. Sometimes they just hold their breath and commit suicide. Actually, I'm very interested in consciousness and communications. It's kind of my field.'

'You're a professor?'

'Recruitment. But I'm very interested in psychic phenomenon. Phenomena.'

'You mean mushrooms. He takes a lot of mushrooms.'

'Tom, have you ever . . .?'

'Long time ago.'

'Course you have.' He bunches up his fist, holds it to his forehead and makes two little screeching sounds.

'What on earth are you doing?'

'Squeegeeing the third eye. Tom knows what I'm talking about.'

'Look, Tom, you can't just—'

'Leave him, Phoebs, he's all right. Nice to finally meet, isn't it? Pretty fascinated to be honest. I mean you've just woken up from like a twenty-year trip, right? A twenty-year *thing*. It must be *bewildering*.'

'It is. Bewildering.'

'See, Phoebs? Told you. And it was the God of Octopuses, right, talking to you? The whole Lovecraft thing. Cuthulu? Cthulhu?'

'No. That is just a story.'

'Everything's a story, man.'

'No. Stories are stories. Everything else is everything else.'

'But he told you stuff? There was, like, a whole mythological framework?'

'Ronny—'

'Let me just grab some more *vin rouge*—'

'I'll do it,' says Phoebe, sighing again, standing up. 'Tom, do you – I mean, can you? Glass of wine?'

'Yes please.'

'Oh,' she smiles. 'Wow.'

'And it was communicating with you on a daily basis? Directly from its realm?'

'Yes.'

'A spirit realm?'

'Yep.'

'Wow.' Ronny sits back and massages his face. 'Wow.' Phoebe is searching through the cupboards. She is wearing pink tracksuit shorts. Oh Phoebe.

'Actually we're trying for a baby,' he says. 'Tom.'

Oh the impossibility of Ronny's face! The cruel perfection of it, of Malamock's whole manoeuvre!

'But when did you get married? I mean what date?'

'I told you all this,' she says from the kitchen. 'Don't you remember?'

174

'About a year ago. We came back from Turkey for it. Sorry, man, we should have invited you.' Phoebe drops a look on him. 'So what was hospital like?' he says, deflecting her gaze.

'Actually,' I say, 'there was someone in there who looked just like you.'

'Me?'

'When I first came back from intensive care. He'd been threatening his wife. He wanted her to have a nose job so she'd have a nose that looked like his. He wanted them to have identical noses. And I said to him "Why didn't you have plastic surgery on your nose? If you wanted to have the same nose as her and she didn't want to have surgery, why didn't you make your nose like her nose?" And he said to me, he said "My nose is better".'

Ronny is staring at me. Phoebe screws off the cap, gives me a new glass and pours us all some red wine.

'And yes I have taken mushrooms. I took a lot of mushrooms when I was an ancient history student. Even more when I was a law student. Lots of mushrooms, before the Octopus God. Although all that is over now. Completely finished.'

'Tom—'

'And I was tripping on a heavy dose of mushrooms and ket once, very heavy, and I had this vision, the whole universe as a book, and the book became a chapter and the chapter became a page, the page became a paragraph, the paragraph became a sentence, and finally a word, the whole universe, the whole meaning of the universe in a single word, and I knew I was on drugs so I decided to write it down in case I forgot it, and then the trip went on and on and on. Anyway, next day of course I had forgotten the word. I ripped up my whole room looking for that bit of paper, but eventually I found it. Guess what the word was.'

'Don't know.'

'*Brickshit.*'

'Ha!' Ronny slaps the table. Kathleen increases the volume on the TV.

'Why did you come over, Tom?' sighs Phoebe.

'I didn't believe you had actually got married.'

Ronny shows me his ring.

'You can't just *turn up*, you know?'

'Sorry. I think I'm going to go now.' I drink my wine down in one and stand up.

'Goodbye, nutbags,' shouts Kathleen.

I dig into Phoebe's eyes for a second then open the back door, stepping down into the garden and go round the side of the house.

'Hey,' Ronny has followed me out. 'Do you want to go out for a beer sometime?'

'OK.'

'But in the meantime, don't do that again. That was fucking weird.'

I touch my head and yawn.

'How did you marry her?'

'What do you mean?'

'How did you do it? Can you remember how it actually happened? Or did you just wake up married one day?'

'I bought her flowers every day for six months,' he says, 'and I've got a massive cock. *Massif Central*. Hey . . .' he stretches his arm out, '. . . joke. Ever done hot stones yoga?'

'No.'

'Just getting into it. You should try it.' Then he turns around and I walk back to the bus stop.

I spend all night smoking and masturbating to pornography and wake up at noon. No punishment nightmares, no dreams of any kind. At the moment of waking I am full of Phoebe wearing pink shorts in her kitchen and it all comes back: Malamock's trick. Perhaps Kiki and Fredericks can't remember seeing anything because He went back in time and changed that too. Has He decided against the stones of darkness? Instead just casting me back into this world alone? Without her? Without Him?

I go into the bathroom and turn on the taps wishing I could know Ronny's secrets and what will happen to him but that kind of knowledge is lost to me now. I take my meds and brush my teeth and get into the bath because I don't know what to do with myself while it's filling and there I have an uncontrollable fit of cackle-eyed pigsobbing.

Bang bang bang goes the door, setting my heart off because I think it's Saul, angry at my crying. I just lie there hoping he will go away until I hear a voice say 'Tom?' and realise it's Megan.

I get out of the bath and tell her what I am doing through the letterbox and dry and dress and let her in and there is Megan. Oh Megan. She hugs me. She looks happy.

'My God, you look so well!' she says. 'You're about half the size!'

'I didn't really eat in there.'

'But I mean the beard! You look ten years younger!'

We sit down in our usual places, Megan in the armchair and me on my bed.

'So. Pretty incredible then?'

'What is?'

'The bildinocycline?'

'Oh.'

'I mean He's left you alone, hasn't He? Tom? Hey . . . come on now . . .' I'm holding my face in my hands. She comes over and sits on the bed with me and holds me for a moment. 'It's all been a bit of a shock, hasn't it, sweetie? Tell you what,

177

why don't I make us a cup of tea and then how's about we go through the care plan, yeah? Have you got your copy? Now first things first, where are we going to put it, because we've got everything on here now, haven't we?' Megan picks up the care plan from my desk and fishes some Sellotape out from her handbag. 'Here?' she says. I nod and she fixes it to a cupboard door in the kitchenette. It's two pieces of paper with boxes that have been filled in. Housing, benefits, medication, daily life. Crisis plan. Warning signs. Activities timetable. Two pieces of paper become one piece, a paragraph, a sentence, a word.

'OK?' she says when we are holding our empty mugs and she has finished going through it. 'So if we agree that one of our objectives is less isolation in the flat, less being on your own, then how do you feel about attending one of the service user support groups? There's a Hearing Voices Network group in Tunbridge Wells that's just started up.'

'Don't you think I might be the odd one out there now?'

'What about trying Crowborough Oak Leaf again?'

'I don't like that community centre. It smells.'

'Tom—'

'I don't like that group. In there just sitting round a table. It's all . . . no.'

'What about trying the Uckfield one?'

'I don't like those groups, Megan!'

'OK, well, how do you feel about going swimming this afternoon?'

'Swimming?'

'Wouldn't that be a great way to start the week? They have an open swim between three and four o'clock at the leisure centre and there's hardly anyone in there. You've basically got a massive new pool all to yourself. Have you got any swimming trunks?'

Megan drives me to the Freedom Leisure Centre. We sit in the coffee shop with one of the instructors while I fill out a form and Megan explains my situation so that I don't have to pay. I get a membership card. The instructor is called Michael and he calls me *mate* a lot. He is perhaps the healthiest person I have ever met. He looks like they have only just taken the wrapping off him.

'Right, mate,' he says. 'Any questions? Do you want to see the gym as well?'

'Does Saul come in here?'

'Saul who?'

'Don't know his last name. Doubt he swims, anyway. Land animal.'

'What, mate?'

'Forget it.'

'Hoooookey cokey, mate. Well, I think we are ready to roll?'

'Tom?' says Megan. 'Are you ready?'

'Am I ready to roll?'

'He's ready.'

'What about "to rumble"? Do you do any rumbling classes here?' A spasm of anger warps through me and I want to scream at both of them but I do not. I buy some goggles.

In the changing rooms I unpack my plastic bag with my towel in it and get undressed. I put everything in the locker, put the 20p in and tie on the plastic wristband with the key on it. I put my goggles on. Instead of going to the pool I go in front of the mirrors and look at myself. My trunks are too small. I have goggles on. I must call Missy.

There are some old people in the pool but the slight echo and warm chlorine smell is somehow comforting. I sit on the metal ladder and put my feet in as an extraordinarily ancient woman finishes her length. 'Hello,' she says, giving me a regal smile. She begins another crossing. I plop into the water and shift over to a free lane. I bob around for a bit and then try front crawl. It is exhausting and by the end of the length I am rolling and heaving out my breaths. I swallow water and cough. I try backstroke but veer out of my lane and collide with the old lady and with my apologies almost drown. I thrash my way to the end and cling to the bar, then get out.

I walk into town and take some money out and buy the cheapest pay-as-you-go phone there is. The teenagers who work in the Waitrose coffee shop haven't seen me in a while and tell me how good I look and that they didn't recognise me without the beard. I sit down with a cappuccino by the window, taunt the froth with my finger and ring my old number. It rings and rings.

'S'that?' says Missy.

'It's me. Tom.'

'Oh fuck man you scared me half to death!'

'Told you I'd call you.'

'Was thinking "what the fuck is that noise?"'

'Told you.'

'Ah shit. Fuck. Shit.'

'Are you OK? What's going on in there?'

'Nothing good. You know. Avoiding Rashid. What's going on out there?'

'It's great.'

'Oh yeah?'

'Perfect, in fact.'

'You'll be OK.'

'Will I?'

'You've got family.'

Through the window blinds I watch two pram-driving mothers approach each other outside the post office.

'What was for lunch?'

'Oh, they hit a new one. A new low. Really, like, amazing shit. How can you fuck up beans on toast, right? Wrong.'

We talk for a bit then the conversation runs out.

MAY

13

A squirrel leads me around the side of the house, jumps into the briar and disappears. I can see Tess disgorging the washing machine, and knock on the windowpane hoping to make her jump. She does not jump. She does not look up. She says 'Hello Tom,' and pulls some socks out of a pillowcase.

Tess opens the front door. A Hoover is dozing across the hallway and the house looks startled by the recent clean. She returns to the utility room where she is feeding the dryer. It is warm and dank and smells of lemon.

'What's that?' she says, pointing at my shoulder.

'Laundry.'

'But I only did you a load two days ago.'

The truth is I have dirtied things so I can come round here but I react in haughty tones.

'I've been doing a lot of stuff outside actually.'

'You've been here most of the last two days. And you fucking left the front fucking door wide open again last night! How many times?' She's pulling the clothes out of the bag with my arm still through it. 'They've got ketchup all over them. Thought you said you been outside?'

'I have.'

'You've been outside with enough ketchup to fuck up three shirts, a T-shirt and these boxer shorts?'

'It was a difficult sandwich.'

'Boxer shorts?'

'I'll put the powder in.'

I start digging powder into the tray. Tess goes into the kitchen. I have to get her back to show me the right settings. Once the machine is shaking, I get the Hoover then follow her into the kitchen, plug it in, and start hoovering.

'Hey! Hey!' she shouts, 'What you doing?'

'Hoovering.'

'Why?'

'I'm good at it.'

'One, I've already hoovered in here, and two,' she stamps off the Hoover, 'I'm listening to the radio if you don't mind.'

'What's all that?'

'What does it look like?'

She pulls the drawer open and takes out a second peeler. We stand next to each other at the sink.

'So,' she sighs, 'what did you do today?'

'Not very good this one, is it? Doesn't catch.'

'Didn't you have any activities today? Any care plan stuff?'

Internet pornography is not, strictly speaking, in my care plan. Nor is Tennent's Extra. Or Facebook.

'I think it's broken. Look.'

'It works fine.'

'It doesn't even . . . just slides over—'

'Tom, in a rare moment of organisation I am actually trying to get the dinner on before midnight. Why don't you go and watch the telly or something?'

'What's on?'

'How do I know?'

'Ow—' I peel off a bit of my finger.

186

'You're bleeding on the spuds!' I turn on the tap to run my finger underneath it. 'Not with them still in the sink . . .' She flicks the tap off, snatches the peeler from me and shoves a roll of kitchen paper into my hands.

'Maybe you should go home and wait for it?'

I can't remember what it is I am waiting for.

'What am I waiting for?'

Tess grips the sink with both hands and drops her head between them.

'Your clothes,' she says quietly.

I go into the living room wrapping some kitchen roll around my finger and watch TV until I realise she is in the doorway.

'I'm going to get you a new peeler for Christmas.'

'Can't wait. Look, bro, I love you and all that, but—'

'You don't want me round here so much.'

'It's just . . . well, you are here more than you were before, even . . . Isn't . . .? I mean, can't you try—?'

'Try what? I've only got my benefit money and I'm still on massive amounts of medication, so—'

'Tom, I know you are. I'm not having a go.'

'I mean what am I meant to do? I can't concentrate on anything, I can't do anything, I'm a fucking zombie!'

'Tom. I am not having a go, OK?' An advert is celebrating old age. I put my head in my hands. 'What about, I don't know . . . make some mates?'

'I have twenty-eight friends.'

'I'm not talking about Facebook.'

'Correction. Twenty-seven, now.'

'Someone defriended you?'

'They were doing this charity appeal for their friend who was ill so I gave them five quid—'

'Tom you can't afford—'

'I know, I know. So when they posted up that she'd died pretty quickly afterwards I asked for my money back.'

Tess bursts out laughing.

'Sorry.'

'It's not funny . . .' I say, but I am smiling too.

'Well you're not such a smelly tramp any more. Throw that dirty old Barbour away – you could, you know . . .'

'What?'

'Meet someone.'

'A girl?'

'Why not?'

'I am in love with Phoebe!'

'Oh I know you are, but I'm just saying, you know – what about a date or something? Nothing heavy. Get your mind off her. Get back in the groove kinda thing.'

'*Groove?* What groove?'

'Christ, you're hardly shy, are you? Seriously, what about Sandy? She knows about all your shit.'

'Sandy Bears?'

'She's always asking after you. Still got a thing for you, blatantly. You're on a promise there – she was nuts about you!'

'When we were kids.'

'Well now she's thirty-eight and divorced. She's quite fit really. Why not?'

'*Hi there, do you want to come out for half a free coffee with me and my Morrisons More card?*'

'Well if you're going be all nunty about it, how're you going to—'

Tess's phone is ringing in her back pocket but it's not her work phone so she doesn't huff and tighten her face.

'Hiya,' she answers, looking at me. 'Yep. Sure. No, that'd be nice,' which means Byron is coming round so I stand up because it is time to leave.

188

'What about some childcare?' I say, peeling off the bloodied kitchen roll from my finger. 'I could look after Ben, couldn't I? Properly I mean. Help you out.'

'Oh Tom . . .'

'You don't trust me.'

'It's a lot of responsibility – you can't doze off with the door open.'

'That's the meds!'

'I know it is, but . . .'

'Are you or are you not struggling with childcare?' Tess opens her mouth. 'Right. I'm not talking about taking him mountain climbing. I'll drink lots of coffee. You can lock the front door. How much is whatsitsname costing you? You can pay me in cheese. Come on, Tess – I play with Ben all the time!'

'That's not the same.'

'Why not?'

Tess stretches up and hangs off the lintel, bending herself, sticking out her tongue. She makes a noise with her throat *gaaaaaaaah.*

14

'No, Tom, of course not,' Megan tucks her hair behind her ears. 'I think you can do anything you want to do, but I also think we might have to be a little more realistic with the time frame, OK?'

'You mean like a fireman.'

'Pardon me?'

'Anything I want to do. Like becoming a fireman.'

'You want to become a fireman?'

'No, Megan, I do not . . .' I am slowly pushing my face together. I let it return to shape. 'But if I had more than two seconds' concentration, if I could just get off the meds, at least the clozapine, I feel I could really . . .'

Megan eases one heel out of her shoe and scratches her instep. She rolls her eyes as if to say 'Here we are, eh? Me, you and this instep' and then lets out a little shiver.

'So,' she says, pushing her foot back into her shoe, 'what *do* you want to do?'

I let out a ferocious sigh.

'Something! Anything! Retrain!'

'Right. So retraining means qualifications, courses, exams, part-time work probably to begin with, and that's only when you're in a position to give up your benefits.'

'What about something unskilled? Cash in hand.'

'That's illegal.'

'What about something unskilled? No cash in hand.'

'Like I said, I'm keeping an eye out for some gentle volun-teering, a couple of hours here and there, because I know you want to get out of the house and do something useful, I know you do, I get that, and don't get me wrong, I think a new challenge is a great idea, Tom, but it's got to be an appropriate challenge. We've got to make sure you can cope with it, OK? And they can cope with you.'

'What about something without skills, without cash, without anything that will worry anyone.'

'Like . . .?'

'Like being a cat. Are there any opportunities for me to be a cat thirty hours a week?'

'That's a lot of hours to start off with.'

'I'm talking cat hours.'

'If you're able to work, Tom, you won't get your PIP – you are opening your post, aren't you?'

'Yes, ma'am,' I salute her. 'Rule number one.'

'I just don't think we're there yet with the work thing. I know you asked Tess for some hours at the warehouse, which she said no to, but can we agree that before you ask anyone else about jobs we're on the same page? I really need us to trust each other that you're going to stick to whatever we decide here about next steps, OK? If someone catches you out and you lose your benefits before you're ready, what's going to happen then?'

'Pluto crashes into Mars. Discovery of a cure for cancer.'

'Come on, Tom. This is serious stuff.'

'Serious as cancer? Rhythm is a dancer.'

'Have you asked anyone else for work?'

I have asked every single person I know. Standing up from

my bed, I walk into the middle of the room and attempt to touch my toes. 'Is this the kind of "first step" they're talking about? Is this an appropriate challenge?'

'Hey' she says, twisting around in the armchair. 'That's not bad.'

'Megan . . .' I give up, hanging in the space around my thighs.

'Look, the benefits issues is one thing, but most importantly we've got to make sure the next experience is positive, you know. I mean look at you – you're doing so well.'

'I cannot get past my knees!'

'We don't want a setback now, do we? And with the sleeping fits and the concentration problems and everything – Tom, going back to work in whatever form means being able to promise someone that you'll be somewhere *on time* and be able to do something, and with the best will in the world right now you—'

I straighten myself with a groan.

'Not being able to do anything or think or stay awake is the meds, Megan! Why can't I come off the meds? Take me off the fucking meds!'

Megan puts her hands on her lap, inclines her head and waits. This is how she puts a conversation into the recovery position. I am ashamed of raising my voice at her but she is the only part of the system that actually comes and sits down in my room.

'Sorry,' I sigh. 'I'm sorry, Megan . . .'

'Why don't I make us some more tea?' she says with a sleepy smile. She rocks to her feet and gives me a hug.

Megan flicks on the kettle and I sit back down on the edge of my bed and look at the books littered everywhere in piles and towers and stacks, books that I can't even read because I can't concentrate for long enough, the words just dissolving into broth, and I am overwhelmed with the urge for an 'appropriate challenge'. Get incredibly drunk. Have a wank.

The tinkle of spoon against mug brings me back to Megan there in the kitchenette, quietly picking her way around my muddled and abandoned cupboards with maternal care and disapproval.

'Megan?'

'Yes, sweetheart.'

'How's about we get wasted? Me and you.'

'I'm not a very good drinker, Tom.'

'Cocktails?'

'Here's your tea.'

Megan sits back in her chair, sipping, as I absorb the warmth of the mug and wonder if we could have been a couple in some other universe.

'How's your love life?'

Megan lets out a knowing cackle. We could be lonely together.

'I think we should focus on the care plan. Look,' she nurtures her tea between her knees, 'why don't we look at the retraining issue at our next CPA meeting? Maybe we can break it down into manageable steps with set goals we can work towards, and then we can integrate those goals into the care plan? So we all know where we are? What do you think?'

'Brickshit.'

'Oh Tom—'

'Oh Megan. *Ohhh Megan!*' I start to sing, '*Ohhh Meeeegaaaan!*' I grip my hands to my chest in operatic style.

'Well that's it then,' she says. 'You should be a singer.'

'*OHH MEEEGAAAAN!*'

'Tell you what. How about this? Why don't we go and have a chat with the employment adviser and then you can— oh.'

'What?'

'Actually she's just been made redundant. Tom, what are those spoons doing on the floor there?'

I don't reply so Megan goes over to the shrine, gathers up the spoons and puts them in the cutlery drawer, murmuring about hygiene.

'To improve socialisation' Megan suggests an adult education course. We won't be sharing like a group, we'll be listening, like a class. She has some pamphlets on local options. There is an ancient history course on a Wednesday morning in the community centre and I share her view that it is preferable to motor maintenance or French for beginners.

Wednesday comes around and we all sit in a circle. The ones that aren't mentally ill are tremendously stupid. I correct Simon the teacher several times. He says the Peloponnesian War 'lasted twenty years' when it lasted twenty-seven. He says the war marked the end of the golden age, when it clearly both caused and contained the greatest moments of Greek intellectual brilliance. Simon defends himself by saying this is just an introduction, which is no defence at all. I suspect that rather than adult education this is some process of de-education and tell him as much and at that point I am invited to leave.

Brickshit.

After much time in the bath listening to Saul's heavy tread above me and considering my next course of action, I search out an old address book among my notebooks and find Phoebe's home number. I ring it and speak to Ronny. I ask him if he wants to meet for a beer. We fix a day and a pub in Crowborough and at the arranged time I go round to Phoebe's. Her nan opens the door.

'Nutbags,' she says, 'you crafty devil.'

'Sorry. I just don't believe in it.'

'My beloved granddaughter has always fallen for people who are a bit lost, a bit screwy. Sound familiar? *Phoebe! Nutbags is here!*'

Phoebe comes to the door. She is wearing a summer dress. She seems caught between several different words at once but then sighs and takes a thick brown woollen cardigan from the coat peg and joins me outside. She puts it on and folds her arms and we start to walk along the houses.

'You really need to internalise something, Tom,' she says, 'OK? I really care about you. You are a very special person to me, and our time together was very special. But I'm married.'

'But I've been reading lots of articles and I know how to make you come now.'

'Oh good grief . . . Tom – Ronny is my husband. But we didn't break up because of Ronny, remember? We broke up because of us.'

'But the Octopus God isn't there any more. He—'

'And if you're feeling better then I'm really happy for you, but I didn't break up with Him. I broke up with you. Eight years ago. Before I got married. To someone I love, Tom. I love Ronny, OK?'

'But it's just a trick! He's gone back and changed everything!'

'Oh Tom. What on earth are you talking about?'

I look up at the stars and lower my voice.

'He came out of my eye sockets, Phoebe. Out of my mouth. Not in a dream – He was there in the flesh, attacking me.' A car drives past us and I make eye contact with the driver.

'But your eyeballs are still there, aren't they? Intact.'

'But He was really there! I felt Him!'

'Feelings can leave, Tom. Doesn't mean they weren't real. Oh babe, aren't you any happier?'

'Well I'm taking my happy pills. Like a good little boy.'

'That's not what I meant.'

'Happiness was never the point!'

'But aren't you? Without Him?'

'No!'

'But aren't you less . . . I don't know – afraid? Aren't you suffering less, at least?'

'Yes but . . . I was – now I'm . . . I don't—'

'You were Job. You were Jacob struggling with the angel. Now you're Tom struggling on benefits.' This is what she could always do. Give everything grace. I touch my head and yawn.

'But I love you.' Her phone rings. It's Ronny but she doesn't answer it. 'It doesn't make any sense if we aren't together, Phoebe, we have to be together, we've got to be able to reverse His trick! Because it's not real! He's just punishing me!'

'Tom . . .' she stops. 'Tom, there's no trick here, OK? I just don't love you like that any more. I love Ronny. I'm married to Ronny, and you've got to move on.'

Nightjars are churring.

'*Let's move on, shall we?* Like that, you mean?'

'Tom . . .'

'You know, in Hilldean, one of the male nurses was having sex with a patient, Roseanna.'

'What?'

'Yep.'

'Are you sure? Then you've got to report it!'

'There's no case. Not unless Roseanna makes the complaint, and anyway, it's all part of the same thing, isn't it? I get it now. It doesn't matter what actually happened.'

'You've lost me. You—'

'He can change it. He can go back in time and change things, he's God! That's what's happened with you marrying Ronny! He's punishing me!'

Phoebe examines me with a tilted face then casts around at the houses and the trees and the night.

'Please, Phoebe . . .'

'Let go, Tom. *Now.*' I am holding her wrists. I release her. 'Listen, there's no going back in time stuff, here's no punishment from above – I'm just your best, last memory. That's what's happening here. And you've— Hey!' But I am walking off down the hill.

When I recover from my thinking I find I don't know where I am and start to panic. Then I come across a sign to the station. I know where I am again. The weight on my chest is terrible.

The next day I go swimming. I go to the far corner of the deep end. I go underwater and hold my breath and imagine the Octopus God emerging from the darkness, a writhing star, beak first, eight giant arms flicking, coiling, coming towards me, siphon swelling, mantle expanded, eyes slit with satisfaction at how alone I am. I run out of breath and come gasping up from the underworld into Freedom Leisure Centre.

In the changing rooms there's a message on my phone from Tess. It says *call me I've got a deal for you* and when I ring her she says she's been thinking about it and what about some baby-sitting one evening, see how it goes and let's take it from there, and I say great and she says no, that's not the deal. The deal is first you have to go on a date with Sandy Bears.

15

I have woken up here again, in my chair, in the middle of the day. I sat down to put my shoes on for a walk. One is still in my hand, my boot with its splitting heel. I wipe my mouth and yawn out another clozapine doze. What time is it? I have a feeling that I have something to do, but that is probably a feeling that I should do something. There is my care plan, taped to the cupboard door. *Coo-eee care plan.*

Saul walks diagonally across the ceiling. He pauses for a moment then walks back the same way. There is a thud. Silence. The pattern repeats itself. What's he doing? I watch the ceiling and try to imagine what could make sense of those noises. He is doing the same thing over and over again. He must be exercising. His phone rings. I can hear the rumble of conversation, but the rhythm of steps and thud is unbroken. Do people who take exercise accept phone calls during their exertions?

I stand up and follow the steps across my flat, stop, walk back, pushing the armchair out of my path. What is that thud? He's still on the phone. Is he dropping to the floor? Or dropping something on the floor? I still have one boot on my hand. With arms outstretched I can easily reach the ceiling. I take the other boot so both are on my hands and start clomping them across the ceiling, mirroring Saul. He stops. I stop. We walk together across our flats. We pause. He runs and that catches me out but when he starts walking again I wait in the middle and join in. There is the thud. I wait for our game to start again but it does not start. I hear his front door close and his footsteps on the stairs.

Saul knocks on my door. I don't open it but he knocks harder and the door swings open because I haven't closed it properly. I'm standing there gloved in boots, and whatever Saul wanted to say no longer fits, so I get in there first.

'What was the thud bit?'

'What?'

'Once across, twice across, thud. What was the thud bit? I couldn't work it out.'

'Why are you banging on my floor?'

I look at my boots.

'I was walking.'

'Just what are you trying to say here? Exactly?'

'I was walking across the ceiling.'

'On your hands.'

'Were you exercising?'

Saul doesn't know what to say next so he shuts my door. Then he opens it again and says.

'You got something to say, just say it – yeah?'

'Are you exercising up there?'

'Get to the fucking point!'

'I just did. I think.' An odd moment passes between us.

'Stop banging on my floor, got it?' He slams my door shut again, walks back up the stairs, opens his door and walks across my ceiling. I put my boots on the floor with my hands still in them and attempt a handstand so my feet can touch his floor but fall over.

I pick up my phone to ring Tess but decide against it because I don't want to annoy her. I ring Missy. No answer, so I leave her a message, reading out the NHS Sussex guidelines for the use of Acuphase I found on the internet. *In the past, Acuphase has often been too widely and possibly inappropriately used, sometimes without full regard being given to the fact that it is a potentially hazardous and toxic preparation with very little published information to support its use . . .*

It cuts me off before I get very far. Then I remember she's not in Sussex. I put my boots on.

The sky is black with raincloud. I walk along the headlands beside the rape, wheat and beans, listening to the calling buzzards and the chip-chipping of a wren. I walk along the fallow fields and heifers run towards me but I know they are just hungry and young and do not fear them like the hikers. I stand in the middle and try to copy how they are talking while they nudge me and swing their dewlaps and then I bellow and they startle. I walk through the wood at its eastern edge. Coppicing hops me through the briney gubber around hammer ponds solid green with duckweed. The land rears and dives from where Romans and medievals dug out iron ore for smelting in their bloomeries. I kick out some slag.

In a clearing among a small cluster of sandstone rocks there is a grove of bright pink azaleas. I lie beneath them to borrow their peace, but hide when I hear dogs yapping. A sweet chestnut has melted down one side of the rocks then pooled onto the ground to form a seat and when it rains I stay there and watch my roll-up being blotted out dead, my jeans polka-dotting as the rain turns furious yet I don't move, I get as wet as the tree. Yet still I cannot enter into these woods as before. I am a ghost now, and cannot share its life. Everything stays behind the glass wall of medication, my blood and thoughts all mixed with lead.

In the evening I listen to Saul and Nika moving about. Sandy Bears has sent me a friend request. I watch television. I drink beer and watch YouTube videos of octopuses, how they change shape and camouflage, a flamenco demon spiralling all its wrists, scuttling across the sand, bunched, guarded, quailing arms gathered beneath; a shrivelled sea-toad that jumps suddenly in all directions, now long and planing, jet-propelled, striped in celadon and white marble, ballooning, brown stippled with black then blushing bright red against the camera crew's torch, hurrying away its own mantle like a waiter's tray. I watch one video after another. They are spider-like, then snake-armed; a parachute, an arrow. They conjure themselves out of themselves. They live alone and die young.

When I'm drunk enough I get up and walk out of my flat into Crowborough. The kebab van is parked outside the Cross. I buy a shish kebab and take it home. I sit on the floor in front of the shrine with the three spoons laid out there and unravel it. 'Meat! This is meat, look! Horrible meat!' I wrap it back up and gobble through the whole thing, the coleslaw and the sauces running all over my chin and clothes and it is sweet and the chunks of meat are chewy and taste only of the sauce. Eating so quickly is exhausting and I am panting and kebab-faced when my stomach convulses and I scramble to the bathroom.

My chest tenses with squalls of nausea and expulsion, the kebab hurtling back out of me, mixing with beer and toilet water into a stinking acid soup. The rhythms of the convulsions are not unlike electrocution and even after I have hawked and spat the last drops I tense myself again and cry out, pretending He is electrocuting me and lie on the floor after this pantomime, gasping. I rock back to my feet, drunk and unsteady, gripping the sink and in front of the mirror, tracing the scar on my forehead, I start twisting myself this way and that. 'I'm going to get my teeth done. I'm going to get my hair done.' Then I investigate myself more closely, pawing at my eyeballs, examining the swivelling ballness of them, the machinery, the meat. Easily replaceable.

'Plop, plop,' I say to my eyeballs.

———

Running through night rain, demented winds change direction, streetlight landscapes pour down, reform, whirl sideways and I am steaming, running uphill, squeaking breaths through my teeth, my whole body slicked with sweat and rainwater and headlights that have become their own animals, things with the taste of my blood, yellow speeding hunters about to savage me right here on the pavement, and if they pass it is only because they are on the way to something worse, some greedy evil, something connected to me, and they will soon be circling back.

I must get to the house.

The bus stop finally comes into view and I am stumbling downhill and almost lose control but I cannot slow down. At the corner, headlights sweep the next bend and I flatten myself against the wall until they have passed, then sprint the rest of the way.

At last I can see the house – the lights are on! I run off the road down the side path, fumbling with my stupid fucking key unable to get the thing into the fucking lock my hands shaking so much I have to hold it with two hands until finally it sucks itself in and I push through the door groaning '*Phoebe?*'

Charlotte is at the pine table.

'Tom?'

She is with two strangers.

There is a man with small inscrutable eyes holding a glass in mid-air. Thin strands of grey hair sweep backwards over his scalp. A little girl with long hair, feet swaying from the chair, stares at me with black eyes and there is something evil about this little girl, horror-movie evil, something wrong, very wrong . . .

'Where's Phoebe?' *Who are these people? What are they doing here?*

'Still at work – Tom you are completely soaked! You'll freeze to death!' The little girl smiles at the word. 'Honestly, get those shoes off!'

'Been for a little swim?' says the man, his voice posh and purring, taking a drink. *Charlotte doesn't know people like this!*

'Hey – hey – Tom? Are you OK?' She is getting out from around the table. 'What's the matter, sweetheart? Come here,' and she ushers me back to the door, 'Let's get you out of those clothes.' The man smiles at me, a quick false smile with yellow jagged teeth.

'Who are they?' I whisper, heeling off my shoes and following her upstairs.

'That's David. Old mate of mine, and that's his goddaughter Marguerite, but sweetheart, what on earth are you doing out in this weather with no coat on?'

'Have they made any phone calls?'

'Who, David? No . . . I don't think so. Why?'

'Did you tell them I was coming?'

'I didn't know you were coming. Tom . . .?' But I am shaking, my hands covering my face. Putting her arm around me she walks me into the bathroom and tells me to get undressed, handing me a towel and a dressing gown. She waits the other side of the door while I strip off. Eventually she knocks, asking to come in, and finds that I have climbed into the bath and pulled the shower curtain across. 'Sweetheart?' I can hear her sitting down on the toilet lid. 'Are you – have you had another fright?'

'Yes . . .' I gasp, and the release of it, the power of saying it out loud, lets out a kind of spasm.

'Can I hold your hand?' she says.

The shower curtain moves and her hand comes through and

I seize it until I can take a normal breath. After a while she says, 'Do you want to come downstairs? Have some dinner, some hot food?'

'But what are they doing here, those people? What do they want?'

'They're just my friends, Tom. It's all right . . .' Charlotte hooks her finger round the shower curtain and peeks in. 'Hey, I know – what about a drink? Bet you could do with a drink. Back in a second.'

I listen to her going downstairs, the rumble of talking, then her footsteps again, the door opening. Her hand appears with a tumbler.

'How much do you – tell you what, take the whole thing.' A bottle of Bell's appears. 'Have yourself a drink and try to relax a bit, OK? Phoebe'll be back soon. Do you want me to stay with you?' And I want to say yes but instead out comes *no*.

'Well you have yourself a bath if you want, or just get into bed, whatever you want. I can bring you some food up when you're ready. Tom?' Charlotte opens the curtain, puts her hand on my knee and wobbles it. 'You're safe here, OK? You're home. Nothing's going to happen to you here. Nobody's going to hurt you, OK sweetheart? I'm here, OK?'

She leaves and I slosh full the tumbler with whisky and down it, gagging against the thick sting as I lie back in the bath, hugging the bottle, whispering prayers to the Octopus God as my heart rattles and the room pulsates.

I hear a creak on the steps. Then another. Then some kind of *clack*, some kind of machine readying itself. I tear back the shower curtain, leaping from the bathtub, yanking the door open but there is no one, nothing.

At the top of the stairs I strain to make out what they are saying about me. The noise of someone coming into the kitchen sends me into Phoebe's room and I curl up in her bed, into the smell of her, the warmth of it, lying there with the whisky bottle. I take another drink. Listen. Their burbling plans. The man's laugh breaks through *HA HA HA* fake and malevolent and what am I doing here I've got to get out of here!

Out of the bed shedding the dressing gown searching desperately until I find some of my clothes and suddenly I can hear Malamock again '. . . must preserve your honour,' and I freeze.

'We have heard the knowledge again of cessation of consciousness,' He says. *A cessation of consciousness*. Is that what's happening? There is a photograph of Phoebe and her mother on her shelf and Charlotte is smiling at me and if these two downstairs mean to hurt me that would mean Charlotte is lying that Charlotte is part of it and – and that can't be right that can't be true because she loves me I know that she would never harm me I know that I'm not thinking straight, my consciousness is just polluted, I'm just dealing with a cessation. 'A cessation of consciousness, Thomas,' He agrees, and I sit back down, tears in my throat. 'Within these categories were a widespread illumination. A longing to cry.' I look at the statuette on the shelf. 'With regard to weapons beyond what is useful. Hold not the spear, the dart, nor the habergeon. The move beyond thought. Stillness.' The man's laughter again, then the little girl's. 'They are joined one to another,' Malamock says, 'they stick.' Charlotte comes back up the stairs.

'Hey,' she says, head round the door, 'Any better?'

She sits down next to me and I let out a tremendous breath. She puts her arm around me. I feel my whole body decompress.

'Do you want to tell me what happened, sweetheart? You don't have to if you don't want . . .'

'I was in traffic, just coming into town, and I had this pulsation. A huge pulsation and I couldn't control it and it turned – and I couldn't reach Him any more, I couldn't hear Him, and there was these cars – they were trying to fucking kill me,

Charlotte! I just ditched my car on the side of the road and ran. I ran all the way here.'

'You know,' she says after a moment, 'once upon a time, I was doing acid up on the Downs with a bunch of friends and I started to get the fear. So I decided I was best off on my own and ran away, only they all thought I was playing a game, so they ran after me. Ooof Lordy! What a dreadful afternoon that was.' Charlotte puts her head on my shoulder.

16

I am in front of the bathroom mirror, squinting, trying to look more handsome. It is surprising how much actual blue there is in my face. I take an extra zopiclone. Missy's advice was 'Don't shit yourself, kiddo.'

I have a new shirt, the kind with patterning that is tight under the arms. *Thank you, Tess.* Black trousers. Leather shoes. I have not worn leather shoes in twenty years and I can't keep my eyes off their shiny dead animal sophistication. There is folded money in my pocket. *Thank you, Tess.* PIP of £53 a week, housing benefit of £134 a week straight to the landlord, £57.90 a week ESA, about £22 a week after food and bills, minus at least 60 g of tobacco, £18, so £4 a week to spare which is not enough for a second date so even if it goes well which it won't Tess will have to pay for every date in the future which is ridiculous. This whole thing is ridiculous! Why am I doing this? In exchange for some childcare which is a favour to her in the first place! This is fucking ridiculous!

Locking up my flat there are two magpies on the paving outside. *Two for joy.* Hayley Fletcher and her kids from the fourth floor are walking across the forecourt and we wave at each other and she tells me I look smart. They get into their Astra and I walk behind the car as it rolls out onto London

Road but after a few steps I halt before a ruffling maple tree because I don't have to do this. I can just go back and send her a text message and say I don't feel well. I can turn off my phone.

The doors of the Crowborough Cross open into a gust of noise and music. I patrol the pub but cannot find her. Relief begins to crest that she has changed her mind but then I hear my name.

Sandy Bears is waiting for me in a booth. She has long dark hair and red rectangular glasses. She looks faintly oriental even though her father is a big man with ginger hair called Alf and her mother is as blonde as the sun. Sandy is wearing a red jacket with a stiff frilled collar, almost military.

'Hi. Hello.' I touch my head and yawn.

'Boring you already?' she smiles, and the thing I am meant to do here is offer to buy her a drink but my hands are trembling so much that I will surely be unable to carry any drinks without spilling them. A prophecy of this embarrassment, a clear and dreadful vision of wine sloshed onto carpet, of fumbling and failure, heats my face to purple. 'All right?' she says. Sandy looks amused.

'Would you like a drink?' I blurt out, and as one half of my mind shrieks blue murder at the other half for letting this doomed offer escape, Sandy says 'Ooh. Yes please. Ginormous glass of dry white wine, please.'

'OK,' I say to the table, thinking *I can't carry anything my hands are shaking*. I look up and her mouth is opening to say something. Certain that it's an inquiry into my ability to perform this most basic task, an inquiry that is embarrassing beyond any tolerable point, I swoop off before she can speak.

A long polished steel bar top runs towards the kitchen and a restaurant area. The fermented smell of beer collecting in overflow trays mixes with the chatter of Friday drinkers. Down-lighters peer feebly onto mauve-grey walls, fruit machines pirouette with light, and outside there is a warm, inviting evening, unattainable and serene with freedoms.

I slot myself between a withered man on his phone with an oddly tight silver neckchain and another with a baseball cap pulled down like a beak. I forearm the sweat from my head, regretting the patch it leaves on my new shirt. It looks like I have sweaty forearms. Who sweats from the forearms?

I glance behind me and see Mr Brigget. He raises his glass at me and I smile weakly, turning away, fearful that he might come over for a chat. Why on earth did I agree to meet her here, where there are people I know?

Longing only to consume enough alcohol that I can return to some approximate sense of humanness I consider downing a couple of quick and greedy shots there at the bar but the size of the shot glasses means my treacherous hands are even less capable of delivering the contents to my mouth than a pint. *Stop shaking!*

'Yes, Tom. What can I get you?'

'A big glass of dry white wine please, Andy. And a pint. Of lager. Stella. With a shot of vodka in it.'

'You want me to pour a shot of vodka into the pint?'

'Yes please.'

Andy pulls a face. The drinks appear on the bar top and I wave over the money but Andy has not added the shot. The change appears beside the drinks but I am frozen by the fear of getting the shot in with shaking hands and am unable to ask Andy to do it for me, even as he asks me if everything is all right, even as he asks me if I want anything else, 'No thanks,' I say, yet it must be done, it has to be done, and as he takes another order from a group of builders one of whom is watching me, I stare at this tiny glass, arm in motion, and seize it with my fingers.

As soon as I touch it my hand quivers. The more I try to control the shakes, stiffening my hand, the more wildly I tremble, wobbling vodka onto the beer mat, my arms stiffening even more, the glass jumping about so much now that I don't have a hope of being able to pour it in, so I just drop the whole glass into the drink. The builder bursts out laughing.

'Just get a call from the taxman did you, mate?'

'No. I've got Parkinson's.' He stops laughing.

Leaving the change, I gather up the other drinks with both hands as if they are a chalice, the most holy sacrament, their weight and size settling my shakes, and with liturgical care I carry them before me down the yellow and red carpeted aisle to our leather pew and place them in front of Sandy Bears. Blazing with relief that I did not drop the drinks or slosh them over her I retake my place, windscreen-wiping the sweat from my forehead with both hands, and then bend myself like a bird into the pint and slurp. I look up to see Sandy quizzing the presence of a floating shot glass in my pint.

'Sorry. I'm a bit nervous.'

Sandy leans over and hooks up the glass with a finger, lays it on the table, sucks herself and says, 'I know you are. No probs. Cheers, then.'

She holds up her white wine with the characteristic ease of a normal person, but I just push my pint along the table towards her and then, once she's clinked it, pull it back. I have another pelican's dip thinking *please please say something else*. Without warning my mouth parps open with 'So why did you get divorced?' Sandy Bears lets out a chirpy giggle. 'I shouldn't have asked you that.'

'Hey, no probs, to hell with small talk, right? Graham ran off with someone else. One of my best friends.'

'Oh.'

'Yep. "Oh".'

'How many best friends have you got?' *What kind of question is that?*

Sandy Bears blinks, and breaks into a smile. I realise my hands are steadying. I gallop more sweet lager down my throat.

'Well I'm not counting Ruth any more. How many best friends have you got?'

'I've got my sister.'

'Oh I love Tess. She's brilliant, isn't she?'

Sandy's phone bleeps. She scans the text message, then watches me through her wine glass as she tips it against her face.

'Tom Tuplow,' she says. 'I can't believe we're doing *this*, can you?'

'No,' I agree. *What is "this"?*

'So do you think I've changed then?'

'Since when?'

'Since you last saw me.'

'I saw you in the window of Café Baskerville about two months ago.'

'And you didn't say hello?'

Do I need to make an excuse about this?

'No.' *I do need to make an excuse.* 'Sorry.'

'No probs, don't worry about it. Since we last spoke, I meant.'

'You haven't changed a bit, Sandy,' I say, meticulously following Tess's instructions. 'You look just the same. You look great. You look beautiful.'

Sandy Bears is blushing. This relaxes me like a shot of haloperidol.

'I'm blushing,' she says. 'Oh God.'

'Hey,' I say, inhaling more lager, 'no probs.'

Sandy pats her cheeks than checks herself in her phone. She gulps some more wine. She is deciding to say something. She shifts in her seat, rotating her glass by its base.

'D'you know I think the last time we actually had a full-on conversation – I mean the two of us type-thing – it was in that old train tunnel by the waterworks in Groombridge, remember? Drinking K cider?'

'A train tunnel?'

'Come on, you remember! There was some party in a barn and we were both looking for it but couldn't find it, so we just stayed in this old train tunnel messing about. You were going out with Abigail Sherman at the time. You were, like, the celebrity couple, weren't you, you two?'

'Oh yeah. Got it,' I say, but I have not got it. I have no idea what she is talking about.

'You were telling me about these books you'd read and stuff and I was sure something was going to happen between us but, you know, *Abi Sherman*. She was so pretty, wasn't she? Gorgeous. What's happened to her?' Abigail Sherman – a forgotten name. She fell off a wall once and I had to take her to A & E. Sandy takes a deep breath and giggles. 'Do you want to hear something daft? Seeing as we're on the "no small talk" vibe?'

'OK.'

'I actually went out with Graham in the first place because he reminded me of you a bit. He isn't clever or anything but he looks like you.'

'He's fat and bald.'

'You're not that fat! Don't do yourself down. No, you've kind of got the same eyes. But he's got a piggy little face. Anyway, I have never ever ever *ever* told anyone that.' Sandy shakes her head in disbelief. *Am I to make a confession too?*

'So—' Her phone bleeps again. She flicks a look at it, then turns it face down on the table, as if that somehow puts it away. '. . . anyway. How've you been then?'

'Since 1992?'

There is the faint smell of caramel from someone vaping in the booth behind me. A Maroon 5 song is playing. I look at my shoes, my shiny leather shoes. Tess has given me strict

instructions not to be miserable or boring. 'I've been – I feel
. . . like a children's entertainer,' I say. 'Out of work.'

'What?'

'Look at these shoes. They're just like a children's entertainer's shoes.'

'Can you do any tricks?' she says. *I used to talk to God.* 'Juggling? Making things disappear?' *Poof! This is an empty booth. I
am in bed.*

'No. Sorry. No tricks.'

'Come on,' she says, pushing my shin with her shoe, 'what
have you got up your sleeve?'

Sandy is evidently very pleased with her joke. I don't know
what to say next. I hover around a few answers but they all
somehow evade me and suddenly too much time has passed and
we have lurched into a brittle silence. I nip at my drink. I am
pleading, screaming at my mind to give me something to say.
Sandy is staring. She sits back, moving her eyebrows around,
the drips from my frozen brain already beading across my back,
moment heaving itself upon moment as I fucking implode—

'Well,' she says at last, 'Anyway. I think you look nice and
I like your shoes.' I fling a 'thank you' at her, a wild guttering
bowling ball at the sticks of our conversation. Then I say, 'I like
your jacket.'

'It's partly silk,' she says. 'And the dress. We're doing the
small talk thing again though, aren't we? Tell you what,' she
says, 'I've got me an idea.' Sandy shimmies herself out of the
booth, goes to the bar and comes back with four shots.

There are no more silences now and I am not trembling but
can watch myself interact with her and listen and think of things
to say and the conversation has the same sort of music to it as a
tumble dryer. A motion is being performed, a looping floppy
waltz of sorts, and I have been thrown in here with these red
clothes and it all just turns and turns and turns.

Sandy Bears works in an administrative role in the HSBC in Tunbridge Wells. She at first refuses to believe that they had been historically involved in the drug business and that among its founders were several opium traders keen to profit from the vast trade in selling Indian opium to China, and indeed the bank recently paid a fine of billions of dollars to avoid prosecution for failing to prevent drug cartel money laundering. When she does accept it, she seems to take this information as a personal attack, which is incorrect. Arguably the liquidity in the banking system from drug cash stopped the financial crisis in 2008 becoming the Great Depression, so perhaps they should be thanked. Sandy says she doesn't want to talk about work. She has been on another date recently which was a disaster because the man got into an argument with somebody at the next-door table and it was embarrassing. Her daughter Betsy seems unaffected by the divorce. She loves her daughter Betsy. Graham is a good father. She cannot deny that about Graham. She wants to go on holiday but can't decide where. She is thinking of giving up Facebook. She can't find enough time to go to the gym. She doesn't like the gym. People who go to the gym all the time are stupid. It is important to go to the gym.

Part of the plan for the evening was the possibility of going to see a film, though I had no idea how we would actually get there as the nearest cinema is in High Brooms. Sandy celebrates the abandonment of this plan as proof of what a wonderful time we are having. She seems also to need to inform the person she's texting of this social victory, so I excuse myself and go to the toilet, sitting down in the confessional privacy of the cubicle.

I realise I am annoyed with her because she has not asked me about my experiences. Perhaps she thinks I don't want to talk about everything I have seen and heard and been through and suffered, how I have lived in another world. So I return to our table ready to give that permission.

'You haven't asked me about the Octopus God,' I say, wriggling into the booth again. 'About the voice I used to hear.'

'Oh,' she says, 'Sorry. I thought you wouldn't want to talk about that stuff.'

'Well, no. It's OK.'

'What do you want me to ask you?' Sandy takes a drink. She is afraid of saying the wrong thing. This isn't fair. 'But it's all gone now, right?'

'Yeah. All gone. I just came out of hospital.'

'I know.'

'And while I was in there, I lost His voice.'

'Oh God. I hate hospitals.'

'My friend Missy's still in there so I'm really worried about her. I'm out here, but she's still in there, you know?'

'That's awful.'

'Yep,' I say.

'God,' she says.

She doesn't know what else to say. Poor Sandy Bears.

'Hey, do you remember James Vickham?' I say. 'Apparently now he's a woman.' So then we talk about James until Sandy takes our glasses back to the bar.

'Who are you texting?' I ask her as she slides a drink over with one hand while texting with another. She has a Black-Berry phone and her thumbs move at incredible speed even though she is drunk now and her hair is in her face.

'No one. Sorry I'm . . .' The text message is sent. She puts the BlackBerry face down on the table. 'I'm not being very nice, am I?'

'What? No—'

'God I was sooooo in love with you for the whole of second-ary school. Do you know that? The whole thing. Every day. And now here we are and it's like, it's like, I want to punish

215

you for that? Or something? Then with the Graham thing it's like . . . it's like, when am I going to get a break? You know?'

'Sand—'

'I know! I know it's not fair. Sorry. I'm pissed, I'm pissed! Whoops. Hey. I've got an idea. Are you hungry?'

I am unsure how to react. If we are to purchase food I need to count my money. This seems ungallant.

'I made a *huge* risotto yesterday,' she says, pronouncing the word 'heee-owage'.

Sandy lives on East Beeches Road. We take the bus two stops down Crowborough Hill and then walk along North Beeches to her house. The night is warm and clear, the dark wooded ridge visible across the rooftops and my nervousness at heading back to her house mixes with the alcohol to produce a light-ness across my chest, a certain euphoric glow that here I am, bowling along the highways of England with a woman. I feel as if I'm on some kind of fairground ride, effervescent sensations beaming out from my stomach. There is the moon.

By the time we are through Sandy's door and I can smell air freshener and patchouli oil we have not spoken for several minutes and I no longer feel drunk. The sharpness of the house lights, the atmospheric sting of being in a stranger's family home, the clunk of the shutting door – my heart pounds out my mistake. I shouldn't have come here. I am not attracted to Sandy Bears even though she is a nice person yet here I am, caught up in a grubby compromise, like the rest of them.

Sandy's first offer is of wine and we sit down to cold sweet glasses of urine-coloured Chardonnay in a kitchen covered with her daughter's drawings. She takes out a Tupperware box from the fridge, yanking the pan out from a low cupboard and only now do I realise how drunk she really is, swaying at the cooker, dolloping out the risotto like a child with Play-Doh. With her back to me I am free to roam the lines of her body, trying to ignite some sexual desire, something that will light up the steps I should take.

'One sec,' she says, and goes upstairs to the toilet. I can hear the jet of her pissing and I look at my wine. I feel ashamed of the loneliness that has bought me here, and finish my glass, whispering a prayer to Him, then fill the glass up again. Sandy's phone bleeps on the table. I look over. The message is from Graham. They have all been from Graham.

Sandy is coming down the stairs. She reappears in the door-way. She has taken her shoes off. Wrinkling her face with a grin, Sandy forgoes whatever she was about to say and instead takes out two plates. She spoons out the risotto and clatters a plate in front of me. She collapses onto a chair, chin resting on her hands.

'Have you got a fork?'

'Oh my God!' she guffaws. 'Sorry!' and leans back on the chair, almost tipping over. She flicks open a drawer to get some cutlery. The risotto is sticky and full of onions.

'Are you OK?' she asks in a light voice.

'This is really good,' I say, nodding.

If I stop eating then I will be faced with what comes next so I carry on eating but the risotto is getting smaller. Sandy's eyes are thin with wine. She is forking up the risotto two grains at a time and there is only the sound of chewing and metal itching against plate. I'm just here because my sister wants me to be here. Somehow my plate is empty. My stomach balls tight.

'Any more?'

'No. Thank you.'

'Tom,' she says, 'do you want to come and sit down next door?'

Not really, but I am smiling and putting my fork down and Sandy is standing up and we are leaving the kitchen, her rounded calves before me. She pushes open her living room door. It is white and smells of synthetic raspberries. Sandy switches on and off lights until there is only one dim bulb at work. She sits down on the sofa and I sit down beside her, looking straight ahead. There is nothing true here, nothing that comes from my heart, yet I do not want to let Sandy Bears down. There is a line of shoes underneath a chest of drawers. She takes my hand. I hear her phone bleep in the kitchen.

'Shall I get your phone for you?'

'Pardon?'

'Do you want me to go and get your phone?'

'My phone?'

'Yeah.'

'Why?'

'It just beeped.'

'Oh,' she says, then, 'Are you all right, Tom?'

'Yeah.'

I can feel her readjusting herself beside me.

'Tom?' she says, her voice commanding me to look at her. 'Do you . . . like me?'

She is squeezing my hand softly and there it is, the lie, that I like her and she's lovely and let's make love and pretend to love. But I know it is a lie, and I don't want to lie to her about something so important because I do like her in the way that she is a nice person but in the time it has taken me to think all this Sandy has let go of my hand. 'Yes,' I reply, finally deciding to lie. There is a soupy image of us reflected in the black of the TV screen.

'Did you like the risotto?' she sighs.

'It was very nice.'

We sit there on the sofa. Some strange, bulky moments pass. I am trying to understand the atmosphere when Sandy says, 'Tom. I'm going to go into the bathroom now and I'm going to be in there for a long time, OK?'

Sandy leaves the room and goes upstairs into the bathroom and locks the door. I look around, at the photos and the awards and a trumpet upright on the windowsill. I go back into the kitchen. I wash up our plates and stack them and leave the house.

It is dark outside as I walk along the road and the moon has gone but I can smell the lilies in someone's garden and am trying to convince myself that I feel OK, that it went OK really. We had risotto. That was nice. I find myself organising the story for Tess so that it will feel normal to her, so that it will feel like progress. *Hey, it didn't go great, but hey, better luck next time. Hey, at least I tried.* Hey, at least it wasn't a humiliating disaster for both of us. Hey, at least I didn't spend the whole time longing for His presence to lift me up above some miserable drunken rutting, some blind unthinking need. Perhaps now I am worthy to look after my own nephew for two hours.

———

I am on a clifftop above the thrashing sea. Down below, cars and coaches shunt away from each other. There are still some walkers behind me coming back from Belle Tout and the Beachy Head pub, but I am cross-legged, tying back my hair, ready to perform my first public obeisance to Him. My left and right side are both warm with His love and even though the wind is harsh and I am trembling, this is how I will endure for my God, bare-chested before the sea . . .

I burst out laughing. Look at me! Scrawny hippy poseur yoga twat! Postcard clifftop Ibiza worship! I have much to learn and look around joyfully to see if any passing walkers can share in this recognition of my own folly, but there is nothing but the gorse. The gorse of course! Where's my horse, gorse?

After a while I just collect my things and put my T-shirt and jumper back on. Then, at the top of the path, He says, 'Run.

219

Leap out. Become rare. A spark of fire,' and so, stilted at first, but then loosening, bounding, galloping wildly down the side of the Seven Sisters, I run at an impossible pace, somewhere between falling and flying, barely breathing, breathless with exhilaration and joy, letting out a cry that carries me all the way down before slowing and steadying to a blissful giggling stop.

'Every shade of fire into my lungs,' He says as I pant, bent over, hands on knees, the sea air stripping out the layers of my old life. This ocean before me, this sky above – it all explodes as laughter! This is my life now! I am God-intoxicated! My solemn oath, my purpose, to serve Him, to prepare and to train, to purify my consciousness, to become Self-Awakened, to await my mission, to feel, to know that there is no difference between me and this ocean foam, this plastic bottle, this Wotsits crisp packet, this visitors' centre.

And then, for the first time, He grants me the golden light.

Shafts of gold rain into my heart. This is what it's like to die, to be born. I am connected to everything, I am everything – oh Malamock!

My soul bursts.

17

What I've decided to do today is cook myself some pasta. I come to this conclusion at about 2.30 p.m. after waking up to watch *Loose Women* and helping them lament the illness of their co-presenter Lynda Bellingham. She is dying of cancer. I regret forcing her into my shower at Hilldean.

'I'm going to cook some pasta,' I say out loud, 'OK then,' but don't move, weary from the effort required to make even this thrilling declaration. How many alarms across how many devices set at brief and constant intervals to incant against the heavy spell of medication? Even they could only prise open a quarter eye as I acknowledged my position once more at the bottom of the morning's well yet still I had to seize the rope, to hoist myself up and out with nothing but sheer will to propel me, bones and flesh pleading for me to let go, to fall back into the comforts of non-existence. Why turn the TV on in the first place? Why fight? Why tumble out of bed like a man with a gut wound, groping for some stimulus, for something that might drag me to the next phase of waking?

Pasta. My mind wanders away, trying to divine where the urge for pasta has come from as I don't really like pasta . . . The advertisements haven't started yet so it is nothing to do with some lady with huge lips slurping spaghetti in Tuscany and giving me the wink. Is it possible that my body is communicating with me via the subconscious? That there is some deficiency in my diet, something I am depriving myself of? But pasta is made out of wheat and I eat bread every day. No, that is a shit theory . . . shit . . . very shit . . . *Aaaaarrrrghhh! Up up up! Get up!* I heave myself up and turn off the television, which feels like a tremendous act of liberation but also makes the flat very quiet. Saul is moving about upstairs.

The showerhead brings me further into the world and, after washing, I take my meds and roll a cigarette and drink coffee, booting up my computer. The brightness of the screen does something to pull me further into the world, and I look at Facebook. Everyone is having a marvellous time. Sandy Bears is having a marvellous time. Phoebe is on a bridge. I turn on Radio 4 with BBC iPlayer. It is *The World at One* with Martha Kearney. Martha is halfway through telling me that one of the oldest Mayan temples in Belize has been bulldozed by a construction company looking for gravel. 'It was thought to be over 2,300 years old.'

'What?' I yawn at her. 'There's gravel everywhere!'

'Archaeologists say that the destruction of ancient temples is an endemic problem,' Martha replies.

I go to the window to check what sort of world we are living in while Martha starts talking to someone else. I roll another cigarette and make another coffee. Why don't they bulldoze Crowborough if they need gravel so badly?

I sit down at the computer and click on BBC Good Food. I begin researching pasta dishes. They have 471 recipes. Pasta with Creamy Greens and Lemon. Summer Pea Pasta. Ten-minute Pasta. Bacon, Spinach and Gorgonzola Pasta. I forget what I am doing for a moment.

'No time to cook?' asks Summer Pea Pasta, but I have lots of time to cook so I click on Silvana's Mediterranean and Basil

Pasta: 'Silvana's fast, easy and healthy vegetarian pasta is perfect for a midweek meal.'

It is midweek. I am a vegetarian. I need to be healthy. I can't really cook so it needs to be easy. The only problem is that it is fast, and I can't do anything fast, but I feel confident that I can slow it right down. I look at the ingredients: two red peppers, two red onions, three garlic cloves, one teaspoon of caster sugar, olive oil, one kilo of small ripe tomatoes, pasta, basil leaves, parmesan. The only thing I think I have is pasta. I go to the kitchenette and open the cupboard.

The cupboard does not respond well to sudden light, accustomed to being left alone in the dark as the food I actually eat comes and goes on the sideboard. Ancient Marmite is oozing in the tar of its own senescence. There are abandoned cereals and tins. A packet of seed has split open. I push things around, looking for the pasta I am sure is hiding out in there. Instead I find a bottle of pasta sauce flowering with a fascinating grey mould that looks a bit like an aerial view of some mountains poking through cloud. After imagining myself as a kind of airplane that looks like a giant face, I throw it away. The closest thing I have to any of the ingredients is a quarter inch of sunflower oil.

I decide to go to the shops. I leave the radio on so that it fills the room with noise that will greet me when I come back. I put on my Barbour and go outside. It is raining and overcast and I don't have an umbrella and remember or half remember a Chinese proverb about running and walking in the rain being the same so the wise man walks so I walk like a wise man until I decide to confront the proverb and simultaneously defend my wisdom because the rain is accelerating down my back. A car with its windscreen wipers rowing furiously beeps and I wave, assuming that the driver knows me but perhaps they do not. Cars are really just like psychiatrists: they only know how to make one noise.

I walk past the Baptist church and Smugglers Lane, up into town, to the statue of Arthur Conan Doyle. I could head up the hill to Lidl but Morrisons is more welcoming and what am I doing again? Pasta. I am cooking pasta today.

I go through the car park and pull out one of the trolleys lined up next to the photo booth. I take the lift up into the shop, skating myself into the aisles and past a huge woman in a mobility scooter who is staring at the mist streaming from tin pipes across the vegetables. A manageress is ticking off two spotty shelf-stackers and I say hello to Michael Hague who I went to school with, but he doesn't reply because he is shoplifting.

People who have lost each other are tutting and turning at the aisle ends. The refrigeration system is broken and there are shelves of cheese buzzing with distress. I find a block of parmesan but have forgotten to write the ingredients down. What were the other ingredients? The parmesan is one pound ninety-nine. I drop it into my trolley, worried because I won't like eating this cheese by itself. What else? The only thing I can remember is the kilo of tomatoes. I go to the veg aisle. A packet of tomatoes is ninety-six pence. One pound ninety-nine plus ninety-six pence . . . equals what? My brain is too clouded and heavy to deal with putting the numbers together. Two pounds? Three pounds? Four pounds? I feel ashamed. Whatever the answer it's too expensive and I can't even remember what else the recipe asks for and now Silvana's Mediterranean and Basil Pasta is just some weird dream, just another thing I can't do. I have drifted towards the meat counter by mistake and am confronted by bloody lumps of beef and lamb and think of the screams and suffering of all these creatures just so they could have their muscles arranged into a happy meat face sculpted by two adolescent butchers.

'Can I help?' says the female one, young and blonde in a hairnet.

'Too late,' I say and walk away, pushing the trolley down the aisles without purpose. Outside huge windows the world shakes with water.

'What's all that?' Ted Atkins is peering into my trolley with a couple of two-litre bottles of cider, one in the crook of each arm as if they are twin babies. He is wearing a bobble hat, his ruddy face clay-fired by the sun.

'I was going to cook some pasta.'

'Oooooh,' he says in a high pitch. 'Pasta, pasta, pasta.'

'Yep.'

'Almost didn't recognise you upright,' says Ted, perhaps because he finds me asleep around town a lot. 'There's a good spot underneath the cheese counter,' he whispers conspiratorially. 'Have you checked her out?' Ted does a mime which I think is of him looking up someone's skirt.

'OK Ted.' But Ted isn't there any more, and I'm not sure how long I've been standing there facing a wall of pasta sauces. I take down a can of tomato sauce that is on special offer for thirty-nine pence. I find some M Savers spaghetti for twenty pence and take out Silvana's parmesan and dump it in the chocolate rack, pushing my trolley into line and queue and pay and look at the people all about me and the cashier who is joking about the weather and think I would prefer every one of their lives to mine and then scold myself because I don't know anything about their lives.

I wrap the pasta and the tomato sauce in a plastic bag and stick it in my pocket. My jaw is hurting. I must have been clenching my teeth.

Out on the road I feel every drop of rain as a personal slight and realise that I'm walking back without the toothpaste I actually need, the toothpaste that I have been trying to remember to buy for days.

At home I discover I have left the front door open and it

is wet inside. The radio is still playing and I take my coat off and shut the door. As I mop up all the rainwater with a towel I notice a packet of spaghetti on the sideboard next to a box of clozapine. It wasn't hiding in the cupboard, it was right there in front of me all the time and I didn't see it. How is that even possible? Now I have two packets of pasta and I don't even like pasta very much. I'm only cooking it to pass the time.

I pull a saucepan out of the sink and fill it from the tap, turn on the hob, and set the pan down to boil. I stand there watching the water as it begins to shift, tiny bubbles firing upwards from the bottom, steam waving up off the surface, the water humming and pitching until it rumbles and starts to thrash. Then I put my hand in.

18

Byron smiles, passing me the coffee. 'It's only three hours,' I say. His smile widens. He is very keen for this to work. If this goes well it means that I'm getting better, aren't I, and she doesn't have to worry about me any more, does she; she can look after Byron instead. She can marry him and move into his house in Eastbourne. He must take ages over his hair.

Tess, bright-eyed and glittering, is sashed by a tiny handbag with a gold strap, Lily is at her friend's house, Ben is in his pyjamas, Byron is wearing a blazer, and I am wearing a bandage wrapped round one hand like a shit Michael Jackson. We won't be later than eleven, Tess is saying, you can put him to bed in a minute, you can read him a— and I break her off to remind her again that I have put him to bed a thousand times.

'He's done it a thousand times!' Byron says, patting me on the arm, which makes me put the coffee down. Byron winks at me and I am uncertain what this means. 'How do I look?' she asks him.

'Gorgeous. Perfect.'

'Tom?'

'Very nice. You look very nice.'

'Why don't you believe it when I say it?'

'Because you say it all the time,' I say, which is true, but it comes out all wrong. What I meant was *it's nice that you say it all the time* but I know it sounded like *you say it all the time it has no meaning* and Byron ices up with a *what is your problem* look for just a split of a split second before plastering it over with a smile, which he is very good at because he used to be a plasterer.

'I hope you have a really nice really great time,' I say with an overspill of earnestness to counter my last comment, but now it sounds like sarcasm. Oh I'm just trying to be normal. Just trying to play it all straight.

Tess says thanks and kisses Ben. We move into the hallway.

'So I'm going to lock the door?' she says.

'OK.'

'But what if there's a fire?'

'Why would there be a fire?'

'What do you think?' she asks Byron, who simply breathes in through his nose and lifts his shoulders. 'You're not going to fall asleep before Ben's in bed are you? Promise? OK – I'm not going to lock the door. Will you drink the coffee now?'

'Doing it right now.'

'Bye then.' And she shuts the door and I can see through the frosted glass she's hesitating and then Byron says something and she's back, shouting through the letter box. 'You're going to put him to bed now then?'

'Right now.'

They leave. I pick up the coffee and take a sip. It is so thick and strong it's disgusting. I put it down again.

'Time for bed, Ben.'

'No,' he says, 'don't want to.'

I sit down on the couch and cross my legs watching him build up a platform of Lego towers, each one made of different-shaped bricks of the same colour crowned with a Lego toilet or a Lego bath. While he is building up one corner with a yellow tower he leans his head on the foot of my crossed leg so that it bends a little under his weight, a tender elegant suspension, and we stay like that until he is finished.

'Look,' he says, 'look.'

'I'd like to live there.'

'You can't.'

'Do you want to go to bed now?'

'What happened to your hand?'

'It was an accident.'

'Did someone shoot you?'

'A monkey bit me.' Ben spins round to face me directly and folds his arms, his forehead heavy with suspicion. 'I was climbing up a mountain looking for gold and it was very, very hot and halfway up there was this tree, an apple tree, and I thought I could sit under the tree and eat some apples away from the sun but when I got close there was this monkey sitting in the tree and maybe she had her babies in the tree or something but she got very angry and started chucking apples at me, which was OK at first because I was hungry, but then the monkey jumped out of the tree and tried to bite me in the neck. I only just got my hand in the way – like this – so it bit my hand instead.'

'Where is there a mountain with monkeys and apples and gold?'

'Crowborough.'

'You're lying.'

'Just behind Waitrose. So I went to the doctor's and he put a bandage on my hand, but it's too late.'

'What do you mean "too late"?'

'Crowborough apple monkeys are very infectious. Won't be long now.'

'Until what?'

'Until I turn into a . . .' I sniff a few times, push out my jaw and talk a few breaths *иии-иии*. I push my chest out, kneel on the floor, hands bent *ооо-ааа-ооо*. Ben wriggles backwards,

229

giggling. I crouch and sniff and pat him on the head with a bent hand then poke around at him as if he is a new object until he turns monkey himself.

We are both making monkey noises bouncing from floor to couch and back again, howling, chasing each other about the room and rolling around until I go into the kitchen area and open the fridge and make a noise that means *do you want something?* And he screeches back a noise that means *yes* so I take out some cheese slices and fling them in his face. I throw up a hand and screech *go to bed* and he jumps up and down screeching *no no no* and I growl and then spring, chasing him across the living room into the kitchen around the table then out the door, up the stairs, and Ben goes into the bathroom, *ooo-oooo*ing now that we're both out of breath.

He picks his toothbrush out from the cup, puts toothpaste on it and brushes his teeth while I pick at the paste with my bent monkey finger, tasting it as if it's something strange, howling with the sweet mint of it. When he has rinsed his mouth out, he monkeys himself into his bedroom and gets into bed and points at the pile of books and says *ooo-oooo-ooo*. I spring onto the bed with one of the books and tumble on him with a badly held upside-down book in my hands. I turn the pages and read the words first in monkey language *aaaa-ooo-aa-oooo-ah*, and then I begin to read the story normally, taking in Ben's head next to mine, how his eyelids lower while he sucks his thumb, the warm biscuit smell of him, how I forfeited this kind of love for Malamock, this sleepy small sweet soft—

I am waking up.

Ben isn't there.

'Ben?'

I swing off the bed, stand up, take in the room.

'Ben?'

I am in the landing.

'Ben?'

I trot down the stairs.

'Ben? Ben?'

The door is shut but there is no one in the living room. I race around the house. No one in the kitchen. No one in the laundry room *oh my God oh my God oh my God* 'BEN!'

Ben makes a monkey noise from the upstairs bathroom. He is looking down the stairs at me *ooo-ooo?*

I take him back to bed and read him another story. He is disappointed that I have turned back into a miserable fidgeting human. Once his light is off I clear up the cheese slices and neck the cold oily coffee and watch TV until they come back.

Tess drops me home and I try to sleep but I can't sleep. I watch television but everything annoys me, the stupidity of it, all these idiots! I try to read but of course I cannot – I can't concentrate on anything! It is all a failure, just one more fucking failure.

I turn off the lamp. My room is lit by the faint blue light of the computer's power cable. It is perhaps one in the morning, or two, or three, and I am gulping, unable to swallow properly, my stomach hovering in my chest, overwhelmed with a sudden panic, a desperate urge to call Tess, to hear her speak some solid words, but to wake her at this time would be unkind *and I must not do it, I should not do it, I am going to do it – no I should ring Missy! Missy won't mind* – this thought shedding itself of Missy, emerging as Phoebe and I consider once again Malamock's trick, how His will makes and unmakes the world. Yes, I am punished. Yes, I am abandoned. Yet the stones of darkness have not come. He has not annihilated me. Does this mean He still holds plans for me? That He may yet forgive me?

My pulse accelerates again. I touch my forehead and feel the sweat. I am hot and my mind lurches towards something un-named and terrible, some kind of falling apart, and I throw back my covers as if that is an act of courage and stand up. Immediately I lose heart. Where's my phone? I've lost my phone and anyway that is a lie, I do not want to talk to Missy or Phoebe or Tess – I want to speak to Him! I want to hear His voice and feel His glory, the light of the otherworld, just one more time, just to hear Him say *Thomas* or—

'Fool!' I say out loud. *Look at you standing naked in the dark unable to decide anything or do anything.* I should listen to music. I should . . . I go into the bathroom and turn the light on and look at myself. 'Coward!' I say, vibrating from self-disgust, and the decision to stop my medication creeps out from under this pitiful fretting, out from between memories of when I last stopped such heavy doses of clozapine and became spectacularly demented, Sheldrake almost scoffing at me when I was practically on all fours in his office as for him this proved the depth of my illness, when it was only proof of the addictive nature of the drug itself, but I was incapable of making such an argument at that moment so it came out in howls.

Out of the bathroom I throw back the curtain of my clothes cupboard, pulling out the bundles and the plastic bags and all the other shit until I find one bag stuffed with medication from previous eras and tip it all out onto the bed. There are enough strips of clozapine here of lower strengths and I place the 750 mg next to the 500 mg and the 300 mg and the 100 mg and the 50 mg and the 12.5 mg, satisfied that there lies my way out. I return to the bathroom and pick up the zopiclone saying to it 'You. Because you do nothing,' and pop one tablet out into the toilet and then pop out one tablet from my current clozapine prescription and cast that into the toilet saying 'you fuck you,' then open the dosette box and take out one tablet of bildinocycline and drop it in and flush. The tablets do not disappear, they only bob around, so I have to push my arm in and send them off round the U-bend and then wash my arm, staring at myself in the mirror. 'One at a time,' I say, wagging a finger at myself like a naughty cartoon thief. Yes, Megan could indeed surprise me with an audit at any moment so I will only get rid of these pills *one at a time!* My cunning is extraordinary, oh yes this is a cunning plan and I am a master, a master of cunning and subterfuge.

'Idiot!'

I go back into the room, turning off the bathroom light and then sit in the armchair in the dark and wait. I watch myself, examining the currents of my agitation, where they are eddying, swelling, until I realise that I am idiotic enough to be secretly hoping that this act alone, this pathetic act of flushing some pills down a toilet will be enough to bring Him back to me. Ha! Thomas the Fool in his armchair naked in the dark. I slap on the wall switch so the main light is on, swivelling the armchair around to face the front door, opening it, sitting down again to face such complete dark as only light can bring. Come and see me! Come in and see the idiot!

It does not take long.

Moths, daddy-long-legs, ladybirds, mosquitoes, a cloud of midges and gnats and even smaller creatures, flying motes of dust almost without a body – they all hurtle in. I am below them, staring up at the ceiling light. A moth lands on the armchair of a type I have never seen before, wings plain and silver, antennae long and curled. There is an enormous constellation of night creatures around the bulb now and then I see something at the doorstep.

Going over, I crouch down, bracing myself against the cold as a huge leopard slug ripples itself into my home. I am looking in at a flat full of insects. It's as if the doorbell has rung and the insects have just found me there, naked on their doorstep.

233

JUNE

19

Richard the Research Assistant looks tired. I notice for the first time how he gulps a little as he talks, how his hands feel like chicken breasts. Soft hands, digestive problems, hair crusading against itself – Richard is a modern.

I make him a cup of tea. He sits down in the chair and I sit on the bed. He fiddles with his satchel until he finds the right PANSS assessment sheet and I prepare to parry. He's wearing a baseball T-shirt with the number 8 on it. *Ha!*

'So,' he says, looking at my hand still lumpy and discoloured. 'How are you feeling?'

'Well, Richard, I have to say, *extraordinarily* well.'

'Great. That's great. Can you explain to me a little bit more what you mean by that?'

'There's a light at the end of the tunnel. I can feel myself getting better. It's as though . . . there's something to live for.'

'Still no voice?'

'No voice. No light. No "*Hello Thomas*",' I say, like a cheesy ghost.

'Any problems with taking the medication?'

'Do you want to check?'

'No, that's fine. You look well.'

'I'm spending a lot of time in the water.'

'Fantastic.'

'Three times a week in the pool. Sometimes four.'

'And you weren't doing any exercise at all before the trial, is that right?'

'I didn't see the point.'

'What do you mean?'

'I didn't see the point of being a hamster, you know, on a wheel going round and round. In a gym or something. I didn't see it as part of a spiritual life.'

'And now?'

'I like it. I like being out of the house. I like socialising with all the elderly and unemployed people there. I know you can't tell me whether or not they're placebos – but are they? Placebos?'

'No one knows. Sorry, Tom. It's all coded. Now then, what are your thoughts about the Octopus God? Do you still believe in him?'

Having this conversation is like a lawnmower across my brain, back and forth, back and forth. There is a rawness to being in the world. Everything is too loud or too bright, too quiet or too dark, as if I have been readjusted to the wrong setting. But I have energy. At Richard's feet are the books I can read again. Herodotus. Rumi. Rilke. *Pleasure of Ruins* by Rose Macaulay.

'I don't believe He talks to me, no.'

'But do you believe he exists?'

'I do believe in God, yes.'

'But do you believe that God is an octopus?'

'I believe that God takes many forms. The divine is within everything, including the octopus, and including you, Richard.' Finger point. Wink. Ho yeah.

'OK, so what's slightly concerning me, Tom, is that there's

238

a very heavy smell of incense in here. Are you praying again?'

'It's true I've been lighting a lot of incense but that's just to get rid of the smell.'

'Of what?'

'Tobacco.'

'You could try giving up?'

'I thought you were in favour of medication.'

Richard points his pen at me, as if to say *you got me there, dude*.

'So you would have no problem taking down this collage on the wall, for example. Dismantling the whole set-up here.' *Dis-mantle*. He doesn't even realise the aptness of his own words!

'Just because I don't hear the voice any more doesn't mean I've stopped being interested in marine biology. Actually I was planning to extend the collage with some other cephalopods. Giant squid. Cuttlefish.'

Richard is writing. I can see by his pen movement he is ringing things: numbers from 1 to 7, from 'absent' to 'extreme'; delusions, grandiosity, emotional withdrawal, poor attention. I make a mental note to download a PANSS from the internet before Richard's next visit and score him while he is scoring me.

'So,' he starts again, 'The Octopus God is real. Yes or no.'

His phone plays its guitar – divine intervention! Richard pulls it out from his back pocket and his face shrinks.

'Sorry,' he says, 'I've got to . . . do you mind?' Richard answers, cupping his mouth, getting up, searching for privacy. I open the front door for him as he bumps about like a summer's wasp, finally flying out. When he returns his face is blotchy.

'Girlfriend problems?'

'I—' he hesitates. I've guessed correctly.

'Have you lost your girlfriend to another man?'

'I don't think we should be having this conversation.'

239

'That's just happened to me.'

'I—'

'It's OK, Richard. I don't really want to talk about it either.'

'It's a bit . . . Sorry.'

'If you turn right past the bins and go into the field you can follow the hedgerow round to the woods. The sweet lime trees smell absolutely amazing at the moment. It's a really nice walk. Might help you centre yourself.'

'Thanks Tom, but I think we should probably continue with the assessment.'

He doesn't ask me any more direct questions about the Octopus God. He asks me if I think I have schizophrenia. I tell him I think I did have schizophrenia and now I think I am recovering from schizophrenia. He looks insanely pleased.

My days pass in prayer. The flat is stripped of alcohol, empty cans and bottles cleared in preparation for His return, every single one dropped into the bin bag with an apology, a plea for forgiveness. On my walks I find things that might please Him, minute masterpieces of His creation, feathers and stones and flowers placed carefully around the shrine. I thank Him for pieces of good fortune like kind words from someone in the street, an 'A' for Lily's homework, things going well for Tess, or just the sun breaking through clouds. I list my faults and crimes and start every session of worship with their acknowledgement, building up to my Great Crime, my rebellion against God, holding my heart out to Him, begging for forgiveness.

Alongside my countless prayers of apology there are three major sessions of worship: morning, noon and night. Sometimes I can spend an hour with my forehead crushed against the carpet before Him, grinding into the floor with humility and submission, trying to clear my mind so that I may once again find His voice.

Sometimes I wake from dreams that have featured Him but they do not reflect the force of His presence and I am left only with the receding fog of my own longing. I have stopped imitating Him, calling out loud '*Thomas*' or '*Fabrications out*' in case that angers Him. When I am not vortexed in prayer or preparing to pray, I am performing good works. I help anyone I can find, anyone in need of assistance, elderly people or lost walkers. Drivers trying to reverse. Animals and insects in distress or danger. I have distracted a dog so that a squirrel could escape down from a tree. I have saved flies from the spider. I have foregone masturbation and considered smashing my computer against the wall out of shame at all the pornography I have watched. At one point I marched it to the recycling bin but then relented and fetched it back. Perhaps I should not have done that. That was a lack of courage. I must show Him I am not a coward. Destroying my computer is the only thing I have wavered on, the only thing I have not pursued to its utmost in humbling myself. Is this what is preventing Him from coming back to me? Am I failing this test? I lean down to rip out the power cable from the wall when my phone plays its glockenspiel. Phoebe.

How I have pined for her to call me, yet now I just grin with determination, offering my phone upwards. 'See?' I decline her call. I am still staring at the mobile's screen when it tells me she has left a message. Perhaps she needs me. Perhaps she has left Ronny or maybe Ronny is dead – but I stop myself and offer the phone up to Him once more. I activate voicemail but when Phoebe starts to speak I delete the message immediately. I place the phone on the table, kneel down at the shrine and wait. Once again I am swept through with self-loathing. Did I think such a pathetic gesture would impress Him? *Idiot!*

I get up again, knees cracking, and sit down to face the computer. In a kind of trance I find myself typing 'how do I get God's voice back how do I contact the spirit world' into Google. The top result is entitled '4 things to do if you can't hear God's voice', yet when I click through it is an article written by someone in prison who believes in Christ. Much of what I find is Christian and foolish and written by people who have clearly never heard God's voice.

As I refine the search to 'making contact with the spirit realm' I come across endless notices and adverts for hippies and charlatans, yet could there be, somewhere here, some kind of genuine intermediary? Could there be someone who can actually help me, someone who can tell me what I am doing wrong? These days apart, savage and unending – are these in fact the stones of darkness? Was it my vanity that imagined an operatic fate, a Promethean hell? Are the stones of darkness really just the walls of my new soul: plain grey and godless?

Eventually I find an institution with credible testimonials, recommended on forums and discussion boards. Audrey Mansfield is the most senior professor at the Academy of Psychic Studies and has been a professional medium for forty years. Though my doubts in all this remain grave, I find myself on a train.

I have not been to London since the day I was hospitalised and sit quietly in my chosen seat, watching the countryside reshuffle itself. I show my ticket without incident. I am not viewed with suspicion by other passengers. I have no pulsations, there is no fear of triggering. How can I ever explain to Tess that everything is wrong?

From London Bridge to Waterloo, on through the cemetery at Earlsfield towards Strawberry Hill. The electronic voice talks occasionally. The sun is going down and the clouds are yellow. We rifle through back gardens, across walkways and balconies of trackside estates but there are no people. It is as if, for the whole sixteen-minute journey, the city is empty. In Wimbledon I walk up the hill into residential streets.

Audrey Mansfield lives in a row of cottages. I check and re-check the address but there is no mistake: it's this little cottage. Number 3. There is no institution, no seat of learning. There is a garden, a gate and the noise of a dog inside.

Audrey is a bright old lady with bobbed dark hair. As I step inside my heart drops further. The house is white and comfortable, patio windows looking out into a garden full of foxgloves and the evening sky. She lights candles. She makes me peppermint tea. She puts her dog in the kitchen. It is only when we sit down with a small table between us with a CD recorder on it that I truly see her eyes. They glow with distant power like a winter sun, and suddenly my misgivings start to lift.

'I'll record everything and give you a CD,' she says, 'because when I'm under I won't remember anything. I'll be talking but if you ask me a question at the end I won't remember what I said so I always like to give people a CD so they can take it home. Have you got any questions before we get started?'

'On the phone you said you talked to spirit guides. Are they former humans or purely spirit beings?'

'Spirit guides are not human, no. One of mine has just told me you came in here with some energy that isn't yours. It's someone else's.'

'Whose?'

'I don't know,' she says with a naughty smile. 'Shall we get started?'

She presses play on the CD recorder and flexes her nostrils, inhaling deeply. 'I'm seeing you in some kind of camouflage uniform. You're cutting through something. Are you in the armed forces?'

'No.'

'But you are troubled. Why don't you tell me why you are here?'

'I used to be able to talk to God, to the Octopus God, but He stopped talking to me and I want to find Him again.'

'You heard a spirit voice, like I'm talking to you now?'

'Yes. But He's gone.'

Audrey inhales through her nose, eyes clenched.

'I have someone coming through. It's a lady. She's very well presented. I want to— oh hello, OK – I want to – she's got very big feet. And she's quite pushy. She's very well presented and I want to lie – like this, like Cleopatra, I want to recline, sort of like this. She's got very big feet for a lady. Has your mother passed on?'

'Yes.'

'Is this your mother who's talking to me?'

'Sounds like her, yes.'

'Ooh – ooh – she's very pushy – wait a minute – she's got something to say – yes, OK, OK – she wants to say – OK! – ooh she's ever so pushy, isn't she? She wants to say . . . she's sorry.'

'What for?'

'Did you fight with her a lot?'

'Not really.'

'But there was conflict?'

'Yes.'

'She wants to say she's sorry. I'm feeling very constricted. I'm feeling—' another deep inhalation '. . . I'm feeling very, I don't know, claustrophobic. Was she a bit overbearing sometimes?'

'Yes.'

'And then remote other times?'

'Yes!'

'Cold even? But then in a moment, in a second, a lot of love. Too much love. I'm feeling suffocated – hang on, hang on! Oooh she's a toughie, isn't she? A real old battler. She says she's sorry.'

'OK.'

'She wants you to forgive her.'

'I forgave her a long time ago.'

'She wasn't sure if you really had. Have you?'

'Yes.'

'Sure?'

'Yes.'

'Do you want to say anything to her?'

'Does she know how I can reach the Octopus God?' Audrey inhales. Pauses. Inhales again.

'What do you do? For work.'

'I'm not in work.'

'How long haven't you worked for?'

'Twenty years.'

'Have you been ill?'

'My experiences make work difficult.'

'Spiritual experiences? Because I'm sensing you are an extremely spiritual person. You've got an old soul – not a very old soul, but quite old. And the spiritual experiences – these were with the Octopus God, the voice you were hearing?'

'Yes.'

'I'm asking your mother now . . .' Inhale. Pause. Inhale. '. . . and she's telling me the Octopus God is real.'

'She just said that?'

'But he's not who he says he is. He's a gyalpo, and a mischievous one at that. Can he be nasty to you?'

'He can be but He can also—'

'You see that's false. Are there rules? Do you have to follow rules? They love rules. Getting you to do things is the closest thing they get to feeling things themselves. They're jealous of the physical world. Of feelings.'

'Yes but—'

'I'm sensing – wait – your mother's going now – quickly, do you want to say anything to her? Quickly!'

'Bye? Mum?'

'She's gone. But my spirit guides – I'm sensing – this spirit – you are a very sensitive person. You've got very porous borders, you see, you're vulnerable to gyalpos like this. Did you ever . . .?' She mimes smoking. 'Wacky backy?'

'I did, yes. Long time ago.'

'Mnnn. You left yourself open.'

'I know. I know that's what happened.'

'You do know, don't you? You are a very, very, incredibly spiritual person, and a very special person, do you know that? You've got light coming off you. Do you play a musical instrument?'

'No.'

'You should. You've got a lot of music in you. I'm hearing – not classical music, sort of folky? Something like that?'

'But the Octopus God – what have I got to do to reconnect with Him?'

'I sense this being is not completely from the light. You have to be careful. This is an important moment. A test.'

'He is testing me?'

'Life – I'm getting – this gyalpo, he confused you with wisdom. There is wisdom there but he's not completely from the light. Wait – I've got someone else coming through. A man. An elderly man. Has your grandfather passed on?'

'But how can I reach Him? And why did He stop talking to me? Is this just punishment for my betrayal or was it really the bildinocycline that—'

'Your grandfather's here. He wants to say something.'

'Can you ask him to wait a second?'

'What?'

'I just – I need to know—'

'He's not very happy about being asked to wait.'

'He was never very happy.'

'Ooof! He's huffing. He's puffing.'

'Can we go back to—'

'You've wasted your life, he's saying. Oooh he's very cross. He's very – I don't know . . .' She blows out her cheeks. 'Was he a drinker? I feel all clumsy.'

'Not really.'

'There's a funny smell.'

'He had bad breath.'

'Oh yes, that's it. Pooof! He's wagging a finger.'

'Which hand?'

'Right hand. Like this. Wag, wag, wag. Don't waste your life.'

'He didn't have a right hand. He lost it in a farming accident.'

'He's got it back.'

'Why's he still so angry then?'

'He's angry with you. Do you want to say something to him?'

'Does he know how I can reach the Octopus God? Do you know?'

Inhale. Pause.

'"*Forget the Octopus God*," he says. "*You're wasting your life.*"'

When the session is over she gives me a CD in a sleeve with the date written on it. We stand in her hallway and I pay her the entire £70 I got from doing the drug trial.

'Hang on,' she says, 'you've still got that energy on your back that isn't yours.' She presses her hands against my back and belly, then runs them up and down, almost as if she's tickling me. She checks my eyes. 'No,' she says, 'still there.' She does it again then puts one foot on the bottom stair and claps her hand over the newel. 'There. Gone now. You are a very special person. I do hope you know that and cherish yourself and don't let anyone or anything take you over, right? Now get out of my house and go have yourself a wonderful life.'

When the train arrives back in Crowborough I get out onto the platform but sit down on the bench, watching the commuters. I take the CD out of its sleeve and try breaking it.

20

Tess is expecting me to be more grateful I think when she grants me the favour of doing her the favour of looking after her children for an afternoon, although still within the controlled environment of the llama farm in Wych Cross. My lack of gratitude is translated as worry. When I say no, Tess, I'm not worried about a llama farm, she says why do you look so tense, and Ben says what's a *lamlafam?*

'Psychedelic chickens,' I say. 'Sheep crossed with donkeys.'

'There are peacocks,' says Tess, 'and llamas.'

She drops us all off at the reception. Lily is complaining but in a theatrical way because she knows I won't interfere with her being on her phone the whole time. Tess has given me money for lunch and we've got two hours before she comes back to pick us up. We wave her off, then immediately fall behind a woman on two walking sticks who moves very slowly indeed. It takes us a full two minutes to get through the double doors into a wall of T-shirts that say *No prob-llama*.

I buy the tickets and feed bags. We get stickers, which Lily puts on her forehead. Ben copies her and so do I. Then we head through another room full of alpaca slippers and hats and knitwear that opens out into a cafeteria and an old Sussex barn converted into a dining room. People smile at us and say hello and then we go outside, picnic tables giving way to a play area with swings, slides, a Winnie-the-Pooh house and a fraying bouncy castle. Moving freely between the picnic tables a tall sleepy white llama, recently shorn, bends his neck to the humans while a peacock squawks and roams. The sun is strong. Everyone is wearing hats and shades and they all give off a particular vibration that is neither wholly threatening nor wholly friendly. I wish I had let Tess smear cream on me as she did with the kids. I don't even have a hat.

We cross the picnic lawn to the stables full of llamas emitting a stewed smell of hay and faeces. Ben runs over to them with his bag of feed. He is wary at first so I feed the animals, their lips tickling the palm of my hand as they snaffle up the pellets. There is something in their eyes that might be sadness or contentment or dreaming or utter stupidity but I don't know, and of course I cannot ask Malamock. Once Lily has fed a few llamas she finds a bench and gets her phone out. Me and Ben go over to the pig pen *Do Not Feed Rita The Pig She Is Pregnant And Will Bite* where the piglets honk and shuffle around a huge knackered she-pig reclining in the shade. Goats mount the fence behind us. The top of my head is burning.

We wander around the goats but Ben is more interested in the four-wheel motorbike a farmworker is using to get around and after the feed bag is empty I look at my phone. We've been here twenty minutes. Suddenly Sandy Bears is coming outside with two elderly women but then I realise it is not Sandy Bears it's just someone who looks like her, yet my pulse rate does not return to normal.

Ben seems happy with the suggestion that we go to the play area. He wants to go into the Winnie-the-Pooh house but there are two boys in there and one of them says 'No. You can't come in. This is our house. No,' keeping his hand on the little swing door. Ben looks up at me. I cannot tell which of these picnic tables contains the parents, so I say to the boy, 'Come on, there's plenty of room.'

'No,' he says, 'we're working. We're doing work in here.'

'Why don't we go over there?' I say to Ben, pointing at another little wooden house on stilts with a slide coming out of it, but Ben shakes his head. He knows all about Winnie-the-Pooh and wants to see what his house looks like. I search around again for the parents then put my hand on the little door but the boy leans out of its window, clamping himself against it.

'No!' he says, 'We're working! Go away!'

'We've all got to share though, haven't we?' I say, but the boy refuses. Ben looks up at me and I look round at Lily who is deeply absorbed in her phone. Then the door flies open. The two boys are wrestling out the little table. They throw out the little stool and come out themselves.

'There you go,' I say to Ben with a little push. 'It's free now. Your turn.' But Ben has been intimidated and is now reluctant. The boy picks up the stool. 'Let's throw it,' he says to his friend, nodding towards Ben, 'at him.'

'No one is throwing any stools at anyone!' I sergeant-major, and suddenly their mother is next to me. She chews and wipes crumbs from the edge of her mouth. She doesn't look at me, she doesn't seem to see me or Ben at all and says, 'Now no messing about, you two.' The boy drops the stool and the two of them run off to the slide. The mother waddles back to her table, still without acknowledging me, and Ben goes into the house and shuts the door. Aghast, I take the sticker off my forehead, watching this sparrow-souled woman in her print dress as she sits back down with her group. Ben comes out of the little house again and takes the stool in. He shuts the door and sits down on it. We are staring at each other through the empty window. He takes the sticker off his head.

Hiding underneath a parasol, the back of my neck burnt and

ringing, I buy the kids fishcakes and chips for lunch. There is a scandal at Lily's school. Two married teachers have run off with each other. She tells us the whole story while the peacock circles our table but all I can think of is the Octopus God. He is here, somewhere, running through everything, yet I cannot see Him, I cannot feel Him, I cannot hear Him! I am buried alive beneath the stones of darkness. Fishcake and chips. Despair and panic. *Is this it?* I am struggling to keep control of myself. Some bikers turn up and have tea and scones.

Once we've finished the fishcakes, Ben wants to go on the bouncy castle. The two boys are on it. I am steeling myself against these mean little gits but as soon as we get there they smile and ask Ben what his name is. Then they're all playing together. They're jumping and falling and bouncing off the walls and laughing and I walk a little way back to where there is a bench for parents, watching the boys, praying out to Malamock to come back to me with all my force and being. Oh Malamock!

Eventually Ben has had enough and is about to climb out when one of the boys bounces behind him, throwing Ben up in the air. He lands awkwardly, slips off the bouncy castle, and hits the ground – *thud* – with his face.

Wailing, lip gashed, nose bleeding, I sweep him up and carry him to the sink to mop his face but it is more shock than pain, and within a few moments he's calm again. Lily hugs him as his shoulders heave out the final sobs, his face red with tears. I've got enough money left for lollipops. We all have one. Ben doesn't seem to mind about the fall any more but I remain exceedingly agitated.

I was on the bench designated for parents. I was as close as I was meant to be. It wasn't my fault. There was nothing I could have done to prevent this. He's a little boy. Little boys fall over. There is no meaning to this.

When Tess pulls up he's licking his second lollipop, holding my hand, and I'm already saying he's fine, everything is fine—

'Oh my God!' she rips off the seat belt, sprinting around the car to hold his head. 'What happened?'

'It's OK. He just fell off the bouncy castle, he's fine—'

'And where were you?'

I open my mouth, all my prepared explanations at the ready, but instead I just take a breath and say, very slowly and calmly, 'Ben falling over has nothing to do with my mental health.'

JULY

21

Folding back the duvet with a final yawn I roll upwards, sitting on the edge of the bed. My line of sight falls directly on the shrine. The spoons are gone.

I stare at the empty space, blinking for a moment then walk over, patting the floor where they were laid out. I spin round, examining the room, then go to the kitchenette and open the drawer where I always keep the spoons now before Megan comes round, but they are not there. I know I left them at the shrine. I prayed in front of them before I went to bed.

I search the bathroom. I look in the cupboards. I look in the fridge. I open the front door and look out, checking on the world, then turn round and stand in front of the shrine again. The spoons have vanished.

Snatching up my phone, I ring Tess.

'Hello Hex— Oh, morning you.'

'You didn't come round last night did you?'

'Oh man did you black out again? What happened? Are you OK?'

'No I'm not drinking. I stopped all that, I told you. Listen, you didn't come round while I was asleep, did you?'

'Tom. What is going on?'

'Nothing, it's fine. So the answer is "no". We're agreed.'

'Hey, what's going on with you?'

'I'll call you later.'

'Tom?'

'Bye-bye,' I hang up then scroll to Megan's number and hover over it but don't call her. If she came round and I was asleep she'd wake me up. She often finds me asleep. Anyway, Megan would never steal spoons.

I call Missy. It goes straight to voicemail. I leave her an excited message. I've been steadily increasing the number of times I pray to Him but last night was the first time I prayed at the shrine *eight times!* Eight is His number! And something's happened! A miracle! *Call me call me!*

I open the front door again just to marvel at the world, to inhale its troubling beauty. Saul is coming down the steps.

'*Bonjour!*' I say to Saul. He pulls a face. 'Saul you didn't – I mean, you wouldn't . . . no.'

'Eh?'

He is carrying two bags and is trying to see inside my bedsit. His tracksuit top says 'Lonsdale'.

'You didn't come into my flat last night, did you?'

'*What?*'

'Didn't think so. Really.'

'What are you trying to say?'

Saul is glaring at me.

'Do you need a hand with those bags?' Saul looks down at his bags. He makes a dismissive little *harrumph* noise, then walks off to his Mini. Oh Saul.

I shut the door and return to the site of the miracle. Now that my being, my soul, is fully possessed with the reality of it I calmly, solemnly, get to my knees, pull out all the stubs from the incense holder and throw them into the bin. I open a new packet of incense and take out a handful of sticks, pushing them into the holder, lighting them all. I light the candle, ring the bell, and then bend down, my face pressed against the floor, readying myself for an almighty prayer when my phone rings. I open my eyes, looking backwards through my armpit. I can see the spoons under the armchair. I must have put them there when I was cleaning.

There is a great heaving wind and the trees creak and shake as if wild things are jumping between them. I walk along a tractor track deep with rainwater, through a patch of wood-land devoured by harvesters and knuckleboom loaders. The beechwood has been thinned recently, their branches left to rot down. Crows call out complaints. I head off the track into dense birch coppicing. The ridge stoops sharply down towards the stream and a grove of scotch pines. Within their circle the ground is dry, brushed with cones and mast, silent except for a woodpecker and the rife.

There I lie down, star-shaped, without Saul and Nika above me, and yell so loud that He must hear me even from the other world. I yell and yell and scream out for Him until the screams turn to blasphemy and then fists of other noise as I sprawl about in the soil, sobbing on the worms.

It is dark and calm when I walk back. Moleish pook-hale cottages peer at me through the trees with their tender golden promises but all I can do is return to no. 1 Etchingham House and open its door and close its door and stand in my stone box with the radio left on and the smell of tobacco and sandalwood incense and the sound of Saul and Nika's television. I go back out and carry on walking along the road. Tess calls but I don't answer.

A breeze combs the trees and leaves them prattling. The road dips and curves and flattens past white cottages clad in shiplap, farm tracks leading to barns and piles of tyres all yellow in the yard light. Headlights swoop past. Through an ironwood I hear a manic rustling and glimpse the white backside of a frightened bolting muntjac, tail upright, and I follow it, breaking through the ironwood into coppiced birch, up the steep bank and out onto a gullied ride. I use the screen of my phone to keep on the track and walk around a group of grey rocks coated in lichen and liverwort. I find a nook formed by a holly trunk squeezing out from the base of one huge striated wall of sandstone and sit down. There is much owl activity, as if they have all suffered some great disturbance, and I roll a cigarette and listen to them, smoking, as the moon recasts the woods in blues and silver. My phone rings. Missy.

'Hey—' she says, then there is a kind of jostling sound and the phone goes dead.

I ring back and no one answers. A couple come through the woods with a powerful torch. They are talking loudly and are dressed in bright colours. They walk through the rocks right past me but I have become invisible so they do not see me or even smell the smoke. Once the cigarette is finished I call Missy again but still no answer. I put both hands in my pockets and tuck myself as far into the nook as I am able.

22

There are lovers beside me fighting over chips, hair sprawling in the wind. I walk along the shoreline to the big wheel. Empty deckchairs. Some kids playing in the sea with a tape measure. I go back up to the road and there is the Brighton Sea Life Aquarium, a group of families and prams outside the entrance. I pay the admission fee in a room full of cartoon creatures.

Children's voices mix with the sound of water tanks. A young girl asks me to sit on a bench in front of a green screen. She takes a picture. There is a television above her and I am on the screen surrounded by an underwater cartoon fantasy. She lets me go and I walk into the Victorian arcade, gothic arches rainbow-lit, tanks on either side: carp, tench, bream, a giant spider crab upright against the glass, catfish pale and lurid. The din of machines is so loud it's like being beneath a train. The lights change in slow disco from blue to green to yellow to red. Another young girl asks me if I want to touch a starfish. I walk past her through the café into a false rainforest with soft woodchip flooring, garish plastic plants and turtles. Then I am in a low corridor with MDF boards spray-painted to look like iron. 'Welcome to the *Nautilus*,' says a voice, 'You are about to embark on a fascinating journey to explore the ocean depths.'

I come out to rousing cinematic music. Water glitters above me. Sharks and turtles and the false face of a stingray glide overhead. On the other side of this tunnel I can see a wall of cartoon octopuses, a tank full of haddock and a narrow window of shogun-faced lionfish. There are silhouettes of octopuses on the floor, the walls full of factoids, directions, appeals for charitable support and protection. I am back in the Victorian arcade. Toilets, video displays, a photo booth. There is a doorway marked *Octopus Garden* and I enter into its dark corners, turning again, and again, and again.

A giant Pacific octopus lies across a flowerpot and an infant's rocking horse, its mantle furious red, arms as if wrapped in caul. Kneeling in front of the tank I lay one hand on the glass and wait. I lay on both hands but the octopus does not come close. Instead, billowing out the cloak of itself, it drifts away from me, now a frosted white.

'Please help me!' I whisper, but the octopus camouflages itself, stone-coloured, squeezing into the furthest recesses of the tank. 'Hey!' I bang both hands against the glass. 'HELP ME!'

'Whoa whoa whoa!' A hand on my shoulder. 'Everything OK there? Sir?' I get to my feet. Bright grey eyes. A thin beard follows the line of his jaw. He says something into his walkie-talkie but I step past him, out through the toyshop, running out into the day.

Cars howl. The sun is losing itself behind cloud. A woman with parted blond hair flicks a look at me from her phone and a moped overtakes a van with great growls of frustration. I wait to cross the road but there are no spaces no gaps until I step out and force myself across against the beeps and shouts. When I am on the other side a rolled down window spits out ugly promises.

I cross the road onto parkland in front of the Pavilion where there are molehills of people everywhere and I sit down next to a couple who are very worried yet pretending to be in love, the man's beard is square and he has tiny Trotsky glasses and the woman has cropped hair and black angular clothing. I call Missy again but her phone is still off.

I can see a girl I would marry, she is perfect for me, she looks kind, but she is already walking off past people asleep, drug people with dogs and beer and I roll a cigarette and smoke, watching their clumsy goings-on. My hand finds a cheap pair of blue plastic sunglasses lying on the grass. I put them on and look up at the sun. My shadow is beside me. I sit there with my shadow and lie down then sit up again and cross my legs thinking about when we were kids coming to Brighton and eating chips and mayonnaise and smelling the sea and wanting to live here so we could eat chips and mayonnaise and be on the beach every day then suddenly I cannot breathe. It's not that I cannot catch my breath it's as if I have no lungs, the air stops in my mouth, as if my body is fake. My brain shutters.

I roar in a huge breath. My hands are on my chest pressing but I cannot be here any more I cannot be in this park and I wipe my forehead from sweat, tumbling myself upwards moving off I don't know where, crossing another road further into town the streets more crowded people yelling information or shopping or hurrying each other to a secret. I walk through street after street feeling calmer, feeling a sort of hatred, the sky pressing flat against the earth. A bus booms towards me and there is a pub on the other side of the road called the Hope and Ruin. This coughs up a kind of laugh.

I go to a cash machine with the credit card I got in the post without asking and take out a thick sheaf of money that isn't mine. Inside the pub there is a stage and junk hanging everywhere. Drinkers are crouched on metal barrels made into stools and it is very noisy, a group standing beside the bar, laughing. The smoothness of the bar top.

'What can I get you?' says the barman.

'What's that one?'

'Kraken?' He taps a bottle on the shelf behind him. It has an octopus on the label. I take off the sunglasses to look at the barman properly. At that moment a cheer goes up and a large pig-bellied man with a beret and white beard flaxened with nicotine comes into the pub. He is wearing a tight T-shirt with a cartoon octopus on it.

'Oh come on,' I say, 'Come on!'

'Single or double?'

'Oh now,' I reply, as if the barman doesn't know, 'I want four doubles.' He nods as if impressed. 'Eight rums.' I put the sunglasses back on. 'That's His number.'

'Is there a conference going on or something?' he says, measuring out the Kraken. 'I've had mathematicians in all day.'

'How many? Eight? Did you have eight mathematicians in today?' The barman doesn't reply. I take out my wallet. The bearded man is being greeted by the company at the bar. He begins to do an impression of how his dog has scared someone familiar to them all. The octopus on his chest is stretching and bowing. I bow back.

Once I have poured the rums into one glass and gulped it down I leave the pub but I do not have anywhere to go. I look around and wait but there is nothing. I go down to the seafront, over the road, past joggers and people walking their dogs, down the steps and across the pebbles to the water's edge. The swell breaks over my shoes and I sit down, taking the sunglasses off. I take my phone out to try Missy again, but Phoebe starts calling. I watch it ring.

The sea looks like it is made of leather, rolls of second-hand greenish leather dissolving itself on an acid beach. I think of praying and decide against it. Talking to a voice that isn't there. 'Mad,' I say out loud, 'even madder,' than talking to a voice

264

that is. I feel the pebbles, pick up a handful and examine them. Stones of darkness.

I sit there for a long time.

'Hey, man – hey – you're getting wet, hey seriously – oh shit . . .' A young woman is peering round at my face. 'Are you OK?' She crouches unsteadily beside me. 'Mate, you are getting soaked.' She has freckles. 'Why don't you come back onto the beach a bit?'

I look back beyond her. She is with two friends, one with a shaved head, the other with red dreadlocks. They are smoking weed and waving. She stands up, offering me her hand. I nod and she pulls me up. We trudge over to her mates.

'Having a bad day, darlin'?' says the one with red dreadlocks.

'Someone left me,' I reply, and they all say 'aaaaaah'.

'A him or a her?'

'Kind of . . . both.'

'Aaaaaaaah,' they say again.

'Over for good or just a bust-up?'

'For good, I think.'

'Happens, geezer. Happens.'

'Plenty more fish in the sea,' says the girl with the shaved head, patting me. That makes me laugh.

'Plenty more fish in the sea,' I repeat, wiping my eyes with my palms, laughing again and they're laughing too. 'And cephalopods.'

'Here,' says the girl with the freckles, passing me a spliff.

'What is it?'

'Skunk.'

I take and examine it, the end burning madly in the wind. Drugs are what bore me down into His world, the most painful and protracted drilling; two years of being strapped to the bit.

'Thanks,' I say, pulling down a deep drag then letting the smoke burn through my teeth. 'You got anything else?' I feel instantly woozy and out of kilter.

'I can call someone,' shrugs the girl with red dreadlocks, 'if you want.'

'Oh,' I say, 'OK. Yes please.'

'He's got pills. Trips. Proper rare, mate. Blotters. Jim Morrisons.'

I give her a thumbs up, then look at my thumb.

She takes out her phone and makes the call, lying backwards and mumbling up at the sky.

'He's on his bike,' she says. 'Be here in a bit.'

'Yeah, man,' growls the girl with the shaved head. I give her the spliff. We sit there and look out to sea and they have a conversation about a friend of theirs called Karen who has moved to America. The skunk is making my heart race. Sounds from the beach, laughter and engines and chatter arriving too fast or from the wrong direction. I am trembling a little. Can these girls see that I am trembling?

The wet loud trudge of someone stomping through the shingle comes towards us. I look up and there is the dealer carrying his bike. He throws it down with a crash. He looks like a bohemian sailor, young and lumbering, a navy cap trying to keep control of curly hair. His teeth are brown. He isn't wearing any socks.

'Easy,' he says and kisses the girls. He nods at me. 'This him then? This you. What can I do you for?'

His smiling face is framed in slate-coloured cloud.

'How many pills have you got?'

'How many d'you want, chief?'

'Eight.'

'Can do.'

'Eight trips as well.'

'Got a party tonight?'

'Yeah, man,' growls the girl with the shaved head again, then, like a seaside Judy, she says, 'that's the way to do it.'

He wriggles a plastic bag from his crotch, counts the trips out and puts them in a little clear bag with the Es.

'So how much is all that then?' I say, taking the spoons out of my jacket. 'Will these cover it?' I look at my hand. Can they see it's trembling? The dealer and the girls stare at the cutlery. 'They're good spoons.'

A moment passes. The dealer and I are staring at each other, but I can see right into his brain.

'Yo. Ain't got time for this, Rach.'

'Hey, man, what are you—'

'OK. Exchange rate for spoons. Spoons have no worth. How about this?' I have my wallet out now, the spoons on my lap, pulling the notes out. I stretch them out to him. He takes the money and counts it saying 'IKEA's that way' then looks at me and gives me a fiver back with the drugs, saying, 'Where d'you find the joker?'

'Exactly what I would like to know. Got any water?'

The girl with the shaved head passes me the beer can she's drinking. I touch my chest and gasp a little because of my thumping heart then empty the bag out into my hand and swallow all the pills and trips at once as the girls say 'Fuck!' and 'Mate! Whoa!' crunching and wincing at the bitterness, tonguing the crumbs out from my molars, swilling, swilling again, swilling them down.

'Thank you,' I say, giving her back the beer and standing up, feeling how drunk I am. The dealer is shaking his head. I put the spoons in my pocket and walk away from them, fast and unsteady, even as they follow me, calling things. After a while they give up.

I carry on along the beach until they disappear and sit down in front of the sea. I take the spoons out and push them into the pebbles one by one. Then I cross my legs, surveying the horizon, until I see my own storm coming in.

23

Humming pocket what? Text message. From T-Mobile.

There are people asleep around me. The three girls are here, a dog, empty bottles of spirits, remnants of a fire.

Something evil has happened. I don't know what, I have only the feeling. Of guilt. Of horror. I have committed some unspeakable crime. It's not a crime, it's a knowledge of something. I have seen something I should not have seen, something endless. How can I still be on this beach? So many things have occurred, so many convulsions, so many becomings. The dog is watching me.

I stand up and stagger away along the shore. Everything is vibrating softly, everything is patterned, the pebbles combed into intricacies by a great master. I am juddering with the cold.

At the water's edge I inhale the sharp stench of wind fleeing sea. There is the burnt West Pier, salted with seagulls. I can hear their echo cry and some hum, some engine at the heart of it all, old and false.

There is no Octopus God. They were right, they were always right. I am wrong. I've been wrong for twenty years, done nothing for twenty years except be wrong and sick and a burden on everyone, and there is nothing nothing nothing but a grovelling of ideas called ordinary life that I've been too stupid to accept. I am not special. I am not chosen. I live on a diet of my own lies. I am a child that won't leave the beach.

A khaki man with a ponytail and a metal detector. Groups of people still up from the night before. A girl with sunglasses dancing to music I can't hear. I am walking beneath the slats and girders of Palace Pier.

People pity me. I am pitiful.

I keep on towards Black Rock until there are no more people, just the high castle walls of the marina, bleak and buttressed. I climb over another groyne and trudge to the marina wall and touch it then turn to face the water.

The sky is clear brown. Drowning is the fate that awaits the world but that was his prophecy and he isn't real. Perhaps everyone will be fine. I don't want to be alive.

I walk into the sea, open-mouthed.

Ankles knees ringing with the icy water, stumbling against waves that swell against my belly, striding, leaping against the crash, half-swimming, grabbing at the sea, thrashing and sinking, swimming out further, sinking down, sinking, sinking . . . I toe off the seabed, stepping off from the earth. *Oh Tess.*

I inhale the ocean.

24

Thomas.

Hero-headed. Lying in a death-soaked field.

Thou take him for a servant for ever? Two spirits, the eyes of all living. Upon the earth there is not his like.

The thought occurred: an ancient road, travelled by people of a requisite condition. The dying man's whole life, every precious thing, upon the mire. Others were firm as stone.

Bring he forth to light. Do not regret what you have done. He would see an ancient city. Followed it. Dr Fredericks. Transmigrants. Ancient road. Direct knowledge.

His experience. His tipsy daze. I have his tongue with a cord. A desolate area; consciousness turns. In his neck remaineth strength and sorrow. Canst thou fill his skin with barbed iron? His head with fish spears?

Thomas. You will not die because you want to die and I will not let you. Thomas.

'Thomas.'

25

'Thomas.'

Something hits my head.

Fingers in my mouth. Heaving up saltwater in stomach-coughs that cut my clothes off. My teeth are rattling. There are people standing over me. Policemen. A paramedic is cracking jokes. 'You've caught a whopper here.' All I know is the cold and the burning in my throat and He has come back to me.

'Thomas.'

My heart is a meteorite.

They wrap me in a blanket and take me on a stretcher into the ambulance. 'You forgot your armbands, old son, didn't you?'

In what seems like less than a breath I am being taken out of the ambulance again in front of the Royal Sussex County Hospital. They lift me onto a yellow trolley and wheel me through the ambulance bay, schools of professionals swimming past each other;

'. . . one of those Polish fishermen on the marina. Yeah. Jumped in and saved him . . .'

'. . . he was on the roof of the car. Already kicked the windows in – I mean he was 20,000 feet and climbing at this point . . .'

'. . . can we dress up as pirates? . . .'

'. . . *In your cotton fields back home . . .*'

'. . . I can't afford no fucking counsellor! All I got is PlayStation!'

'. . . hypothermia. OK? Can you hear me sir?'

In a room beside a blue plastic curtain I can see the feet and chests of men in other bays. They put a brown tube into the crook of my arm and I lay there beside the drip. The ceiling is very low. Electrodes are taped to me, my chest covered in wire jewellery.

'What are his obs? OK. Sats? . . . Have we had a blood gas on him?'

'Do not enter by one the waters by measure. Who hath prevented this holy life. It is not they.'

'You will always protect me,' I whisper.

'Pride,' He says and my right side turns hot with the onset of electric punishment *I almost believed them I almost turned myself into water* His voltage shaking my body, the curtains wrenched back further, an oxygen mask on my face and shouts of 'he's seizing, he's seizing' but I do not hold myself against this pain as all the times before, I do not resist it or strike myself rigid, armoured in fear. I look to the ceiling past the faces bent over me and give myself to the pain. *The pain is real. You are real.* 'Forgive me,' I say without sound as it feels like a thousand spikes are running through my flesh – and then, emergent from the ceiling, comes the golden light.

It falls upon me, shafts of warmth from heaven and I feel the truth of His love, of the whole universe, not just down my left side but all across my soul. I understand how my doubts, my betrayals, have caused Him such great sorrow but those doubts are gone, utterly gone. Oh Malamock!

They take off the mask and ask me questions and I nod or

274

shake my head wishing they could see the golden light soaking into my being. I have an erection.

'I am not crazy,' I say to the nurse at the end of the bed. She too is covered in golden light.

'I bet that's what you tell all the girls.'

'I was confused.'

'Your temperature dropped a little low but you're going to be fine, sir, OK?' she says as another nurse arrives over her shoulder, looking at my erection and disappearing before her laughter shows. 'Clearly.' I roll my head back to the ceiling.

'Don't contact my sister please.'

'You've been with us before, haven't you, Mr Tuplow?'

'I don't want her to know I'm in here.'

'It's the doctor's decision I'm afraid, OK? But seeing as you're responding and conscious that's probably going to be fine.'

The golden light dwindles but I am still aglow. Nurses and a consultant move around me until there is a great flurry of screaming from another bay. They pull the curtain shut.

I wiggle out of the blanket that still covers my legs and lie there, listening to the ward around me, the screaming that abruptly stops, the wheels, the opening doors, the conversations between people moving away from each other.

'. . . tell me something then?'

'I love you.'

'Something I don't know?'

'. . . no, he's come in from Bognor.'

'Got a password for him?'

'Can't think of anything to do with Bognor.'

'It's his birthday, isn't it?'

'That's why he's here. Too much birthday.'

'So the password's "birthday" . . .'

There are consultants wearing red jump suits, nurses in blue, anaesthetists in purple, ambulance crew in green, porters in

T-shirts, policemen in black. I am wheeled into a room without windows, only blue curtains, beds, and that smell again, the wine of disinfectant, perhaps even the same brand I once drank to disinfect myself and ended up here, in my own bowels.

A youthful man with a hipster moustache introduces himself as a registrar called Philip. He has not yet learned how to talk and look people in the eye at the same time. He tells me I am in the Clinical Decisions Unit and he is part of the Mental Health Liaison Team. He tells me that I am lucky. One of the Polish men that fish from the end of the marina wall saw me go under and jumped in, dragging me out onto the beach while his friends called 999. A policeman appears and tells me the man is called Laslo. Then Philip muddles through questions about my medical history.

'You're not going to section me, are you? Philip?'

I retch and he holds my arm.

'OK there, Mr Tuplow?'

I roll back onto the pillow and nod.

'Is there a phone I can use?'

'Do you want to call your family?'

'I need to call my friend Missy.'

'Let me see what I can do. Now can we turn to what happened this morning?'

'Is there any kind of breakfast here? I think I should eat.'

'It'll be coming along in a minute. Now you say you—'

'I had an epiphany, you see, but I really can't go to hospital. I've got to go home.' *Because I have seen what it means to live your life,* I am thinking out to Philip as he smiles at me, *and that threw me into the sea. But He has thrown me back, for my life is yet to be lived!*

Philip asks me if I was trying to commit suicide and I tell him I was doing the opposite and when he looks confused I tell him I too was confused, and high. Philip finds me a phone but once it is in my hand I know of course there is no point in calling Missy. She's been Acuphased.

Breakfast arrives, a plastic tub with beans and some stubby sausages in it, but now I cannot eat. Powerful waves of nausea are making me sweat.

'You are my Lord God,' I whisper, 'as real as these beans.'

I am so hot now I would almost like to go back to the sea for a swim. This thought makes me laugh but laughing to yourself is not wise when trying to convince a Mental Health Liaison Team you are ready to go home. A kind of vertigo overwhelms me. I grip the bed as if on a fairground ride, revolving, spinning, and shut my eyes but that makes it worse. I concentrate on the curtain rail and eventually it slows.

'Philip! Excuse me?' He comes over.

'I just wanted to check that no one has called my sister. I really don't want to worry her—'

'Sorry, Mr Tuplow, but I actually think she's been contacted already.'

'But I asked – I said not to ring her!'

'So you're not going back to an acute ward or anything like that, which is good news, isn't it? But we don't think it's a good idea you go home on your own, plus the doctor needed to check some information, make sure this isn't part of a pattern? Look, I know it's embarrassing but it is probably for the best in the long run if everyone involved in your care knows what's happened, OK? Excuse me a second—' I sink back onto my bed as Philip disappears but catch despair in one hand, examine it and throw it away. I close my eyes and pray to the Octopus God. I pray for Missy.

I am sorry they had to cut up my Barbour but it was time for a new coat. I feel doped and elated and anxious about Tess and Missy and intensely hung-over and exhausted but at least not so nauseous now and Malamock tells me to sleep so I try to sleep.

After I have been lying there for what seems like hours I start to worry that the nurses have forgotten about me.

'Are you there?' The Octopus God does not reply but Philip and Luciana appear. Their shift is ending. They say goodbye and introduce their replacements Flavia and Alexi and Curtis. It is Curtis with skin the colour of housing brick and hair like moss who brings me a lunch of wet vegetables and rice and I nod through his questions, desperate to be forgotten about again.

After lunch Curtis takes the drip out and tells me they are going to let me go home that evening. Tess is coming to collect me. I fall asleep for most of the afternoon, waking to a headache and thirst and more thoughts of Missy and Tess and the miracle of His truth, of how he has come back to me, how He worked through Laslo to save me – the golden light! I brace myself for my sister's arrival, but as the evening sets in and I am running through what I will say to her, I see Byron approaching my bed.

'Oh Jesus man, Tom . . .'

'Where's Tess? Why are you here?' I close my eyes and martial my resources. 'I want to talk to Tess.'

'Your sister doesn't know anything about this. Are you ready to go or—' but he stops himself because Curtis and Flavia are saying goodbye. He dumps a bag of clothes on the end of the bed and sits down beside it. I take out a tracksuit from the bag. It is white with green trim.

We leave the ward, descend in a crowded lift, head through a corridor with a long painting of dolphins and then out between the ambulances. I look up behind me at the tower, this same tower where I was awakened. The Royal Sussex: my Calvary, my Hira, my Bodh Gaya. There are people smoking and shouting at each other. We walk down the hill. There are nurses and ambulance crew leaning against a wall, smoking in silence. We get to the car park in front of the Cancer Centre and into his

Audi. I am faded with fatigue and nausea and want only to be lying down on my own in the dark.

'They rang the house phone,' he says, revving the engine. 'And there was something, you know . . . I knew it was about you – I never answer that phone. She was upstairs getting ready for work. Jesus Christ, Tom!' he says, his voice suddenly high, 'Don't you think you've put her through enough?'

'Don't you?'

We haven't got out of the parking space yet but he cuts the engine and turns.

'Say again?'

'Don't *you* think *you've* put her through enough?' He gives me the murder eyes. 'Why don't I just get the bus?' I say, undoing my seat belt.

'Oh no you don't.' He snaps the engine back on, pulling out. 'Me and you are having words.' So off we drive through Kemp Town.

'OK, Tom. You are not going to tell her what happened today, got that? Because it will finish her. Fucking warning you. She can't – she's already halfway to cracking up again. She doesn't deserve any more of your shit!'

'I asked them not to call her! I don't want her to know either, OK?'

Byron accelerates. The sky is a grim yellow. He takes a call. We say nothing else to each other until we're on the A26 outside Crowborough.

'Anyway, thought you were meant to be feeling better,' he says, 'So what's this? What's the "cry for help" all about?'

'What "cry for help"?'

'Well if you really want to kill yourself you don't do it on Brighton beach, do you? All those people about. You go somewhere a fuck sight more remote and do it. Beachy Head or wherever.'

279

'Is that a suggestion?'

He tries to overtake but fails because of a van hurtling the other way. He drops back into place, cursing.

'You believe things would be better between you and my sister if I was dead.'

'Oh don't be ridiculous!'

'Because it's not true, you know.'

'And the fuck you know about what's true! Off in your own self-centred fucking selfish little Never-Never Land, you are! You're like a fat Peter Pan—'

I burst out laughing.

Byron, bewildered, flicks his eyes between me and the road.

'Fat Peter Pan . . .' I say, drawing a long breath and then start giggling again. There are giggles bubbling out all over the dashboard. Byron begins to smile despite himself. 'Fat Peter Pan! Oh, that's brilliant, that's the funniest—' The giggles are tickling Byron now. 'Oh dear,' I say, 'Oh dear, oh dear . . . fat Peter Pan . . .' There is a lay-by with a burger van parked up in it.

'Pull over! Pull over!'

'Why?'

'Quick!'

He dips into the lay-by and we shunt forward then fly back as he brakes. I shake out the last of the giggles, wiping my eyes and sighing. I take off my seat belt.

'What you doing?'

'I'm not going to tell my sister anything because I love her, not because you threaten me.'

'Threaten you?'

'Thanks for the lift,' I say, getting out of the car.

'Tom,' he says, 'get back in the fucking—' but I shut the door. 'Tom,' he says again, out of the car himself now. 'What do you think you're doing?'

'I'll walk the rest. It's not far.'

'Get back in the car. *Now.*'

'No, Byron. *You* get back in the car.'

'Tom!' he moves around the Audi towards me but I move away.

'Get back in the fucking car!'

'Or what?'

'*Tom . . .*' He is getting ready to pounce.

I look over at the people by the burger van.

'Do you think I care about screaming my head off? I'm a madman. I'm a fat Peter Pan.'

'Just get in will you! For God's sake!'

Byron doesn't know what to do.

'Please,' he says. 'Tom.'

'Please,' I say, 'Byron.'

'You fucking—' he starts, then leans his head against his fore-arm on the car roof. '*Aaaargh!*' he shouts into his arm. Then Byron straightens up, furious. 'D'you know what?' he says, getting back into his Audi. '*Fuck. You.*'

Byron accelerates past me. His face is tight and dark. He zooms out onto the A-road.

'Fat Peter Pan,' I say to the Octopus God. 'That's the funniest thing he's ever—' But a weighty pulsation travels through me mixing with the force and noise of passing engines. Two drivers at the burger stand are watching me. Their faces become cloud.

Suddenly they are helping me off the ground. They are saying things I cannot really make out.

'Are you sure?' one of the men says and I am nodding. I have to tell them many times that I am walking home and I faint all the time, it's OK, it's not far, and there is no one they can call for me, thanking them, waving them off, stepping onto the verge towards Crowborough as the cars shriek past and I move unsteadily through tottle grass and yarrow.

281

I drew a pirate on the bed sheet lying next to me and I am in trouble. Tess is in trouble, though she did nothing. We have been in the dark since the door slammed, listening to the music coming from downstairs and the voices and the laughter. 'I'm hungry,' says Tess. She is sucking her thumb, sniffing on her teddy's ear, her hair in bunches wearing pyjamas with an apple on it. I pick up the biro off the floor and draw a picture of an apple on a piece of paper then tear it off and give it to Tess and she eats it and we are giggling and I draw a cow and give it to her and she eats it and I draw a pirate and she eats him too then I try the door and it's unlocked.

We go out onto the landing giggling as the music changes to singing, someone on their own singing, and people are joining in and we are pretending we're singing, clomping around the landing with our fists as microphones. There is a wardrobe on the landing and we get in it then get out of it then go to the top of the stairs and listen. We can smell cigarette smoke. Someone is making noises and there is shouting then a clap of laughter. Tess slides down a step on her bottom and I say no stop no and she stops then I slide down on my bottom past her one step and she says no stop no, then she bottoms past me one step and I say no stop no and then the living room door opens and a woman in a black frilly dress comes out. She is wearing a motorbike helmet. 'Oh God there!' she says. 'Hello?'

'We had a bad dream,' I say. Tess is giggling.

'Oh goodness dearie me,' says the woman.

'My leg fell off.' I am sitting on my leg, hiding it. 'Look.'

'Your leg fell off?'

'The devil ate it.'

'Boohoo,' says Tess. 'The devil ate our legs off.' The woman calls out for our mother and we scramble up the stairs and slam the bedroom door shut but get into the wardrobe. We close it carefully, listening for her to come up, but she doesn't come.

————

By the time I get home night is trying to fall. I kneel down to light the incense and candle, ring the bell and pray to my true living Lord, the Octopus God.

'Tom!' *Bang bang bang.* 'TOM!'

I open the door. My sister stands lost. The minute hinges of her face have been loosened; her features have a slackness, her cheeks bright red as if newly struck. I am wearing Byron's tracksuit.

'You idiot!' she clasps me. 'You fucking idiot!'

'Hey – hey—'

'You want to go back to hospital again? Do you?'

'Tess—'

''Cause I'll fucking cart you right back! What are you doing?' – she is beginning to scream – 'what the fuck are you doing! Trying to kill yourself?'

'HEY! HO! Calm down!'

'Byron said—'

'Whatever Byron told you is bullshit—'

'He went to the hospital? He left you on the side of the fucking motorway?'

'We had an argument, OK? Have you spoken to the hospital? Have you spoken to Philip?'

'Who's Philip?'

'The mental health team registrar. Tess, whatever Byron told you, I did not try and top myself, OK? Ask Philip. Come on—'

'Then what the fuck is going on, Tom?'

'I just went to Brighton and got wasted, really, you know, old-school wasted and I met these girls and stayed up all night

283

with them on the beach and in the morning I went for a swim and this Polish dude—'

'*Dude?*'

'Tess, I did not try to kill myself! They only rang your place to check how I've been lately. How have I been lately? I've been good, haven't I? I mean He's gone, hasn't He? The Octopus God has gone!'

I can feel Him. Everywhere.

'Why are you laughing?'

'Because this is all so ridiculous! Byron didn't even talk to the nurses! All he knows is that they pulled me out of the sea and he filled in all the dots himself. As usual. Tess, please, come on . . .'

I go to hug her but she won't take it. A car turns into Meadowside Close, flaring us in its headlights. My sister's eyes are quivering.

'Tell her,' says the Octopus God suddenly, 'that I am here.'

'Look, can we talk about all this tomorrow?'

'*What?* No we fucking cannot, Tom!'

'Tell her.'

No I can't tell her! Not now!

My right side heats.

'Do not deny me.'

Please! Not now! I can't do it!

'Sorry Tess I – I can't do this now, I'm very tired, you've got go I'll see you tomorrow—'

'*What?* Fuck off, Tom!'

'Tell her.'

I can't!

My right side is on fire. I push her out the door, locking it just as Malamock strikes me and I am crumpling over with the pain, holding my mouth so that she won't hear, she won't know. She is banging her fists and rattling the handle.

'*Tom!* What the *fuck?*'

'Tell her.' And I know this voltage will stop, this biting spitting sizzling pain will stop if I tell her but I am holding my whole face shut shaking on the floor, trying to relax into it like in the hospital but I can't because Tess is shouting and rattling the handle and now I bite my hand.

'Tom! Let me in! Let me in there right fucking now, do you hear me!'

The pain increases and I want to scream it out but I cannot, I cannot let her see or know or hear—

'Tell her.'

. . . and so to my stuffed hand my throat tells Him *no* even as the pain begins to subside and I can unroll, lying on the floor, breathing.

'Open this fucking door!'

'I've told you what happened and I'm in no mood for an interrogation, all right? I can't handle it! OK? *Please!* Just *leave me alone!*'

There is silence.

'I'm sorry,' I whisper to Him. 'I can't hurt her any more.'

'Tom?' she says, quieter now.

'Leave me alone!'

I close my eyes and wait. I can feel her through the door.

'Let me in, Tom,' she says, 'Please.'

'*Go away!*'

'Come on—'

'JUST FUCK OFF WILL YOU!' I shriek, 'LEAVE ME ALONE!' and then cover my face with shame.

After a few moments I hear her walking off. Saul says something to her from his window. I crawl to the shrine and light the candle and beg for forgiveness but I cannot feel Him and gather myself up on my knees in panic, rocking and praying. *Please don't leave me again! I just don't want her to suffer!*

'Thomas,' says the Octopus God and I roll onto my side, weeping. Saul and Nika change channel. Tess starts her car.

Unable to sleep I send Tess an email, hesitating at each word, each letter, fearful of His reaction. Once I send the first without punishment I send another and then another until finally she replies but it is just a line of kisses, no words.

Towards two o'clock in the morning He says, 'To see her,' in tones soft enough that I am able to fall asleep though I click awake in the dawnlight. After prayers I stay knelt, waiting, until He says, 'Not to wait,' and I march into the woods unsure of what He might do but unable to do anything else because I must see her, I must be moving towards her.

These woods are once again illumined by His presence. Every shape and shade, every wisp and whisper. We come out into a grove of orchids and in their delicacy I feel again how deeply I have hurt Him.

Out from the treeline, we walk alongside Jockey's Field to the stile. I push up on one leg and see the Audi but I feel a firm, gentle constriction on my left side so I step backwards and sit down in the damp grass behind the hedgerow. Here is the High Weald, full of God, Downs country breathing in then out towards a dun horizon.

I hear Byron's voice.

'Seriously, babe. Can easily blow it off. Serious, now.'

'I don't want you to get into any trouble,' she says, 'Kids!'

Carefully I raise my head to see Byron ushering Lily and Ben into his car. Tess is in pyjamas, her face rinsed and jagged. She is smoking and fidgeting and Byron keeps hugging her, whispering things and kissing her. A heavy shame tugs me down, lowering my head as he turns back to the car. I listen to the doors slam and the engine rev, the spit-crackle of tyres on small stones, the shush of the tarmac as he turns onto the road, his engine noise brightening even as it disappears.

'She's just not ready yet,' I say.

At the front door I knock and push it open and Tess's head pokes around the corner, the rest of her body gathering itself until she is all there, coming closer, pale and suffering, eyes still with the night left in them.

'I'm—' But she has thrown herself around me.

'Don't you leave me,' she whispers.

In the kitchen she makes us tea. Malamock is right there beside us and I struggle with relief and gratitude as He lets me lie again about the girls and being high and how I was trying to make some friends, like she said, and yes I thought I was getting somewhere with one of these girls, like she wanted, but look what happened. Once again I made a proper dick of myself and ended up in hospital with everyone thinking I'm suicidal because they looked at my record and jumped to the wrong conclusion and all because I fancied a swim and got knocked out by the fisherman's boot that's why I'd swallowed all the water not because I tried to drown myself, and how sorry I am. I don't want anyone to worry about me any more, ever again. I am sorry. I am so so sorry.

She has both hands on her mug though it is long since finished.

'You're acting weird,' she says.

'I'm still adjusting.'

'To what?'

'To this. To ordinary life.'

'Fuck's sake,' she sighs, taking out a cigarette, 'is that what you call it?' She lights the Silk Cut, gulps the smoke and jets it from her cheek.

'What time are the crisis team coming?'

'Ten.'

'Will Megan be there?'

287

'Think so.'

'Tom. Look at me. Are you hearing it again?'

'No.'

'Promise me?'

'Tess, I'm still taking the bildinocycline and it's still working. Honestly.'

'But the three months is up soon, isn't it? Trial's over. Then what? Still burning your little sticks, aren't you? Still got your little fucking shrine thing.'

'Tess, I can't hear Him any more. He's not there.'

'It's that simple, is it?'

'That isn't simple, Tess. That isn't a simple thing at all.'

'Yeah?' she says, wriggling off the stool. 'Well I tell you what is a simple thing,' cigarette aloft, filling up the kettle at the sink, 'you do anything like this again and I will kick your fucking head in. I'm not even joking.' I have caught her in another hug and she is saying to my neck, 'You won't need a psych ward, you'll need accident and emergency. You'll need a fucking wheelchair.'

'Then you'd have to push me everywhere.'

'An electric one.'

AUGUST

26

Tangled and sweaty from punishment nightmares of Tess drowning, He drives me from my bed calling me 'fool' and 'wretch' and 'coward'. Once in the bathroom He electrocutes me and I hit my cheekbone on the sink as I go down. He electrocutes me over breakfast, the plate and chair upended. I ask Him if this will stop when Tess comes round and He says nothing. My phone buzzes with a call from Missy. Since she was Acuphased again my calls often go unanswered so I leap on the device and say hi, hello, how are you doing, are you OK?

'What's wrong, Tom?' she says, and He makes me drop the phone. When I've picked it up again I feel Him clench both my sides like a fist about to close. 'Tom?' she's saying, 'Hey? You there?' Tess beeps the Polo outside. Malamock casts the phone from my hand.

In the car I am fidgeting and unsettled and keep touching my face. Tess asks me again and again if I am OK. I gabble off lies. I slipped in the bathroom. I've got gastric flu. I have a fear of scanners. My right side grows hot and I think He will electrocute me again but instead He says, 'Lick the window.' I am paralysed by this command. 'Or she will know.' The heat increases, my right side already tingling with the onset of electrocution.

'Tom!' she gasps.

'There was some sugar on it.'

'Licking the fucking window? What are you now, a dog or something?'

In the waiting room of the Queen Victoria Hospital in East Grinstead an elderly couple sits next to us on plaid plastic chairs underneath a painting of a ship. She smells of wax, both hands resting on the pommel of her cane. She is in loose, embroidered clothing. The knot of his pale-blue tie is oversized.

'And what are you here for?' she says, leaning against me. 'Keep forgetting your house keys too?'

'Hearing a voice. The doctors are testing my brain.'

'Oh,' she says. 'Me too. I hear a voice now. It says,' and, like an old frog, she croaks, '*battery low.*'

'That's your hearing aid,' says her husband.

'I know, I know.'

'I'm glad you're finding this all so funny,' he says. He takes a handkerchief out of her handbag to wipe his eyes. She pats his other hand. The nurse calls my name and Tess smiles but her face is weighed down with concern.

I change into a dressing gown. The radiographer leads me in and I lie on a platform in front of the huge teal portal that will see my mind and is made by Siemens. The ceiling tiles are the same as my room in Hilldean. The radiographer has a shaving rash on his neck. Earphones are put either side of my head and I'm given an alarm button to hold in case I become claustrophobic. The machine hums with the sound of cooling helium. He affixes a white metal mask over my face.

There is classical piano music playing in the headphones. The radiographer presses a button, the platform interring my body within the bright plastic tunnel. The noises change, loud electronic stabs of different notes and volume. After several minutes

292

the radiographer's voice comes into the earphones to tell me that another sequence is underway.

'You reneged on a bargain,' says the Octopus God suddenly, 'when you entered a solemn oath to me.' A huge pulsation wobbles through me, a wave of fizzing and destabilising energy. Panicking, I start to fight it – the fear of triggering – my thumb moving onto the alarm button *no no no!*

'Mr Tuplow? Is everything OK?'

I picture Missy telling me that I'm a dickhead. *Don't be a dickhead, you're fine. Don't be a dickhead. Dickhead, you're fine. You're fine. You're fine* and I think of her in her oversized hoodie and concentrate on this image of her and think only of her and as suddenly as it came the pulsation passes.

'Mr Tuplow?'

'Why are you being like this?'

'Accept suffering,' says the Octopus God.

'I accept it! I accepted death!'

'Accept everything. So to be overwhelmed.'

I cannot control my breathing, my face doused in sweat, trying to wrestle off the metal face mask. The radiographer runs into the room.

Tess smokes constantly as we drive home, flicking ash out of the window and looking at me. A plane thunders the air above us and she grips the wheel, peering upwards. Once heading back down Beacon Road she turns into the Morrisons garage, steering Polly the Polo into one of the bays. I stare out at the shaggy limbs of the carwash while she clunks around at the back corner of the car, the spew of petrol whirring and grinding. With one hand on the pump she bends down and examines me through the passenger window. I get out of the car and go into the shop.

'Oi!' she calls after me, 'What you doing?'

The door tinkles. A blue-haired woman beyond the sweets murmurs some kind of greeting but I go straight into the toilet, shutting the door and sitting down, hoping perhaps I can wait here and He will leave or not really sure what I'm doing but Tess cannot see me in here.

'You reneged,' says Malamock, yet again.

'But we've been through . . . you know how sorry I am! How I have been punished!'

'As the divine can be sharp. Sharp stones under him. Kneel.'

I get to my knees facing the toilet bowl relieved that He is just commanding me to prayer. I close my eyes putting my hands together but then He says. 'Lick the bowl.'

'What?'

The door tinkles. I hear Tess's voice. 'Or she will know,' says the Octopus God. '*What are you now, a dog or something?*' Then suddenly He heats my right side almost to the point of electrocution. I bob my head into the bowl, just touching the ceramic with the tip of my tongue. I am getting to my feet again when He clenches both sides of me.

'Flatten the tongue,' He says forcing me back on my knees. '*What are you now, a dog or something?*'

There is old piss in this bowl and the stench of ammonia and lemonish cleaning fluids sears my brain and I retch, my tongue ungloving itself, bending downwards as in shocked and submissive despair I lick one side dinner-plate clean and throw myself back on my feet, tongue stretched out away from itself, fussing on the sink taps so I can dowse myself but He orders me to close my mouth. I taste salt.

Once He has let me spit water several times I leave the toilet, fighting the urge to cry. There is Tess, waiting for me.

'Direct knowledge,' He repeats, but then again, in the mocking tone, as if mocking Himself, '*Direct knowledge.*'

'You OK?' I nod and she puts her arm in mine. We are out

on the forecourt. 'Did you just have another panic attack?'

'I just want to go home.'

'Shit man, what is going on today?'

When she pulls up in front of Meadowside Close I want to leap from the car certain that He will wait until the very last moment of being with her before He starts to torment me.

'Hey—' she says because I am struggling with the door to get it open. 'What's the matter . . .? Hey!'

'I'm just – I've got to do something.'

'Easy, easy, calm down. I'm going to drop by later so—'

'No! Don't!'

'What?'

'I'm going straight to bed.'

'Bed? Tom, the crisis team are coming at three—'

I shut the door and march to my flat. I don't look back. I concentrate on the door, the key already in my hand.

I prostrate myself. Blasphemous thought-forms bubble in the distance. To combat them I pray in a loud voice, contorting my body against the floor. Once the praying is done I go to the bathroom and remove the last trial pill from the dosette box, holding it in front of myself in the mirror then up to Him before I cast it into the toilet bowl and flush.

I run a bath. Afternoon light breaks through the frosted-glass window laced in cobwebs, catching waves of steam. I become aware that Malamock is watching the spider with me. He is watching from every point in the universe, and I am watching from my bath, but we are watching it all together, the spider, the Octopus God and I. The spider moves, quick and nipping, as if in stop-motion.

———

I can see the ambulance arrive and take another look round. Is it all tidy enough? I shout out to Phoebe's grandmother Kathleen that they're here, watching the paramedics open the rear doors, Phoebe climbing out. Then comes the stretcher.

We have made up her bed in the living room and Charlotte is making jokes, playing Cleopatra as her litter-bearers carry her through the door into the throne room, Kathleen treating her daughter's forthcoming death from bone cancer as an entirely predictable occurrence in a world set up to pester her.

'Oh give over!' she curses, unable to read a medicine label once everything has been laid out. 'Who's meant to read this? The bloody mice, is it, or what now?'

When the ambulance leaves Charlotte pulls us all round and instructs us that there is to be joy. She scoops a tear off Phoebe's cheek with her forefinger and inspects it like dust, then sniffs and tastes it.

'*Bleurk*,' she says, 'you been on the Marmite?' Now she is tired. Now she wants to rest. Jaw muscles corrugate her face. She lies in her hair.

In the kitchen Phoebe is sobbing into my shoulder, trying to muffle the noise of it. When she has steadied herself we go out the back door and round to the step beneath the French windows, looking out across the houses. Holding both my hands she kisses them and says *thank you* and I pull her against my chest and she is sobbing again.

'She is just preparing for a journey,' I say. 'She's a Self-Awakened One, travelling into pure consciousness itself. Into pure love.'

'Oh fuck off with that, Tom,' says Phoebe, sniffing. She can't get her cigarettes out of the zip pocket in her handbag. I try to help her and she tells me to fuck off again.

27

I can hear their voices as I come up the ridge to the edge of what was a thick growth of Scots pine, harvested and mulched but not yet replanted. They are standing by a Polaris and a Shogun. A grey-faced Bavarian mountain dog yaps and bounces with a cocker spaniel. My phone rings and it is Tess again. I decline the call and it pings with a text: *Getting fed up with this!!!*

A man in green trousers, an army jumper and a red baseball cap sits astride a trap, loading clay pigeons. There is a tall young man in a checked shirt showing another in dirty white trainers how to shoot. He is wearing ear defenders, positioning and repositioning his cheek against the stock. Long hair done up in a topknot. They are all drinking.

'What you got there, Huge?' says Baseball Cap, taking a swig of beer as Tall Man leans down into a cardboard box full of cartridges.

'Number 3,' he says, which makes Baseball Cap cackle. 'They're for killing foxes really,' breaking the barrel for Top-knot and slotting in the cartridges, 'you watch the kick now.'

The dogs have smelt me coming out of the treeline and start barking as someone cries 'Pull!' and two discs spin out over the bare ground. Tall Man puts his fingers in his ears while

Topknot lets off two shots and misses. Everybody laughs. The dogs are close now, barking madly.

'Red dog!' shouts Baseball Cap, taking a swig of his beer, 'Come here!' They have all turned to see me except the shooter who breaks the barrel, two fuming cartridges leaping out from the shotgun, the dogs leaping about me, eyes sparkling as they slobber and threaten. 'Red! Flinty! Come here!' orders Baseball Cap, marching towards me. 'Get away! Come here!'

When he is close they heed their master and turn towards him. 'Shut up, Red! Quiet now!' he says, grabbing the mountain dog by its luminous orange collar. 'Sorry, mate,' he says, throwing his head towards the forking ride, 'you might want to head more that way.' He's got his hands on both their collars now. 'They can't work out why there's nothing to fetch. Driving 'em barmy.'

'Oh, OK,' I say, 'No problem.'

'Hey,' he says, looking at me more deeply, 'it's Tom, isn't it? Tess's brother? Shut up, Red!'

'Yeah, I'm Tom.'

'So I heard you're feeling much better these days,' and I am so surprised by this, from someone I don't know, that it triggers a thought reply I can't control – '*not any more*'.

'Yep much better thanks see you then—' I say, hurrying out the words, face runnelled with a half-smile, already stepping away from him when suddenly every muscle, every bone in my body locks stiff, stuck as in the old nightmare, a statue unable to speak. I am tugging at my own limbs. I have no power over myself. Malamock has paralysed me. My face reddens, bristling with sweat.

'Tom?'

I am pleading with Him to let me go, to let me get away from them. *I'm sorry! It was just a thought-form!* Baseball Cap lays his hand on my shoulder. 'You all right, mate?' He turns to the others who are coming over now and soon they all surround me and still I cannot move. *Let me go!*

'Tom? Mate? You all right there, what's going on?'

'What's up with him?'

'Dunno . . .'

Topknot is peering into my eyes.

'Hello? Hello?' Topknot waves his hand in front of me then says 'Fuck me, what's the matter with him?'

'Can you talk?'

'Can you hear me? Hello?'

'Look at him!'

My phone starts to ring.

'It's him. It's his phone – Jesus, look at his face!'

'Maybe he's having a heart attack or something. A stroke or something.'

'Answer it then!'

'Why me?'

'Tom, I'm just going to get your phone, all right, mate? I'm just going into your pocket? Yeah? OK . . . Oh shit – it's his sister.'

'Answer it!'

'Hello . . .? Yes, no, this isn't Tom. Tess, listen, it's Jack here. Jack. Yeah that's it. Listen, we're up in the woods and we just met your brother and he's having – well I don't know what but he don't look so good, you better – kind of stuck. Kind of a seizure or something. But he's upright. No, he's conscious. Upright. On two legs, yeah . . . I dunno. He can't speak he's just – I don't know, Tess, you best come and – OK.' Topknot is taking a picture of me with his phone. 'We're up by – beyond that. You come off Corseley Road by Penns Rocks Cottage, straight up past Rocks Farm keep on the track going straight all the way to Minepit Woods? Yeah. Yeah. Exactly. On the right-hand side there. We're just in there . . . OK, wait

299

a second – Tom, do you think we should call an ambulance for you? . . . He doesn't look too keen on that idea, Tess. No, no he's awake and everything, he's just frozen up, like. I don't really know how else to describe – OK then. OK. Yup.' He switches the phone off and tucks it back into my pocket. 'Sister's on her way, mate, yeah? Two minutes. She's at home and she's jumping in her car now. You feeling any better?'

'*Not any more*,' says the Octopus God, releasing me. I stagger forward, gasping and bewildered.

'Tom?'

They are gawping.

'Sorry,' I say, 'happens every now and again, it's just a kind of, it's just a – it's a . . .' Why am I lying? The dogs bark. 'I'll call her back – sorry, sorry . . .' I say, hurrying off into the woods as they jibber-jabber behind me.

I call Tess and tell her not to come and that I am fine I just got frightened because they came over with dogs and guns and I panicked but it's fine everything is fine don't get in your car, don't come over and she tells me to stay right fucking there she is coming over whether I like it or not and I tell her I am in the woods she won't find me and I haven't got any time and I can't see her because why because why not because why because I am late I'm going to see a friend and I'll call you later what friend what friend I'm fine I promise I just got scared I'm fine I'm fine what friend?

All the way to London I just stare out the window and away from everyone, watching the countryside rip itself to pieces as He curses me repeatedly – 'fool' 'coward' – but also other words, garbled things I do not understand and sometimes it's as if He is talking to someone else.

Once I am on the platform of London Bridge station I go straight into the underground system. There is construction

300

work everywhere, shouts and drills darting out from behind new walls and the escalator isn't an escalator any more it's a wall. I need to go outside and cross the road and head down a different escalator and then I am in the station that I recognise.

Huddled into a Jubilee line tube by a crowd of foreign children all in brightly coloured clothing. They chatter loudly with braced teeth and blond hair swept this way and that. Malamock remains silent but without menace, as if lost in other thoughts.

I step out of the carriage at Baker Street and find the Metropolitan line. At Uxbridge I ride up the escalator, examining the face of each descending passenger. Then I am out through the barriers. There is the bench. I am back on the triggering ground.

Heading up to the bus queue, I take my place on board a U4 to Hilldean Hospital. I sit right at the front. The driver wears sunglasses and has scars that go from the side of his mouth to his jaw. We sway along the road, picking up pace, passing through houses and waste ground then a golf course and huge cylindrical buildings ringed with cars, playing fields and running tracks. Then I can see the hospital. The bus stops and I get out, thanking the driver who doesn't reply. Malamock has begun to hum. I cross the road and head around the main building to a curved wall of opaque glass beside white double doors: Hilldean Psychiatric Unit.

There is a woman with a great curl of braided hair fixed upwards from her head bent over paperwork in the reception kiosk. She senses I am there and then breaks into a huge smile and asks me how I am and how she can help me. I tell her I'm here to visit Missy Davids and that I am her uncle because only family are permitted to visit and she looks at me quizzically then checks and says she doesn't have any record of it and I tell her there's been some mistake because it has been arranged and she tells me to wait there a second so I sit down on a fixed row of grey plastic chairs that face the security doors. I can see into the unit.

A healthcare assistant I do not recognise is above me and introduces herself as Diana. She tells me there isn't much visiting time left but they are willing to make an exception because Missy doesn't get any visitors and she knows things are complicated but it would really help her recovery if I or other family members try to visit more often. I follow her to the security doors and she presses in the code and we pass through no man's land to the second set of doors. She prods in the next code and the doors click, and she lets me through. I am back on the unit. Disinfectant. Boiled vegetables.

We head up the corridor to the nurses' station. Rashid is inside, leaning against the wall. He sees me then, expressionless, raises an arm, like the final upswing of a shop window Chinese cat.

Diana turns to see that I am no longer right behind her and I shuffle on past Rashid and down the next corridor, the smoking garden now visible behind the exit door. We are at Missy's room. Diana knocks on the door, says her name, then walks away. I check the corridor but Rashid has not followed me.

Missy is cross-legged on the bed in her onesie, the sleeves pulled over her hands, hood over her face.

'Well, well, well,' she mutters darkly. 'Something really fucked up must have happened for you to come here.'

'Surprise.'

She throws back her hood and stares at me in shock. Missy has lost even more weight and looks grey and skeletal and bad, very bad.

'Sorry, they wouldn't let me in otherwise I should have—' But she is on her feet and I have her in the heavy overcoat of a deep hug.

302

'Was thinking it can't be him,' she says to my neck, 'My uncle'd never show his face. What you doing here?'

She pushes me back a little so she can examine me and asks me if I am all right and halfway through telling her I'm fine I stop lying and tell her not really, I'm not really fine, and I had nowhere else to go no one else I wanted to see because I am scared of being near my sister. She pulls me down to sit beside her and I tell her everything that has happened but I can feel Him listening to me so often try to change the subject, fearful of reawakening his anger, but she makes me carry on. When I am finished she says, 'You're worried about Him. Aren't you?' I cannot answer that. Then she says, 'Can I talk to Him?'

'What?'

'And I don't want you to talk to Him for me, I want to talk to Him myself, you know, direct.'

'You don't have a telepathic connection.'

'He's God, isn't He?'

'Please, Missy, don't—'

'Don't what? I just want to thank Him.'

'Thank Him?'

'For saving your life. He stopped you drowning, didn't He? And after what you told me about back in the day sounds like He turned up twenty years ago when you were losing your shit big time. Basically, He came along and protected you. So I want to thank Him. For looking after you. Can you tell Him that? Can you tell Him "*thank you*"?'

We wait for His response. I am hugging my knees, unsure of what Missy is up to. What if He becomes angry and strikes me here, in the unit? If I am seen electrocuted, maybe they will detain me. What if Rashid comes in? Why have I come back here? I can be trapped here!

'Accepted,' He says. I exhale.

'Good,' Missy smiles and suddenly we are both watching her,

303

the Octopus God and I. 'I was in the main hospital,' she says, 'I fitted in the shower. Banged my head. Arms came out the sockets again.' She rubs her fingers together.

'Just saw Rashid.'

'Yeah. That cunt's still here. Kiki's gone. Loads of new staff now. They spend the first couple of weeks convinced that they can cheer you up then when they realise they can't – then it's your fault. Hey, but check this out, right, they brought these two in, one in the evening and one in the morning, but same day basically yeah, one was like Lithuanian or something, Eastern European, white, anyway, and this other one was Somali, yeah, Somalian, right? And they both thought they were Jesus. Black Jesus was at breakfast telling everyone he was Jesus and in comes White Jesus saying no no no, I'm Jesus. Fucking brilliant. There was this other girl Jenna in here who was my mate for a bit and me and Jenna were like well, come on then, one of you two turn the water into wine then we wanna get pissed up. They really fucking hated each other. Kept getting into fights and calling each other the devil and we was like, that's not very Christian. Rashid Acuphased Black Jesus. White Jesus got sent home. See what I'm saying?'

'Where's Black Jesus now?'

'Dunno. Disappeared. Same day Jenna left. She didn't even say goodbye, the bitch.'

We are sitting on her bed and I hug her but at the point I would let go I can feel she isn't letting go.

'You're not eating much then,' I say eventually.

'Fuck off,' she says and we carry on hugging.

A nurse I do not recognise comes into the room and says visiting time is over. She stands there in the doorway waiting for us. I help Missy up and when she is upright we keep holding hands and walk back down the corridors together, Missy nodding to patients and staff. Almost everyone is new, except her.

The nurse tells us to wait for Diana who will take me out and we just stand there facing the security doors as if waiting for a lift and I can feel her grip tightening and I pray to Him *please help her* but in answer here is Rashid.

'What you doing, T?' he says. Missy looks at the floor.

'Waiting for Diana.'

'Who?'

'She's going to take me out.'

'Ain't no one here called Diana.'

'She's—'

'Only relatives are allowed as visitors, Tom. You know that. You're not a visitor. You live here, remember? You're staying with us.'

He crosses his arms, tuts, and shakes his head.

'What?'

'Tom?' he leans into my face. 'Come on. Dr Fredericks wants to see you.' He puts his hand on my arm. 'Chop-chop. Meds time.' I look down at his hand. Then he lets go, points at me and says, 'Aaaaaah! Got you! Look at your face, man.'

Diana arrives. 'Hey D,' he says.

A walkie-talkie fixed to Rashid's belt crackles out his name. He picks it off and starts talking into it, opening the security doors, first one set and then the second, wedging them open for a delivery man balancing a stack of boxes on his barrow.

'Well there you go,' says Diana and I hug Missy again. I walk off into reception and then turn back and there she is in the doorway, the other side of no man's land, lost in her oversized onesie.

Another healthcare assistant re-wedges one of the security doors that has come loose. Rashid helps a second deliveryman guide his veering dolly truck into the unit and once they have gone past Missy, she blinks. Then Missy just starts walking to-wards me.

She is beside me. She is taking my hand.

We walk out past the empty reception kiosk. We walk through the main entrance also hooked open, a white lorry reversed up to it with two other men offloading its supplies. We walk out between the cars and onto the road, hurrying as if we are both desperate for a piss but we do not break into actual running until we turn the corner and see the bus coming. I show my pass and pay for Missy and we drum our feet up to the top deck, staring out through every window until the bus churns away from the kerb.

'I was praying for Him to free you! And He did it! He did it!'

Missy is grinning. She says, 'Holy fucking shit. Holy fucking shit,' over and over again the whole way to the tube station. We get off the bus and cross the square past the bench towards Uxbridge station, its entrance large and shadowed and promising to hide us and where else is there to go but Crowborough?

28

The journey home passes in a kind of dream, as if we are floating, borne along by some special dispensation. Barriers seem to
open for us without payment. People leave their seats just as
we enter the carriages so we can sit down, once even leaving a
shopping bag on the floor so that when the train leaves London
Bridge we have sandwiches and fruit and cans of drink. London
rolls itself back up, the countryside streaming out from underneath it as we eat our picnic in glowing silence, my heart full of
gratitude and wonder. Missy keeps giggling.

In Crowborough we walk through the town, people I know
saying hello to us and this seems otherworldly to Missy, some
other England, a forgotten toytown. Part of me is hoping we
will bump into Phoebe. I repress it.

Once we are through the door of number 1 Etchingham
House, I give her a tour of the servants' quarters, the ballroom,
the dining room, the conservatory and the stables. I am about to
make the tea when the white light crackles above us.

'Put her out,' says the Octopus God.

I put the kettle down.

'*What?*'

'Put her out. Be detached.'

A shadow of white light falls on Missy's face though she cannot see it.

'But we can't do that! We've just . . .' And I feel a heat, not divine, a flush of childish frustration and embarrassment. 'But it's not fair!'

He constricts my right side and I am against the wall, red and twisting. Missy is holding me, unsure of what to do and I see myself through her eyes and I know she must not leave, that I need her, yet the Octopus God is my living truth and though neither protest nor defiance is the answer still I must find progress.

'Just wait, just stay – I need to speak with Him – just a . . .' I go into the bathroom and shut the door.

Sitting on the edge of the bath I summon my whole spirit, looking down at the plughole. When I return, the Octopus God is speaking. His command is clear, but where resentment and exasperation rise, instead I lower myself to the bathroom floor, to the damp red knotted bathmat, and kneel. I bow my head.

'Dear Lord, I simply ask you to allow me her company, to help her, after all her suffering, as befits my mission here on earth to follow the spirit path and to do good, always following your laws and truth, my Lord God, Malamock, the Foundation Spirit, the First Transmigrant. This I ask of you. I hold out my heart in my hands to you, oh Lord.' I empty myself of everything but belief and confidence in Him and that, if He wishes it, I will expel her. I will abandon her. '*Please*.'

A long moment passes. It looms and squeezes and grinds and then . . .

'Accepted.'

'Thank you!' I spring to my feet. 'Thank you, thank you!' and I fling open the door with an enormous grin.

'Wow,' says Missy. 'Good poo?'

I make the tea, rattling through our escape again now we are safe, now we can relive it, and as I talk I feel almost as if the golden light is upon me, a cold fresh warmth, a knowledge that now I can explain myself to Him! I can ask and He can give!

'So, look, you take the bed. Seriously. I can—'

'Joking aren't you? I don't want your smelly bed. I'll take the bath.'

We make her up a bed in the bath. It fits her perfectly as she is so small, though she does not like the spider on the window-sill. Missy has never been in the countryside before, and her fear of insects is very funny.

She sits in Megan's chair while I pray and give thanks and then I cook us lentils and it begins to rain and we watch *I'm a Celebrity . . . Get Me Out of Here* as Saul and Nika argue upstairs.

'You're like an outlaw now.'

'Naaaa,' she says, 'outlaws are wanted.'

In a pre-emptive move I ring Tess. I tell her I am fine over and over again and that I've just been out and about and no I haven't had any more panic attacks, actually I'm feeling pretty good again but no I don't want to her come round right now I'm really tired I'll be round tomorrow when she's back from work. Promise. Promise. I promise.

The next morning after prayers and toast and tea I find Missy a top and put on my kagoul. I am excited to show her my woods. We walk out onto High Paddocks, along headland waving with ox-eye daisies and cow parsley, mallow, yarrow and mint. We hoist ourselves over the gate and into Jockey's Wood. Sorrel carpets the rides. The woods quiver with sunlight, and in this light I perceive His light, breaking through into our world, and give thanks. Megan calls but I don't answer.

We trample over blackberry brambles and stumbling bracken, bistort and butterbur, pulling twizzled and broken branches down from where the canopy has caught itself. Along the ghyll then we head back up the rise to show her one of my favourite trees, a gigantic gorgon beech mounded in rock that grabs the hill, huge tentacles resting on sandstone lumps that continue to grow out in warped shapes of things unborn, memories from other creatures trapped and manhandled in the wood, wrinkled at the bends like sealskin. The bark is greenmarine slick, and we clamber about these marooned limbs, balancing, clinging, ahoying ourselves out across the High Weald, so strange and wonderful to be with Missy here, the first time I have seen her joyful and unguarded.

We scale the gate and canter down the knoll that steeps back to the stream. We stop at the pillbox, walls damp with lichen, the scratched entrance covered by a butterfly bush. Once inside I explain its purpose and we peer through the embrasure imagining Nazis before struggling back out into peacetime and the tinkle-lilt of blackbird song.

The sun comes out behind us and for a moment we are burnt into the grass as shadows. Missy keeps muttering, 'Can't believe you live here . . .' as the stream takes us to a wooden footbridge and then we come back up the valley through more alders and chestnut, inhaling the tang of wet moss and fern cover until we reach a blasted oak and I explain the lightning scar. A sudden wind in the trees sounds like the ocean and it rains again though lightly, the chamber of my kagoul hood picking out the sounds of certain droplets, my boots rubbing them against their own shushing of the ground. Megan calls again. She leaves a message. We cross another bridge through the clodgy field all glutted with slub and boggery to where the gate buckles Rocks Wood and there, hidden within, I lead her to my vale of sandstone rocks.

As we walk through their canyons and gullies, I explain to Missy how they are silt deposits left behind by retreating water. Before this was the forest of Andredsweald, and before this was the forest of Anderida, this whole area was a great brackish lake that stretched to northern France. These huge rocks are simply boulders of crusted sand, biding their time for the water to come back. 'So really we're all just squirming about,' I tell her, 'on an ocean floor.'

Two roebucks cross the ride. They are close enough to see the black of our woodland eyes then jolt off into the brambles. This first meeting with wild creatures like herself holds powerful magic over Missy. She is lost in the shaken bushes. 'Ba,' she says. 'Ba-ba-wha-what the fuck, man!'

I show her where the young deer are killing yew trees by scuffing the bark with their antlers to clean off the velvet. I name several species of butterflies and translate noises for her like a magpie's rattle and the dull knock of distant shotguns. I am happy telling her all about my woods but then Malamock scolds me for boasting. 'She wants to know!' I say out loud, but in judgement of my vanity there is sharp hot pain in my right side and I collapse against her; a dog that's been tugged, reminded of its collar.

I am quiet the rest of the way home. As we climb over broken fencing onto High Paddocks Missy says, 'Can I ask Him a question?' and when He tells me it is permitted she says, 'Why do you punish Tom?'

'Preparation and training. Fabrications, out.'

'Why can't he eat meat or have sex?'

'Achieving orgasm. A banquet. The fowls of the air. Do not pursue these forms of death. They break from complete and ancient right concentration. Knowledge of the path.'

'What does that mean?'

Meadowside Close comes into view across the pinstriped field. Missy chews her fingernail and is about to say something else when my phone rings.

'Oi!' barks Tess, 'Did you go to fucking London yesterday?'

'Yes. Yes I did, yes.'

'Why didn't you tell me!'

'Did tell you. Told you I was going to see a friend.'

'You went back to Hilldean?'

'To see my friend. Missy.'

'The fuck do you think this is, Tom? Fucking *Shawshank Redemption*? You busted her out?'

'I didn't "bust her out". They left the doors open and we walked out. Tess—'

'Where is she now?'

'Tess, she's been getting abused in there basically and—'

'Is she still with you?'

'No.' Missy picks up a stick. 'We went as far as the tube station together then she chipped.'

'She "chipped"?'

'"*I'm chipping off*", she said. And off she chipped.'

'You're being weird.'

'That,' I say, bending backwards to the sky, 'seems *unavoidable*.'

'Had Megan on the phone.'

'And what did Mega Megan have to say?'

'Said you could get into all sorts of trouble! Harbouring a criminal and all that.'

'You're making this up now.'

'Well she did say your mate's got a violent record and is, you know, basically disturbed.'

'You try being in that place for a year!'

'So do you know where she is?'

'No!'

'Are you sure, Tom?'

'Yes I'm sure! I wish I did!'

'All right! Calm down . . . fuck's sake . . .' Tess sighs. 'So are you coming round later then?' Missy throws the stick away.

'Sly Stallone and Pele request my presence at a certain sporting event.'

'Yeah, well. Try not to waste any cops,' she says, 'on your way home.'

Tess hangs up. Missy crouches down like a tracker.

'I'm in,' she says, nodding, fingering the grass.

'In what?'

'The praying thing. Fucking need some help.'

———

We are kneeling in front of the shrine, hands closed in prayer, eyes shut.

'Dear Lord,' Missy repeats after me, 'Malamock, the Foundation Spirit, the First Transmigrant. We thank you for protecting us, for showing us the path to freedom. Please guide us. Please keep us free.'

I pause, but Missy carries on.

'And please make sure I never ever go back there. Please, please, please.' I open an eye to see her face clenched in prayer. I can feel His warmth towards her. She opens an eye, checking on me. We have one eye on each other, four hands, four legs.

'You will bring him back to me,' He says, to her.

That evening I cook us some rice and vegetables. I leave Missy watching TV while I go round to see Tess, stopping myself from any parting comment, any expression of glee that Missy is actually eating, wary that drawing attention to the act might derail it.

Once more I wade through Tess's questions and repeat my lies over and over again. I repeat the story of our escape and again try to explain what Acuphase is like, what Rashid is like, how Missy was being treated, how I don't know where she's gone. I feel His warmth down my left side even as the lies pour out. I'm still adjusting, I tell her, to ordinary life, to normality – the consensus perversion.

I walk back home through the woods. When I get near I start

panicking that perhaps someone has turned up and taken her back to Hilldean but as I get to my front door I can hear the TV. She smiles at me as I come in then carries on watching *Pointless*, as if this is our home. I go into the bathroom to brush my teeth, and then look at the cushions and blankets in the bath. Will it be snug in there? It's really a kind of cot. What meds have I got to offer her so she doesn't turkey? I grip the sink, looking up at myself, at how I am now, the scar on my forehead.

'Thomas,' He says, a vast and profound warmth suddenly blossoming across my chest and neck and down my spine. 'A thought arose. Your mission.'

'My mission?'

The ribbon of white light appears before me. I fall to my knees. *Oh God!*

'Stillness. Thomas.'

I still my mind. We take a breath together and out from the deep silence knowledge arises. It is just there, without me chasing it: I am to be a lawyer again.

Now, suddenly, like summer lightning, I see, I understand what was preventing me from receiving my mission all this time: it was me! My own impatience, my ceaseless striving, my worrying! Malamock is beyond thought. He has been guiding me to migrate beyond thought. To be a Transmigrant. To wake up from myself. To be Awakened. This is the dilemma of consciousness, of birth and death, of ego and form. What exists? Name and form? Nothing exists. Only stillness.

'You are my soul,' I say to the Octopus God. I am weeping.

'Thomas,' he replies, 'I forgive you.'

29

The sea is pale gold, the sky white with heat. A line of fishermen in front of us are spaced out against the railing with folding chairs and mounds of plastic bags. Some tie on bobbers and sinkers, others are threading the eye or reeling in, butt caps wedged against their bellies, cigarettes balanced. They are chatting, gesticulating, gazing out to sea. Everyone is Polish.

We ask for Laslo and get sent down the marina wall, the name called out in front of us until a stocky young man with a shaved head, narrow eyes, and a nose that looks pinched off at the end greets us suspiciously. We shake hands. He has not recognised me and I explain that I am the one he pulled from the sea, prodding myself, pointing down at the waves, vomiting noises, until he understands.

'Thank you,' I say and embrace him.

'No problem, no problem,' he says, explaining in Polish who I am to his friends. They stand around us. I hold up a plastic bag.

'It's a present.' And one of them translates for him and he smiles, takes the bag, peers in and starts laughing. I've bought him a whole flat-bodied skate.

'Big fish,' I say about myself.

'Big fish! Big fish!' he says. Everybody is laughing.

He reels in his line then hooks the skate on the end and we stand together as his friends take photos with their phones. I take the hook out of the skate and pretend to hook my lip with it and there are some more pictures. I hug him again and he whispers something to me in Polish which I both don't understand and do understand.

We wave goodbye to Laslo and the other fishermen and walk down onto the shore. I point out to Missy where everything happened. It's Saturday and there are washed-up people everywhere. Laslo jumped a great height to save me and we look up at them all fishing there as we sit down. Missy closes her eyes against the sun and I say that I was just wondering about her parents. She never talks about them.

'I think they just fell off the world,' she says. 'Lost their grip, let go and just aaaaaaaaaah fell off into space.'

'You think the bodies are still floating around up there?'

'Frozen solid.'

Missy picks up some pebbles. She throws them away one by one. 'You know, it's like that. It's like you are floating around in thick black space. You can't feel anything. Can't feel your own body. Like, kinda like this *speck*, lost in a massive endless void of nothingness. Like you're dead but somehow you haven't died. And you panic – you fucking panic big time, but there's nothing you can do . . . and it goes on and on for ever. That's what Acuphase is like. And then things do start to happen. The tripping-out shit. These things come, these *monsters*, and they're attacking you – and you can't move, you can't wake up . . .' Missy bursts into tears. She curls up in a tight ball. I put my hand on her shoulder, unsure of what to do as a couple with a terrier stomp past us. They try to stop themselves looking at us and then sit down, their dog jumping back and forth, barking at the sea.

I am sitting on the hospital bed and feel perfectly calm, perfectly serene. This is my first ever time in hospital and I have had many visitors but finally I am alone. I can open my heart to this great thing that is happening to me, this thing that has been building since that day in the Aquarium and though I do not understand it I know it is something incredible. There has been much distress and I have experienced many earthquakes but now I feel calm. It is the eighth of October.

I sit cross-legged on the bed, gripping the slender chain that the nurses found under my bed, a tiny gold Christ on the cross. No one I know wears or has such a chain, yet it has appeared under this bed, a sign of goodness and purity and suffering. I close my eyes to concentrate on the world around me and try to slow my breathing. I inhale through the nose and out through the mouth, breathing in this smell of disinfectant, exhaling the noise of the ward, the closing of a door, the voices in conference with one another. Somewhere there is a radio playing. I can hear a plane overheard. I sense the street outside and something happens in my left arm.

It feels as if it is being gripped. I open my eyes and there is nothing visible yet my left arm is wrapped in something, it is being held tightly, it cannot move, and though I flush with panic I see the Christ chain on the sheets in front of me and surrender to this sensation, the urgent warmth of it: love. Love is coiled around my arm. The sensation disappears.

A few hours later I hear the most indescribably beautiful music being played on instruments I cannot name. I go into the corridor to find its source and I know they all think me mad because they can hear nothing. This music is for me alone. It is a sign. I lie back down on my bed and try to listen to it but I am trying to capture it and so it dissolves. Again I compel myself to

317

meditate, to open myself in preparation for whatever is trying to make contact when suddenly a ferocious, ripping pain shoots up my spine.

I cry out, falling backwards off the bed onto the floor. Nurses run in and, as I struggle, they heave me back onto the mattress. I buck against them. The pain is like metal spikes piercing my back. They turn me over as I howl and a doctor arrives, a young woman with her chignon wrapped in her collar. She is checking me and I am injected. The cloud of it rushes up my arm into my brain and shadows me over. I fall unconscious.

When I wake the doctor tells me there is nothing wrong with my back, no trapped nerve, no slipped disc, everything is fine. She leaves and I am alone again. The pain must have been of a spiritual origin. When the sedation clears I get out of bed and look out from this hospital tower across Brighton to the sea. Sobs mount in my throat because never have I been more confused, though never have I been more certain. The words 'Where are you?' come out from the depths of me and in reply a vast white light flashes back from the sky. I fall backwards in shock, and then I hear a voice, both distant and close.

The voice says, 'Thomas.'

'Who are you?'

'Malamock,' says the voice, 'I am the Octopus God.'

Three orbs of golden light appear from nowhere. They circle me. Then, one by one, they enter the crown of my head.

I am remade.

30

'Mr Tuplow, you were in Hilldean acute psychiatric ward, is that correct? And you had a friend in there, Missy Davids?' Megan inclines her head, crosses her legs, then leans forward as if she wants to grab my hands. Oh Megan. The policeman looks up at my octopus collage.

'Anyone want a biscuit?'

'No thanks.'

'Actually I'm lonely,' I say, repeating Malamock. The cupboard curtain wavers ever so slightly but neither Megan nor Detective Constable Gable notice. Is Anne Frank laughing?

'Oh Tom . . .' sighs Megan.

'Yes and I went to visit her the other day because she is so miserable and because that place is pure hell, when we were saying goodbye, she walked out with me. They left the doors open. That's what happened.' I give them a powerfully conclusive smile.

'This is serious, Tom.'

'I am being serious. Have you ever been Acuphased?'

'Mr Tuplow, can you tell us what happened then?'

'Well, we got as far as Uxbridge station and then we had a row.'

'Why's that?'

'Well, I used to hear a voice. Megan's probably told you. A voice that no one else could hear, but Missy and my voice were good friends, so when she wanted to talk to Him and the voice wasn't there any more she left in a bit of a huff.'

'Did she say where she was going?'

'She was going to find my voice. He's an octopus.'

'Right,' says the policeman, again exchanging glances with Megan, who tucks her hair behind an ear, 'and where might the voice be? If it's no longer . . . in your head.'

'Hawaii?'

'You think she's gone to Hawaii.'

'That's where He comes from.'

'No messing around please, Tom. Come on.'

'I'm not messing around!'

'So she didn't come back here with you? London's the last time you actually saw her?'

Someone, in a car quite close, honks their horn several times. This policeman looks exhausted. He has red-eye.

'London is the last time I saw her, yes. By the way, Detective, as you're here, I would like to formally open an investigation into abuses at Hilldean psychiatric unit. Can I talk to you about it?'

'Do you have any evidence?'

'I've got witness testimony.'

'And these witnesses are psychiatric patients,' says DC Gable. I sit back in my chair. 'Mr Tuplow, if you have allegations to make about Hilldean I suggest you make a formal complaint—'

'I am making a formal complaint.'

'. . . by writing a letter to Hilldean. To whoever was the senior doctor there.'

'Oh right, yes. A letter to Dr Fredericks. Not wildly effective perhaps. Did you know that it is impossible to get legal aid for clinical negligence cases? I live on benefits.'

'But just now, we need to stay focused on Missy Davids because it is very important we find her, Mr Tuplow. Do you understand? She has absconded from lawful custody.'

'Oh I do understand. She doesn't have any money.'

'Has she been in touch since you last saw her?'

It suddenly strikes me how similar this situation is to a supermarket loyalty card. The loyalty only goes one way. The right to exercise the law only goes one way.

'Tom? Has she called you or anything? A text? Email?'

'No, she's pretty pissed off with me. Do you want to check my phone?'

'You are telling the truth, aren't you, Tom?'

'And nothing but the truth. I don't think she actually has a phone though. What else do you want to know?' DC Gable makes an uncomfortable throat sound and stands up. 'Already?' I say.

'You've been very helpful,' he says. Megan stands up too. She looks quite cross. The policeman opens the bathroom door and looks in.

'Oh it's not there any more, I'm afraid.'

'What isn't?'

'Hawaii.'

'Goodbye, Mr Tuplow.'

'It's seventeen hours by plane. You may have to stop in California.'

'This isn't funny, Tom,' says Megan, giving me a stern look.

'I'm not being funny, Megan. Stop saying that.'

'If she gets in contact you've got to tell us. You know that, don't you?'

'Hey, do you want to come swimming with me this afternoon?'

'I'll call you later,' she sighs, giving me a prim little hug.

'Bye-bye,' I say to DC Gable, waving them both off, 'Bye-bye now.'

When the door shuts I watch them through the eyehole until they disappear.

'Clear!'

And out from the cupboard curtain tumbles the fugitive Missy Davids.

'Was He helping you?' And when I say yes, she starts clapping above her, clapping all around her head, the way footballers do when they leave the pitch.

Missy isn't happy about being stuck inside on her own but we don't have any bread or toilet paper. I tell her not to answer the door or turn the TV up too much or go near the windows.

'I'm not stupid,' she says. 'How long you going to be?'

I walk into Crowborough and take out yet more money on the credit card they sent me. I buy enough food for a week or more so that we don't have to go into town again and hurry home to her, the plastic bags cutting into my fingers.

As I turn the corner into Meadowside Close I am swept through with despair. How long can we live like this? What are we going to do?

'Never stray from the way,' replies Malamock, 'the requisite condition,' and my despair leaves, but there is Byron's Audi parked in front of the flat and now I am swept through with panic, Byron leaning against the car, swiping through his phone. He puts his phone away. Straightens himself.

'What are you . . . is Tess in there?'

'She's at work – calm down.'

'You're not – you haven't . . .' I'm looking at the door. I exhale. 'Why didn't you just call me?'

'Because you never answer your phone to me, Tom. As well you know. Look, can we just talk about your sister's birthday for a moment please?' He sees that I have forgotten. 'Right,

OK. So me and the kids are giving her a surprise party tomorrow? Lynn and Adam are coming, nothing big . . .' I put down the shopping bags flexing the blood back into my fingers. 'Half eight? I'm going to take her out for a drink first after work.'

'I'll have to check with my secretary.'

'*Badoom-tish*. It's a surprise. So. Don't be late. Can you manage that?' he says, getting into his car. 'You know, you could buy her something. You could do something for her for a change.'

Byron drives off. Saul is at the window.

Though the jacket has remained on the coat hanger, the trousers have slipped off to join the wedging of other stuff in the bottom half of the cupboard. Although I do not have an iron, and indeed have spurned ironing as an inappropriate concern for someone following the spirit path, we clear space on the floor and lay out the trousers, covering them in heavy books overnight. It doesn't work as well as I'd hoped but the creasing is less of a serious problem than the fact they don't fit. I bought this suit during my pupillage. I can get into the jacket just about, if I don't try and button it, but I can only wear the trousers with the zip open and a belt on. I shave off the beard that has now regrown and though it was not in my plan I ask Missy if she thinks I should carry on over my head as well. So, crouched by the sink with a towel round my shoulders, Missy shaves my head.

I put on the most acceptable shirt I can find and examine myself in the mirror.

'I know there is vanity in this but it's just part of the present,' I say, but Malamock remains silent. When it is time to leave I light incense and we pray together. I ask Him that the evening will go well.

'I wanna come,' she says, sad and pouting. 'I wanna to go to a party.'

'We'll do something tomorrow. Promise.'

'Bring me back some cake then,' she grumbles. 'Fuck yer party.'

She is leaning against the door. Holding the carved wooden box I have as a present for Tess, I pull on my jacket sleeves and straighten up, gesturing for her approval. She gives me a cock-eyed thumbs up. 'You look like a lawyer,' she says, and I brighten. 'For tramps.'

Though the ground is dry I am worried about getting the suit trousers dirty and pay uncommon attention to my steps. The heifers in Park Grove field watch as I come down Gorse Bank. They barge and nudge me as I step around the poached mud and into their scrum, patting and swaying with them, holding the box aloft. They seem to be in a good mood. We move across the field together.

Once I am through the woods and at the top of Jockey's Field I can see the Audi is not there. I am not late!

The hallway is perfectly silent and I shut the door calling out 'Hello? It's Tom?' There is a release of noise from the living room and Ben comes running out and pulls me by the hand. The room has been decorated by every type of streamer and garland, *Happy Birthday* in all different colours and shapes, Christmas decorations repurposed, the whole room fluttering with gold and silver. Wine and bowls of crisps and cakes and Ben is wearing a waistcoat. Lily is wearing make-up and a dress and she kisses me, checking me up and down. 'You going to do singing or something?'

Lynn is there with her husband Adam, tying balloons to the cupboard handles.

'All right, sweetheart? Look at you! My God!'

'Thought I'd make an effort.'

'Like it, like it . . .' she says, coming over to hug me while I shake hands with Adam. Lynn has many moles on her face and a long muscular neck, hair pulled back into a bun. 'Just trying to whip a few more of these balloons on – want to give us a hand, like?'

'Sure.'

'Drinkypoos, Thomas?' Adam asks. His arms are completely covered in tattoos and he has a huge fanning beard that is grey around the mouth then becomes tawny brown.

'No thanks.'

'Thought you were back on the sauce these days?'

'Not drinking?' says Lynn, thoroughly shocked.

'Not drinking, not masturbating.'

'Whoa – children alert!' she says as Adam sniggers. 'But thanks for keeping us in the picture there, Tommy Boy, *Jeez Louise* . . .' She hands me a packet of balloons and I put the wooden box on top of the fridge. Lynn directs everyone to finish off the decorations but it is only a few minutes before we hear the tyre-crunch and she herds us into position, her and the kids behind the sofa, me and Adam behind the curtains. Wrapped in fabric I hear the door shut and then Tess's voice and know that she is already pissed, her voice light and tinkling. The door handle rattles and then her voice becomes a clear gasp. They all jump out and call *surprise* only I have become caught up in the curtain so by the time I emerge everyone is looking at me.

'Surprise!'

Byron is finding this very funny. Tess claps her hands over her mouth then rushes over to me, rubbing my scalp, taking in the suit.

'He looks like a bouncer,' says Lynn.

'For a bouncy castle,' says Byron.

'Not before time though,' says Tess, examining my head, 'you were looking a bit patchy.'

'Happy birthday,' I say, and we hug, Adam turning on the stereo to Russ Abbott's 'Atmosphere'. He seems very pleased with himself and starts dancing with the kids.

'Thanks for making such an effort,' Tess says, 'Not seen you in a suit since . . .' and she whistles off the years.

'It was Byron.'

'Really?' She is giving him a smile.

'Well . . .' he readies himself for the credit.

'Yeah. He told me not to come so I thought, fuck you, I'm coming in a suit.'

Tess bursts out laughing and Byron sighs. Lynn gives him and Tess a drink while we're all pulled into a dancing circle. Tess looks happy though tired, Adam switching to 'Happy Birthday' by Hot Chocolate and then other naff classics. Everyone whoops as Byron scoops her up for a tango kiss and when he whispers 'Happy, babe?' his eyes are wet.

'You could've invited a few more people,' she says, 'not just these layabouts.'

'Oi!' Lynn pokes her in the armpit and then the friends are dancing together until 'We Are Family' comes on and Tess gathers us all up. Me and Byron have our arms round each other and it's OK. Byron even pats me.

Tess pulls me to the sideboard and glugs out wine for us both but I say no no I've stopped all that I told you. She screws the lid back on, still staring at me.

'It's my birthday. Just have one.'

'I don't want to.'

She searches my eyes, full of suspicion.

'My birthday?'

'I need a clear mind, Tess. The booze wasn't doing me any favours, you know that.'

'Clear mind for what?'

'So I can sort myself out. Get my plan together.'

'What plan?'

'It is being formulated. You'll see.'

'Mnnn . . .' says Tess, examining me. 'Hey, listen, I've had an idea about a girl for you. Mate of Lynn's actually.'

'No way.'

'Look, I know it didn't go so great with Sandy but you've got to—'

'Absolutely no way.'

'Have a drink then.'

'No.'

Tess is very close to my face now.

'Promise me he's not come back, he's not hurting you.'

'Promise.'

'Don't you leave me,' she hisses, 'Don't you leave me alone in all this.'

'All right?' Byron is beside us and we both fake a happy yes to him and Ben is pulling her back into the dancing circle and she downs my wine and takes hers along.

'Wait, I got you something,' and I pull her back, taking down the wooden box from the fridge, a carved Indian box with protruding hinges that I once kept hash in and then stones and shells.

'What is it?'

She opens the empty box and says 'I knew you were coming for a magic show with that fucking suit.'

'Can't do the trousers up.'

She puts the box back on the fridge and says, 'Come here, dafty,' pulling me into a hug, and I say 'Happy Birthday, sis.'

'They find your mate yet? Missy?'

Beside us the kids start up a burping competition with all the Orangina but Adam beats them. Lynn brings in the birthday cake with candles and the lights down and the song and the blowing and the wish-making and the cheer. I eat a vast amount of cake, smuggling a slice wrapped in a serviette into my pocket for Missy. Everyone is drinking and dancing, Adam and Byron squabbling over which rave tunes from the early nineties to play until the kids and the girls just sit down laughing, watching us three do the moves: 'big fish, little fish', 'Bez', 'look at my two screwdrivers'.

———

Kathleen and Phoebe are both asleep upstairs. It's my shift and even though it is nearly three in the morning Baron's Down Road is strangely lively, two female voices somewhere laughing, their heels clacking loudly down the street. Someone is parking. Someone is driving past, headlights fanning through the blinds. Charlotte's hand spiders over mine.

She is awake again. She wants to say something but must take breaths in preparation. She blinks, parts her lips. She must take another breath, weighted and rusty.

'What,' she gasps, 'do you want me to say to Him?' She deflates a little with the spent effort.

'Who?'

'The,' she breathes, 'Octopus God if,' she swallows, 'I see Him over there. Old,' she breathes again, 'Malamock,' resting into His name with a smile.

'Say hello from me. Shake His hand,' I say, gently shaking hers.

Her chest lifts and lowers. She wants to speak again, eyes brightening, flaring her nostrils, dragging up more energy.

'I need,' she gulps, closing her eyes for moment, pausing, opening them again, 'six more hands,' smiling at her own joke, the caps of her teeth showing, and there is something about this smile, the courage of it, the way it lifts her old face back out from the skull, that makes me cry. She squeezes my hand, so lightly, and suddenly I cannot control myself and everything I have wanted to say floods out of me, how much I love her, how I don't want to lose her, how it seems so short this time I've had with her, how I wish she had been my – 'Thomas,' she says, then, after a struggling, rattled breath, 'stop moaning.'

———

'I don't think we should go out today,' I tell Missy as we have our breakfast. 'It doesn't feel safe.'

'Fuck off,' she bobs the teabag then slings it on the table, 'seen how sunny it is out there?' I remove the oozing offender. 'No feds in the woods. Is there?' I open the bin and cast the teabag in, wiping off the brown puddle with a huff but Missy seems oblivious to such messages of disapproval.

The sun is already strong, and we walk through the fields and Rocks Wood then out through the pines and rotting stumps bearded with moss onto a public footpath that cuts past Rocks Farm, through spring beans destined for Egypt, past bullfinches and the oast house and down the other side of the valley. Cows pull themselves up from their grazing to watch us smell their baked and flaking pats strewn across the grass.

There is a fenced copse in the middle of the field and as we come alongside a young man with pale ginger hair in a side parting, his shirt sleeves rolled up past his biceps, stands at the edge with a radio tracker and a spade. He lifts his hand to us, the bleeping from the tracker intensifying as he sticks it into the hole he's dug. He puts down the madly beeping tracker and takes out a trowel, arms bent into the hole.

'Chased a pheasant down this set,' he says, grunting, and there is a sudden muffled jangling as he rolls backwards. A Harris' hawk with a bell on its neck erupts out of the ground, shaking and squawking, flying straight up above us into the copse. Missy gasps.

At the bottom of the field we climb onto Orznash Lane, an ancient boastal track that will take us through the land unseen. Arched in cedar and oak, farmers have patched its potholes with broken tiles, a burnt-out car folded neatly up onto the track-side. Holden Wood one way, Gill Ridge and Crowborough the other.

'What are we doing?' says Missy.

This old green lane is steep-sided with bracken and brambles that tumble onto our ankles. Slowly the dog prints and weeds become tarmac as we head towards Eridge and the lane turns into a drive. We come out past a new-build brick cottage and farm buildings, a chalked hopscotch on the road. 'What am I going to do, Tom?' says Missy, hopscotching out the question again. 'What. Are we. Going. To do. Tom.'

'Trust in Malamock,' I reply, 'Never stray from the way.'

Along Forge Road we keep to the fields, and once we have arrived home again I peer round the hedge to check for Tess or Megan or the police but there is just Saul and Nika standing beside his Mini. They are in the middle of intense conversation. We skirt around them to the front door but as I take out my house keys I realise Saul is marching towards us.

'I'm sorry,' he says to me, sincerely. Then he grabs Missy's arm.

'Oi!' she says tugging back, but he has wrapped up both her arms, interlocking them with his own, palms against the back of her head. It is some kind of move.

'What are you doing?'

'*Tom!*' Missy is shrieking, '*Fucking get him off me!*'

'I'm sorry,' he says to me again, Nika coming over, finishing off a call.

'The police are on their way, OK?' she says, laying a hand

on my shoulder, 'So let's all just stay calm until they get here.'

'The police?'

'They told us to call them if we saw her – we saw you leave this morning and, well, they should have been here ages ago really.'

'*Fuck off get off!*'

Missy is shouting and struggling, trying to back-kick Saul's leg and squirm free. Nika gives me a gentle squeeze.

'She shouldn't be walking around outside like that.'

'Outside?'

'It's not safe, Tom,' she says, 'for anyone.'

Saul is ordering Missy to give in. He is hurting her.

'Two spirits,' says the Octopus God, 'the moment of companions,' and He heats up my right and left side and all across my chest but this is not the onset of electrocution, this is something new.

I run into the parking area and scrape my latchkey as deeply as I can the length of Saul's Mini. He makes a high-pitched noise, like an unoiled brake. Saul drops Missy.

Shedding his slippers he charges over and shoves me from his car. He takes in the damage then grabs me by the shirt, punching me in the side of the head, then in the back of the head, again and again, until there is a slapping sound and the punching stops.

I uncover my head. Saul is on the tarmac. He is groaning. Nika is running over to him and Missy is pulling at my hand.

'What did you do?'

'I just hit him!'

'With what?'

We run through the hedgerow and out onto High Paddocks. We keep running along the headland until at Gorse Bank we stop at the trunk of a storm-felled beech, heaving out breaths.

'Where are we going?'

'What did you hit him with?'

She shrugs and we run down the side of the ghyll. Crossing the treeline into the woods, I look back to make sure we're not being followed but against the sky I see three figures on the ridge. One of them is a policemen. He calls out.

We accelerate into the trees though it is easier on the ride, sloping upwards past the temple to Jockey's Field. A siren wows Corseley Road so we dip back away from it to the stream. Missy is doubled up against an alder, wheezing and pale, but I pull her along and we are back on a footpath running past a brightly coloured jogger who sees we are not part of the same activity. We run through Sawmill Field and over the stile into Rocks Wood.

'Where the fuck are we going?' she hisses, desperate with exhaustion. A herd of deer erupts through the overgrowth and we follow on behind them to the rocks, scaling up the side of one huge boulder and then lie still, fifteen feet off the ground, camouflaged in yew growth and holly. Missy is breathing heavily. I peer back down the wooded hillside.

'But what did you hit him with?'

'Think he hit his head on the ground. See them?' she whispers. I shake my head.

Satisfied that they are not coming up towards us and must have kept alongside the stream towards Groombridge, I lie down, trying to recover the pace of heart and lungs.

'You knocked Saul out. I can't believe it.'

'Wanker,' she says, but then we hear voices.

I raise my head and see flashes of blue uniform coming towards us from between the trees. Gesturing to Missy that we must move or be surrounded we slide backwards off the rock and run straight into a narrow gulley through jagged sandstone corridors. We wait, listening, moving carefully away from their shouts.

'Cessation,' says Malamock and we freeze but I can't hear anything – until suddenly there is the crackle of a police radio, right below us. I step gently backwards, forcing Missy to do the same so we are behind a 130-million-year-old corner watching the uniform pass.

'Anything?' he shouts, and someone replies 'No!' and I can hear Saul shout 'Not here!'

I raise myself to see over the gulley and survey an empty canyon. We run into it, the trees beyond waiting to cloak us, when I hear my sister shouting 'Tom! Tom!'

She is coming into the canyon. We have just enough time to drop and roll into a low cave at the foot of the scarp. 'Tom!' she shouts again. Her footfall comes nearer, then further away again, and I think she has carried on and missed us when I hear a noise close to my head and know we are undone. I roll backwards to face her. There is Ben.

He is smiling. I put my finger against my lips. He copies me.

'See him?' his mother calls from afar.

'No!' he shouts back, grins, runs off, and we lie there, shouts coming from everywhere. They have not swept the rocks and carried on. They are circling, checking.

Though our faces are so close she is a blur, still I can see Missy's fear. I dig into my pockets and shove all the scrunched-up money I've got there into her hands. 'OK?' I whisper. She is nodding and gives me a furious kiss against my jaw. 'He will save you,' I say, because I know that He will. Then I roll out into the canyon, stand up, and stride towards the voices.

'Hey,' I call over to Tess and Ben, 'what are you doing here?'

'Fucking hell, Tom!' she says, then shouting, 'Here! He's right here!'

There is a great shuffling and out pour the pursuers. Saul rushes at me making all sorts of unattractive assertions but is held back by police fingertips.

'All right now, Mr Tuplow,' says the policeman, approaching me. He has a charming face. Soft eyes and a wise frown. 'Where is she?'

'The station.'

'Eridge?'

'By now, I should think.'

Ben is grinning. He is having a wonderful afternoon. The policeman takes a step away, talking to the voice on his shoulder. Nika and Saul gabble furiously at his colleague.

'*Tom?*' gasps Tess.

'What?' I shrug.

'What do you mean – "*what*"?'

'Saul was breaking her arm! And she doesn't want to go back to that hellhole. You want to swap places with her?'

'Mr Tuplow,' says the charming policeman, 'you're sure she's gone that way?'

'Yes.'

He is inspecting me. He looks back at the rocks as if he has just finished painting them, then goes over to Saul and Nika, discussing things with the other officer. He tells us we're all going back up to the road. Tess is still staring at me, hands on hips, and I turn away from her as we are herded through the pines onto a tractor track, following it out onto the driveway that leads to Corseley Road. Once we're collected there, the charming policeman tells us to wait with his colleague. He goes back to the rocks.

He means to catch Missy out.

Tess is trying to talk to me but I am ignoring her. Ben breaks a stick over a tree stump and Saul bawls something at me that sounds like *fricka-bricka*. A muffled cry comes from the woods.

The policeman orders us all to stay put as he darts back down the tractor track into the trees but I bolt after him, Tess telling me to stop, then chasing after me, everyone zigzagging back down the mud-lumped furrows.

Missy is in the trees, cornered by the two policemen.

She is running from one trunk to another but they are flanking her and she is caught behind by a rhododendron bush. She sees me and screams '*DO SOMETHING!*' but she is not screaming at me, she pleads with Malamock because it seems as though hope is gone – but it is doubt that has gone, my doubts in God.

They close in on her, hands out, knees bent, coaxing her as if she is some kind of wild horse.

Missy stiffens.

'Sparks of fire leap out,' says Malamock.

Both her arms fly forward, thumbs twitching as if she is asking for a light.

'What doesn't exist? Lamentation.'

She convulses. Her eyes roll white.

'God is always painful.'

Missy falls.

SEPTEMBER

31

Stanmore Orthopaedic Hospital is spread out over parkland like a 1930s military barracks. The Jubilee Rehabilitation Centre is a semicircular brick structure with men and women on the benches outside smoking and wrapped in plaster. Missy's ward is female-only, the windows are large, the room light-filled and colourful even though the stench of disinfectant and mashed potato is the same as all the other places.

Missy wears a baseball cap and a double sling with a kind of Gore-tex waistcoat that fails to keep her shoulders in place, squares of different textures like denim, sandpaper and wool sewn into the sleeve of her sling as she can no longer feel things unless she is looking at them. The fit was so severe her arms came out of their sockets again but the doctors can't get them back in. This is how He delivered her from Hilldean.

I give her the chocolate and tobacco, which she takes with a smile. There is a young girl in the bay beside her, curled up and listening to her iPhone while the other women are throwing conversation at each other from the beds.

'Nathalie, you haven't met Tom?'

'Hiya Tom.'

'Look what he bought me—' *Clack* goes her shoulder socket,

Missy's head hovering up to one side, eyes slitting, breathing off the pain.

'Bless.'

'No biscuits this time?'

'Don't be such a greedy cow, you!' I get a wink from a huge woman on crutches stalking by. I offer to roll Missy's cigarette for her but she says she needs the practice. She must keep her arms moving, take the oxys, do the physiotherapy and constant visualisations of them going back in the sockets and staying there. 'I'm a Tyrannosaurus rex,' she says, wiggling hands that stick out from the slings at her ribs. 'Raaaaaa!'

We go outside through the fire exit to smoke. There is an old milk churn out there for an ashtray and a man called Duncan with a titanium knee. His old knee had cancer, so they took it out and left him with a spider of white scarring. They trade affectionate insults and when we are alone again I show her my phone. It's got a picture of her as the screen saver and she tells me I'm soft, I'm a softy. She tells me a psychologist has given her a post-traumatic stress disorder diagnosis after her experiences at Hilldean.

'So what's your news?'

'Saul's dropping the criminal damage charge and I'm dropping the assault charge. Even Stevens.'

'And me? Still nothing?'

'I honestly think he's too embarrassed. Being laid out by a girl like that. I think he wants to forget that bit.'

'Don't you bump into him all the time?'

'Yeah. Can't really avoid it. He did threaten me in the car park.'

'What did you do?'

'I offered him some wild flowers.'

'Ha!'

'Now he's just ignoring me. Win–win, really.'

'So how's it going with the Facebook detective shit?'

'Well I haven't found Roseanna, but I've found Price . . .'

'How's he doing?'

'Hard to tell. He posts mostly conspiracy stuff and music videos. Found Chanelle. Loads of pictures of her baby boy.'

'Not for long. She grew up in care. They'll be whipping that baby off her pretty soon.'

'Anyway she's up for the whole class action thing. Has put me in touch with some other people who've been in Hilldean.'

'Look at you,' she kisses her teeth, 'Do your thing, chicken wing!'

'A consistent body of testimony from the maximum amount of former patients. That's the key to get this thing rolling. Critical mass. And if we can't find a civil rights specialist to take us on and force a judicial review, then there's always journalists. Get an investigation going. Going to be a long haul though but as long as . . .'

A girl with short dyed blond hair pushes open the door. She is wearing a blue tennis dress and has crutches on both arms, elbows shaking wildly. I catch the door for her and Missy hooks out a rotting plastic seat from the corner of the yard and knees it behind the girl so she can topple backwards and rest. She lets out a gasp but follows it with a huge grateful smile and exhales.

'Hello you,' she says to Missy. 'Saw you go out.' They kiss each other, Missy leaning down to grip the girl's collar with her dinosaur hands.

'This is Tom,' Missy says once they've stopped kissing. 'My best mate. This is Kirsty.'

'Heard a lot about you,' says the girl. 'You're well famous.'

'Am I?'

They start kissing again. I prod my phone as if to answer it. This is how I talk to Him in public now, so those unchosen are left undisturbed.

'This is not my path, my requisite condition,' I say, walking away towards some trees, 'You are my Lord God. You are my path.'

'There came the Rightly Self-Awakened Ones. Complete with parks, groves and direct knowledge. Everything, because we had the freshness and vitality, there came everything, the divine.'

I turn back to face the rear of the ward. Missy is talking to Kirsty, holding her hands while at the same time checking that I am all right, that I am not being seized by divine anger and dashed against the ground.

This is acceptance.

OCTOBER

32

Despite much wavering and Tess trying to change the date, the eighth of October is unequivocally upon us. I spend all afternoon in the woods, walking through beech mast and hazelnuts, climbing on top of a sandstone outcrop to sit among the ferns, my back against the nook of a yew, elbows resting on bracket fungus. I have even debated whether it would be wise to restart certain medication just in the run-up to this event but there are to be no more tablets ever again, just my Lord the Octopus God, a table, plates, glasses, and the raw liver of truth.

It is important to me that I pay for this dinner, that it is my invitation, an affirmation of my independence, so after much consideration I invite Tess and Byron to the Wok Inn Chinese restaurant in Crowborough due to resource issues. I imagined this summit in grander settings and indeed took a seat in many salubrious restaurants in Tunbridge Wells and East Grinstead to feel out the appropriate atmospherics but Malamock identified this as a tactic of delay. It will only be after my qualification as a barrister that I can afford to take my family out to Hotel du Vin.

Saturday night. The Wok Inn restaurant is two rooms split by a thin bar that welcomes you with a reclining Buddha, chipped and lacquered. Surrounded by red flowering wallpaper I sit in the corner table by the window watching the ghosts of other diners as rain pelts the glass. Traditional flute music floats above a soundtrack of waves and on one wall there is a large painting of travellers using a tree branch as a raft while some creature rides a swan above them. I yawn and touch my head, nibbling at the prawn crackers like a giant hamster. A hairy-faced grandma with a bruised nose and tombola torso pours a bottle of beer into her mouth and suddenly I crave that taste, that sedation, but take out my phone and say into it: 'Forgive me. I love you with all my heart.'

There are three glum-looking generations of the same family, three straw-coloured women with wine glasses filled to the top slowly stripping a pig's rib of its flesh. A father at the table beside me is scolding his daughter, 'Get your feet off the chair and sit round properly!' as she plays a game on her phone that generates squelching noises and the sudden trill of prize-winning. The mother has straight long hair that hangs from her head like a tablecloth. She is picking from a plate of noodles. There are eight people in this restaurant.

'But you're a good drawer,' she says to the teenage girl, who is also on her phone.

'I need a proper art pencil,' says the teenager. 'A proper art rubber, proper art paper, proper art everything.'

'My ears are too big,' says the little girl. None of the pictures in this restaurant are hanging straight.

'You're winding me up now,' says the father, 'get your feet off that bloody chair.'

Tess and Byron walk into the restaurant. Now there are ten people in the restaurant not including staff. Oh Tess. She is excited, shaking out an umbrella. I have told her I have an important announcement to make. They hook their jackets on the clothes rack. My heart is pulsing.

Tess and I hug, then I open my face to Byron because I want

346

this to be a new start. He nods a curious hello. The Chinese waiter gives us menus. He has troubled, swollen eyes and bushy hair that falls in front of his ears.

'Just three persons?' he says, starting to clear the fourth setting.

'No,' I say, 'there's someone else.'

Byron and Tess are two owls peering over the laminate.

'Who's that then?'

'I've invited someone else.'

'Megan?'

'No.'

'Whatsername – Missy?'

'Tom, with her, you're not—?'

'She's just my friend. As I keep telling you. Over and over again.'

'OK, OK. Don't get all touchy. She's just, you know, pretty young.'

'Speaking of touchy – they got her arms back in yet?'

'Not yet.'

'Still in the hozzie?'

'She's living in West Drayton. With her *girlfriend*.'

'Who is it then?'

'It's a surprise.'

'Oh Jesus. Think we need to order some booze, sharpish.'

'So I've got a little bit of other news.'

'You're moving?'

'Shut up, Byron.'

'Oh it's a joke, it's a joke . . .'

'So,' I take a deep breath, 'I have decided I am going to be a lawyer again. Contacting all these former Hilldean patients has really helped get my mind back into it. I've been going through my law degree stuff and my certificate's lapsed, so I'll have to sit some exams again to requalify, but just for some bits, and under the Equality Act they have to take my experiences into account, and I've already done my pupillage, so I won't have to do that again—'

'You? Are going to become a lawyer?'

'I've got a first-class law degree.'

'That's twenty years old. That you got before you went—'

'Byron—'

'There's a few firms that specialise in mental health issues. I think I can get a tenancy at one of them, and before you ask, Tess, I have talked it through with Megan and I know it's going to take time, I know that. I'm going to go very slowly, not put myself under any pressure I can't handle. Just going to see how it goes – like this Hilldean class action thing. Just something to work towards. I'm going to start volunteering at this place in Brighton. Gledhill.'

'How are you going to afford it though?'

'I'm just volunteering. Just a few hours a week.'

'But after that. What about your PIP?'

'I don't know right now, but I'll find a way. That's the meaning of all this. I know that now.'

'Of all what?'

'Of everything that's happened. I need to master the law. To help people. That's my mission.'

'People with mental health problems?'

'In the face of the chaos that is coming. The law will be what remains of civilisation. The law and faith. And the law is a kind of faith, they have the same deep roots. Because it contains doubt, and doubt is an article of faith, not its opposite. I understand that now. I think that's one of the reasons I always loved the ancient Greeks so much. Even Zeus cannot subvert the law, so—'

'Are we ordering or are we waiting for the mystery shopper here?'

'Shut up, Byron! Hey, look, whatever it's for, it's amazing

that you've got a plan and a goal and everything. Good for you.'

'I feel much stronger. I feel like I've reached a point where I am who I am, so—'

'That drug really was a total fucking miracle, wasn't it?' she says. 'Look at you – you just look totally different. You're not being, you know, tortured any more—'

'And neither are we!'

'Seriously, Byron, if you—' Byron makes a zipping motion across his lips, hails the waiter and orders a pint. Tess has a glass of wine. I ask for water.

'Do you want to give 'em a bell though?' says Byron. 'Seriously, I'm proper starving. What? I am!'

'He doesn't have a phone.'

'Oh.' Tess's face flattens. 'It's a "he"?'

The little girl beside us has started talking in an American accent. 'Oh my God,' she says, 'I'm, like, so cute.'

'Not all this again,' says the mother.

I shuffle on my seat. Take a breath.

'Tess, Byron: I wanted to invite you both here to tell you how well I'm doing and really, basically, to sort of, well – you are my family and I need you to accept who I am—'

'Here we go. I knew it. What's his name – Clarence? *Ow!*' Tess has pinched the skin on Byron's hand.

'And I know that goes both ways, I know that, and Tess, look, I know I've never really accepted Byron, I know that, and I have certainly done my bit in keeping things between us hostile, and I want to apologise.'

'I'm not going to tell you again,' says the father, 'sit round properly and eat your food.'

'Anyway I don't like Harmony any more,' says the teenager, 'she's always hanging around with Becca now, and me and Crystal don't like her.'

349

'And what I want to say, Byron, is thank you. For looking after my sister. I know my experiences have put a real strain on your relationship, and that has not been fair on either of you, and I want to apologise for that too. So – sorry.' I offer my hand to Byron across the table.

'Is this for real?'

Tess nudges him and he takes my hand and shakes, though his grip has nothing in it.

'OK,' he says, 'OK then. OK.'

'Well I never,' she says with a grin.

'Can we order now?'

'Why are you always such a wanker?'

'What? Anyway, you going to tell him our news then or what?'

'In a bit.'

'What news?' I say.

'Not now, just . . . anyway, where's your mate?'

'He's coming,' I say, and there above them appears the ribbon of white light. I feel a tingling in my neck and the warmth of His love down my left side.

'Tom? You OK?'

'He is here now.'

'Who?' and they both turn to the door.

'You've never been properly introduced.'

'Tom?'

'I'm going to use an empty chair. I think that's going to make it easier for both of you.'

'What?'

'If you could direct all your questions and replies to the chair next to me, even though it will be me speaking obviously, that will make this—'

'Oh no . . .'

'I want you to meet my Lord, Malamock, the Octopus God.'

'Is this a joke? Are you fucking with us? Tom?'

'This is not a joke, Byron, no.'

My sister has covered her mouth. She sits back. Her chest is leaping.

'Tess, listen to me. I hear a voice. That voice is real. That is the voice of the Octopus God. It is part of who I am and I need you to accept that. In fact it's twenty years ago to the day, October the eighth—'

'I mean what gets me,' Byron is swaying, 'what just gets me, right, is – *can't you see what you're doing to her?*'

Tess is sobbing and shaking her head. The other diners have stopped talking.

'Oh no, Tom no . . .'

'Tess, look at me. I'm not ill. No pulsations, no triggering. I'm doing fine. I just hear a voice no one else can hear.'

'And how is that not ill?'

'I can manage my life, Tess. I'm having . . . Tess, I'm not mad. Have I been acting mad?'

'You invited an empty fucking chair to dinner!' shouts Byron.

The diners stop eating.

The waiter comes over and Tess apologises and we all sit there in silence as the room picks itself up, cutlery begins to scrape, murmurs unfold into speech. The family watch us, raising eyebrows at each other.

'Byron, just give us a moment, will you please? Go get a kebab or something.'

'Babe—'

'I just want to be alone with my brother for second, OK? Please?'

She seizes his hand and holds his face and kisses him. He wipes the tears off her cheek with his thumb. He kisses her again and whispers something to her then stands up. He tears

351

his jacket off the coat rack. *Tingalingaling*. I see him walking up the road in the rain. He puts his head in his hands.

Stretching across the table I take my sister's fingers, the ribbon of white light above her.

'I am the Octopus God. I am older than the universe.'

'Oh Tom,' she says, 'then you'll be a child for ever.'

Author's Note

Bildinocycline is a fictional drug. It is loosely based on minocycline, a drug being trialled in the UK at the time of writing for the treatment of negative symptoms in patients with an early onset schizophrenia diagnosis. Its anti-inflammatory properties are thought to calm microglia activation in the brain. Minocycline is an antibiotic, commonly used for the treatment of acne.

Clozapine is a widely prescribed anti-psychotic. Acuphase is used in the NHS.

My cousin Ed Metcalfe died in 2011 at the age of forty, having suffered with a schizophrenia diagnosis for twenty years. This book was inspired by his death and is dedicated to his life.

Jasper Gibson, East Sussex

Glossary

CBT – Cognitive Behavioural Therapy

CC – Care Co-ordinator

DLA – Disability Living Allowance

DSM-4 – Diagnostic and Statistical Manual of Mental Disorders fourth edition

ESA – Employment and Support Allowance

ICD-10 – International Classification of Diseases tenth edition

PANSS – Positive and Negative Symptom Scale

PIL – Patient Information Leaflet

PIP – Personal Independence Payment

RA – Research Assistant

Section 2 – compulsory detention in hospital because of a mental health disorder as defined by the Mental Health Act for up to 28 days.

Section 3 – compulsory detention in hospital because of a mental health disorder as defined by the Mental Health Act for up to 6 months. The section can be renewed or extended by the clinician.

Acknowledgements

Zara and Jonty Colchester. Patrick Gibson, Beatrice Gibson and Nick Gordon.

Vicki Kennedy.

Dr Jacqui Dillon.

Pat, Peta and Maria Kennedy. Shauneen Lambe. Professor Bill Deakin. Professor Robert Bentall. Dr Joanna Moncrieff. John Weatherall. Edward K Penny. Sam Sproates. Dr Matt James. Alan Hendry. Susanna Simmonds. Magnus and Pete from the Royal Sussex. Richard 'Speedy' Byrne. Miles Cleret. Lloyd Hudson. Roland Marks. Ben Maschler. Toby Tripp. Jonny Benjamin. Hugo Campbell. Forbes McNaughton. Woody and Scarlett Gibson. Christoph Hargreaves-Allen.

Will Goodlad. Chloe Aridjis. Nat Turner. Kate McCreary. Jane Maschler. Rowan Somerville. Laura Fairrie. Seorais Graham. Thomas Forwood. Lewis Heriz.

Maria Alvarez. Darren Biabowe Barnes. Jake Smith-Bosanquet. Kate Burton. Alexander Cochran. Matilda Ayris.

Ellie Freedman. Rosie Pearce. Seán Costello. Peter Adlington. Cait Davies. Virginia Woolstencroft. Jen Hope. Esther Waters. Inês Figueira. Steve Marking.

Hugh and Frances Gibson. Effie and Phiz Phizacklea. Amelia and Paddy Lyndon-Stanford. Mick and Lulu Sadler. David Ambrose.

Johnny Flynn.

Amy Strickland. Farah Cleret. Nicholas Ridley-Wilson and Steven Derbyshire. Toby Macdonald. Matt Court. Lloyd and Kam Hudson. Louisa Havers. Holly Mirza. Roland Marks and Beth Rycroft. Laura Fairrie. Mike and Pawna Spencer-Nairn.

With special thanks to Lee Brackstone for taking the plunge, to Clare Conville for her wisdom, and to Crispin Somerville for his enduring belief and friendship.

Above all I would like to thank my wife Daisy Sadler: reader, editor, anti-muse.

About the Author

Jasper Gibson was born in the Peak District, Derbyshire in 1975. He is the author of one previous novel, *A Bright Moon For Fools*.

Help us make the next generation of readers

We – both author and publisher – hope you enjoyed this book. We believe that you can become a reader at any time in your life, but we'd love your help to give the next generation a head start.

Did you know that 9 per cent of children don't have a book of their own in their home, rising to 13 per cent in disadvantaged families*? We'd like to try to change that by asking you to consider the role you could play in helping to build readers of the future.

We'd love you to think of sharing, borrowing, reading, buying or talking about a book with a child in your life and spreading the love of reading. We want to make sure the next generation continue to have access to books, wherever they come from.

And if you would like to consider donating to charities that help fund literacy projects, find out more at **www.literacytrust.org.uk** and **www.booktrust.org.uk**.

THANK YOU

*As reported by the National Literacy Trust